EAST GERMAN
SHORT STORIES
AN INTRODUCTORY
ANTHOLOGY

Translated and Edited by
PETER E. and EVELYN S. FIRCHOW

University of Minnesota

TWAYNE PUBLISHERS   *1979*

Published in 1979 by Twayne Publishers,
A Division of G. K. Hall & Co.

Printed on permanent/durable acid-free paper and bound
in the United States of America

First Printing

177416

Book Design by Audrey James Augun

Library of Congress Cataloging in Publication Data

Main entry under title:

East German Short Stories
An Introductory Anthology

Bibliography: p. 251
1. German fiction—Germany, East—Translations into English.
2. English fiction—20th century—Translations from German.
3. Short stories, German—Translations into English.
4. Short stories, English—Translations from German.
I. Firchow, Peter. II. Firchow, Evelyn Scherabon.
PT3740.I5   833'.01   78-21686
ISBN 0-8057-8159-5

For
Raimund and Hildegard
Scherabon

CONTENTS

ACKNOWLEDGMENTS

The authors wish to thank the following persons for help in preparing this anthology:
Prof. Dr. Eberhard Brüning, Leipzig; Mr. Jacob Steinberg, former president of Twayne Publishers; Mrs. Karleen Kosiak-Sveum, Minneapolis.

We are indebted to the following publishers for permission to translate and include certain short stories in our anthology:
Aufbau Verlag, Berlin und Weimar: Willi Bredel, *Der Auswanderer*; Stephan Hermlin, *In einer dunklen Welt*; Hermann Kant, *Ein bisschen Südsee*; Günter Kunert, *Märchenhafter Monolog*; Siegfried Pitschmann, *Die wunderliche Verlobung eines Karrenmannes*; Anna Seghers, *Der Ausflug der toten Mädchen*; Erwin Strittmatter, *Schneewittchen*; Bodo Uhse, *Die heilige Kunigunde im Schnee*; F. C. Weiskopf, *Ein verhinderter Sankt Franziskus*.
VEB Hinstorff Verlag, Rostock: Ernst Böttcher, *Ein Beispiel und ich*; Franz Fühmann, *Der Jongleur im Kino oder Die Insel der Träume*; Manfred Jendryschik, *Briefe*; Kristian Pech, *Podiralla geht zum Zirkus*.
Mitteldeutscher Verlag, Halle/Saale: Werner Bräunig, *Unterwegs*; Wolfgang Buschmann, *Ein Dorf und viele Dörfer*; Eduard Claudius, *Das Opfer*; Joachim Nowotny, *Pimpusch*.
Union Verlag, Berlin: Johannes Bobrowski, *Mäusefest*.

In addition we are grateful for the translation rights granted to us by Fritz Rudolf Fries for *Die zweite Beschreibung meiner Freunde*. Stefan Heym allowed us to include his short story *Babik* in his own translation which first appeared in *The Cannibals and Other Stories*, Seven Seas Books, Berlin. Finally our thanks go to Erwin Strittmatter who kindly sent us a copy of his short story *Schneewittchen*.

INTRODUCTION

A truly artistic work is completely, irrefutably convincing and bends to its will even the heart which resists it.
Alexander Solzhenitsyn, *Nobel Prize Lecture.*

What is most immediately surprising about the literature of the German Democratic Republic is that it should exist at all. Surprising, that is, not because the GDR should have writers who are worth reading and writing about, but because those writers should belong to, or at least be perceived and generally accepted as belonging to, a new "national" literary tradition. How very odd this is in a nation which has barely reached its thirtieth birthday can best be appreciated by looking at the situation in the Western half of Germany, where there is no national literature in the same sense, no "literature of the Federal Republic of Germany." In the Western half, there is German literature—not German literature plain and simple, perhaps, differing as it does in a variety of important ways from German literature up to 1933 (or 1945), but still recognizably part of the larger and older tradition.

Why? The chief reason, one seems forced to conclude, is that the literature that is written in the Federal Republic of Germany is written merely *in* and not necessarily *in behalf* of the Federal Republic. It is German literature because it happens to have been written in the German language, by German nationals, and was published usually within the political boundaries of a German state. Not so, however, with the German Democratic Republic, where literature is by definition an expression of the social and political ideals of the state—because if it is not, it cannot be published. Hence the literature of the German Democratic Republic has a consistency (or even uniformity) which allows one to consider it as a literary unit separate from the main body of German literature.

In this there is both strength and weakness. There is the

strength of producing quickly a large quantity of (officially certified) literary work, a verbal portrait in which a people can learn to see itself as it is supposed to be, a portrait of GDR man in a GDR literary tradition. But there is also the weakness of making that tradition artificial and only partially true, of portraying not a living face but a mask, with possibly Dorian-Grayish results. The situation here, as so often, is analogous to that of the Soviet Union, with its initial rejection of much of the received tradition of Russian literature in preference for an "instant" Soviet tradition. Inevitably, despite times of relaxation and liberalization—the intermittent "thaws"—the new tradition has proved too narrow to accommodate the vision of a number of truly creative writers; and, inevitably, these writers have either been forced to yield or to fall silent or to seek an audience elsewhere. That was the case with Mayakovski, Pasternak, and Solzhenitsyn in the USSR; and it is the case with Stefan Heym, Wolfgang Biermann, F. R. Fries, and Reiner Kunze in the GDR.

The birth of a new literary tradition—and that of a new nation—can never be easy. Like all births it is and must be accompanied by bloodshed and suffering; and this was all the more true in the case of the GDR, where birth was also at the same time amputation. The story of the collapse of Nazi Germany, of the partition of its former territory (as of 1937) into six separate segments—four occupied areas and two others incorporated into Poland and the USSR—has been told so often and is so well known that it need not be repeated here. What needs to be stressed, however, is that the borders of the Soviet Zone, as fixed by the Potsdam Agreements, were new in the east and in the north-east, as well as in the west, so that the geographical identity of what in October 1949 was to become the German Democratic Republic was utterly different from both the immediately preceding Third Reich and the earlier Hohenzollern Reich and Prussian Kingdom. To a degree which it is difficult to gauge precisely but which one feels nevertheless sure must be considerable, the very novelty of the geography of the GDR permitted and even enforced a new consciousness—a new self-consciousness—upon the inhabitants of this territory, a consciousness which the inhabitants of the Western Zones, where the borders remained much as they had been, except of course towards the east, did not share. Symptomatic of the difference is that in the East the job of building up a new

Germany was habitually referred to as "Aufbau" (Construction), whereas in the West it was termed "Wiederaufbau" (Reconstruction).

The Nazis and their disastrous war had reduced Germany to a chaotic heap of physical and moral rubble. Into this literal waste land there flowed, along with the conquering Soviet armies, a great number of returning exiles, many of them members of what had been until 1933 the largest and most powerful Communist Party in Western Europe. These men and women were determined to reverse the defeat which they had suffered at Hitler's hands twelve years earlier, and to establish a state as intensely red as he had tried to make his brown. This first meant gaining political control, a task in which they could count on the active assistance of the Soviet Military Government, but in which they could also count on the—more or less passive—resistance of some of the other pre-1933 political parties, especially the Socialists. With the fusion in early 1946 of the Communist and Socialist Parties of the Soviet Zone into the SED (Socialist Unity Party), this obstacle was removed and the way cleared for a thorough revamping of the political and economic machinery of this part of Germany.

One of the first and probably the most popular and successful actions of the new regime was to carry out the land redistribution program called for by the Potsdam Agreements (an action later portrayed, along with the start of the subsequent and less popular collectivization of agriculture, in Erwin Strittmatter's widely read novel, *Ole Bienkopp*). Similarly, all large industrial holdings were removed from private ownership, again in accordance with the Potsdam Agreements stipulating the break-up of large industry, and gradually transformed into "VEB"s or "People-Owned Corporations." Today only small businesses employing fewer than ten workers constitute the last remnant of private enterprise in the GDR. Neither of these articles of the Potsdam Agreements was, one might add, carried out in the other occupied zones of Germany, nor were former Nazis excluded as rigorously in the West from positions of influence, especially in the educational and judicial systems, as they were in the East—as rigorously as the Nazis had once excluded former Communists. All of this involved a vast amount of effort over a considerable period of time. New agricultural and industrial management had to be created, new teachers and

judges trained, new texts written and published to take the place of those that had to be burned. As Konrad Franke suggests in *Die Literatur der Deutschen Demokratischen Republik* (1971) [The Literature of the German Democratic Republic], these reforms meant that in one part of Germany at least the program of the Revolution of 1848 had finally been carried out—that is, in an economic if not in a political sense.

Unlike the Revolution of 1848, however, the "Revolution of 1945-49" was one which came from above rather than from below. Inevitably, therefore, from its very beginnings the socialization of the Soviet Zone proceeded along paternalistic —not to say, Prussian—lines. Symbolic of this paternalism is the fact that the only real workers' revolution to take place on German soil in modern times was the so-called fascistic, counter-revolutionary uprising of June 17, 1953, which was put down more rapidly and brutally by the Government of the GDR, assisted by Soviet tanks, than the King of Prussia had suppressed the bourgeois revolutionaries a century earlier. It is in this sense of a party bureaucracy claiming to carry out a revolution in the name of its sometimes reluctant working class that the famous lines of the most famous poet of the GDR, Bertolt Brecht, are to be understood:

> After the uprising of the 17th of June
> The Secretary of the Writers' Union had
> Leaflets distributed in the Stalin Allee
> In which it was said that the people had
> Lost the confidence of the Government
> And could only regain it by
> Working twice as hard as before.
> Wouldn't it be simpler, then, just to have
> The Government dissolve the people
> And elect another?

This kind of paternalism—along with occasional unsuccessful "Oedipal" attempts to do away with that paternalism—has also been a leading feature of the cultural policy of the GDR. Though antithetic to modern Western ideas, which prefer to see in the writer a Shelleyan unacknowledged legislator of mankind, there is something to be said for turning the writer into an acknowledged handmaiden of the legislator, especially if that legislator is in possession of the one and only true law. Which, in

any Marxist state, he by definition is. A writer in such a state, therefore, theoretically cannot help but endorse the actions of his government, since those actions are in accordance with the immutable laws of dialectical materialism and with the progress of the human race, even when in practice they may seem to be blatantly at variance with basic human decency. Ideas like "freedom" and "honesty" do not exist in a vacuum, as they tend to do in the West where it is up to the individual to fill these words with meaning drawn from his own personal experience, but are clearly defined in relation to a systematic interpretation of history and society. Hence it is, and it should not be surprising, that we find statements like the following taken from a collection sponsored by the Central Committee of the SED, *Kultur in unserer Zeit* (1965) [Culture in Our Time]: "In the sphere of artistic creation, too, freedom is achieved precisely through the agreement of the creative act of the individual with the objective needs of social progress. Socialist society makes it possible for the artist, by working for the interests of the people as a whole, to do full justice at the same time to the basic humanistic function of art. The real social preconditions of socialism provide a guarantee that there can no longer be any contradiction between this basic function of art and the aesthetic demands which the ruling working class makes on artists in the name of the people as a whole." So, too, with the remarks on "honesty" in Erhard John's *Zum Problem der Beziehungen zwischen Kunst und Wirklichkeit* (1960) [On the Problem of the Relations Between Art and Reality]: "We must vigorously resist all attempts to operate with an abstract concept of honesty. Such as: an artist, writer or philosopher is honest when he says and writes what he thinks. . . We cannot therefore let ourselves be hoodwinked by an abstractly conceived 'honesty' but we have to ask what the writer thinks and feels, what he is fighting and engaging himself for artistically. Most profoundly do we hail the honesty of a Maxim Gorki and Erich Weinert, a Pablo Neruda and Nazim Hikmet, a Hans Marchwitza and a Bruno Apitz, who stake their honor on perceiving and proclaiming by artistic means the great truth of our era, the historical mission of the working class and the legitimacy of socialist development, and on showing that the working class conscientiously receives into its hands all the great and worthy productions of mankind's cultural history up to now, and cultivates them and develops

them further." A Western skeptic might see in these statements the unmistakable handiwork of Orwell's Ministry of Truth, but even so it should be remembered that this sort of relativized morality is by no means a novelty introduced by socialist states. On the contrary, the greatest and oldest model for it is the Roman Catholic Church which, with its index of forbidden books, its doctrine of infallibility, and its power to excommunicate unbelieving and recalcitrant members, bears a far more than passing resemblance to the workings of a socialist state like that of the GDR. Just as the Church "inevitably" replaced the late imperalist phase of Rome, so too socialism will "inevitably" replace the late capitalist phase of bourgeois domination; and just as the Church has its holy texts and dogma, extending into all areas of life, including art and aesthetics, so, too, with the "developed" socialist societies.

Indeed, in many ways a state like the GDR is best understood as a paradoxically atheistic theocracy of a militant type, eager to convert the heathen bourgeois and to stifle all traces of heretical revisionism. The parallel holds true right down to the preoccupation with meetings and congresses to establish and promulgate policy, attended by party bishops and cardinals, or, in the case of Socialist Internationals, a kind of papal council, hosted by the *servus servorum*, the worker of workers, in Moscow itself. And as is only right and proper in a political church, decisions to join the party often take the form of quasi-religious conversions: as, for instance, in the case of at least one writer included in this anthology, Anna Seghers.

The literature of the GDR, as we have said already, has a certain uniformity or consistency of orientation. This does not, however, mean—as it is sometimes understood to mean by uncritical commentators—that this literature is either an indistinguishable and undistinguished mass of propaganda, or that it is monotonously predictable, or that it is aesthetically contemptible. One should remember that Chaucer, Dante, Saint John of the Cross, Pascal, Newman, Gerard Manley Hopkins and Evelyn Waugh were all devout Catholics, and that this important—indeed crucial—fact by no means prevented their work from reaching the very highest aesthetic levels. Socialism, to be sure, has not yet produced a Dante, or even a Waugh, but then it has not yet had a thousand years of extremely variegated history behind it, as the Church did in the case of Dante. Certainly in

Brecht socialism produced an artist of truly international stature, and, as the evidence of this anthology may indicate, it has fostered and is fostering talents worthy of serious critical attention.

The point that must be remembered here is that all dogma—social and religious, as well as aesthetic—is liable to interpretation and to individual manipulation, within a certain range at any rate. That range or spectrum has grown enormously broad in the case of the Roman Catholic Church; in the case of the socialist states, and particularly in that of the GDR, it is still comparatively narrow, though by no means so narrow as not to allow for some variation of treatment. It is here, in the question of the willingness of the Party to allow for a greater range of literary response to the conditions of socialist society, that the real aesthetic crux of socialism lies; if the Party is tolerant, if it has the courage to see in opposition not treason but loyal criticism, then socialist society can be fertile soil for a genuine socialist art. If not, if it lacks that courage, then socialism will be fruitful artistically only as a movement to react against rather than to act with, however ambiguously. It is the difference, say, between Catholicism, with its rich Catholic literary tradition, and Scottish Calvinism, with its rich anti-Calvinistic literary tradition.

So far, the literary history of the GDR has unfortunately leaned more in the direction of Calvinism than Catholicism. It is not merely the mass of literary hackwork that is being churned out annually in the GDR—socialist allegories as dull and barren as those of any pious medieval monk or fanatical convenanter—but the insistance on the highest governmental levels that art in general and literature in particular should express party policy. Typical of this attitude is Walter Ulbricht's censure, in 1965, of the Deputy Cultural Minister, Witt, for failing to note "ideological manifestations of skepticism and alienation" in a novel by Manfred Bieler, *Das Kaninchen bin ich* (1963) [I'm the Rabbit]: "It all hinges on this simple question: Do we believe that a couple of artists or writers can write what they like and determine the whole development of society? That's the question we're concerned with here, and that question you've answered with 'yes' and the Politbureau with 'No!' " In the GDR, answering "yes" or even "maybe" to the question of authorial independence, in other words, was and still is tantamount to advocating

the overthrow of the SED—a treasonable act for which a variety of punishments, from prison to loss of citizenship to expulsion from the party to loss of livelihood to refusal to publish, can and will be imposed.

This assertion of Party primacy in cultural affairs has been a consistent feature of the history of the GDR. In 1954 Otto Grotewohl, first Prime Minister of the GDR, announced that "what is right in matters of politics is absolutely right in artistic matters as well." Some fifteen years later, Kurt Hager, a leading cultural official put in a claim for what amounted to Party infallibility: "Our Party is approaching its 20th Anniversary. Louis Fürnberg wrote that beautiful song, 'The Party is Always Right.' That's true of the past, and that's true of the present and the future." This beautiful song, by the way, runs as follows:

> She [the Party] has given us everything,
> Sun and wind, never stinting
> And where she was, was life,
> And what we are, we owe to her.
> She has never flattered us.
> If ever we lost heart in the struggle
> She simply patted us gently on the back:
> Don't falter!—and in a trice we recovered.

This, in any terms, is simply drivel, no matter how well-intentioned; and any cultural policy which bases itself on such drivel is bound to fail. It was this assumption of artistic infallibility, as a corollary to political infallibility, that led to the so-called Bitterfeld Way, the largest-scale attempt so far in the GDR to force literature systematically into a single, officially endorsed direction. The name derives from the electro-chemical plant in Bitterfeld, a town near Halle, where in April 1959, under the auspices of the Mitteldeutscher Verlag [Central German Publishing House], a conference was held on the relationship between writers and workers. Walter Ulbricht was there and in his address to the participants urged workers and writers jointly to "storm the heights of culture," to fuse work and art in order to produce socialist art, an art which would concern itself with the problems of contemporary socialist man. As a result, veteran workers began to reach for their pens, to keep artistic journals recording their daily experiences, to publish stories and anec-

dotes; and writers rushed to don hard-hats, grasp unfamiliar tools, join work crews, factories and collective farms with a view to writing stories and novels based on their new roles.* The results, measured by serious aesthetic standards, were predictably unpromising: trivial, if well-meaning sketches by workers of the kind contained, for instance, in *Nachricht vom Schreibenden* (1969) [News from a Writing Person]; or rather mechanical, polished, and often unreadable documentary reports by the professionals.† In some cases where a genuine work of art threatened to emerge, as in Werner Bräunig's projected novel about the uranium miners in the Wismut district, the Party acted quickly to stifle the impulse. Perhaps the only novels of the Bitterfeld type ever to appear that were also genuine novels were Christa Wolf's *Geteilter Himmel* (1963) [Divided Sky] and Hermann Kant's *Die Aula* (1965) [The University Auditorium], both of which, ironically, rejected the Bitterfeld preoccupation with "ordinary" workers in favor of focusing on intellectuals of working-class origin.

Bitterfeld was only the most notable and widely publicized instance of Party manipulation of literary life in the GDR, and in its militant banality it is probably best understood as a reaction against the "excessively" liberal 4th German Writers Congress of 1956, at which Stefan Hermlin, Stefan Heym, Anna Seghers, Arnold Zweig and others voiced sharply worded criticisms of Party cultural policy—something that was not to happen again for twenty years, until the aftermath of the enforced exile and de-naturalization of Wolf Biermann in late 1976. Bitterfeld was really the logical consequence of the inflexible Party sponsorship of the doctrine of "socialist realism," an artistic theory officially formulated and endorsed during the Soviet Writers Congress in 1934, at which the notorious Stalinist Zhdanov

---

*This program had already been enunciated in its essentials by Ulbricht as long ago as 1948, as he himself pointed out at Bitterfeld, and a few writers had already written "factory" novels. Also, it had been customary for some time for Party Congresses to set specific themes for writers, often having to do with similar subjects, such as agricultural reforms or the lives of factory workers.

†How spontaneously the workers took to their new literary role or how much they enjoyed reading books about themselves by professionals is, however, questionable. The popular pulp novelist, Harry Thürk, for instance, was once confronted by a group of miners who told him that they would like more adventure and detective stories, whereupon he replied that they ought to demand books dealing with their own lives and problems.

played a leading role. The West German critic, Marcel Reich-Ranicki, has suggested that socialist realism might therefore more aptly be called "Stalinist classicism," and there is undoubtedly a kind of ponderous monumentality about certain products of socialist realism that is reminiscent of the Stalin Allee in East Berlin. Basically, socialist realism is a development of bourgeois realism (or "critical realism" as it is sometimes called), but unlike bourgeois realism it does not criticize the conditions of society, since these conditions, created as they have been by the historically necessary rule of the working class, cannot be criticized. According to Zhdanov, the positive functions of socialist realism are: to examine carefully the life of workers; to become a school for socialism by having the writer obey Stalin's dictum to be an "engineer of the human soul"; and to portray not objective reality but "reality in its revolutionary development."

A great mass of theoretical literature exists on the subject of socialist realism, its nature and origins (especially in the letters of Marx and Engels); and there have been some remarkable attempts, notably by Georg Lukács, to develop a kind of "socialist realism with a human face." In the GDR, however, particularly after the abortive 1956 Hungarian Revolution in which Lukács took part, such efforts were generally discredited. "Stalinist classicism" was once again the order of the day.

Socialist realism may most simply be thought of, in respect to the GDR, as selective realism in a socialist society; and this is certainly how it is usually conceived of in GDR Party discussions: as a literary technique which serves to *reflect* the *typical* features of the social and technological achievements of this new state (often by way of contrast with the failures of bourgeois society in general and the bourgeois societies of West Germany or Nazi Germany in particular). Aside from merely reflecting, however, it may also have a more dynamic and active function, namely to enhance or speed up the development of socialism. The official adoption of socialist realism as the only possible literary method for a socialist society has been useful in a variety of respects, not least in justifying a continuing Party involvement in aesthetic matters. In hindsight, it has also formed a part of the rationale for the decision (made early in 1946) to accept the "German Classics"—Goethe, Schiller, Lessing, Heine, Hauptmann, Mann, etc.—as part of the progressive German

literary tradition culminating in the socialist realist literature of the GDR. And, in addition, it has permitted an exclusion of so-called formalist bourgeois literature, on the grounds that such literature is nihilistic and harmful. Hence a writer like Kafka is not considered a suitable model for GDR writers.

The case of Kafka is especially interesting because Kafka was the subject of the last serious attempt to alter the aesthetic dogma of the GDR in a direction which would permit writers greater access to modernist literary techniques. This took place at the "Kafka Conference" in May 1963 near Prague—a conference also attended by a delegation from the GDR—at which Ernst Fischer put forward a radical thesis that alienation was an emotional-intellectual condition not confined to bourgeois society exclusively, but present also in socialist society, as an inevitable result of the inordinate complexity of modern technological conditions; and, further, that this alienation would only disappear when a communist form of society replaced the socialist form. As a consequence socialist realism could not be considered a method but only an attitude which the socialist artist held in respect to his society, an attitude moreover which could include criticism of the bureaucrats who administered that society. Though shortly thereafter—apparently as a result of this conference—a limited edition of Kafka was allowed to appear in the GDR, the official response to Fischer's attempt to rehabilitate Kafka was unmistakably negative. Conflict there might be in GDR society, but if so it was occasional, aberrant, individual conflict; certainly there was and could be no conflict of a systematic sort such as Fischer had posited in his concept of alienation. Modernist snakes were to be denied visas to the proletarian Garden of Eden, or at best allowed in for only brief, possibly antidotal visits.

With all this, it is perhaps not surprising that the everyday life of the writer in the GDR is not an easy one. As Werner Brettschneider remarks in his study of literature in the GDR, *Zwischen literarischer Autonomie und Staatsdienst* (1974) [Between Literary Autonomy and Government Service], the writer in the GDR is continually balancing on a thin line dividing him from denunciation on the one hand and a National Prize on the other. Even writers such as Erwin Strittmatter and Alfred Kurella, now so highly regarded that they are used as models in the schools, have occasionally been either in danger of censure

or have actually been censured severely by the Central Committee of the SED—not to speak of more suspicious sorts of writers like Stefan Hermlin, Günter Kunert, Christa Wolf, Ulrich Plenzdorf, and, of course, Stefan Heym.

Those who have had it least difficult of all perhaps are the oldest generation of GDR writers, that is, those who were born roughly in the closing years of the last century and the opening years of this, writers who reached maturity and in some cases fame in the Weimar Republic, who almost to a man and woman suffered the hardships and humiliations of exile during the Nazi period (or else imprisonment and worse), and who returned filled with hope and enthusiasm in the years immediately following the war, ready to build up a truly humane socialist state. Undoubtedly many members of this older generation—including such writers as Bertolt Brecht, Arnold Zweig, Bodo Uhse, Ludwig Renn, Anna Seghers, Willi Bredel and Johannes R. Becher—suffered greatly as their dreams were confronted by the actual facts of life in the GDR, but at any rate they had the satisfaction of enjoying a secure place in the new society, relatively exempt from the criticism often heaped on younger writers, and more or less free either to rest on their laurels or to write on subjects dealing with the bourgeois past—often their own personal past—rather than with the socialist present. Their work, on the whole, is marked by the struggle to achieve a socialist society, and not by that society itself. Their best work, indeed, tends to arise out of opposition to bourgeois or fascist society; and they seem either to continue to draw strength from the memories of that opposition or to decay and fall silent.

To write of the past—even the quite recent past, such as the war—soon came to be considered an attempt to escape facing the realities of the present. The second generation of GDR writers—those born roughly in the first three decades of this century—were most acutely and often agonizingly caught in the conflicting claims of the past and the present, because their memories were full of the intense experience of the years of Nazi domination, because some of them (like Franz Fühmann) had even been enthusiastic Nazis themselves, because they needed to understand their place in the past before they could cope with their situation in the present. At the same time, these writers were still young enough at the end of the war to be influenced strongly by the new directions in which the Soviet Zone (and later the GDR)

was moving. They are the "transitional" generation—the generation of Strittmatter, Hermlin, Bobrowski and Kant—whose work is frequently and sometimes poignantly concerned with that very process of transition, of the guilt of the past and the promise of the future, of childhood in a Nazi nightmare and manhood among the growing pains of a socialist state.

It is only with the third generation—those born after about 1930 and including writers like F. R. Fries, Wolfgang Biermann, Werner Bräunig and Ulrich Plenzdorf—that one can really date the beginning of GDR literature as such. This literary generation is the first to be wholly or at least decisively shaped by the conditions of a socialist society on German soil and to be free (or as free as any German generation ever can be) of the guilt attached to Germans who lived through the Nazi period and the war as adults. It is the first generation for whom the GDR is the "ordinary" experience, the first generation which has never really known anything else. Hence, not surprisingly, the work of this generation tends to be concerned with "ordinary people"—as Werner Bräunig observed—with their "ordinary" conflicts and concerns. No longer is it necessary to pore guiltily into the past or smile fixedly into the future, to denounce opposition or revision or to exhort undying loyalty to the resolutions of the latest Party congress; now it is enough to examine, more coolly and even cold-bloodedly than ever before, the facts of what life is like for an intelligent and rather skeptical young person in the GDR.

Unlike the young skiers and swimmers of the GDR, this youngest generation of writers may not have attained an international reputation in the equivalent of the literary Olympics—in terms of prizes and awards—but then serious writers are not "produced" or "coached" in quite the same way that skiing or swimming teams are, despite the existence of the Johannes R. Becher Institute for Literary Study in Leipzig, an Institute which was originally designed to do just that. "Storming the heights of culture" requires more than conscientious drill and good organization. Even so, and even because this new generation seems less disposed to allow itself to be herded than its predecessors, it contains the seeds of remarkable literary promise. It is they, more than anyone else—aside from grand-old-men like Brecht—who may do most to disprove that famous prophecy about the future of the arts under communism made by

Heinrich Heine in his preface to the French edition of *Lutetia*: "This confession that the future belongs to the Communists, this confession I made in a tone of anxiety and terror, and that—alas!—was no pretense on my part. Indeed, I can only think with fear and trembling of the time when these gloomy iconoclasts will come to power. They will pitilessly break all the marble statues of Beauty with their calloused hands, those statues that are so dear to my heart; they will smash all those entertainments and fantastic trifles of Art that this poet so loved; they will destroy my groves of laurel and plant potatoes in their place; the lilies that neither span nor labored but were as marvellously clothed as King Solomon in all his splendor—they will tear them out of the soil of society, unless they get busy on the spinning wheel; the same fate will befall the roses, those idle brides of the nightingales; they will drive away the nightingales, too, those useless singers, and—oh!—my Book of Songs will be used by the grocer to make paper bags into which to pour coffee and tobacco for the poor old ladies of the future. Oh! I see it all coming and I am seized by an unspeakable melancholy when I think of the fate with which a victorious proletariat threatens my verses, a fate that will annihilate them and along with them the whole of the old romantic world."

Heine, one can now safely say, was wrong—wrong at least about the fate of his own verses, which have been officially cherished and republished in lavishly edited form. He was wrong too about the laurels and potatoes, but not entirely wrong: the laurels have not been replaced by potatoes, but GDR official-dom is intent on growing laurels as if they were potatoes. But he was right about the lilies: they, alas, have had to learn to spin.

Perhaps the best and certainly the easiest and most pleasant way to gain a quick overview of these orchards of literary laurel, these fields of literary lilies and potatoes, is to turn to a good selection of short stories. Unlike most Western countries, where the short story as a genre has steadily lost in popularity since the Second World War, in the GDR it is still one of the most widely used and beloved forms. There are several reasons why this should be so: because the short story is a relatively new form in any German-language literary tradition, which until recently had preferred the somewhat longer novella-form;* because the

*We have also included some novellas in this anthology, notably Anna Seghers' "The Excursion of the Dead Girls" and Erwin Strittmatter's "Snow White."

short story has a historic and honored place in Russian and Soviet literature, to which literary bureaucrats in the GDR look for guidance; because the short story, generally speaking, is easier to produce than the novel, and in a society which is hyper-conscious of meeting or exceeding quotas this is an important factor; because the short story can be both less and more political than longer narrative forms, in that it can either be all surface, in the way a novel almost never can be, or in that it can suggest criticism obliquely and apparently innocuously as the more "important" novel cannot; and, finally, because there is an audience for the short story in the GDR, in journals and newspapers as well as in collections and anthologies.

Ideally, dipping into an anthology of short stories like the present one should be like taking a bus tour through a strange country. One stops at all the main cities and sees all the notable sights, some of which one likes more and others less; sometimes one is bored and sometimes excited. In the end, one's memories tend to grow a little muddled and it is not always easy to distinguish one place from another, though invariably there will remain an intense and detailed recollection of a very few places and experiences. To those few places—and those few authors— one should return and probe more deeply; explore them thoroughly until one gets to know their secrets, until one ceases to be a tourist and gets to be as close to a native as a stranger ever can be.

That has been the aim of this anthology. Like all anthologizers, we have tried to make ours representative, though of course we are perfectly aware that no general anthology worth its salt can ever be representative of the mass of the literary production of any country. It can and should only be representative of the best—in this case, of the best that has been thought and written in the form of short story by men and women who are or have been considered part of the GDR literary tradition. The best is always elitist and never represents the average, though it may be "typical" in the sense given that word by Georg Lukács, who thought of the "type" as an "extreme situation" embodying an essential historical process. In any case, we have tried our best to provide our readers with a sense of the development of the short story, both formally and thematically, in the GDR, during the lives of three literary generations. Unfortunately, due to circumstances beyond our control, we have not always been able to

include every writer, or for that matter every story, we had originally hoped to include. Two of the most obvious omissions are Bertolt Brecht and Ulrich Plenzdorf; we regret their absence and can only say that the compilation of anthologies—like the planning of bus tours—is fraught with unforeseen difficulties and sudden surprises, not all of them pleasant.

THE EMIGRANT

WILLI BREDEL

One cold February morning a strange creature sat on a wooden bench among the bright, slender birches in front of the airport restaurant: small and slight, dressed in a long dark overcoat and in very tight, dark-striped pants, a gray checked cap pulled far down into his heavily marked and furrowed face. His head was hunched down into the collar of his coat and only his hands—rubbing his thighs and knees nervously—gleamed like bright dots against his somber, shrouded body. Behind the big windows of the restaurant one could see people sitting at small tables covered with white linen. The man must have been feeling very afraid and seemed to be freezing, and he looked shyly around and up at the control tower where a big swastika flag was flying. As he lowered his eyes again he remembered that he still did not know what time it was and he looked up once more. The second hand was moving quickly across the clockface. Still twelve minutes to go. Maybe the plane was late too. He had hesitated a long time and had mulled everything over a hundred times, first one way, then another. Now, after having been threatened with murder, every minute he had to wait was torture.

Arno Talborn, who was sitting here on the bench feeling afraid and freezing, knew that around noon he would be in Amsterdam—in other words, saved. From there he would be going on to America. And he never, never planned to return. Would he ever see his son Bruno again? He had been in prison for the last two years and was supposed to stay in for another six. Would they really release him after six years? Nobody knew exactly. . . . In six years his son would be thirty. From twenty-two to thirty in prison: it was unthinkable! So don't think about it. . . . Two years ago they had arrested Bruno and it was soon known that they had tortured him; then there was a rumor that

they had killed him and buried him in Eilenriede; and Talborn's wife jumped out of a window and he—he had cursed his son then. What business of his was it to get mixed up in politics? And on top of that with the Communists. A Jew and a Communist—no wonder the Nazis got doubly riled up about that. He himself had always steered clear of politics and had always kept out of the public eye. Sure, he had voted the Social Democratic ticket since the Revolution, but nobody knew about that. He was a businessman and people in business had to keep neutral. His customers had usually never noticed that he was a Jew; most of them were Aryans and many of them even—as he had always known—anti-semitic. But he was a businessman. What did selling flour and bottled beer, sugar and canned goods have to do with politics?

When Bruno joined the Communist Youth Organization, Talborn had only let him do it after Bruno had sworn not to get involved publicly. The boy had kept his word too until the Reichstag fire. But in the worst days when it was doubly wise, as Arno Talborn believed, to keep in the background, the boy did not merely stay with those who were being persecuted but even, so it appeared, had taken up a leading role among them. And so, after a period of living outside the law, restless and continuously hounded, the unavoidable had happened. With one stroke old Talborn lost his wife and son. He had already lost half of his customers. Then came the threats against him. His relatives in America offered to help. Now he was sitting at the airfield with his plane ticket in his pocket and the steamship ticket waiting for him in Amsterdam. He could not stay another day in Linden without running the risk of being lynched.

It had not been an easy decision for Arno Talborn, not only because of his son. Forty years he had lived in Germany and more than thirty of those years in Hanover, out there in Linden. Now at the age of fifty-six he was supposed to go off alone into the unknown with hardly more than a few dollars in his pocket.

"Who are you?"—Arno Talborn jumped up, frightened. In front of him stood a towering SS-man. Before he could answer, the man asked: "And why are you sitting out here in the cold?"

"I'm not allowed inside," answered Talborn. The SS-man did not understand that and looked at the pale and trembling little figure.—"Your name?"—"Arno Israelite Talborn."—"Ah soo . . ."—The man in uniform sneered contemptuously and

was about to walk on; then he changed his mind. "You're planning to leave the country, right?"—"Yes, sir."—"With a pile in your pocket, huh?"—"No, sir."—"Then what <u>have</u> you got in your pocket?" the SS-man suddenly screamed. "Cash, jewels?"

Shaking with fear, Arno Talborn looked up at the man who had abruptly turned angry. Why had he lost his temper? After all, his answers had been short and to the point. He pulled himself together, squared his shoulders and replied as firmly and steadily as he could: "No, sir, only underwear, some soap, a toothbrush and so on."

A mocking grin began to form at the corners of the SS-man's mouth; he narrowed his eyes and fixed the Jew with a malicious stare. "Soap? As if a pig like you ever washed. A toothbrush? Your breath stinks enough to make me sick." He paused a moment to reflect. Alone, without witnesses, he was not authorized to examine anybody's baggage. The filthy rat might even complain later that he had stolen his stuff.

"My baggage has already been searched." Arno Talborn saw the SS-man eyeing his suitcase.

"Did I ask you, bonehead? Open this stinking little package up. Come on, come on!"

A plane was making its landing approach. Passengers were leaving the restaurant. Suitcases were being wheeled off on a cart. Arno Talborn did not see any of this; his hands, grown clumsy from excitement, tried to open his small suitcase. "Hurry up, hurry up! Are you trying to pull something on me, you pig?" the SS-man threatened. Finally the suitcase sprang open and Arno Talborn heaved a sigh of relief. "See, Sir?" He rummaged around with his hands among the shirts and underwear, showed him socks, a pair of slippers. "Or would you rather check for yourself?"

"And what have you got hidden behind that?" The SS-man pointed at the lining of the suitcase and flashed a piercing look at the Jew.

"Where?" asked Talborn antonishedly because he did not see anything except the cover of the suitcase in which there was not even a small pocket.

"Where?" the SS-man yelled at the top of his voice. "There of course. Behind it!" He leaned down, ripped the lining in two with a jerk and reached inside. He found nothing.

"Talborn!" a voice called. Arno Talborn answered: "Here!"—
"What are you doing over there? Come on over here!" Only now
did Talborn notice that a plane was standing on the airfield and
that the passengers were getting in. He pointed to his suitcase
and the SS-man, "Inspection, sir. I'm coming! Right away!"—
"Shut up, you pig!" the SS-man hissed at him between his teeth,
watching the official running over to him, "Pack your stuff
up."—"Haven't you checked your things through customs yet?"
the airport official asked. "Oh yes, sir! But the gentleman
here . . ."—the SS-man cut him off and said: "The fellow was
behaving suspiciously."—"I see." The official avoided looking
at the man in uniform. He handed Talborn his passport and
shouted impatiently: "Well, then hurry up, otherwise you'll be
left behind."

Arno Talborn wedged his suitcase under his arm even though
it was not properly closed and ran off towards the airplane. The
official followed him. As Talborn was climbing up the short
gangway, he felt his arm being held back. The official asked him:
"Are any of your things missing?"

"No, no of course not," Talborn cried out, terrified as if he had
been accused of a crime.

*　　*　　*

Arno Talborn had found a seat near the exit. He was very
happy about that because that meant he would not have to look
into anybody's face. In front of him there were only the backs of
heads and necks. He made out seven passengers besides himself,
five men and two women. Four seats were empty. Nobody paid
any attention to him. They had only looked up because he had
arrived late.

Now Arno Talborn was flying. He would never come back. But
his son was in the prison at Celle. Four bare walls, a square hole
with bars in it, a bunk, a bucket . . . Two long years already—and
three times two years to go . . . Wasn't Gertrude better off in the
cemetery on the Linden Hill? Wouldn't it have been better for
him to follow her? America. The word did not mean anything to
him. He might just as well be taking a trip to the moon. America!
His brother-in-law whom he could scarcely remember owned a
bar in Topeka. What was the point of his going there?

When he looked out of the window, he saw the bright metal of
the wings and below them the massive undercarriage with a

slowly turning wheel. If he leaned forward a little he could see below him villages and country roads that were thin as lines and straight as arrows, and individual small fields and dark patches of woods. When gentle, wind-blown clouds drifted past, the clear visibility vanished for seconds . . .

An infinite sadness came over Talborn. He was forced to excape like a criminal. Anybody who felt like it had the right to humiliate and insult him.

What did that man in the uniform want? Did he really believe that he was smuggling valuables out of the country? He thought of all the insults he had endured over the last few years, malicious insults, without cause, without meaning. To humiliate others, to demean them, to hurt them—for many people that had turned into a sport, an amusement . . . Why America? Why? Should he not have stayed after all and hanged himself like Nathan Roth, the jeweler in Goethe Street, or gassed himself like the Goldschmidt family in Waldersee Street? They had wanted to kill him, and he had fled. 'Why am I running away? What do I want to do in America? I'm running away while Bruno is sitting in jail . . .'

"Sir, would you like to have a map showing our flight route?" A steward opened up a folded, longish-looking map. "If you look over to your left, sir, that's Minden. We'll be over it in a moment." Talborn did not look at the map, he looked at the man who spoke these words to him. It was only rarely that anyone was nice to him. Very rarely. "Would you care perhaps for a cup of coffee?" the steward asked. "Yes, yes please," Talborn answered, overwhelmed with gratitude.

Minden. Talborn leaned towards the window. Red roofs, towers, embedded in a wreath of dark woods. He had been in Minden, in a small hotel; and he had been in the Teutoburg Forest, Gertrude and he; and Bruno had still been little, wild and full of high spirits. Gertrude had spoken incessantly of some disaster that was still to come . . . some disaster . . . no, the disaster came later . . . and the boy hadn't done anything wrong. He called himself a Communist, and he and his friends had stuck together even after it was forbidden. For that he now had to pay with the best years of his youth. 'What will the boy think if he finds out that I've escaped to America? To this day he doesn't know that his mother killed herself because of him . . .'

The steward stepped out of the galley right behind Talborn's

seat. "Your coffee, sir." Along with it came a little bowl of cream and another with sugar. "Thank you very much."

'A nice man,' thought Talborn. 'An uncommonly nice man in these times.' He tasted the coffee and his spirits revived a little. The steward, moving past with an empty tray, said: "We're just flying over the border now, sir."

"You don't have an entry visa. And your special passport expires in three weeks.* Where is it that you want to go?"

"To America!" answered Talborn softly; he sensed the approach of a new misfortune, pulled his head down into his jacket again and looked anxiously up at the official of the Amsterdam airport. There was something unspeakably meek about his big, dark, somewhat protruding eyes.

"Do you have any money?"—"Oh yes," he whispered.— "How much?"—"Twenty-five dollars."

The official looked at him surprised and annoyed. Was he trying to play the fool? Now Talborn even smiled, a shy, apologetic smile. Unfortunately for Talborn the official interpreted this smile as mockery; his face became bureaucratic and hard: "You have to go back."

"Excuse me? . . . What did you say?" Arno called out after him. But his voice no longer reached the angry man.

*   *   *

Two hours later Arno Talborn was in the plane again, flying back on the same route. The steward had come and distributed maps of the flight route. Talborn was asked if he wanted coffee and he had refused. Everything was infinitely indifferent to him. He would get off in Hanover, return to Linden, to his dead wife. The border guard was right: what was he, Talborn, going to do in America? Innumerable people lived in America and they certainly were not waiting for him. The whole business of emigrating was a stupid idea. He belonged in Hanover, in Linden, where his wife lay and where his son would come back—after six years. He certainly would not have sold his store in such a rush if he had not received that threatening letter. What did he care about the sale price . . . he could not take the money along with him to America anyway. It was out of the purest magnanimity that the Small Business Bank had deposited the money in his son's

*In Nazi Germany passports issued to Jews were stamped with the word "Israelite."

account. He had given away his store—no, they had stolen it from him.

'They wanted to kill me if I didn't take off immediately.' Perhaps that fellow Heidemann who had afterwards bought the store had actually written the threatening letter? 'Let 'em kill me . . . Let 'em kill me . . .' Since having come to fear life, he no longer was afraid of death.

Arno Talborn was seated again, hunched up among the cushions, in the rearmost seat of the plane. He was a long-suffering man. That of all people he, a man who did not like many Jews himself, had to suffer like this because he was a Jew! For example, what decent person could respect somebody like Eugene Winkelstein? He knew his mansion near Berlin with its immense park. Whenever he thought of that park, he never envisioned trees, plants, arbors and running fountains; instead he saw a vast military cemetery with one wooden cross next to the other and in the middle of it Winkelstein's palace. Could one respect somebody like that? Was it not terrible that this man was a Jew? But was that his fault—the grocer Talborn's fault—who had been a soldier himself, had fought in the battlefield for Germany and had worked hard and honestly his whole life long? His brother-in-law in Topeka had advised him to turn to Eugene Winkelstein; he could help him, he had innumerable connections. A man like that remained untouched despite his palace amid the wooden crosses, despite his being a Jew. That rich people were always spared unpleasantness was something the little storekeeper understood quite well and he had never expected it to be otherwise. So too, under different circumstances it would have seemed self-evident to Talborn that great disaster should pass Eugene Winkelstein by, but now he was outraged by this injustice.

The plane began a steep descent. Talborn saw a church tower going past, a broad meadow approaching, then a few hedges which the plane barely cleared, a jolting impact, he had landed in Hanover airport again.

"You?" the surprised airport official asked.

"My visa wasn't there even though they had assured me here that it would be. There must have been a mistake. Or an oversight." Arno Talborn spoke these words in a quick stammer. "I am going to put off my trip. And find out exactly what happened."

"You will get your passport back in the Dispatcher's Office," the official said. "Over there in that little annex."

Talborn would much rather have kept his receipt and left the airport without delay; he was afraid of meeting the rude SS-man again who had accused him of smuggling money. But what could he do? He took his little suitcase and went over to the elongated building and stopped at the entrance with "Dispatcher" written over it. His heart was hammering in his chest. His head felt dizzy. He had a premonition that it would turn out badly. He walked in hesitantly—his hand shook as he grasped the doorhandle. He had not yet had a chance to look around properly when he heard a shout of exultation: "My Jew! Why here's my Jew again!"

Arno Talborn turned around and recognized the young SS-man. Now he was trembling in his whole body, incapable of speaking a word or walking another step. In a moment he saw himself surrounded by a whole troop of uniformed Hitler soldiers. The tall young SS-man whom Talborn already knew stepped up very close to him. His face was radiant, his malicious gray eyes exultant, his wide mouth laughing. "You worthless little punk: they wouldn't accept you, eh?" he asked. "Could it be that they caught you smuggling jewels, eh?" And the eyes grew even more malicious and threatening. "No, no," screamed Talborn. "Oh no, sir . . ."—"Why did they send you back? Hurry up, answer!" Talborn looked around confusedly. What should he answer without arousing these people's hostility to him even more? An SS-man said: "Well, they're slowly beginning to get the idea out there and saying no thanks to Jews. Kill the whole rotten lot of them."—"My visa was not there."—"Why wasn't it there?" the SS-man asked and narrowed his eyes, like an animal about to pounce.

"A mistake, sir," Talborn stammered. "Probably a mistake. Or perhaps . . ." he hesitated fearfully. "Or perhaps what? . . ." the SS-man probed. "Perhaps . . . or perhaps an oversight," Talborn brought out with difficulty. "What? What?" the SS-man screamed. "You want to accuse us, you dog? Blame us for an oversight?" He extended himself to his full height and commanded: "Hands to your pants seams!" Arno Talborn let his little suitcase drop and placed both arms tight against his legs. "You're going to be punished for your insolence," said the SS-man, and at the same time he slapped the Jew resoundingly

in the face as he stood at attention. The latter reeled back from the powerful blow and held up his hands to protect his face. "Didn't I order you to keep your hands at your pants seams?" And he hit Talborn again and every one of the uniformed men against whom he reeled pushed him away. "Insolent, brazen, shameless animal! Bloodsucker of the German people! Rapist! Child killer! Hyena!" Every blow, every shove was accompanied by an insult. Finally somebody kicked Talborn into a corner of the room. The SS-men dispersed laughing and talking loudly. One of them screamed at Talborn to get up and stand with his face to the wall. The beaten man got up laboriously and staggered over to the place that had been indicated to him.

For two hours Arno Talborn was forced to stand with his face towards the wall; now for the second time he was in the plane en route to Amsterdam. The steward distributed maps; he did not give one to Talborn. He asked the passengers if they wanted coffee. He did not ask Talborn. He went past him as if he was not there. The SS-people at the Hanover Airport had drawn his attention to Talborn. Talborn had had to pay ten dollars for his second ticket. Counting the tip for the SS-man who had gone to get it because Talborn had not been permitted to leave his place by the wall.

This time he was not sitting in the rearmost seat but with the other passengers. Without being able to help it, the tears ran down his deathly pale face; his small slight body shook periodically with nervous attacks. An older lady behind him offered him coffee out of her Thermos bottle. He took it and drank greedily. Then she handed him a ham sandwich. His face wet with tears, he thanked her with a smile. Somebody said: "My dear lady, he's a Jew."—"That's percisely the reason," she answered and added: "Thank God, I am not subject to the barbaric laws of your country." The passengers remained silent. The woman however rummaged about in her pocketbook, pulled out a little card and handed it to Talborn: "If you need any help abroad," she said loudly so that everybody could her, "I am at your disposal." Talborn, who had not dared to eat the ham sandwich for fear of causing another scandal, thanked her effusively in whispers and immediately felt a terrible fear of the man who sat three seats behind him on the other side of the window.

But when the plane began its descent he nevertheless heaved a

sigh of relief. He thought he was saved. He did not know that the problem with the visa was still unresolved and that the SS-man had sent him on this hopeless journey as a joke.

Arno Talborn spent the night in the guard room of the Amsterdam Airport. All his appeals had not been able to weaken the resolve of the officials: nobody was allowed to enter without a visa. Besides the authorities were already taking care of the matter. Contacted by telephone, they had promised in Hanover to secure the entry permit from the Dutch consul in Berlin. In the meantime there was no other choice but to send Talborn back again; the Germans had to be prevented from casually dumping offensive elements of the population over the border. "Kill me," Talborn had whimpered, "but don't send me back!"—"We don't kill people here," the Dutch official had replied.

In utter despair, knowing that the chain of torture and humiliation had still a long way to run, Arno Talborn sat apathetically in the plane. The chief of the Amsterdam Airport had given him a letter for the chief of the Hanover Airport. In an official tone the Dutch official requested that the emigrant Arno Talborn only be permitted to leave when in possession of a visa. Since said emigrant desired to continue en route to the United States of America, a transit visa would be sufficient, a document which could be secured without difficulty from the Dutch representative in Hanover. Talborn did not know what was in the letter. He did not care either. He did not care about anything. "The flying Jew's here again!" the SS-men yelled for joy and dragged Talborn off in triumph to their dispatching office. "Well, you scarecrow, nobody wants you. The rest of the world declines the offer of scum like you," one of them said scornfully. "But we're supposed to tolerate them," another one screamed. "A little more quiet, please," shouted the SS-man who had been the first to question Talborn. "At least wait until the passengers have left the airport." One of them pointed to the letter which Arno Talborn was holding in his hand. "What kind of a letter is that?" the SS-man asked and pushed his face with its infuriated, malicious eyes and mouth pursed in fury right up against Talborn. He fell back in horror. "For the chief of the airport."— "For whom?"—"For the chief . . ."—"For whom?" Talborn retreated even further, right up to the wall. "For whom, you uneducated pig?"—Finally Talborn understood. "For the *Hon-*

orable Chief!" But he did not succeed in avoiding a slap in the face.

His torturer took the letter out of his hand and opened it. "Imagine," he said to the other SS-people who were looking at him full of curiosity. "The chief of the Amsterdam Airport advises us to keep the Jew."—"Well, he makes him sick too," one of them said. But the SS-man holding the open letter in his hand, screamed in outrage: "Who does he think he is to get mixed up in our affairs? We are masters in our own house. This eternal interference in purely German affairs . . . well, I'm going to teach that fellow a lesson." He turned to Talborn: "And you, you crud, off with you to your place. Hurry up, over there in the corner. With your monkey's snout up against the wall. And don't move or there'll be hell to pay."

The SS-people of the airport guard enthusiastically continued their sport with the "flying Jew." To make sure they were safe from any possible consequences, they established a file for the case and sent it off to the appropriate office. They knew that it would take plenty of time before they would get an answer. Arno Talborn had to pay another ten dollars for a ticket to Amsterdam.

He started to cry quietly. Not to Amsterdam. He was ashamed to arrive there again without a visa. The SS-men stood around him and held their bellies, ready to burst with laughter, because Talborn's old face was disfigured from crying. "Not to Amsterdam. Let me go home." He wanted to escape from these SS-people. He trembled at the thought that they might ask him about his son. Then again mad, desperate ideas of revenge shot through his brain, ideas that brought him close to insanity. 'If I only had a gun,' he thought, 'I'd shoot, shoot these animals until they were dead.' He furtively formed his hands into fists as he thought this. But he was old and weak. His torturers on the other hand were young and strong; and they had guns, and on top of that they had the legal right to use those guns. 'Oh!—I should have killed myself, like Nathan Roth and Goldschmidt did,' he thought in his deathly misery.

"The plane for Amsterdam is leaving at 2:25. You're going to be on it! Stand up straight! Straight! When you're coming from Germany, you always stand up straight! The world out there has got to see at once that we've got law and order here." The SS-man who said this to Talborn could hardly hide a grin. Howls of

laughter broke out around him. "Here's your ticket. Regards to your Dutch friend. Tell him that if you disgust him, he can always send you back. We—we'll be waiting for you!" Again the whole bunch broke out in howls of laughter.

Escorted by two SS-men, Arno Talborn was sent off for the third time on the Amsterdam flight. He found a seat again in the last row, pulled his head down deep into his jacket and, resigned to his fate, closed his hurting eyes.

"Hey, Gerhard," one of the SS-men shouted, "should I hang the sign up? I'm sure they're going to send him back. Probably even today!" He fastened the sign up over the entrance to the Dispatcher's Office. Proud of his idea, he looked around.

Sudden loud cries of horror. The airport officials ran out over the airfield. One of them cried out: "Somebody's fallen out of the plane!"

On the banks of the Leine River lay a small, smashed-up body. "The Jew," shouted the SS-people who had run over.

Arno Talborn's corpse was carried to the "Dispatcher's Office" and through the door over which hung a sign surrounded by garlands: "A Hearty Welcome."

THE SACRIFICE

EDUARD CLAUDIUS

He heard the howling hiss of the bullet; he huddles up more closely behind the stone that he is pushing ahead of him like a protective shield. Doesn't notice that he's only moved three meters forward on the asphalt . . . away from the corner of the wall that provides protection and up to the point where his memory is jarred by the whizzing of the bullet.

That hiss—that's how it was then. Every hiss was followed by a piercing pain. That it was a pain of the soul he only realizes today. Then he was an eight-year-old boy.

He looks at the valley, bare, dry, only covered with olive trees. In the background of the other half of the valley stood the manor house, fairly high up as if it had been built to overlook everything right up to the grayish-green trees on the hills on the other side. He feels now that he's pushing the stone ahead—hot from the sun—how he would often lie then like this in the valley, holding fast to stones, pieces of wood and trees torn apart by the years and the burning sun. How far away all that is despite the nearness of the memories.

The enemy machine-gun—the target of his hand grenades—is silent, overwhelmed by a flood of rifle-fire from his comrades. He shoves the stone forward. Crawls forward. He feels the earth warm under his body. So was his mother's gentle nudging when she used to wake him as a boy in the morning. You couldn't resist it even if you were burdened down with the waking irritability of the new day. Strange that he'd never seen his mother in the morning in her bed, a heap of straw in a corner of their hut. Then you staggered into the dawn, lying dully between day and night. Out of the neighboring huts, standing glued to each other on the way to the hacienda, came the noise of awakening life, the bleating of sheep, the squealing of pigs, the cries of children, the scolding voices. He staggered up the road;

the ground still cold to his bare feet from the night. The stables surrounded the manor house. He had to go into one of the stables and tear open the door; the woolly balls of sheep's bodies welled up into the road and he followed them. It was his job to herd them during the day; not a hard job really.

How ridiculously easy that job seems to him now when he thinks of the task of silencing the machine-gun. There were something like three hundred sheep, but what was that compared to today. To be sure he has two well-loaded, home-made handgrenades . . .

He grabbed for his belt, afraid that he might have lost or forgotten them. The cold crept up his legs, for he felt he had left a great deal behind him that was worth living for. The warmth of the earth . . . Two handgrenades. In front, the machine-gun. Behind, life. The warmth of the earth under the noon-day sun. He is already further away from life, from his memories, than he was a few minutes ago, because he has managed to crawl three meters forward. There are at least thirty more to go before he reaches the point where he can throw.

Actually the sheep always stuck together in clumps. You had to watch them pretty frequently but there were hours that you could spend looking at the sky. Clouds like herds of sheep grazing towards the horizon as if there was better grass there: in the distance. It was lovely to watch when you knew that the Master had already taken his morning walk. You could never let yourself be caught by him when you were lying, dreaming and staring into the sky.

Once he lay in the shadow and thought about the furrows that the twisted olive trees had in their bark. The furrows in the olive trees, the parched earth, the furrows in the faces of the people.

He listened to the talk of the old people. Some had traveled beyond the boundaries of the estate. Cities were supposed to exist there. They called them cities. Lots of houses standing together, and they were supposed to be tall, twenty or even thirty meters tall. He had to laugh at these bare-faced lies. How could that many houses stand together in a heap? There wouldn't be any room for the stables; and sheep can't crawl up the walls, after all. There wouldn't be any more room for olive trees or for sheep to graze under them . . . He wasn't entirely sure of his laughter. Grown-ups knew a lot, the men who had strength in their arms, the women who could nurse the children.

When one day an old man told him that towards the south—
and he pointed in some direction with his emaciated hand—
there was an ocean and towards the north as well, his faith
wavered again. How could that be? Here where he was, where he
lived, there wasn't even water all year long in the brook, and
there where the ocean was supposed to be, water, water as far as
you could see . . . ? Where was it supposed to come from?
Somewhere. Where was it supposed to go? Anywhere. Impossible. He only believed one thing; that it was blue like the sky over
him on days when there were no cirrus clouds to put streaks into
it. That's the only thing he believed.

And he contemplated the sky again and again. It was blue. It
wore stars at night.

He would have to see this ocean someday. And his longing to
leave all this grew, the old estate, the olive trees, the wretched
huts along the road, the skimpy food. If out there there was an
ocean on which ships could sail—ships that in his dreams took
the strangest shapes—if there were towns out there where one
didn't need to herd sheep and still was able to live, then he
wanted to get out of here. He had to see all that: he wanted to
have more to eat too than a beet in the morning, potato soup at
noon and another potato soup with olives in the evening.

Suddenly he is torn out of his memories. Something is moving
behind the sandbags over by the enemy machine-gun.
Memories, dreams—they've all left him. Now he only sees the
house in which a few soldiers are providing cover for the
machine-gun; he sees how a body moves over there, jumps up,
throws something, then collapses at the sound of a shot.
A handgrenade explodes in front of him; it was meant for
him.

He was often bothered by hunger pangs during those days
under the olive trees while he thought about the broad expanse
of the world; hunger drove him to think about food. He looked at
the sheep. He didn't know what numbers were. But he knew this:
the earth would buckle under his feet and bury him if the
thoughts that pained and tortured him were to take shape: if he
were to . . . It wouldn't have to be anything bigger than a little
lamb, though he actually felt most sorry for the little animals . . .
The final straw was a heavy blow he received right in the middle
of his face from his Master, and then he decided not to go hungry
for once.

He stole a knife from his mother. Waited until his herd was grazing in the furthest corner of the valley.

For three days he lived off the young meat. In the evenings he would nevertheless try to eat his soup, tried to put the old expression into his eyes, for he felt that something in him had changed.

His mother did not say anything. Remained silent even when one evening the Count had them summoned. It was strange that everybody from the huts came. That deceived him too.

The Caballero let them all wait. The men stood next to each other in the courtyard and smoked acrid tobacco and the women talked about pigs and sheep, not succeeding very well in hiding their anxiety.

Then the door opened and for a moment he saw through the gap between the door frame and the round figure of the Master into the brightly lit hall. Saw the colorful walls, the glaring women and men who hung there in painted effigy. The Master stood in the door. There was silence in the courtyard. The Master had a horsewhip in his hand. It seemed to the boy as if everyone ducked.

He can't remember anymore what words the Master spoke. He only remembers the terror that crept up into his body: a stupefying, deadly terror. Now parts of sentences come back to him: ". . . and he cut the throat of the little animal . . . gorged himself for three days on stolen goods . . . as the Lord well says: mine is the revenge, but earthly justice . . . we have to once . . . and for all put an end to this . . ." He thought then: now he's going to drive me away. Didn't feel any grief about that. He saw the herd of sheep grazing in the sky. "I don't want to stand in the way of parental authority; I don't want to hurt so weak a child. Therefore his mother is to . . ." Thus spoke the Master and handed the horsewhip to my mother. She stood woodenly in front of him, nodded stupidly with her head.

It won't be as bad as all that, he ventured to think happily; mother probably won't hit as hard as the Master would have done. . . .

"Don't you want to take off your clothes?"

He shrank back from the ravenous maw of the man who had a belly and wobbly cheeks. And since he still stood there frozen, the man tore off his old, dirty, ragged pants. He stood naked in front of the people. The man signaled to the mother.

He felt happy again: his mother was really not hitting him hard . . . for that he would . . . oh, what should he give her for that . . . ? Tomorrow he'll . . .

"It won't hurt to hit him a little harder!"

That time it hissed through the air; that time it dug deeper into his flesh.

"Harder!"

Hatred burned in him against the man, against his mother who was beating him, against the man with the ravenous maw and the fattened belly. His hatred burned more intensely than the blows.

"Harder!"

That hissed and burned. His body was hot against the coolness of the night and his blood coursed in waves, red waves, through his body. He saw his mother's face: distorted, covered with perspiration. In turning jolts the house, the dark landscape and the star-sprinkled sky began to sway. His knees started to give way; he felt a warm, gentle wetness trickling down his back; the hissing and howling of the whip grew steadier as if his mother was enjoying herself. The landscape, the people blurred into a dark spot. A blunt, dead weight pressed his body towards the ground . . . he still felt the warm breath of his mother . . . He pulls his hand back suddenly. What's trickling so warm down his finger? Red and sticky. He smiles. It trickled then, it trickles now: blood. Don't think, don't brood now. He has to go forward; it's still thirty meters and now, pushing the stone with his finger smashed by a bullet . . .

A salvo from his comrades standing at the wall behind him gives him a chance to slide forward another three or four meters. He gropes for his handgrenades and he feels some of that same joy he felt then when he woke up and saw his mother—her face streaming with tears—soothing the wounds on his back and dabbing cool, alleviating oil on them.

Strange that he can't keep his thoughts under control. The task that he has before him is so difficult that it really requires all his thoughts, nerves and feelings. And he's dozing! His comrades behind him are waiting. Somewhere in the distance in the streets at his back, he hears the noise of crowds of people. They're singing songs, screaming their outrage and hatred into the streets, into the hot summery July air.

One day his mother did not get up any more. A few neighbors

went with him to the cemetery, wondered why he didn't cry but simply screamed several times. Like an animal.

Three days later they found his hut deserted. He went wherever the roads led him. Today it really made you smile to think that you had sought the great world, the cities, the ocean, the blue sky, the fat pastures of the cloud-sheep; and that you had believed that if you found them everything would be fine, that all the pain that time brought with it would be blown away as if by a gentle wind. What was it that he'd actually expected in those days?

He was fourteen years old. After he had seen the ocean, had listened to the roaring waves on an empty stomach for eight days, had stopped marveling at the blueness and the multitude of water, and had not found the fat pasture of the cloud-sheep, he had gone back into the cities. He worked for a trader as a mule-driver. It wasn't a bad life; it wasn't a good one. You trotted on behind the animals and in the evening you sank down dead-tired into some corner of the stable, melancholy with solitude, burnt out from the sun, your feet hurting from the country roads, your heart full of sadness. The corner belonged to him. So did the heavy smell of the mules that burned your eyes. One night—maybe half a year later—when he couldn't sleep, he saw himself. He saw a boy, lean, his eyes black and burning, trotting after the mules during the day and lying at night in a heavy, drugged stupor. And he wondered if that was he. If that was what he should be. He got up a quarter of an hour earlier than usual and escaped on foot into the country-side. ... Forward! He had to move forward. His comrades' rifle-fire gets more intense, as if they wanted to warn him. The pain in his smashed finger burns through the blood. If the crowds arrive before he's finished off the machine-gun nest, there'll be a bloodbath. And up to now, really, everything has gone well: they had taken the military camp; only this machine-gun, manned by officers, was still holding out.

He slides and crawls forward. The bullets whistle over him, next to him. When they hit the stone in front of him—his armor—there's a splitting crash. Two of the machine-gun crews are spraying the wall from which his comrades are giving him cover. They are firing through little cracks in their fortification, so they must have rifles as well ... Then, back then ... he found a construction job one day. He carried stones, lugged sand in

little baskets, sweated bitter sweat that tasted salty on his tongue. He found himself brooding over the question: is the world beautiful, is the world ugly?

The ocean is beautiful. The cloud-sheep that he'd once seen— they were beautiful. The cities are full of light and life. The happiness you have is bitter and tastes like sweat on your tongue: salty. In the gleaming cafés the men and women sit, slender and with bright red lips. He sees the women of his brothers, his fellow construction workers: their wombs protrude from child-bearing, their faces are carved with wrinkles . . .wrinkles like in the bark of the olive trees, wrinkles like gashes in the earth lying under the noon-day sun. They eat their salad unspiced and raw. The men and women in the cafés drink coffee with milk, sweet liqueurs. For him and his friends there's the drugged forgetfulness of bitter wine. If they want women, they have to go to certain houses. And he goes to them. Girls: honorable, decent girls . . . those you have to marry. He was too young for that.

Sixteen years old. And even so he already recognized in rough outline the laws of his time; a time that was not his time. He only existed in that time and was allowed to serve its people. He knew that after painful brooding. He started to experience a tomorrow in his dreams; he made childish, painful attempts to separate himself from today. But time stood like a barrier in front of him . . .

Until one day somebody stopped him. A guy who worked with him on the construction site. Slender face with a sharp nose. He saw too that his eyes were good but otherwise he saw—beaten and kicked dog that he was—nothing. When they talked to each other, they lay down under the olive trees on the outskirts of the city. He listened to the man who must be almost thirty.

There is nothing but faith in him. And a little clarity. He pours out himself and his life in words of outrage: "I was hungry. I just wanted to eat. I was beaten. And worst of all—they made my mother beat me. Now I know—each blow rebounded on her. The blows hurt her more than they did me . . ."

Years of apathy. The mules. The ocean. The cloud-sheep. The cities. Hunger. And at the same time sky and sea, both blue. And cities and houses which you build but you can't live in. Aren't allowed to. You build for the others. Women that rock their hips

when they walk across the street. They're not for us. People like us have to go to certain houses.

The man next to him remained silent. There was goodness in his eyes. And he, the sixteen year-old boy, followed his older comrade. In the evening he didn't go to the bars, to the houses any more. They went to meetings. At first he felt shy but then he opened up again. He was overwhelmed by the greatness and power of the thoughts that whirled about him. He would talk with his older friend until late in the evening; no, the older friend taught him. The world was transformed; hatred and love grew in him and gushed out of him in fiery words. When he heard of Lenin and saw his face, he was reminded of the mountains and the seas and the cloud-sheep that sought for better pastures. And he knew: someday everything will belong to mankind.

He was fired after a strike. He had to go to another city. Then again into another. He got to know his country. He knows the rough lands of Estremadura; he only seeks the gentle sun of the Levante when he can't help it any more; in Barcelona he's put in jail for four months. He wanders through Don Quixote's land-scape again. In the cities, among isolated groups a trace of his work remains. He doesn't have a friend but he has comrades. In the autumn of 1934 he's arrested in an Asturian city with a gun in his hand. Sentenced for life. When after months of hard labor there's an amnesty proclaimed, men and women and children are waiting in the streets for them. Singing. He never felt the power of a song, of the International, as intensely as then . . .

And now its roar draws near, that powerful song, the shouts and heavy tread of the approaching crowd, the increasing fury of the machine-gun fire: flooding over everything like a wave, flooding over him and his thoughts—he's got to move forward . . . forward! A glance at his smashed finger: it's only a shapeless bloody mass now. The bullets chirp, they hail down on the stone, they buzz past him above and to the side. Behind him he hears one of his comrades at the wall utter a gurgling scream. The officers shout for joy . . .

And then February came. The days were like a smile of spring. He warned repeatedly against exaggerated optimism.

As he moves his body up a little, a bullet rips his cap from his head. He flinches. That was foolhardy. Nothing must happen to

him yet. Not yet. Later? It would be nice to be able to stay alive. We will win and then what was the future will become today. For a moment he feels the pain in his hand so intensely, so sharply that he turns pale. Sweat covers his forehead. Soon he'll be nineteen. Maybe one day a woman will come to him . . . He thinks—quite briefly, quite fleetingly, as he crawls forward—how will that be. . . .?

Behind him the roar of the crowd surges closer. About twenty more meters to crawl before you could say with certainty: the machine-gun is finished.

It would be nice to shape the earth and its people, to remake oneself anew, to know: today is fulfillment.

Now that it occurs to him he's filled with joy at the idea that this battle against the machine-gun is already today, is the dim dawning of the great, bright day. He has to move further up . . . still further. His comrades' faith in him demands it.

The crowds of people will soon be at the corner of the next street and march out into range of the enemy machine-gun. They're not frightened by the yapping of the rifles. He smiles. It's nice to know: my sacrifice will not be in vain.

How was it, this morning? A stream of men and women swept up surging against the military encampment. Rifles barked, bullets whistled—but they stormed forward, irresistibly forward.

He crawls up closer. The crowds sing, sing; the song vibrates in all his nerves; he feels the song physically. They mustn't come too soon. If worst comes to worst he could try from here . . . no, he mustn't; he has to be dead sure of hitting them on his first throw because when he stands up . . .

He knows he's going to die. All his anxiety has vanished abruptly. He feels cold like he never has done before in his life. He crawls forward, centimeter by centimeter. The machine-gun is now focusing all its fire on his stone. Do they think they can shoot through his stone? Stone-splinters fly about his head. He feels a gentle weariness in his left leg, a pain; he feels something trickling warm down his calf . . .

As long as you don't hit my head or my right shoulder, you haven't gained a thing!

It's as if they wanted to drown out the noise of the approaching crowd with their machine-gun. Won't help you any more. Five

meters to go, he thinks. Slides forward. Ventures to look around. Sees a bright wall gleaming in the sunlight. With the holes black in it, and behind them—he knows—are his comrades.

The crowd won't hold back because of the gunfire. They're now singing "The Young Guard." His comrades, who have noticed that he will soon have reached the point where he can throw, are shooting like mad. Too bad that we didn't have a machine-gun too—that would have made it a lot easier. Hold it. Now he can reach them. Slowly he pulls the handgrenades up his body, pushes them before him behind the stone. He takes the cap off one, tests it. The fuse is OK. He lights it. Estimates the distance once again. Hears the song, "The Young Guard", behind him. Now the people will be streaming around the corner of the wall—now!

He gets up, throws, hears the explosion of the grenade. Hears screams, sees clumps whirling up in the air, feels suddenly something hot in his chest, sinks back.

Sees the blue sky above him, hears the steps rushing forward, sees the blue sky again and, losing consciousness, catches a glimpse of feet wrapped in rags standing next to him. And then he's lifted up. . .

But he doesn't feel that anymore. And in death his face was like the faces that watch the cloud-sheep that wander across the sky towards the distant green meadows.

BABIK

STEFAN HEYM

(Translated by the author)

Babik leaned idly on the handle of his spade, and surveyed his house. My house, he thought, and then, slowly, as if he were leafing through an album of old photographs, he thought of all the places he had lived in: His father's low-roofed, crooked-walled hut back home, near Katowice; the cheap, cold rooming houses in Pittsburgh and Cleveland; the miners' slatted shacks here in Goldsborough where he had paid for bed and board, always living with a family and yet not a part of it, never quite alone and yet always lonely.

A man must have a house, he thought—and now there it was: With a concrete foundation, and four beautiful straight walls of good timber, and a black roof and a red chimney, windows in every wall to let in plenty of light, and even a small porch from which five steps led down to what would be the pathway as soon as he bought gravel and put it down.

Babik creased his forehead. As soon as he bought gravel . . . There were so many things to be bought. He had planned the house, not all at once as other people do to whom a house means just a place to stay in when it rains. He had thought about his house when he crouched at the black face of the coal and hacked away at it, when he sat at Mike's Club and Bar nursing a beer for a whole evening—and over the years, the house had taken shape in his mind.

There would be the kitchen with a fine, white-enamelled electric range, with a gleaming sink and hot and cold water running into it from a shiny faucet. Next to it would stand a big refrigerator that opened with a soft click, like a man clicking his tongue before a good meal, and in the refrigerator would be two dozen cans of beer dewy with cold, and eggs, and butter, and

three different kinds of sausage, and a fried chicken, and oranges, and a chocolate layer cake. The walls of the kitchen would be light blue, and along the border of the ceiling he would paint a band of red flowers.

And then there would be a bathroom, with curtained-off shower and a real toilet to sit on and flush when you're through with your business. He'd had enough of stumbling to some God-damned rickety outhouse where the big green flies tickled his rear and the stench of three months worth of dirt from six or eight or ten people seemed to crawl under his skin.

The bedroom would have flowery wall paper, and a big, soft, wide bed with white sheets and a feather quilt, and a rug so that his bunions didn't scream when he got out of bed and set his feet on the cold, hard floor.

And finally a living room—a large table and chairs so a man can have company, an upholstered sofa with many pillows for the lady guests to lean against, a cupboard to hold the dishes and glassware and the set of Classics some salesman had talked him into buying, and pictures on the walls, two pictures to each wall, with gilt frames.

Such a house he had planned. Into such a house you could bring a woman without having to blush. In such a house you could say to her: "This is my house—do you like it?" And what woman wouldn't like it? What difference would it make then that he wasn't good-looking and that he couldn't talk fast in a language he never had had the chance to learn well, that he danced like an elephant and that the smart-cracks and jokes which came so easily to other men never would come from his lips? No difference at all.

Babik sighed. Years ago, it might not have made any difference. But now he was too old. His hair was still black, not a strand of gray in it, but the rest of him had shrivelled; his mouth and his eyes had sunk in, his ears stuck out like the handles of a pot, and his skin was ribbed like a washboard. Only his arms were sinewy and supple as always, the arms that dug the coal out of the Pennsylvania hills, ton after ton, how many thousands of tons of coal?

Babik gripped the handle of his spade and jammed the blade furiously into his plot of ground. Woman or no woman, a house was a house. So it had taken him forty years to save up the three thousand dollars he figured he needed to start it! But at least he

had something to show for his life's labor—look at the others, paying rent to the coal companies for their miserable shacks, with a brood of kids that ate up every penny the men ever made! And it wouldn't have taken him forty years, either, except that the depression hit the country and the money he had in the bank was suddenly gone.He had had to start all over again. And dollar by dollar he had wrapped into newspaper and shoved into a self-made belt which he carried around his lean belly. He'd rather be buried with it under a mountain of rock than trust another bank!

The belt was empty, now, but he had the house and the piece of land on which it was built. He smiled with grim pride; he felt like a conqueror, and in a way he was, even though what he had conquered wasn't quite what he had dreamed of.

No, it wasn't what he had dreamed of at all. Babik turned over his soil, spadeful by spadeful, jabbing the blade into the land as if he wanted to hurt it for something bad it had done to him.

With the land the trouble had begun. He had figured everything so carefully. Many a night he had sat up in his bed, a notepad balanced on his knees, and had added and subtracted and crossed out and added again—what this would cost and that; the materials, the labor; what he could do himself and for what he would have to pay others, and how much.

But when everything was figured out and he had his three thousand dollars, the land had gone up. And timber. And concrete. And nails, and wire, and roofing, and fixtures, and labor—up and up. Mike, who ran the Club and Bar, had told him, "Babik, you're a fool. Hang on to your dough. We ain't the kind of people can afford real estate. But if you got dough, you got something. If worst comes to worse, you can always drink it away."

He had cursed Mike. He knew, if he didn't start building the house then, he'd never build it, and he would die with nothing, nothing to show for his whole life. And when he thought of that, Babik felt real fear, a fear that sat in the pit of his stomach and was a thing with teeth that gnawed at his guts. And it wasn't just fear of a wasted life, it was fear of an old age, living on a measly pension maybe in the back room of Mike's Club and Bar or maybe in some other hole in the wall, creeping about drearily. He'd seen enough other old men whose strength had gone into coal and who hadn't been clever enough or thrifty enough or

systematic enough to get something out of the coal for themselves.

He had built the house, and when the last dollar was spent, it was ready and stood, not a mortgage on it, not a penny owed, all his, all Babik's, his house, his property!

The conqueror's smile softened and became almost tender. Babik picked up the spade and shuffled toward his house. At the bottom of the stairs that led to the porch, he deposited the spade and carefully wiped his muddied boots on a sackcloth. Then he went up to the porch. He took a key out of his pocket and fumbled with the lock. He didn't need to lock the door, he had good neighbors, and anyhow, he had been right there on his land. He just liked to lock up his property and to unlock it when he came back to it. Never before in his life had there been a house to which he had owned the key.

The door opened smoothly on its hinges. Babik entered. The deep frown that took the place of his smile made his face grotesque.

From the small, bare foyer, the doors to the kitchen, the bed room, and the living room were open. In the kitchen, he had a kerosene burner and an old chair with a few unwashed dishes on its seat, and a banged-up bucket now half full with some empty cans and torn papers. An iron bedstead with a thin mattress, a striped pillow, and two second-hand army blankets furnished his bed room, and his living room was empty but for the set of Classics piled on the window sill and a bicycle leaning against the wall. Well, why shouldn't the neighbor's kid use his house as a garage?

Babik sat down on the bed. He sat very straight and listened. But no sound came, no voices of guests laughing or talking and clinking glasses, no woman's voice calling him for dinner. Babik looked at his hands that were resting on his knees. He looked at his black-rimmed, cracked nails, at the broad, plump, gnarled fingers, at the scar that ran whitish across the red back of his right hand. With these hands he had built the house, and they were strong enough to dig the tons of coal that would go into getting the furniture and the electric range and the shower and toilet seat. He wasn't finished by any means, he was only fifty-eight, not a white hair on his head—

He reached under the pillow and pulled out a much-fingered slip of mimeographed paper. The date on it was more than a half

year old. "Notice!" it said, then a few lines, and then his name typed in, and a few more lines, and a scrawled signature.

He wasn't finished by any means, neither with his house, nor with his life. What if they did put in a new loading machine in the mine? Couldn't he learn to handle it? Or couldn't they let him dig elsewhere? There were coal seams running all through the mountain, and the Company owned the whole mountain. Couldn't they find one tiny corner under the mountain for him to work in?

"Babik! Hey, Babik!"

He was so glad to hear a voice, any voice, even Mike's hoarse, gruff voice that he let him go on calling a few times more before he opened the house door. Mike was coming up the path, his jacket open, the knot of his tie pulled down, a splotch of sweat on his shirt where it bulged over the top of his pants. Some of his reddish-gray curls were ridiculously stuck to his reddened forehead, and he was slipping in the mud of the path and the puddles. The man who followed him was walking carefully, balancing along the drier spots, and clutching an umbrella and a briefcase with one hand, and a fine gray hat with the other.

Babik frowned. Strangers, especially well-dressed ones, made him suspicious, and Mike had no business being out of his Club and Bar at this time of day when the men, coming back from the mines, were likely to drop in for a quick beer.

At the porch steps, the two of them stopped.

Mike coughed and wiped his face and said, "I thought I come up and see how you are."

The stranger said nothing. He just looked, appraisingly.

"What do you want?" Babik called out over Mike's head.

"You're Joseph Babik?" the stranger demanded.

"Sure he's Babik!" Mike said, with an attempt at eagerness. "I told you that I'd take you right to him, didn't I?"

"Can't we go in?" asked the stranger, hooking the handle of his umbrella over his arm.

But Babik was still blocking the door to his house. "What d'you bring *him* for!" he complained, as if Mike were a kind of Judas.

Mike's pale blue eyes were begging. "Don't you think he'd have found the way without me, too? I just thought, maybe, it'd be better if I was here when—" He broke off and, more firmly, added, "Anyhow, he came into the Club and asked how to get to

your house. For Christ's sake, I can go if you don't want me here! . . ." But he made no move to leave.

"Let's go in!" said the stranger, clamping his hat on his head and advancing up the steps. Babik moved aside. The stranger walked by him into the house, gave it one brief glance, hesitated, and then made for the living room. He searched for something to sit on or lean on, found only the seat of the bicycle, supported his briefcase on it, opened its flap, and pulled out a document.

Then he turned around to face Babik who slowly came through the door, prodded by Mike.

"I'm from the Goldsborough County Welfare Department, Mr. Babik," he began. "You made an application for relief?"

"I got no more unemployment insurance coming," Babik said slowly, "I must have something to eat." And then, with more certainty, "But I don't need rent money. I got my house!"

"I see," said the stranger.

"I've been looking for work all over," said Babik. "I've been working in the mines 'round here all my life, and they know me, and they've promised me . . ."

"Yes, we know," said the stranger. "We have investigated your case." He sounded a little tired, or perhaps a little impatient. "You aren't due to get your pension for another two years?"

"And he won't get it at all if he doesn't find work," Mike put in helpfully. "But he'll get work. He's strong. It's just because they put in the new machine, and he's a hand loader, and they say he's already too old to learn the machine."

"Yes, we know," the stranger said again. "When we investigate a case, we find out all about it." His lips stretched into a thin smile that was meant kindly.

Except that it froze Babik. "The chair," Babik said. "I'll get you the chair from the kitchen."

"Don't bother," the stranger waved him off. "You'll just have to sign here on this paper. Then we'll get you the money." He pencilled a cross next to the space where Babik would have to put his name, and handed the document over.

Babik began to read the close print, but gave it up after the third or fourth line. The paper was full of long words that didn't mean a thing to him.

"What is it, Mister? What do you want me to sign? I already signed the relief application—"

The stranger's thin smile reappeared. "I thought you knew, Mr. Babik. It's a property assignment."

"Yes?" said Babik, not quite understanding what was meant and yet sensing the danger to himself and his house.

"Well, it's like this, Mr. Babik. We're here to help people who've got nothing—no job, no money, not even a house. But you've got a house, you've got property. You wouldn't want to take money that you're not entitled to, would you? You wouldn't want to take money away from those who have nothing at all?"

"No," said Babik. His face showed the effort of his thinking. "I don't want to take anybody else's money. I just want relief. All my life I worked, except when I was out of a job; then I got relief. You can't let me starve!"

"Nobody's going to let you starve, Babik!" Mike was wringing his hands. "That's what the gentleman is here for, don't you see?"

"Yes, yes!" said Babik, "but what does he want me to sign?"

"I told you already, Mr. Babik—a property assignment. You sign over to the county your title to your house and your piece of land, and then we'll put you on the relief rolls."

"But the house belongs to me," said Babik. "I built it. I paid for it. For twenty years, I saved for it, and for twenty years before that—but then the bank went broke."

The stranger shrugged. He was not smiling any longer. "If you sign over the title of your property, Mr. Babik, it obviously no longer belongs to you. Of course, the county won't throw you out, we'll let you live in it for a while. We'll just keep it as security, so we know you'll pay us back as soon as you have a job. You're a property owner; in your case the relief money is like a loan the Government grants you. The Government, that's all the taxpayers. You don't want the taxpayers to lose their money on you, do you?"

"No," said Babik. "I just want relief. I don't want as much relief as you give the others, because I got my house and I don't need money for rent."

"But we can't give you relief as long as you have the house!"

They wanted to take his house. Babik's knees trembled. Because they took his job, they also wanted to take his house; the Government man had finally said it.

"You don't get the point, quite!" remarked the stranger, observing that Babik had stepped back to lean against the wall,

and pitying him a little. "We're very considerate! We could tell you to sell your property and not be a burden on the taxpayers! But we don't! We give you relief and hold your house until you have a job and can pay us back!"

"And if I don't get a job?" There was no tone to Babik's voice. "What's the sense of kidding myself? They don't hire men like me. And I've got two years to go till I get my pension, and I won't get the pension if I don't work steady for those two years. I only got the house. What do you want to take it for? It's a big Government, what do they want with this little house, just four bare walls and a roof. . . ."

Babik's voice broke.

The stranger, embarrassed, took off his hat and patted his hair. "I'm sorry, Mr. Babik. I don't make the rules." He held out the document and almost pleaded, "sign here."

Babik took the paper. Slowly he tore it to pieces and let the pieces fall on the floor.

The stranger put on his hat. In the door, he said: "If you reconsider, let us know."

Then he was gone.

For a while, there was silence between the two men in the empty room. Finally, Mike said softly: "I told you, if you'd kept the dough. . . . They didn't have to know about it, the way you carried it around your belly! You could have gone on relief and laughed at them! But you had to go and build a house, show them that you had something, be a property owner!"

But Babik didn't hear. His face was shrunk more deeply than ever, and he seemed to have turned entirely into himself.

THE EXCURSION OF THE
DEAD GIRLS

ANNA SEGHERS

No, from a great deal further away. From Europe." The man looked at me smiling as if I had said: "From the moon." He was the owner of the Pulqueria on the road out of the village. He stepped back from the table and, leaning motionlessly against the wall of the house, began to look at me as if searching for traces of my fantastic origin.

Suddenly it seemed just as fantastic to me as to him that I should have been banished from Europe to Mexico.—The village was surrounded by organ cactuses like the palisades of a fortress. I could look through a crack at the gray-brown mountain slopes that, bare and wild like the mountains of the moon, repudiated by their very appearance any suspicion that they had ever had anything to do with life. Two pepper trees glowed at the edge of a completely barren canyon. Even these trees seemed more to burn than to blossom. The innkeeper had squatted down onto the floor beneath the gigantic shadow of his hat. He had stopped looking at me, he was interested neither in the village nor in the mountains, he looked motionlessly at the only thing that presented him with immeasurable, insoluble mysteries: the absolute void.

I leaned against the wall in the narrow shade. Refuge in this country was too questionable and too tenuous to be called safety. I had just gotten over months of suffering from an illness that had laid me low here, even though the various dangers of the war hadn't been able to do anything to me. Although my eyes were burning from the heat and from tiredness I could make out the part of the road that led out of the village into the desert. The road was so white that it seemed to be etched into the inner sides of my eyelids as soon as I closed my eyes. I could also see at the

edge of the canyon the corner of a white wall. I had already caught sight of it from the roof of my hotel higher up in the larger village that I had clambered down from. I had asked at once after the wall and the hacienda or whatever it was, with its single light as if it had fallen from the night sky; but nobody could give me any information. So I had set out for the place. Though I was weak and tired and therefore found it necessary to stop for a rest here already, I had to find out for myself what this house was all about. Such idle curiosity was the only remnant of my old love for travel, an effort made out of force of habit. As soon as that curiosity was satisfied, I would return immediately to my prescribed place of lodging. The bench on which I was resting now was the last point in my journey, in fact the furthest point west that I had ever been on this earth. The desire for out-of-the-way, extravagant expeditions which had once occupied me in earlier days had long been sated, even to excess. There was only one expedition left that could still spur me on: the journey home.

My hacienda lay, like the mountains themselves, in the glimmering mist; and I wasn't sure whether that mist consisted of dust reflecting the light of the sun or of my own weariness enveloping everything in a fog, so that what was near seemed far away and what was distant stood out like a fata morgana. I stood up because I was rather annoyed at my tiredness, and in doing so the mist in front of my eyes cleared up a little.

I went through the gap in the cactus palisade and then around the dog who lay sleeping and covered with dust, absolutely motionless like a corpse with his legs spread out in front of him. It was shortly before the rainy season. The open roots of bare and twisted trees clung to the cliff, in the process of turning to stone. The white wall drew closer. The cloud of dust or perhaps of weariness which had already lifted a little now grew denser, not dark in the dips of the mountains like clouds usually were but shiny and glittering. I would have believed it was my fever if a gentle hot breath of air hadn't driven the clouds on, like patches of fog, towards the other slopes.

There was a gleam of green behind the long white wall. Probably there was a spring there or some small stream that had been diverted and so irrigated the hacienda more than the village. Even so it looked uninhabited, a low house that had no windows on the side facing the road. The single light of

yesterday evening, if it hadn't been a mirage, had probably belonged to the caretaker. The lattice work, unnecessary and long decayed, had broken out of the gate. But there were still in the archway the remnants of a coat of arms washed out by uncounted rainy seasons. I seemed to recognize what was left of this coat of arms as well as the stone seashells in which it rested. I stepped into the empty gate. To my surprise I now heard inside a gentle, regular squeaking. I took another step forward. I could now smell the vegetation in the garden and the longer I looked into it the fresher and stronger its greenness grew. Soon the squeaking became more distinguishable, and among the bushes—growing increasingly thicker and more luxurious—I saw the steady up and down movement of a swing or a seesaw. Now my curiosity was aroused so that I ran through the gate towards the swing. At the same moment somebody called out: "Netty!"

Nobody had called me by that name since I was in school. I had learned to react to all the good and bad names which friends and enemies had called me, to the names which had been imposed on me over many years in the streets, meetings, parties, rooms at night, police interrogations, book titles, newspaper reports, protocols and passports. Sometimes as I lay sick and unconscious I had even hoped for that old, early name, but it stayed lost, the name which I deceived myself into believing could make me healthy again, young, happy, ready to live the old life with the old friends, a life irretrievably lost. Alarmed at the sound of my old name I grabbed my braids with both hands, although my classmates had always mocked me for doing just that. I was surprised that I could still grab my two thick braids: so they hadn't cut them off in the hospital after all.

The stump of the tree onto which the seesaw was nailed seemed at first also to stand in a dense cloud but very quickly it separated and thinned out into a mass of wild rose bushes. Soon individual buttercups glowed in the ground mist that welled out of the earth through the high and thick grass; then the mist drifted away until dandelions and geraniums were clearly distinguishable. And in between there were brownish pink tufts of quaking-grass which trembled when you just looked at it.

At each end of the seesaw sat a girl; my two best school friends. Leni shoved herself powerfully off the ground with her big feet covered with square-buttoned shoes. I remembered that she was

always inheriting shoes from some older brother. The brother, to be sure, had already died in the fall of 1914 in the First World War. I wondered immediately why one couldn't notice in Leni's face any trace of the grim events that had spoiled her life. Her face was as smooth and clean as a fresh apple and there wasn't the slightest mark in it, not the slightest scar from the blows which the Gestapo had given her when they arrested her and she had refused to incriminate her husband. As she swung up and down, her thick Mozart-braid stood distinctly out from the back of her neck. Along with her heavy close-knit eyebrows she had in her round face that determined, rather energetic look which she had put on for every difficult undertaking, starting from the time when she was a little girl. I knew that wrinkle in her forehead, in her otherwise mirror-smooth and round apple-face, from all the other occasions, from difficult ball games and swimming competitions and school essays; and later too from excited meetings and leaflet distributions. I had seen that same wrinkle between her eyebrows for the last time when, during the Hitler time and shortly before I had fled for good, I had met my friends for the last time in the city where I was born. She had also worn it on her forehead earlier when her husband hadn't met her where and when he was supposed to. It was clear that he had been arrested at the printer's that had been outlawed by the Nazis. She must also have knotted her eyebrows and mouth when they had arrested her too very shortly thereafter. The wrinkle in her forehead that had earlier only emerged on special occasions now became a permanent feature as they let her starve slowly but surely to death in a women's concentration camp during the second winter of this war. I wondered in the meantime how I could have forgotten her head, shaded by the wide ribbon around the Mozart braid, since I had been sure that she had kept her apple face with its scored forehead even in death.

Marianne, the prettiest girl in the class, was perched on the other end of the seesaw, with her long thin legs crossed in front of her on the board. She had put up her ash blond braids in buns over her ears. There was nothing but happiness and grace to be seen in her face, carved as nobly and regularly as the faces of the stone statues of girls from the Middle Ages in the Cathedral at Marburg. You could see in her as few marks of heartlessness or of wrongdoing or lack of conscience as in a flower. I myself forgot at once everything that I knew about her and was pleased to see

her. A jolt went through her straight lean body every time that she quickened the swing of the seesaw, without pushing herself off from the ground. She looked as if she could even fly away effortlessly, with a carnation between her teeth and her firm little breasts in the washed-out dress of green linen.

I recognized the voice of the elderly teacher, Miss Mees, looking for us, right behind the low wall which separated the courtyard, where the seesaw was, from the restaurant terrace. "Leni! Marianne! Netty!" I didn't grab my braids anymore from surprise. It wouldn't have been possible for the teacher to call me by any other name when I was together with the others. Marianne pulled her legs off the seesaw and as soon as the board swung down towards Leni's side, she put her feet down firmly so that Leni could get off comfortably. Then she put an arm around Leni's neck and carefully picked some blades of grass out of her hair. Now all that I'd read or heard told about both of them seemed impossible to me. If Marianne held the seesaw down so carefully for Leni and picked the blades of grass out of her hair so affectionately and with so much care and even slung her arm around Leni's neck, then she couldn't possibly have dropped from her lips the reply that she couldn't be bothered about a girl who sometime, somewhere, had once chanced to be her classmate. Or that every penny which was spent on Leni and her family was thrown away, was an attempt to defraud the state. The Gestapo officials who had arrested both parents, one after the other, let it be known in front of the neighbors that Leni's child, left behind unprotected, ought to be put into a National Socialist reform school at once. Whereupon the women of the neighborhood intercepted the child at the playground and kept it in hiding so that it could go to Berlin to stay with her father's relatives. They hurried over to Marianne to borrow money for the trip because they had seen her some time ago walking arm in arm with Leni. But Marianne refused and said that her own husband was a high Nazi official and that Leni and her husband had been rightfully arrested because they had committed crimes against Hitler. The women were afraid that she would even denounce them to the Gestapo.

It crossed my mind to wonder if Leni's little daughter had a scored forehead like her mother's when they finally came to take her away to the reform school after all.

Now both of them, Marianne and Leni, one of whom had lost

her child through the fault of the other, went out of the little garden where the seesaw was, with their arms around each other's necks, their heads pressed against each other. Suddenly a sadness came over me, and I felt, as I often did when I was at school, a little excluded from the shared games and warm friendship of two others. Then they stopped once again and took me into their midst.

We followed Miss Mees up to the restaurant terrace, like three ducklings behind their mother. Miss Mees limped a little and that, together with her big behind, made her look even more like a duck. On her breast, in the V-neck of her blouse, hung a big black cross. I would have stifled a smile, like Leni and Marianne, except that my amusement at her comic appearance was diminished by a respect that was hard to reconcile with it: later on she had never removed the massive black cross from the opening of her dress. She had gone quite openly and fearlessly to the illegal services of her sectarian church wearing this very cross instead of a swastika.

Rose bushes were planted along the restaurant terrace on the Rhine. They seemed, compared to the girls, so regular, so perfectly straight, so well cared for, like garden flowers compared to wild ones. The smell of coffee penetrated temptingly through the smells of water and garden. The buzzing of young voices sounded like a swarm of bees coming from the tables covered with red-white checkered cloths and standing in front of the long, single-storied restaurant. At first I was drawn closer to the river bank so that I would be able to look at the limitless sunny breadth of the countryside. I pulled Leni and Marianne to the garden fence and we all looked down into the river flowing green-blue and glimmering past the restaurant. The villages and hills on the opposite bank with their fields and woods were mirrored in a network of reflections. The more and the longer I looked around me, the freer I was able to breathe, the more rapidly my heart was filled with happiness. For almost unnoticeably the heavy pressure of melancholy, which had lain on every breath I took, vanished. By merely looking at the gentle hilly landscape, happiness and the joy of life grew out of my blood instead of gloom, just like a particular strain of wheat grows out of a particular air and soil.

A Dutch tug with a chain of eight barges steamed through the hills reflected in the water. They were carrying lumber. The

Captain's wife, with her little dog dancing about her, was just sweeping the deck. We girls waited until the white foam behind the convoy of barges disappeared into the Rhine and nothing else was to be seen anymore in the water except the reflection of the shore on the other side merging into the reflection of the garden on our side. We turned around and headed for the coffee tables, with our waddly Miss Mees in the lead, but to me she didn't seem funny at all anymore, with the cross on her breast that waddled too and that for me suddenly had become a fact and as significant and solemn as an omen.

Perhaps there may also have been among the school girls a few who were sullen and mean; but in their colorful summer dresses, with their bouncing braids and merry curls, they all looked fresh and festive. Because most of the seats were occupied, Marianne and Leni shared a chair and a coffee cup. Little snub-nosed Nora with her thin voice and two braids wound around her head and wearing a little checkered dress, poured coffee and passed out sugar as unselfconsciously as if she had been the innkeeper's wife herself. Marianne, who otherwise usually forgot her former schoolmates, still remembered this excursion vividly when Nora, who had become the leader of the National Socialist Womens' Organization, later greeted her as a fellow countrywoman and former schoolmate.

The blue cloud of mist which emerged from the Rhine or still from my overtired eyes, cast a fog over all the tables where the girls were sitting, so that I couldn't distinguish clearly anymore the individual faces of Nora and Leni and Marianne or whatever else they were called, just as no single umbel can be differentiated from among the confusion of wild flowers. I listened a while to the bickering about the place where Miss Sichel, the young teacher who was just coming out of the restaurant, should sit down. The cloud of mist in front of my eyes drifted away so that I was able to recognize Miss Sichel very clearly as she walked toward me, as freshly and brightly dressed as her pupils. She sat down close by me and nimble Nora poured the coffee for the favorite teacher; in her eagerness to please she had even rushed to wind a couple of jasmine boughs around Miss Sichel's seat.

If her memory had not been just as thin as her voice, Nora would surely have regretted that action later on when she was the head of the National Socialist Womens' Organization in our

town. Now she looked on proudly and almost infatuatedly as Miss Sichel put one of these little twigs of jasmine into the button-hole of her jacket. During the First World War she would still be happy that she had the same working hours as Miss Sichel in the section of the Womens' Organization which gave food and drink to the soldiers who were passing through. But later on she would insult this very same teacher, by then already shaky with old age, and chase her away from a bench on the Rhine because she had wanted to sit down on one that was forbidden to Jews. It suddenly went through me as I sat next to her, like some grave omission of my memory, as if I had the higher duty to remember even the tiniest particulars forever, that Miss Sichel's hair had not always been snow-white in the way I remembered, but that at the time of our school excursion it had been a fragrant brown, with only a few white strands at the temples. There were so few white hairs that one could still count them, but they overwhelmed me as if here today I had come up against a footprint of time for the first time. All the other girls at our table were happy along with Nora that the young teacher was so close to us, without suspecting that they would later spit at Miss Sichel and mock her as a "Jewish sow."

The oldest girl of us all, Lore, had had real boyfriends for quite some time already. She was wearing a skirt and a blouse and had reddish, wavy hair and had, in the meantime, gone from one table to the next and distributed pieces of cake that she had baked herself. All sorts of invaluable domestic talents were united in this girl, partly having to do with the art of love and partly with the art of cooking. Lore was always extremely cheerful and pleasant and ready for fun and games. The loose way of life that she had started to live unusually early had been strictly censured by the teachers, but it had never led to marriage and not even to a really serious love affair, with the result that when most of the others had long become respectable mothers she still looked as she did today, in school, in a short dress and with a big, red, sweet-toothed mouth. How could it be possible, then, that she should have met with such a terrible end—suicide by a bottle-full of sleeping pills. A disappointed lover—a Nazi—had threatened her with concentration camp because her unfaithfulness to him constituted so-called racial dishonor. He had lain in wait unsuccessfully for a long time so as to surprise her at last with her forbidden lover. Even so, in spite of his

jealousy and lust for revenge, he was only able to prove his accusation when, shortly before this war started, the air warden had forced all the residents to leave their rooms and beds during an air raid exercise and go down into the basement, Lore and her forbidden lover included.

Secretly but not unnoticed by the rest of us, she now gave a leftover cinnamon star cookie to Ida, who was also remarkably pretty, clever and adorned with countless little natural curls. She was Lore's only friend in the whole class since Lore was looked at rather askance by the others because of her amusements. We speculated a lot about Ida's and Lore's good times and also about their (mutual) visits to the outdoor swimming pools where they would meet their athletic chums for swimming. I just don't know why Ida, who was now furtively nibbling on the cinnamon star, was never affected by the secret tribunal of the mothers and daughters, perhaps because she was the daughter of a teacher and Lore the daughter of a barber. Ida put a stop in due time to her loose life but she too never married, because her fiancé was killed at Verdun. Her grief drove her to take up nursing so that she would be of use at least to the wounded. Since she didn't want to give up her profession when peace came in 1918, she joined the Deaconesses. Her beauty was already a little faded, her curls already a little gray—as if strewn with ashes—when she became a supervisor of the National Socialist nurses; and even if she didn't have a fiancé in this war, her desire for revenge and her bitterness were still alive. She impressed upon the younger nurses the official instructions which warned against speaking to POW's and against false services of pity while taking care of them. But her instructions to use the recently arrived bandages exclusively for their own men were of no avail whatever. For into the place of her new activity, into the hospital far behind the front, they dropped a bomb which blew friend and foe to smithereens and naturally her curly head as well, through which now once again Lore drew five manicured fingers such as she alone in the whole class possessed.

At the same time Miss Mees struck her coffee cup with her spoon and ordered us to deposit our money for the coffee into a china dish that she was just sending around the tables with her favorite pupil. Later on she collected money with just as much ease and aplomb for her church, a sectarian one the Nazis had

proscribed. Accustomed to such jobs, she had in the end become its treasurer—not exactly a position without risks; nevertheless she had collected the offerings just as efficiently and naturally. Now her favorite pupil, Gerda, jangled the collection plate and then took it over to the innkeeper's wife. Gerda was attractive and adroit without being beautiful; she had a skull like a mare, thick, coarse hair, strong teeth and lovely brown, protuberant eyes which also reminded one of a faithful horse. Right after that she ran back—and here too she resembled a little horse, always galloping off somewhere—in order to ask permission to leave the class and take the following ship back. She had found out in the restaurant that the owner's child was seriously ill. Because there was nobody else there to take care of her, Gerda wanted to help the sick child. Miss Mees allayed all of Miss Sichel's fears and Gerda galloped off to her nursing job as if to a party. She was a natural nurse and lover of mankind, born to be a teacher in a sense which has virtually vanished from the world's vocabulary, as if she had been chosen to look after whatever children needed her; and she always and everywhere found people who were in need of her help. Even though her life finally ended obscurely and pointlessly, still nothing she had done was lost, not even the least significant of her efforts to help. Her life itself was easier to obliterate than its traces. Those went on existing in the memory of many whom she had once chanced to help. But who was there to help her when, though she begged and threatened, her own husband hung out the swastika flag on the first of May? He did so to conform with the orders of the new government, because otherwise he would have been fired from his job. No one was there to calm her down when she came back from the market and, seeing her apartment decorated so hideously, she ran up full of shame and despair and turned on the gas. Nobody helped her. In that hour she remained hopelessly alone, no matter how many people she herself had helped.

A steamer blew its whistle on the Rhine. We craned our necks. On its white beam was written in gold script "Remagen." Although the ship was far away I could read the name easily with my poor eyes. I saw the wisps of smoke over the chimney and the bullseyes of the cabins. I watched the water in the wake of the steamer continually being smoothed out and starting anew. My eyes had in the meantime grown accustomed to this familiar world; I saw everything even more clearly than when

the Dutch tug had gone by. There was a clarity about this little steamer "Remagen" on the broad still stream, skimming past villages and ranges of hills and drifts of clouds, a clarity that nothing had damaged, that nothing could damage, that nothing in the world could dim. I had myself already recognized the familiar faces on the deck of the steamer and in the bullseyes, and now the girls were calling out aloud: "Mr. Schenk! Mr. Reiss! Otto Helmholz! Eugene Lütgen! Fritz Müller!"

All the girls cried out together: "That's the Boys' High School! That's the senior class!" Like us, their class was making an excursion. Would they stop here at the landing? After a brief consultation Miss Sichel and Miss Mees ordered us girls to line up in rows of four, since at all events they wanted to avoid having the two classes meet. Marianne, whose braids had come loose on the swing, started to pin up her pigtails over her ears again. Her friend Leni, with whom she had been sharing her chair since they had been on the swing together, ascertained with her sharper eyes that Otto Fresenius was on board too. He was Marianne's greatest admirer and favorite dancing partner. And then Leni whispered to her: "They're going to get off here; he's signaling with his hand."

Fresenius, a dark-blond, lanky boy of seventeen who had already been waving insistently from the ship for some time, would even have swum over to us in order to be with his girlfriend. Marianne put her arm tightly around Leni's neck. Her friend—of whom she later pretended not to have the slightest recollection when they asked her for help—was to her like a real sister, a faithful adviser in the joy and anxiety of love, conscientiously delivering letters and arranging secret meetings. Marianne, who always was a lovely, healthy girl, developed into such a marvel of delicacy and grace through the mere proximity of her boyfriend that she stuck out from the rest of her schoolmates like a fairy child. Otto Fresenius had already told his mother, with whom he shared his secrets, about his liking for Marianne. Since his mother was herself pleased about his happy choice, she thought that sometime later, after a suitable interval, there was nothing that would stand in the way of their marriage. And they did in fact get as far as an engagement party, but never to a wedding, for the bridegroom was killed already in 1914 in a student battalion in the Argonnes.

The steamer "Remagen" now made a turn toward the landing

pier. Our two teachers, who had to wait for the ship coming from the opposite direction in order to get us girls home, immediately started to count us off. Leni and Marianne looked intently in the direction of the steamer. Leni turned her head around so inquisitively as if divining that her own future, too—the course of her own destiny—depended on the union or the separation of this pair of lovers. If it had depended on Leni alone instead of on Kaiser Wilhelm's mobilization and, later, on the French snipers, both of them would surely have made a couple. She instinctively felt how well these two young people suited each other in heart and body. In that event Marianne would never have refused later to take care of Leni's child. Otto Fresenius would perhaps have found the means even earlier to help Leni to escape. In time he would probably have impressed on the lovely, delicate face of his wife Marianne such an expression of justice, of shared respect for humanity, that she would never have denied her schoolmate.

Spurred on by his love, Otto Fresenius—later on a bullet in the First World War was to rip apart his stomach—was now the first to come down the gangway and walk toward the garden of the restaurant. Marianne, who never removed her hand from Leni's shoulder, gave him her free hand and let him hold it. It wasn't only clear to Leni and me, but to all of us children that these two were lovers. They gave us for the first time a real conception—not derived from dreams, not read about in poems or stories or classical dramas, but real and genuine—of what lovers are, just as nature herself had planned and produced them.

With one finger still hooked in his, Marianne's face revealed an expression of complete submission, turning now into an expression of eternal fidelity toward the tall, lean, dark-blond boy. Later on she will grieve like a widow dressed in black for him, after her letter to the front is returned bearing the stamp "Killed in Action." In these dark days in which Marianne completely despaired of life, the same Marianne whom I had seen worshiping life with all its joys, great and small, the joys of love or the joys of a seesaw, in those same dark days her friend Leni, whom she was now holding in one of her arms, would make the acquaintance of Fritz, on leave from the front and belonging to a family of railroad workers in our town. While Marianne was for a long time enveloped in the black cloud of her despairing sweetness, in the gentleness of her profoundest

sorrow, Leni was at the same time glowing like the ripest, rosiest apple. That is why both friends were alienated from each other for a time in the ordinary human way that grief and happiness are divided by a great gulf. After the period of mourning was over and after various meetings in cafés on the banks of the Rhine, where Marianne would sit with her fingers intertwined as she did now and with the same expression of eternal fidelity as now on her longish gentle face, Marianne would establish a new relationship with a certain Gustav Liebig who had survived the First World War unscathed and was later to become an important SS-officer in our town. That is something Otto Fresenius would never have turned into, even if he had come out of the war alive, neither an SS-officer nor an agent of the local Nazi government. The spirit of fairness and integrity which already now unmistakably marked the features of his boyish face made him incapable of that kind of career, of that kind of a profession. Leni was somewhat troubled when she found out that her classmate—to whom she was then still devoted like a sister— had accepted this new fate, one which promised fresh joys. Then as now she was much too foolish to realize that the destinies of boys and girls taken together make up the destiny of a nation, the destiny of a people, and that for this reason in the short or long run the grief or happiness of her schoolfriend would cast shadow or sunlight on her own life. Now I was just as aware as Leni of the unspoken, inextinguishable vow on Marianne's face, which was resting, almost as if by chance, on the arm of her lover—the guarantee of an indestructible union. Leni drew in a deep breath as if for her it was a special joy to be the witness of a love like this. Before they, Leni and her husband, were to be arrested by the Gestapo, Marianne was to hear her new husband Liebig—to whom she had also sworn eternal fidelity—utter so many contemptuous remarks about the husband of her school-friend that she herself soon lost the sense of friendship for a girl who was looked upon with such contempt. Leni's husband had resisted with all his might joining the SA or SS. Had he joined, Marianne's husband, who was a stickler for rank and order, would have become his superior in the SS. When he noticed that Leni's husband disdained the organization which he held in such honor, he brought his negligent fellow-countryman to the attention of the authorities in the little town.

Gradually the whole class of boys along with their two

teachers had disembarked. A certain Mr. Neeb, a young teacher with a little blond moustache, bowed towards the two women teachers and then quickly cast a piercing glance over us girls, looking instinctively for Gerda and noticing that she wasn't among us. Gerda was still in the restaurant nursing and watching the sick child of the innkeeper's wife and didn't know anything about the crowd of boys outside in the garden. And she didn't know either that her absence had already been noticed by Mr. Neeb, whose attention had been drawn to her on other occasions because of her brown eyes and her eagerness to help everyone. Only after 1918, after the end of the First World War, when Gerda was herself already a teacher and they both supported the school reforms of the Weimar Republic, were they to really get to know each other in the recently founded "Federation of Determined School Reformers." But Gerda remained more faithful to the old desires and ideals. After he had finally married the girl whom he had chosen because of her convictions, he would soon set a higher value on living together in peace and comfort than on their mutual ideals. And so he, too, hung the swastika flag out of his living room window, because if he didn't the law threatened him with the loss of his job and hence no more food for his family.

It wasn't I only who had observed Neeb's disappointment when he didn't see Gerda among the crowd of girls, the very same Gerda whom he would so single-mindedly seek out and make his own, thereby sharing in the guilt of her death. Elsie was, I believe, the youngest of us all, a chubby girl with thick braids and a round mouth as red as cherries. With apparent casualness and indifference she observed that another one of us, Gerda, had stayed in the restaurant in order to take care of a child that had fallen sick. Because she was so small and unremarkable all of us soon forgot Elsie, just as one forgets some promising bud in a rosebush; she had not yet become involved in any amorous entanglements of her own, but she loved to find out about those of others and to poke her nose into them. Now she learned from the way Mr. Neeb's eyes lit up that she had guessed right, and she said, as if by chance: "The sick-room's right behind the kitchen." While Elsie was testing her insight in this way—and she was able to decipher Neeb's thoughts much better with her shiny child's eyes than the eyes of an adult would have, clouded as they are by experience—she would have to wait a long time

for a love of her own. Because before he did anything else, her future husband Ebi, the cabinet-maker, first went to war. At that time already he had a goatee and a little potbelly and he was much older than she. When after the peace, he turned Elsie—still plump and stub-nosed—into a master-carpenter's wife, it suited him very well that in the meantime she had learned bookkeeping in commercial school. Cabinet-making was important to them as well as to their three children. Later on the cabinet-maker was in the habit of saying that for him business went on as usual whether there was a Grand Ducal or Social Democratic Ministry in the provincial capital of Darmstadt. He also regarded Hitler's coming to power and the outbreak of a new war as a kind of disastrous natural event, like a thunderstorm or a blizzard. But by then he had already grown fairly old. And in Elsie's bushy braids there were also a number of gray strands. He probably didn't find much time to change his mind when during the English bombing raid on Mainz, he, his wife, his children, and their apprentices departed this life in a space of five minutes, and were converted along with his house and his workshop into dust and ashes.

While Elsie, as firm and round as a little dumpling and not to be split by anything less than a bomb, jumped into her place in the line of girls, Marianne stood in the farthest corner of the last row so that Otto could still stand next to her with his hand in hers. They looked out over the fence into the water where their shadows merged into the reflections of the mountains and the clouds and the white wall of the resort inn. They didn't say anything to each other, they were sure nothing could separate them, neither the counting-off into rows nor the departure of the steamer, nor even later their death in leisurely old-age among a troop of children.

The older teacher of the boys' class—he had a habit of shuffling and clearing his throat and the boys had nicknamed him "The Old Man"—came across the landing pier into the garden. He was surrounded by his students and they sat down quickly and greedily at the table which we girls had just left. The innkeeper's wife, who was happy that her sick child was still being taken care of by Gerda, brought out her fresh blue-white China with the onion pattern. The head teacher of the boys' class, Mr. Reiss, started to slurp his coffee. It sounded as if some bearded giant were slurping away.

Reversing the usual order of events, this teacher experienced the dying-off of his young pupils in the subsequent and in the present war in black-white-red and in swastika regiments. He, however, survived everything unscathed. For he grew gradually too old not only for fighting but also for making remarks which might have led to his being arrested and put into a concentration camp.

While the partly well-behaved, partly scampish boys who were dawdling around "The Old Man" resembled legendary hobgoblins, the swarm of girls in the garden below was twittery and elfish. When we were being counted off it was noticed that a few girls were missing. Lore was sitting with the boys, because she was always staying as long as she could in masculine company, just as much now as during the rest of her life—a life, by the way, which met with a bad end because of the jealousy of a Nazi. Next to her a certain Ellie was giggling because she had just discovered her dancing school partner, Walter, a chubby-cheeked little fellow. The short little pants which, to his dismay, he was still wearing, fitted a little too tightly over his firm behind; later on, though a rather oldish but still quite good-looking SS-man, he would in his capacity as chief of transportation carry off forever Leni's husband after his arrest. Leni continued to stand carefully at an angle so that Marianne could exchange a few last words with her lover, but she didn't have the least presentiment about how many future enemies were surrounding her here in the garden. Ida, the future Deaconess nurse, was whistling and trotting down towards us in a series of droll dance steps: the round saucer-eyes of the young boys and the slanting, relaxed eyes of the old coffee slurper of a teacher rested contentedly on her curly head, bound round with a velvet ribbon. Once in the Russian winter of 1943, when her hospital is unexpectedly under bombardment, she will remember that little velvet ribbon in her hair and the white, sunny inn and the garden on the Rhine and the boys arriving and the girls departing.

Marianne had let go of the hand of her Otto Fresenius. She also no longer had an arm around Leni's shoulder; she stood in the row of girls alone, lost in amorous reflections. In spite of the fact that these are the most earthly of all sensations she now stood out from among the other girls by virtue of an almost unearthly beauty. Otto Fresenius returned to the boys' table, side by side with the young teacher Neeb. The latter behaved himself like a

good comrade, without mocking and asking questions, because of course he was looking for a girl in the same class and because he respected the love affairs of even the very youngest of his pupils. Since death was to tear away this particular boy, Otto, so much more quickly from his beloved than the older teacher, he was granted during his short life eternal fidelity and was spared all evil, all temptations, all meanness and shame, to which the older man was to fall victim when he sought to rescue for himself and for Gerda a position paid for by the State.

Miss Mees, with the heavy, indestructible cross on her breast, was watching carefully over us girls to make sure that none of us would make off to her friend from dancing school before the steamer came. Miss Sichel had gone off to look for a certain Sophie Meier, and finally found her on the seesaw together with a boy, Herbert Becker, who just like her was delicate and wore glasses, so that they both looked more like brother and sister than a pair of lovers. Herbert Becker ran off as soon as he saw the teacher. I later saw him many times running through our town, grinning and making faces. He still wore glasses and had the same sly boyish face when I met him again a few years ago in France just as he was returning from the Spanish Civil War. Miss Sichel scolded Sophie because of her running around so much, so that Sophie had to clean her glasses that had gotten wet with tears. Not only the hair of the teacher, in which I now again perceived with astonishment a mixture of gray strands, but also the hair of her pupil Sophie, now still as black as the ebony of Snow-White's hair, was to become white all over when both of them together were deported by the Nazis to Poland in a railway carriage, stuffed full of people and sealed from the outside. Sophie had grown completely old and wizened when she suddenly died in the arms of Miss Sichel, more like a sister than a former pupil.

We consoled Sophie and cleaned her eyeglasses when Miss Mees clapped her hands as a signal to move off to the pier. We were ashamed because the class of boys was watching how we were being marched off and because they were all amused at the crooked, duck-like waddle of our teacher. Only in my case was the sense of ridicule diminished by my respect for her demeanor, one that always remained unchanged and that neither the summons to appear before Hitler's People's Court nor the threat of prison could change. We all waited together on the landing

pier for the rope to be thrown to land from our steamer. The way the boatsman caught the rope, the way he wound it around the peg, the way the landing bridge was set up seemed to me terribly dexterous, a welcome to a new world, a guarantee of a successful voyage, so that all journeys across the unending seas from one continent to another grew pale and fantastic in comparison, like the dreams of children. Such trips would never be so exciting, so true-to-life again in their smell of wood and water, in the easy sway of the landing bridge, in the gnashing sound of the ropes, as the beginning of that twenty-minute trip down the Rhine toward my home-town.

I jumped up on deck in order to sit near the wheel. The little ship's bell rang, the rope was pulled in, the steamer turned. Its white, glittering bow of foam dug into the river. I suddenly thought of all the white furrows of foam which any number of ships had ever plowed in the oceans anywhere. The rapidity and finality of a journey, the bottomlessness of the water as well as its accessibility have never subsequently been able to impress themselves so powerfully on my mind. Then suddenly Miss Sichel stood in front of me. In the sunlight she looked very young, dressed in her polka-dot dress with her firm little breasts. Looking at me with her clear, gray eyes, she said that because I liked to take trips and because I liked to write essays, I should write a description of the school excursion for the next German class.

All the girls in the class who liked the deck better than the cabin below, rushed up around me and jumped up on the benches. The boys were waving and whistling from the garden. Lore whistled back shrilly and was loudly scolded by Miss Mees, while on shore they kept on whistling in the same rhythm; Marianne leaned far over the railing and didn't let Otto out of her sight, as if this separation could already be forever like the one later in the 1914 war. When she could no longer distinguish her boyfriend, she put one arm around me and the other around Leni. Along with the touch of her lean, bare arm I felt the sun shining on the back of my neck. I, too, looked back towards Otto Fresenius who continued to stare after his girlfriend (now leaning her head against Leni) as if he could still see her and remind her forever of inviolable love.

With our arms drawn tightly around each other, we three looked upstream. The slanting light of the afternoon sun on the

hills and vineyards ruffled here and there the white and pink blossoms of the fruit trees. In the waning sunshine a few windows glowed like the flames of a fire. The villages seemed to grow in size as one approached them and when one had hardly passed them they seemed to shrivel up. That is the congenital desire for travel, a desire that one can never satisfy because one only grazes against everything as one passes by. We steamed underneath the Rhine bridge which the troop trains would soon be crossing in the First World War, full of the boys who were now drinking their coffee in the garden and all the other schoolboys in the country. When this war ended, the Allied soldiers advanced over the same bridge and later on Hitler with his untried army reoccupied the Rhineland, until the new troop trains would roll off all the country's boys to die in a new world war. Our ship went past the little island of Petersau on which one of the piles of the bridge rested. We all waved to its three little houses, which ever since we were little had been as familiar to us as the little houses in the picture books with fairy tales about witches. The little houses and the fishermen were mirrored in the water just like the village on the other side. The fields of rape-seed and wheat growing beyond the margin of pink apple trees climbed up the slope of the mountain to the little church tower in a swarm of gable roofs tucked into each other and forming a Gothic triangle.

At one moment the evening light would give us a glimpse of a valley with a single railroad track leading into it, at another moment it would shine on a distant chapel, and everything peered quickly once again out of the Rhine before it vanished into the twilight.

We had all grown still in the soft light so that we could hear the cawing of birds and the factory sirens from Amoeneburg. Even Lore had fallen completely silent. We three—Marianne, Leni and I—all hooked up arms with each other, becoming one with what was quite simply part of the great union of all the things on earth and under the sun. Marianne was still leaning her head against Leni's head. How was it then possible that later on betrayal and madness could enter her mind? So that she thought that only she and her husband had a lease on love for this country and that therefore they could in good conscience despise the girl on whom she was now leaning, and report her to the police. Nobody ever reminded us, while there was still time,

75

of this trip that we had taken together. No matter how many essays were still to be written about our country and about its history and about the love for our Nation, it was never mentioned that our troop of girls—now leaning against each other and moving upstream in the slanted afternoon sun—were part of that country.

An arm of the river was already branching off toward the lumber pier where freshly hewn and sawn lumber was taken off in rafts to Holland. The town still seemed to lie far enough away so that it could not make me get off and stay, even though its pier, its rows of plane trees and warehouses along the shore were much more familiar to me than any entrance to any of the foreign towns where I was subsequently forced to stay. Gradually I began to recognize the familiar outlines of streets and gables and church towers, intact and familiar like long vanished places in fairy tales and songs. The day-long school excursion seemed to me at one and the same time to have taken everything away as well as given it back.

As the steamer now made its approach to the landing and the children and idlers leisurely crowded up for our arrival, we didn't seem to come back from an excursion but from a journey that had taken years. No bomb craters, no fire damage were to be seen in this familiar, teeming, medieval city, so that my anxiety was soon calmed and I felt at home.

Lotte was the first to say goodbye—almost as soon as the ropes had been thrown on land. She wanted to go to the evening mass in the cathedral, the bells could be heard already as far down as the landing bridge. Lotte wound up later in a convent on the Rhine island of Nonnenwerth, from which she was then transferred along with a group of other nuns over the Dutch border; but their fate eventually caught up with them. The class said "Goodbye" to the teachers. Miss Sichel reminded me once again of the essay for the German class and her gray eyes gleamed like finely scoured pebbles. Then our class broke up into separate groups going home in various directions.

Leni and Marianne went arm-in-arm to the Rhein Strasse. Marianne still had a red carnation between her teeth. She had fastened another carnation to the ribbon of Leni's Mozart braid. I still see Marianne with her red carnation between her teeth, even while making nasty replies to Leni's neighbors, even while lying with her half-charred body in the smoking tatters of her dress in

76

her parents' house. For the fire brigade came too late to save Marianne, when the fire caused by the bombs began to encroach on the houses on the Rhein Strasse where Marianne was just visiting her parents. Her death was no easier than Leni's, whom she had disavowed and who died slowly in the concentration camp of hunger and disease. But because of the disavowal Leni's child survived the bombing attack. Because the Gestapo had taken it away to a distant Nazi reform school.

I trotted off with a couple of schoolmates in the direction of Christhof Strasse. At first I was full of anxiety. As we turned away from the river toward the center of the town, I felt something weighing heavily on my heart as if an irrational, evil thing was going to happen to me, perhaps some terrible news or some calamity that our sunny excursion had frivolously made me forget. All at once I understood clearly that it was impossible that the Christhof Church could have been destroyed during a night-time bombing raid because we were listening to its bells sounding the angelus. I had had no reason whatever to dread going home this way, although it had stuck in my memory that this central part of the town had been completely destroyed by bombs. It also occurred to me that the newspaper photograph which showed all of the alleys and squares razed to the ground or destroyed might have been wrong. At first I thought that perhaps, following Goebbels' orders, they had rebuilt a fake city with incredible speed in order to deceive people about the extent of the damage, a city in which no stone rested on another in the same way that it had before but which nevertheless gave the impression of being intact and pleasant. After all we were long used to this kind of simulation and deceit, not only in connection with bombing attacks but also on other occasions more difficult to comprehend.

But the houses, the staircases, the fountain stood as they always had. Even Braun's Wallpaper Store displayed its samples of flowered and striped wallpaper, although it was to be burned down in this war together with the Braun family, after only having had its display windows smashed in the First World War by a spent anti-aircraft shell. Marie Braun, who had been walking along at my side, went quickly into her father's store. The next of the homecomers, Catherine, ran over to her tiny little sister Tony. She was playing beneath the plane trees on one of the stone steps in front of the fountain. The fountain and all of

the plane trees had of course been blown to pieces long ago, but the children weren't deprived thereby of an opportunity to play, because their last hour too had struck in the basements of the surrounding houses. In that attack little Tony died in the house that she had inherited from her father, along with her little daughter, as tiny as the little girl she was today, blowing water out of her plump cheeks. And Catherine too, the bigger sister who now grabbed her by her hair, as well as her mother and aunt standing in the open door of the house (who both greeted them with kisses), they too were to die together in their family's house. At the same time, Catherine's husband, a paper-hanger and her father's heir, was helping to occupy France. With his short moustache and paper-hanger's thumb, he considered himself to be the citizen of a nation that was stronger than other nations—until the news reached him that his house and his family had been blown to pieces. The little sister turned around once more and sprayed me too with the last drops of water that she had saved up in her cheek. I ran the rest of the way home alone. In Flachsmarkt Strasse I met Liese Moebius, pale and wan, who was also in my class but because she had had pneumonia couldn't take part in any excursions during the last two months. Now the angelus tolling from Christhof Church had lured her away from home. She rushed past me with her two bobbing, long, brown braids and with a pince-nez on her little nose, as quick-footed as if she was running to a playground instead of to evening mass. Later on she begged her parents to let her join the convent in Nonnenwerth along with Lotte. When Lotte was the only one to get permission, Liese became a teacher in an elementary school in our town. I kept on seeing her sometimes running to mass with her pale, pointed little face and with the pince-nez perched on her nose just like today. She was treated contemptuously by the Nazi officials because of her piety but even her transfer to a school for the retarded—which under Hitler was considered contemptible—did not bother her at all because she was accustomed by her faith to all kinds of persecutions. Even the most rabid Nazis, the most treacherous and spiteful neighbors became quite gentle and mild as they sat around Liese during the bombing raids. It then occurred to the oldest among them that they had already sat once in the same dark basement with this same neighbor Liese, when the shells exploded in the First World War. They now crowded up close to

the despised little teacher, as if by virtue of her faith and her calm she had already once appeased death. Even the most impudent and derisive among them were then disposed to assume some of the faith of the little teacher Liese. In their eyes she had always been timid and fearful, but now she crouched confidently among the grayish-white distorted faces in the artificial basement light, while the bombs were dropping outside and the city was almost completely destroyed. This time including Liese as well as her religious and irreligious neighbors.

The stores had just closed. I passed through Flachsmarkt Strasse in the midst of the turmoil of people going home. Just as their houses were still untouched by explosives, from the first great test of 1914-1918 as well as from the most recent major bombardments, so, too, their comfortable, thoroughly familiar, lean and chubby, mustachioed and full-bearded, warty and smooth faces were still untouched by guilt, untouched by looking on and tolerating this guilt out of cowardice, out of fear of the power of the state. And yet they will soon enough get their fill of exaggerated state power, of overbearing commands. Or did they come to develop a taste for it? Like the baker with his twirled moustache and round little pot belly at the corner of the Flachsmarkt where we always bought our Streusel cake, or the streetcar conductor who was just now clanging past us? Or was it the calm of this evening with the quick steps of the homecomers, with its sound of the Angelus bells, with its six o'clock whistles of distant factories, was it the simple cosiness of the everyday working day which I now enjoyed like a reinvigorating drink? Did all of this have something repulsive about it for the children who soon greedily inhaled their fathers' reports about the war and who longed to exchange working clothes covered with flour or dust for uniforms?

I felt another twinge of fear come over me as I was about to turn into my own street, as if I had a presentiment that it was destroyed. The feeling soon vanished. For already along the last stretch of Bauhof Strasse I was able to take my customary and favorite way home, under the two great ash trees forming a triumphal arch between the right and left sides of the street, touching each other, undestroyed, indestructible. And I saw already the white, red and blue islands made up of flower beds of geraniums and begonias set in the grass and lining the street. As I entered, I felt against my forehead an evening wind stronger

than any I had ever felt before. It blew a cloud of leaves out of the pink hawthorn bushes that seemed to me first to be gilded by the sunlight but that were really colored sun-red. As always after a day's excursion, I had the feeling that I hadn't heard for a long time the whistling of the wind as it came up from the Rhine and was caught up in my own street. I was tired through and through so that I was happy to be in front of my house at last. Only it seemed to me unbearably hard to climb up the stairs. I looked up to the second floor where we had our apartment. My mother was already standing out on the little veranda, decorated with boxes of geraniums and overlooking the street. She was waiting for me. And how young she looked, my mother, much younger than I. How dark her smooth hair was, compared to mine. Mine of course went gray early while hers still didn't show a single strand of gray. She stood up there erect and happy, destined for a domestic life full of hard work, with the usual joys and burdens of everyday existence, and not meant for an agonizing, cruel death in the remote village to which she had been banished by Hitler. Now she recognized me and waved to me as if I had been away on a trip. She always laughed and waved this way after excursions. I ran as quickly as I could into the hallway.

I stopped short before the first landing. Suddenly I was much too tired to climb up the stairs as fast as I had wanted a moment ago. A gray-bluish fog of tiredness enveloped everything. Yet at the same time everything around me was bright and hot, not dim as it usually is in entrance halls. I forced myself up to my mother. The steps, immense in the mist, seemed to me unattainably high, impossibly steep as if leading up the side of a mountain. Perhaps my mother had already gone out into the hallway and was waiting at the staircase door. But my feet simply refused to move. Only as a very small child had I felt an anxiety like this: that some disaster might prevent me from seeing her again. I imagined how she was waiting for me in vain, separated only by a few steps. Then with a sensation of relief it occurred to me that if I should collapse here from exhaustion my father would of course find me immediately. He wasn't dead at all, he would be coming home any moment now that work was over. It was only that he was fond of stopping at the street corner to chat with his neighbors for rather longer than suited my mother.

One could already hear the clatter of supper dishes being set out. Behind every door I heard the hands clapping while kneading the dough in a familiar rhythm. I found it strange that

people made pancakes in this way: beating the dough flat betweeen two hands rather than rolling it out. At the same time I heard the violent clucking of turkeys coming from the courtyard and I was puzzled why they were suddenly raising turkeys in the courtyard. I wanted to look around but the very intense light from the courtyard windows blinded me at first. The steps were blurred in the mist, the staircase opened up in all directions into a bottomless pit like an abyss. Then clouds formed in the window niches and quickly filled up the abyss. A distant thought still crossed my mind: what a pity, how nice it would have been if Mother had embraced me. If I'm too tired to climb up the stairs, where will I get the strength to get back up to the village in the hills? They're expecting me there by nightfall. The heat of the sun was still strong; its rays never burned more intensely than when they hit at an angle. As always it seemed strange to me that there was no twilight here—only an abrupt transition from day to night. I pulled myself together and now started walking more vigorously, even though the staircase was lost in an unfathomable abyss. The banisters turned and arched out into a massive stake fence made up of organ cactuses. I couldn't tell anymore where the mountains stopped and the clouds began. I found the road to the inn where I'd sat after coming down from the village up in the mountains. The dog had run away. Two turkeys that hadn't been there before were now feeding in the roadway. The innkeeper was still squatting in front of the house and next to him a friend or a relative was squatting too, lost in thought or not thinking at all. At their feet the shadows of their hats kept them company. The innkeeper didn't move a muscle when I came back; I wasn't worth it; I had already become part of the usual order of his sensory perceptions. I was now too tired to move another step; I sat down at my old table. I wanted to go back up into the mountains as soon as I had caught my breath a little. I wondered how I was going to spend my time, today and tomorrow, here and there, for I now felt an immeasurable flow of time, unfathomable like the air. For we had been trained since childhood to subjugate time in some way instead of submitting humbly to it. Suddenly I remembered the assignment my teacher had given me to describe our school excursion in detail. I planned to start working on it at once, tomorrow—or even this evening—as soon as I'd recovered from my exhaustion.

SAINT CUNIGUND IN THE SNOW

BODO UHSE

I got to know Steffie through young Lernau. One day in the late summer of 1937 he brought her up to me. Actually I didn't find their visit particularly convenient since I wanted to work, but Lernau in his oblivious way made himself right at home in my easy chair. Steffie kept standing shyly on her long legs next to her friend, a little put out by his unduly intimate manner—one which in fact was out of place considering the great difference in age between us.

I was touched by her embarrassment. I took out a bottle of cognac and she came into the kitchen with me to help wash out the glasses in which some water colors had gone dry. Then we had a drink.

"This time they really got it!" Lernau said triumphantly. He was talking about the rowing regatta last Sunday when the Würzburg University team had been beaten in the eights.

"You've got to admit," I objected, "that the Würzburg team was basically better, except that they had to row on the outside."

"What do you mean by that?" Lernau blustered only too ready as usual to pick an argument.

"The river is too narrow. You can't have three boats racing alongside each other there," I explained.

Steffie sat on the squat African hassock which I had inherited from Ullmann when he left for France. She had folded her hands over her knees. Every now and then she would give me a velvety look with her big, brown eyes.

"The positions had been decided by lot beforehand. And if the Würzburg team was unlucky, that's their problem. In any case they got beaten." Lernau's opinion was unshakeable. Only now did I remember that he was a member of the victorious Bamberg Rowing Club to which the better class of people in our town belonged. So I let him have his fun and poured him another drink. Lernau started to fool around.

"If your head bothers you," he shouted, "throw it against the wall! If it doesn't stick, put it back on."

He had a few of these phrases which he had a habit of repeating. He laughed quite loudly at his own joke and then wanted to tell me the story of poor Mrs. Gabelsberger who had been surprised with her lover in the Botanical Gardens. The whole town was buzzing with it already. I interrupted him and asked him about his work.

At the moment he was painting his "Striding Warrior." "Completely self-contained," he said. "You understand? The colors hard, the outlines sharp as knives." He jumped up and ran around in the studio. His blond hair fell down onto his forehead, he laughed out of a crooked mouth. He was always laughing, laughing about everything.

It was as if Steffie was bewitched by him. Lernau kept on talking about his picture: "An expression of our time. Hard, magnificent, dangerous. A symbol of warlike Germany. Banners are what we have to paint: banners!"

He stopped by the table and emptied the glass that I had filled for him again. He probably believed at that moment what he was saying. But I was sure he believed it only at that moment. I thought of his earlier work. He had once had a way with his paint brush. How he had been spoiled!

Years ago he had been offered a job in the western part of Germany, a job that had turned out to be disastrous for him. The New Museum—supported by industrial interests—had started out originally to use its great wealth to foster an art that sought for objective expression. But later, after the captains of coal and iron had discovered their "social conscience" and had decided to side with the brown tyranny, with re-armament and a new war, they had demanded under the gray sky of the belching smokestacks a "Steely Art" to match it. They had demanded an aesthetic expression of their hunger for power and higher profits, something that in literary terms was called the "Longing for the Thousand Year Reich." A lot of people had left the Essen Institute at that time but not Lernau. He had hastily adopted the pathos of the big lie and now painted striding warriors.

I felt it was my duty to really talk to him for once. But I didn't do it. Nobody talked about important things in those days.

Yes, it was the hallmark of those years not to talk about what was important. Nobody had the courage to speak it out loud or

write it or to let it come out in one's pictures. It was against the law! So everybody was careful. In the end you didn't even think about thinking about it. Not only because it was against the law; not only because we'd been conditioned by the habit of thinking it was against the law. But because the encounter with the important things was painful for us; that's why we were careful to avoid such encounters.

And of what use could my advice be to young Lernau? I knew in advance that he wouldn't pay any attention to it. He was determined to be successful and he found success lying right in the middle of the road he was pursuing as a "striding warrior." He was known, he always got good, sometimes lavish reviews. The first rays of fame were beginning to bathe him in a promising light.

They had never said very much about me even in earlier days, and at that time I was as good as forgotten. And so it was Lernau who criticized me: "You sit around in your little room here and go to pot! The big world outside keeps on moving."

He was especially insistent that day, probably because he wanted to make an impression on Steffie. I was annoyed at being forced into a role that his attitude forced me to play. For since I couldn't say the essential thing, I had to take refuge in all sorts of excuses.

"Let the world keep on moving," I said. "It's my job to paint pictures. I've been taken up by other things long enough. First I studied law because my father wanted me to. When he died and I thought I was free, the war came. Four long years! After the war I went to work first in a bank because I didn't have any money. So I got to be thirty-two years old before I could start painting. I've had a lot to catch up with. Let the world move on: I'm going to paint!"

Lernau laughed and recited:

> "I'd like to own a little garden
> And bask in the shade of a tree.
> How grand to dig up my radishes.
> God bless you. It's nothing for me."

This time our conversation didn't end as usual in a quarrel. On the contrary, Lernau had a suggestion to make to me. I was to submit two pictures to the Munich exhibition that was being

planned for the spring. It had some patriotic name that I've forgotten. I was completely surprised, especially when Lernau explained that he had been authorized to make the suggestion. An official written invitation was to follow.

Steffie was bored by our talk. She stood up and wandered through the studio. She seemed to feel shy at my pictures, or at any rate she avoided looking at them. She went to the window and looked down at the river. When the mill started up and the floor of my studio groaned, she turned to us with an exclamation of surprise.

Lernau examined me attentively when I once looked over towards Steffie as she stood with her silent good face by the window. I liked her and he, with his vanity, was proud of it. He was showing off with his young woman as he did with his muscles or with his ugly but whimsical horsehead.

After the two of them had gone, I went back—still marveling at Lernau's offer—to my sketch books.

I was looking for a landscape which I had once made a rough sketch of: the upper Town Hall Bridge with the statue of Saint Cunigund. I finally got tired of rummaging around for it. I took my sketchbook and went over to the Town Hall Island. It was only a couple of hundred yards away from my studio in Eckert's Mill.

Once on the bridge I got down to work immediately. But it just wouldn't come out right. At that time of day there was a lot of traffic (by the standards of our town) and the people bothered me, stopping and looking over my shoulder.

I shut my sketchbook and went home in a bad mood. On the way I tried to think where I might have put the sketch but I just couldn't remember. Finally I gave up the idea of painting the bridge of St. Cunigund. I gave it up without having a real reason for it. And I was sorry about it too because now I didn't have a set project for the next few days—and I liked my life to run according to plan.

That evening I spent at the window doing nothing. I should have been busy making my preparations, putting the canvas on the frame, choosing paints and brushes.

The little river murmured past the old mill wheel with its slowly rotting boards. For years now the mill had been powered by modern turbines but the grinding operation still made the

whole building vibrate. Once in a while a fish would jump out of the water and dive back in with a clapping sound.

I thought about Lernau and his girlfriend. What a difference between them! He was intemperate and at the same time despotic, and he took unheedingly whatever he needed to add to his glory from no matter whom. I sensed that I had to be on my guard with him. But she was full of devotion and gentleness and didn't belong to these times. I translated her back into the period when Rilke's and Hofmannsthal's poetry still met with a living response. I even took her further back: hadn't Dehmel and Liliencron sung of her? They were the poets of my youth.

I broke off my train of thought with a jolt. The mist was rising from the river and I had to close the window. At my age, women really were no business of mine. I didn't like living alone. I could have managed a little affection, but playing the lover—no, that didn't agree with me anymore.

I turned on the light and reached for a book and decided to watch my step. That's how bad it was with me already on the first evening after I'd seen her.

I also acted according to my principles when I met Steffie again. After all our town is quite small and you can hardly avoid running into people. I met her often from then on, sometimes in the Shooting Gallery Café where I drank my coffee, sometimes on my rare walks into town. I pulled myself together and was very cool to her. Even so she seemed happy to see me. Lernau popped up repeatedly in my studio and he frequently brought her along. She grew talkative during these visits, which now delighted me, and even got up enough courage to tease me a little. But I pretended not to notice. I hid myself behind my age, as if behind a protective wall. "Kids" I called them and clothed myself in the guise of a father.

I played the role well enough to deceive Lernau. But to the extent that I had tried to use it to save myself, it was useless and too late. I took advantage of my role to get as close to Steffie as possible; wasn't it obvious and natural that I should be allowed to smooth her hair solicitously away from her forehead? Soon there were little, harmless secrets between us, and on her side a heartfelt trust. In a short time I had gotten to know more from her and about her than Lernau could ever have found out because his conceit made him inattentive. Every day she drifted closer to me.

At that time I told Lernau that I didn't have any pictures for the spring exhibition. That is, my studio was full but none of the pictures seemed suitable. Basically I felt that I didn't belong in this exhibition. Lernau suggested half jokingly that I should make a portrait of Steffie. I accepted at once and we set a day for the first sitting.

I hadn't painted a portrait for quite some time and so I got the idea of looking at some of my older work. I brought down the dusty canvases from the attic. What I saw when I set up the pictures in my studio filled me with a burning dissatisfaction. I couldn't manage to be impressed by even a single one of them. I had played the color contrasts off against each other too calculatingly and probably too brashly as well. And all the backgrounds were wrong! Where they needed light, they were dark; where they should have been more two dimensional, I had forced them into violent perspective.

Behind the fleshy and yet so sour face of the merchant Bing—what joy I'd derived from the light on those full, reddish-blue cheeks—stretched inexplicably a stormy landscape. Bing was killed during the fire in the synagogue. Didn't one recognize his violent end in his face? Hadn't I inscribed it on his forehead in the painting?

I was overwhelmed as I looked around now at my pictures: I had collected a gallery of the dead, an exhibition of murder victims and suicides.

I had painted twelve portraits during the last few years. Nine of my models were dead now. They hadn't just passed away but had died in various unnatural ways. The painter Marcus, for instance, had been found floating one morning down in the grate in front of the mill wheel; or Geyer's Florian who worked in the brewery had been shot. Of course I'd heard about their deaths because the news spread even though nobody ever said a word about these things. But what hadn't occurred to me as I received the news of their deaths, what hadn't occurred to me was that they had all gone through my hands, that I had painted them.

Now, looking at their pictures one after the other, it seemed to me that their faces were all marked with a sign. I had marked them. For didn't they look like dead people in these pictures that I had painted while they were still alive?

Dressed in a jacket of blue linen, with his red child's face topped by blond hair, there sat Matthew, the son of the carpenter

who made my frames. His half open mouth wasn't laughing, it was screaming—in horror at a gruesome death. I had painted him two years ago when he was fifteen. Even his parents hadn't found out what happened to him. Old Scheuffele in his shop had shown me the letter that the government had sent him. The tears had dropped quietly out of his old man's eyes onto the paper. Matthew had died suddenly in a work camp and had immediately been buried nearby in the cemetery of the village of Frankenheim.

I'm usually not superstitious but now I thought I saw on the faces of the other ones—the three who were still alive—the sign of a bad end.

The three had very little in common: Captain Carl Söldner, gallant and worldly; Neusel, the editor, bald, intelligent and unscrupulous; and then the old woman peddler whom I painted in the market place next to her stand with the radishes. Death flickered about their mouths and a horror was reflected in their eyes which they could have known nothing about when they sat for these pictures for me.

I kept standing among these portraits until nightfall, continually comparing the pictures of the dead with those of the living. Confused and tortured by a sense of malevolent responsibility, I finally cut up the last three pictures with a knife that I took from the kitchen and burned them. I actually felt better afterwards.

I laughed at my fears with a kind of forced laughter. Was I to blame that my models had been hanged and drowned, shot and beaten to death? It was the fault of the times. It was just that people died more quickly and less peacefully nowadays. I couldn't help that.

There have been other painters who have had bad luck like this with their models. Who would think of blaming Hans Holbein for Thomas More's death? It wasn't he who had ordered Anne Boleyn to be beheaded. He hadn't determined the fate of the beautiful, unfortunate Jane Seymour.

He had painted all three and others besides who had become victims of their times as my models had become victims of ours. He had painted the victims and—the face of his times—their murderer, King Henry.

I was terribly excited. At that time one had to work out everything for oneself. If Ullmann had still been there, I might have been able to talk it over with him. But Ullmann had been

living in France for over a year. Now I wondered if I shouldn't have gone with him after all.

When Steffie came the following day, she was wearing a pale-pink dress with a white ruffle around the neck that stood up stiffly against her chestnut hair and accentuated her neckline. She was a little embarrassed and looked more beautiful than I had ever seen her. She sat down by the window overlooking the river. But the light there was too harsh. We moved the heavy easy chair further into the studio.

Then I set up the easel. I squeezed the paints onto the palette, slowly and clumsily. I was hesitant to make the first brush stroke. I was seized again by a sense of insecurity, a superstitious terror. I wanted to throw away my brush and palette.

Still the temptation that emanated from her quiet beauty was stronger than my fears, and even stronger was the hope for a few uninterrupted hours of her company and the task of painting this gentle, luminous face, a face that was human as few faces were at that time. For the faces had changed too, had grown colder, more expressionless, flatter. Do you really believe that it doesn't leave a trace in the faces when the people who belong to those faces keep silent about everything? Of course not, but only people like me can see that.

And so I began with a trembling hand. I used a dark, heavy blue for the background. An inward fervor shone out of Steffie's face as in the pictures of saints in the early Middle Ages.

I usually talked with my models so as to distract them a little. But this time I couldn't find any words to say, so I asked her to sing a song. Since the old folk songs had become popular again for some years now, she knew quite a few of them. At first she simply hummed quietly to herself, changing melodies now and then in search of the right one. Through the half open window the smell of decaying wood drifted up from the river along with an early morning mist. The mill machinery rumbled and the whole house trembled.

Steffie sang.

I worked. I swore and cursed as I put the paints on the canvas. Then, suddenly, I stopped. I was overcome by disillusion and the old fears rose up again. I laid palette and brush down on the table and hung a cloth over the canvas.

"No, that's not the way," I said grumpily.

She looked at me like a child who has just been caught doing something wrong.

"These new paints aren't worth anything," I explained to her. "I've got to go see if I can't get any better ones."

Later Lernau came by to pick her up. He was beaming with importance. He had received a special commission that had to do with setting up the spring exhibition in Munich. Just what it was exactly I couldn't quite grasp. But I knew that he was in touch with all sorts of "artistic administration big cheeses" and with other influential people. He announced he would soon have to leave on business. How happy I was to hear that! But Steffie trembled as she put her hand on my arm when leaving.

After the second sitting Lernau and I had a stupid quarrel. I was nervous and still depressed by my superstitious fears. That made me irritable and I couldn't tolerate the self-complacency with which Lernau played the role of my protector and patron.

"Yes, if it weren't for me," he actually said, "you'd still be lurking in your dark little corner. But you just wait, a man of your talents shouldn't be hiding himself away anymore. We'll pull you out into the light all-right."

He said more of this kind of thing. In former days I had simply accepted it and defended myself by denying my convictions, just as I had done the first time Lernau had come to see me with Steffie. But now I couldn't do that anymore. I loved Steffie and did not want to conceal from her how I really felt. So I threw caution to the winds and came out with everything that I had learned laboriously to suppress during those years.

I probably didn't act very shrewdly in my excitement.

"I don't need your help," I screamed. "You've chased hundreds of people away; you've forced hundreds of others to remain silent. You don't let them work; you don't let them exhibit. Now you're embarrassed by the gaping holes in your museums. You want to fill them up. And that's where I come in too: a stop-gap, eh?"

"My God," said Lernau impatiently and looked at me in sham horror, "have you lost all faith in yourself?"

"My self-confidence is healthier than yours," I declared sharply. "I don't find it necessary to shore myself up with exhibitions, flattering reviews, and well-paid commissions."

"Now you're constructing a theory out of your lack of suc-

cess," Lernau said unmoved and with an air of inner superiority. "You're bitter, old man, and I can really understand that. You used to talk quite differently, didn't you? I remember a conversation with that red-headed Ullmann . . ."

"He had more talent in his little finger than you do in your whole hand!"

"He did, did he?" Now Lernau started to get riled up too and I was pleased that I had broken his calm façade.

"But in any case he had to make tracks, your friend Ullmann, eh?" Lernau said. "Another one of those Jews of whom there's never been a lack in your house. And I really don't understand why you're bothering to defend him now. Back then anyway you always used to be in each other's hair."

Lernau was beginning to calm down again. He even laughed.

"Remember when Ullmann was talking about the loneliness of the artist, his detachment, his inner and outward freedom: how you lost your temper then! You were the one who talked of the need for an art solidly entrenched in reality—yes, those were your very words! Well, what more do you want: I'm rooted in reality. Art must have a mission, must fullfil a function—that was another one of your arguments. You said: Art needs to be commissioned. Well, I—"

"How you manage to twist things around!" I interrupted him. "I spoke of two kinds of commissions: a material and a moral commission. You can't have missed that. I guess you've succeeded with the material commission, but I can't see a trace of the other one in you. Because what you call reality, that is precisely what's the lie!—Sometimes I wonder," I then went on, "what is actually worse: your autodafé's or what you call creativity. In any case the only things worth seeing in your museums are those blank spots where the pictures you've banned used to hang." I couldn't restrain myself any more and came down hard with both of my fists on the big work table. What I had otherwise never admitted to myself—the consciousness of the barrenness and the bitter dryness of our life, the fruitlessness and the narrowness—overwhelmed me so terrifically that I hammered on the table as if it was the gate of a gigantic prison in which we were all of us imprisoned.

I ripped open a drawer and threw on the table prints of the pictures that had been removed from the museums—prints that I

had to buy secretly because they had been taken out of circulation.

"Look at that," I screamed at Lernau and probably got a little pathetic. "Look at them. Those are the heralds of our agony. In these colors burns the impulse for freedom. In these forms resides our longing for the shadow of eternal truth."

I grabbed Steffie's arm. "Look at it," I said. "They can't blind you forever. When you see these pictures, don't you feel what it means to be a human being? How good and evil our blood is? How weak and magnificent our spirit?"

The sheets lay in front of us on the table; good, carefully executed and craftsmanlike prints. His head flushed, young Lernau stepped up to the table. He lowered his big, somewhat bulging eyes. Using only his fingertips, as if he found it revolting to touch them, he turned over one sheet after another.

"It's a real mixed bag," he said, "but your collection does seem to be complete. All Jews—just look—here's Kollwitz too with her stench of poor folks."

I stood next to him trying to catch my breath. "Barlach," continued Lernau, "of course, he's absolutely essential. And whom have we here? Well, well: Rembrandt! I've got to admit you're really up to date. His status hasn't been quite settled yet. Lehmann-Hildesheim calls him the ghetto painter and that's my opinion as well, if you'd care to know—"

Lernau didn't smile, he bared his teeth and grabbed the sheet—"Joseph Recounting His Dreams"—and tore it up. I'll remember the sound of that tearing paper until the day I die: that's how sharp and evil it sounded. I jumped forward to grab Lernau's arm. But before I could reach him, Steffie had got to him. She bit him so hard in his hand that he screamed.

"Are you crazy, Steffie?" he yelled and put his bleeding hand to his mouth. The two halves of the sheet dropped to the floor. Steffie didn't bother about Lernau; she knelt down on the floor and fitted the two halves of the torn sheet together with a delicate, healing gesture. She remained huddled on the floor, crying.

"There's iodine on the night table," I said to Lernau and turned to Steffie.

"Don't cry," I said and then stopped. No, I couldn't console her; it looked too disconsolate inside my own self.

"Yes," I called out and in my grief felt ecstatic at her spontaneous, passionate act. "Yes, do cry! Cry: there's reason enough. Scream, scream so that the whole world hears you!"

Lernau had pushed away the curtain separating the adjoining room where my bed was. He let water run over his hand to cool off his wound.

"Do cry," I said to Steffie. "Don't hide your tears. Cry if you can't do anything else . . ."

I put my hands on her trembling shoulders, my wrinkled hands, covered with dark hair and shot through with bulging veins in which the blood flowed only wearily.

Lernau turned off the faucet again and came back into the room. He was still rubbing his injured left hand. He had dampened his blond hair with water and combed it back so that his forehead was exposed. His face was naked.

"You'll regret it—sooner or later," he remarked drily. Steffie got up and let him take her out of the studio. At the door she looked at me again with a sad, meaningful look. I heard the sound of their steps dying away on the wooden stairs.

What in the world had I done? What had come over me to make me say all those things one should never say? I had a little pension and I was independent. I didn't have to rely on commissions and I was able to live my own life. What was the point of getting myself involved in what Lernau called the world?

I had talked the way Ullman had spoken that last evening before he left for France. But then he had only spoken that last evening, and only to me whom he trusted.

"Come along," he said. "Come along; the air's getting too thin here." But what was I going to do in France or wherever the road of emigrants led? I belonged to this Franconian landscape with its white, half-timbered houses, its hills and streams, with its blond, brown-eyed girls, with its treasures of the Gothic, the Renaissance and the Baroque. This was the space in which I lived; this was the air I breathed. But I was afraid of Van Gogh's hot sun.

What preoccupied me most during the next days wasn't Lernau's threat—though despite his youth he had influence and could certainly harm me—but my concern for Steffie.

I had grown so accustomed to her and now I missed her. What was strange was that I didn't meet her anywhere, neither in the

Shooting Gallery nor on my walks that I now purposely extended.

To my astonishment Lernau popped up with her again one day in my studio. At first I didn't know what to make of it but one look into Steffie's eyes calmed my fears.

Lernau shook his head and laughed, with his blond hair flying in all directions.

"If my head bothers you, throw it against the wall! Here, take it," he said and acted as if nothing had really happened between us.

I didn't let on how very relieved I felt. I even said: "Lernau, in your heart you really admit I'm right."

"Hold it, hold it," he said and pressed his hands against his ears. "Let's not start off with that again."

Now I should have insisted stubbornly, as I felt instinctively, but at that moment I could think only of Steffie, and I trembled at the idea that she might be taken away from me again. And I accepted everything without protest, all of Lernau's smooth words which should have warned me, his jokes and laughter and then the news that lay behind his magnanimous gesture of forgiving and forgetting: he was leaving for Munich. He'd been offered a government job with a high salary.

"See, that's why I came here, despite everything. Steffie trusts you; you're her fatherly friend,"—how he wounded me by saying that!—" and I know you'll look after her well."

We drank a bottle of wine in reconciliation and farewell. Lernau wanted to see Steffie's portrait but I refused to show it to him. He didn't insist.

"Now it's onward and upward along life's golden highway," Lernau said. I wished him a good trip.

It was remarkable that after he left I didn't make any progress with Steffie's portrait. I felt self-conscious since I was alone with her now in quite a different way than before. She seemed to sense that too. At first she told me now and then about the letters she received. Lernau sent me his regards. Later on she didn't mention them any more. A worried look came into her face. Probably she wasn't getting any more letters. Slowly her face began to change. An expression of patient suffering, a streak of hardness that hadn't been there before, were etched into it; and the gentleness and softness that had stamped her face up to then

vanished. So she grew and matured under my eyes. I loved her all the more and thought that she had become more beautiful.

But I never had so much difficulty with any picture as with her portrait. I started over again three times and couldn't finish. Finally I began to wonder if it was really just my dissatisfaction with myself as an artist that lay behind it or the change in Steffie's looks or even the wish simply not to finish. For undeniably I was seized again every now and then by the terror that had overcome me when I looked at my old portraits. And then there was still another reason for me to try to make the job last as long as possible.

It was nice to have Steffie around. She helped me keep the studio in order, she brought me flowers, she made coffee for us in the afternoon. Sometimes she even looked after my clothes. I was pleased at these little signs of intimacy; I enjoyed the quiet, industrious hours with her, the tranquil conversations, her quiet laughter when in the heat of my work I started to swear.

Sometimes I thought that it would be nice to live with her. These ideas shocked me, I admit, but I couldn't help myself. I didn't have any control over myself anymore. I was driven, just as the river under my window was driven towards the sea. That river was now full of ice floes because winter had come very early and with great intensity; it had snowed and it was freezing. In the corners of the big window overlooking the river, ice flowers were opening their mysterious fans.

Yes, I loved Steffie. I knew what it was that worried her and trembled at the thought that one day she would come and tell me that Lernau had written her and that everything was fine again. My heart skipped a beat when I heard her coming up the stairs. I listened anxiously for her step and I heaved a sigh of relief when I realized that it was the same hesitant, trailing, rather melancholy step to which my ears had grown accustomed.

Then I opened the door and looked into her face and the friendly and yet hard smile on her lips—and then I was happy!

Of course I kissed her hand, I put my arm around her shoulder and pulled her over to the easy chair by the window. We looked down at the river and the ice floes. I loved her.

In the meantime I'd changed my mind and had started to paint the upper Town Hall Bridge with its statue of St. Cunigund. I did it in order to provide myself with a distraction from the dangerous passion that had seized me. Besides I wanted to overcome

the difficulties which Steffie's picture caused me. I wanted to prove to myself what a great guy I still was. Every morning at the break of dawn I would crawl out of bed and drag my easel and canvas over to the upper Town Hall Bridge. Even before I reached it my fingers were ice-cold and numb despite my fur gloves. And so I had to warm them up first over the little cast-iron pot full of hot charcoal—an old-fashioned device that gave me good service. Here my work progressed more quickly than I had expected. And one morning I discovered that the picture was finished.

I was satisfied with it and wanted to show it to Steffie. So I set it up on the easel.

She was late that day. I sat waiting impatiently in my studio, narrowing my eyes and examining the picture: the bridge of light, gray-white stone with the noble figure of the Saint standing on the edge, with the little river in the background, covered with ice floes. Snow and white clouds in the sky. White on white—nothing else. It almost dazzled one's eyes. The color had almost devoured the forms: they were only left hanging loose in the swoop of the bridge into space and anchored in the frail, erect figure of the woman bowing her crowned head gently down over her praying hands. White on white on white.

Was I satisfied? No, I suddenly revolted against the monotony, against the colorless, hopeless rhythm in it.

I took my palette and squeezed colors onto it, whatever colors came to hand—ochre and Prussian blue and carmine—though I didn't know what I was going to do with them in my landscape of snow. But then I made up my mind, grabbed my putty knife and smashed a blue window into the whitish gray winter sky.

I was painting on wood. The easel groaned under the blows of my putty knife and kept on edging away. I kept painting, swearing and cursing in my usual way until I had driven the easel almost up against the wall. Then I stopped and wiped the sweat from my brow. All that dumb excitement over a little bit of Prussian blue! That color really hung now like a flag affirming the joy of life in the white of the picture.

I lit a cigarette and looked down on the Regnitz. The mill works were grinding, the house was groaning and humming. But what had happened to Steffie?

When I turned around again, the Cunigund picture seemed completely alien to me. What a cheap piece of joy that blue

triangle was—insipid, shabby and prosaic: a way out that was just too easy! Like a big coarse lump it squashed the whole picture together, destroyed the frosty solemnity that had been in it and vulgarized its ceremonious severity. That's how gross and stupid that blue looked.

I pulled the easel out of its corner again, dragged it squealing on one leg across the uneven floorboards and started to cover up the blue hole in the sky again. Only a little bit of it was to stay, only a short, hopeful tinge.

Then I mixed a little more ochre into the white of the snow covering the bridge railing, but only enough to brighten somewhat the arch that spanned the picture. It was to be whiter even than white.

I had to move the easel back from the wall three times into the middle of the room until I had finally completed the job.

Then I felt tired and at the same time very lonely. What was the matter with Steffie?

I was freezing and my eyes hurt me. They probably couldn't stand all that white. I'd used four tubes on the picture, four big tubes.

"You're throwing money out of the window, you old fool," I swore at myself.

Steffie came with the twilight. I went through the room to meet her. She didn't excuse herself. We sat down at the broad window and watched how outside twilight turned into night. That happens quickly in winter. First the things, the houses on the other side of the river, and the Church of St. Joseph lost their color and then their form. The squat, angular church tower flattened out into a silhouette; the houses turned to shadows. Soon we couldn't even distinguish the ice-floes anymore that were swirling past on the river under the window. The street lamps on the bridge twinkled at us. In their glow we watched the snow sinking down in single flakes.

We listened intensely as if we were waiting to hear it fall.

"It's snowing," I said. Steffie huddled herself up in her chair; she must have been freezing.

Then I said: "If you look over towards the lights, then you think you can feel the damp flakes on your eyebrows."

Steffie didn't reply. That made me sad. I had worked the whole day and waited so long for her. Now I was tired and would have liked to show her the Cunigund picture and heard her praise it.

Then she started to talk about Lernau. She hadn't mentioned him for months. But now a letter had come from him at last. The pages rustled in her hand.

I wanted to turn on the light but she wouldn't let me. Huddled up freezing in the chair she talked into the dark. Lernau had written to her that it was over. He had gotten engaged in Munich. Steffie also mentioned the name of the bride. She came from a very influential family.

I could hardly wait until she had finished. Then I told her everything, everything that I felt for her. The darkness and her abandonment made me daring. Steffie slid out of the chair and bent down over me. Silently she stroked my head with her hand; then she left like a stranger. As she pulled the door shut behind her, two brushes rolled from the table and fell to the floor. For a long time I heard the bright, quivering noise of the thin pieces of wood.

Steffie did not return and her portrait remained unfinished. I only sent the picture of St. Cunigund in the Snow to Munich for the exhibition. The jury turned it down, but that wasn't all. The picture was not sent back to me but forwarded to a special exhibition of "degenerate art."

A FRUSTRATED ST. FRANCIS

(For Lilly)

F. C. WEISKOPF

Americans love to call their United States God's Own Country, and there is hardly another country in the world where the Lord's Word is quoted so abundantly by as many people as there. But to quote does not necessarily mean to heed, as witness the following incident which occurred around Christmas time 1946 in the city of New York.

A citizen of Brooklyn by the name of Jim O., who had managed in a short time to advance from shoeshine boy to the owner of a bar and poolroom—not because he was particularly shrewd or hardworking, but rather because he possessed the gift of inducing people to laugh, drink and spend their money—this Jim O. was just in the process of settling his accounts on Christmas Eve, when all at once and without warning he felt the overpowering urge to go out and divide twelve percent of his income among the poor and unfortunate. As he was later to say at one of the numerous interrogations he was forced to submit to, he had received the inspiration for this plan while counting the fifty-cent pieces, which, because of the soft tinkle of silver, had reminded him of a long forgotten children's legend about St. Francis, the charitable saint.

It was a clear, frosty night and the stars sparkled above the shadowy outlines of the skyscrapers like the chrome on a brand-new Packard limousine. The cheap dives of the Bowery were crowded with part-time peddlers, unemployed men and beggars—in other words, with down-and-outers of all kinds. O. entered the first likely joint, climbed onto a chair at the counter and gave a speech. He said that he couldn't stand eating his Christmas turkey while all of those present had to be satisfied with eating a dish of macaroni costing a dime or a cup of coffee

and stale doughnuts. For this reason he was inviting his honored audience to order for themselves any food and drink they desired. The bill would be paid for by him.

The response to his speech was quite different from what O. had anticipated. Some of the guests loudly doubted his sanity, others ridiculed him as a poor joker or felt insulted and began to swear at him, and one person even threatened to call the police. Not one of them took O.'s offer seriously. It took a long time to persuade three or four guests to come with him to the next police station in order to be officially convinced that the acceptance of his offer of a free meal did not entail any hidden obligations.

Frowning, the sergeant on duty listened to O.'s explanations. But since he was in a Christmas mood and since he also wanted to continue a very successful game of pinochle—he had to interrupt his game because of this strange visit—he decided that the police had no objection to the project of the man from Brooklyn. But, of course, O. would be responsible for any damages resulting from his goddamned strange whim to be charitable!

After returning to the joint—where in the meantime quite a few curious people had gathered together with the original guests—O. ordered that everything be served up that was available both in the kitchen and the cellar, and in addition he gave a five dollar bill to everybody who got up full from the table.

When it became apparent that his money would not be sufficient to give something to everybody, our man from Brooklyn—who was brimming over with St. Franciscan brotherly love—gave away his watch, his ruby ring, his hat and his silken shawl so that nobody would have to leave empty-handed. The two last items were brand-new: O. had just received them as Christmas gifts from a young and rather wealthy widow with whom he was carrying on a serious relationship.

After everything was over he sat down on the threshold of the joint and cried tears of emotion and satisfaction. "I bet," he said to a newspaper reporter who visited him a few days later when the incident had stirred up general attention, "everybody in my place would have acted exactly as I did; I feel like a Rockefeller ten times over. So help me God!"

The appearance of the crying man and the news of his generosity attracted a quickly growing crowd which soon stop-

ped all traffic so that the police had to take action. However, O. got away with a simple warning.

He drove home, threw himself into bed and slept through all of Christmas Day—he was exhausted not so much from being up the whole night but rather from the many emotions he had experienced. Late in the evening a telegraph messenger awakened him. The rich widow sent him a telegram telling him that she was through with him; she was tired of spending her holidays alone, disapproved most strongly of his association with the bums of the Bowery, could not find any excuse before God or men for the way in which he threw honest dollars practically down the drain, and she asked for the return of her gifts to him.

O. gave a tip worthy of a bank president to the telegraph messenger waiting for his reply, threw the reply form of the telegram into the trashcan and—like the day before—went off with a new bundle of money to the Bowery.

Since the dives were still comparatively empty, O. began to pass out money to passers-by, loiterers and drivers whom he met while slowly walking down the street. Most people believed that he was giving them advertising flyers or fake money. Only one old man did not seem to think it unusual that a stranger was giving him money for no reason at all, but this old man was completely drunk. O., however, did not let himself be distracted from his gay and generous mood even though the souls of the recipients of his gifts were hardened, cynical and distrustful. Rather, he continued to pass out his green bills left and right until all at once he felt a hand on his shoulder and heard a voice telling him to come along—there could be no doubt about the official character of this order because of the stern joviality of the voice addressing him. Before he knew it he found himself in a police car between two hefty sergeants and was driven to the main police station, where—so he was told tongue-in-cheek— somebody was eagerly awaiting him.

This somebody turned out to be the police doctor in a white coat with a stethoscope around his neck and a shiny mirror on his head. O. was told to take off his clothes, which he did most obligingly and indulgently so as not to be considered a spoil-sport. When, however, the examination went on and on—the doctor had started it immediately and with great seriousness— O. remarked still indulgently and in good humor that there must

be a curious misunderstanding since he was in the best physical and mental health and completely sober. The doctor replied smilingly—and it was this smile which caused shudders to run down O.'s back for the first time—that this was all very well but first Jim was to give his exact address, then list the names of the months in proper order, then deduct three from eleven, then walk across the room with closed eyes, and so on and so forth. After going along with all of the orders of the doctor for some time, O. finally decided that he had had enough and he refused to continue to take any more part in this monkey-business, as he called it. At this point the white-coat gave orders to take him away immediately, for he seemed to have been waiting for just such an opportunity.

The next two days our friend spent in the psychiatric observation ward at Bellevue hospital. He was just about to be introduced to a sizable study group as an exceptionally interesting case, when a certain needle manufacturer with influential connections, who was a friend of O.'s, managed to have him released.

Finally home again, he also made the discovery that thieves had taken advantage of his absence and had opened his safe. After these experiences anybody else would certainly have turned into a convinced misanthrope. Not so Jim O. When the above-mentioned newspaper reporter asked him whether he was filled with justifiable bitterness after what had happened to him, our man from Brooklyn quietly shook his head and replied: "I can't deny that I'm a little hard-nosed about fraud and such-like foul tricks. After all I haven't been standing ten years behind a bar counter for nothing, and a poolroom, by God, isn't exactly a Sunday School! With my experience, I really ought to be the most cold-blooded and hard-hearted guy under the sun. But I'm not. I'm simply not made that way. Patience has always been second nature to me. Also," he added after a minute of thoughtful silence, "I'm insured against theft and any loss by the Mutual Indemnity Insurance Company."

FEAST FOR MICE

JOHANNES BOBROWSKI

Moise Trumpeter is sitting on the little chair in the corner of the store. It's a little store and it's empty. Probably because the sun that's always coming in needs the room, and the moon too. The moon also always comes in as he passes by. Yes, the moon too. He came in, the moon, at the door and the bell on the door rang only once and very softly, but perhaps it didn't ring because the moon came in but because the little mice are running madly and dancing around on the thin floor boards. So, the moon came and Moise said, Good Evening, Moon! and now they're both watching the little mice.

But it's really different every day with the mice; sometimes they dance one way, sometimes another, and always with four legs, a pointed head and a thin little tail.

But my dear Moon, says Moise, that isn't the half of it; on top of that they've got a kind of little body and you wouldn't believe all of the stuff they've got in it. But perhaps you can't understand that and, besides, it isn't different every day but always exactly the same, and that, I think, is what's really so very remarkable. It's more likely you that's different every day although you always come in by the same door and it's always dark before you sit down in here. But now be quiet and keep your eyes peeled.

See, it's always the same.

Moise lets a bread crust fall down by his feet. The little mice scurry up closer, a little distance each time; a few even get up on their hind feet and sniff the air a little. See, that's how it is. Always the same.

The two oldsters sit there and are pleased and at first don't hear that the door of the store has opened. Only the mice heard it right away and are gone, completely gone, and so quickly that you couldn't say where they've run to.

A soldier stands in the door, a German. Moise has good eyes;

he sees: a young man, no more than a schoolboy who actually does not know what he wanted here now that he's standing in the door. Why not just take a look how the Jews live, he probably thought outside. But now the old Jew is sitting there on his little chair and the store is bright with the moonlight. You would like, maybe, to come in, Mr. Lieutenant, says Moise.

The boy closes the door. He isn't at all surprised that the Jew speaks German; he just stands there and when Moise stands up and says: Come, sit you down. Another chair I don't have, he says: No thanks, I can stand. But he takes a few steps into the center of the store, and then three more steps towards the chair. And when Moise asks him again to sit down, he does sit down.

Now you be real quiet, Moise says and leans up against the wall.

The bread crust is still lying there and, look, the mice are coming back again. Like before, not a bit slower, exactly like before, a little distance, then a little further, up on their hind feet and sniffing and the tiniest of snorts that only Moise hears and maybe the moon too. Exactly like before.

And now they've found the crust again. A feast for mice, on a small scale, to be sure, nothing special, but not an everyday thing either.

There you sit and watch. The war is a few days old already. The name of the country is Poland. It's completely flat and sandy. The roads are bad and there are a lot of children here. What else is there to say? The Germans have come, so many that you can't count them, one of them is sitting here in the Jew's store, a very young one, a stripling. He has a mother in Germany and a father, also still in Germany, and two little sisters. So, you're getting around in the world, he'll be thinking, now you're in Poland, and maybe later on you'll be going to England, and this Poland here is completely Polish.

The old Jew leans against the wall. The mice are still gathered about their crust. When it's gotten even smaller an old mother mouse will take it along with her and the other little mice will run after her.

You know, the moon says to Moise, I've got to be moving on a bit.

And Moise knows already that the moon is uncomfortable because that German is sitting around there. What can he be wanting? So Moise only says: Stay a little longer.

But then it's the soldier's turn to get up. The mice run away; you can't understand where they all could have disappeared to so quickly. He wonders if he should say good-bye, so he stays standing a moment longer in the store and then simply walks out.

Moise doesn't say anything; he waits for the moon to start talking. The mice are gone, vanished. Mice can do that.

That was a German, says the moon, you know, don't you, what these Germans are like. And because Moise keeps on leaning against the wall as he did before and doesn't say anything, the moon says somewhat more insistently: You don't want to run away, you don't want to hide, oh, Moise. That was a German, you saw that, didn't you. Don't tell me that boy wasn't one or in any case not a bad one. That doesn't make any difference anymore. When they've run over Poland, what's going to happen to your people?

I heard you, Moise says.

Now it's completely white in the store. The light fills the store right up to the door in the rear wall. Where Moise is leaning, completely white, so that you would think that he's becoming more and more one with the wall. With every word that he speaks.

I know, says Moise, you're quite right about that; I'm going to get into trouble with my God.

THE JUGGLER AT THE MOVIES
OR
THE ISLE OF DREAMS

FRANZ FÜHMANN

I had never seen him before until that day and now I know I'll never see him again. The doorbell had rung; it was one o'clock in the afternoon and the doorbell had rung the way it usually did around that time. I wanted to get out of the library where I'd been rummaging around for my father's anatomy books. They had declared these absolutely off-limits for me and had also kept them, a little apprehensively, hidden from me. I was going to mosey across the corridor to the door (in earlier days I would have rushed but now, after having held down this job for half a year, I just moseyed), when it occurred to me that I wasn't supposed to open the door to anybody today. I was alone in the apartment. Mother had gone with the maid and the office receptionist over to the next village where they were selling extra-juicy pears; and Father was far away making house calls and wouldn't be back before three. Bad luck, you poor fellow out there; I can't help you.

I was just about to return to the bookshelves when the doorbell rang again. And if the first time the bell had rung briefly and timidly as usual, this time it had an insistently loud ring to it. I had never experienced that before. Up to now there had been at least a pause of some minutes before one of those beggars who were in the habit of coming by every noontime for our scraps would dare to ring a second time; and if he dared, he pushed the button even more timidly the second time than the first. Suddenly I felt annoyed at not being allowed to open the door when I was alone. What was going to happen anyway? After all, I was ten years old and would be going to prep school next fall.

I went out to the corridor and saw dimly a slender figure standing behind the opaque glass pane in the apartment door. Who could that be? Suddenly all those taboos made me angry: the taboo not to play with the children next door because their parents worked in a factory and, even worse, didn't go to church on Sundays; the taboo not to get dirty and not to slide down the hill on the bottom of my pants when the snow thawed, like all the other children did (who of course wore clothes that were patched); the taboo not to accompany the organ-grinder on his route through our long-drawn-out little town; the taboo not to leaf through my father's books; the taboo not to talk to anybody no matter how much you liked him and at the same time not to be unfriendly to anybody you couldn't stand; and above all, of course, the taboo not to go to the opening tonight of the first movie theater in town. My father was going to give a dedicatory speech there as Chairman of the Municipal Cultural Society— and then they were going to show a film, "The Isle of Dreams." The isle of dreams—and I, who loved dreams like I loved fairy tales, so much that even during the day they would overwhelm me: I wasn't supposed to sail off to those isles? And I wasn't supposed to be even allowed to open the door when the bell rang and I was alone? What the hell, I would; after all, wasn't I ten years old and going to attend prep school next fall?

Suddenly—all of this happened in a matter of seconds— suddenly I hated my job as well: the job of opening the apartment door for the beggars; telling them to sit down on the steps and giving them as much soup as I saw fit or mashed potatoes or sliced dumplings with a little gravy or other leavings of our lunch; setting the food down on their knees and wishing them a hearty appetite as they started to dig in right away and slurp and gulp the food down. That had been my job for the last half year and my father had made me do it because I was lazy in school, and to make me see with my own eyes where on the steps of life, quite literally speaking (this was the eighteenth step from the ground floor up to our corridor and it was covered, as the whole staircase was, with a brownish yellow, rather well-worn carpet with a lily pattern) people like that landed. That is, people who hadn't learned anything properly and therefore wouldn't amount to anything. At the beginning I had loved the job and tried to do it as well as I could. Now I hated it.

The doorbell had rung a third time and now I rushed to the

door, and as I ran I wished that some unheard of adventure would happen to me, that some oriental fairy tale would break up my monotonous life, a life surrounded by the taboos and rules of propriety of my class like an insurmountable wall. I wished that Haroon al Rashid were at the door or Ali Baba with his open-sesame key or maybe even Sinbad the Sailor who would sail off with me to The Isle of Dreams—and why not: it was possible, wasn't it? I grabbed the doorhandle and then it occurred to me that my father had often told me that there were bad people who would abuse children, but I had never been able to imagine what that was. What was that supposed to mean: abuse children? Suddenly I wished for a moment that a murderer would step over the threshold. I was thirsting for adventure. I'd take care of him all-right. After all, I was ten years old and would be going to prep school next fall.

As I flung the door open, I saw—utterly disillusioned at first—that he looked almost like all the other men who were in the habit of ringing our doorbell at noon: badly shaved but well washed (oh, I could tell that now at a glance), dressed in a suit that was trying to look proper although patched at the sleeves, knees, jacket-pockets and no doubt at the seat of the pants too, head bowed, eyes focused on the tips of split shoes and, in this attitude of humility, stammering the following words shamefully and nearly inaudibly: "I only wanted to ask, young Sir, if maybe there are some left-overs from lunch?" This man who stood in front of me was unshaved but well washed; his suit was patched at the sleeves, at the knees, at the jacket-pockets and no doubt at the seat of his pants too; his dirty gray shoes were gaping at the tips, but his head was not bowed and instead of looking at his gaping shoes he looked me straight in the eyes; and that confused me.

I took a step back.

"I'd like to speak to your father, please, young Sir," he said to me and put his foot in the door—something nobody else had ever dared to do.

"Then you'll have to see him during his office hours," I said. "His office is on the ground floor and his hours start at three, but today he's only taking people with appointments."

"I've got to speak to your father privately, young Sir," said the man and stepped into the corridor.

Now I got really scared.

"My father won't be back until three," I said and sensed at once that what I'd said was colossally stupid. Suddenly I was afraid as I'd never been before: it was the fear of the little boy lost in the woods with the wolf approaching and the hunter far away. The man shut the door behind him; the hinges creaked softly as he closed it and that creaking cut into my stomach and spleen like a saw. I felt sick. The lock clicked shut; that's how the lock clicks in the man-eater's den. We were alone: him and me and the deaf walls all around. Suddenly I understood the rule of not opening the door to strangers when I was alone in the house. The man moved towards me—what are you baring your teeth like that for, man; what big eyes you have, man; what huge claws you've got on your hands, man—and the man moved towards me; I moved back and the man followed me and was standing already in front of the door of the only room from which I could have called down to the street for help and past which I'd run like a fool. All the other windows which I could still reach faced the courtyard or the garden; and both of those were a flight down and there was nobody there. Suddenly I felt what I'd never felt before: the sound of blood pulsing through my heart. I moved back towards the kitchen door at the end of the corridor, scraping the floor with the soles of my feet as I did so. The man followed me. All at once the corridor was as short as my breath.

Wasn't there any diamond-like wall coming down between him and me? Where were the angels coming to help me with flaming swords? Something heavy and bulky was pressing upward painfully from the pit of my stomach, higher and higher up along my throat; it started to fill my gullet and choke me.

I swallowed and gasped.

"I can give you pork roast with cabbage and dumplings," I stammered hoarsely, "a really big piece of meat; it's left over— we were expecting guests." And as I said this something strange in me immediately perceived my third blunder. The guests were supposed to arrive in the next couple of minutes and I could hear them already on the steps—*that's* what I should have said, the stranger in me with a jingling laugh—but I'd said the opposite; and the man came irresistibly closer without answering and looked fixedly into my face.

He was the murderer and he was coming for me. The apartment door was unreachable. The only door leading to a window from which I could have called for help lay behind the man's

back. There was only one choice left: to tear the kitchen door open, excape in one leap into the kitchen, close the door behind me, jump through the kitchen window into the courtyard and then, if I was still in one piece, escape from there into the street. Yes, that was my salvation and I looked frantically over to the kitchen door, when I was horrified to see that the key was sticking in the lock from the outside and that the murderer couldn't fail to grab me before I'd be able to pull the key out. For I now knew that he was a murderer and, now that it was too late, I all at once—in an epiphany of raving fear—understood all the taboos and rules. Too late, too late . . . My skin grew damp, my brain melted away. One kick, I was still able to think, because I already knew the spot where a kick could paralyse somebody, but then the murderer was already almost touching my chest with his body and I couldn't lift my foot anymore to give him a kick; and as I moved back a last step I felt in my back the cold steel cylinder of a gun barrel: so his accomplice was at the kitchen door already! My knees shook; I started to tumble backward, when my shoulder-blades hit up against wood and just as I was about to collapse I realized that it was the kitchen key that had been sticking in my back. And I tried to grab hold of it with my wobbly hands without turning around, but by then the man had already laid his murderous right hand on my shoulder; and then my underpants got dirty, and then I wanted to pull all my strength together one more time in order to push the man away but I didn't have the strength to breathe anymore. And then I thought that I'd have to drop to my knees and beg the murderer to spare my young life. But by then the corridor had turned completely black and I didn't see the murderer anymore and didn't see anything anymore and heard my heart and heard a loud humming noise and the corridor hummed and as it hummed the darkness started to clear and became gray and there the murderer lay on his knees in front of me.

All this happened in the time it takes to draw three breaths but to me it had lasted an eternity, an eternity of suffocating semi-consciousness halfway between fear and death and interrupted by spurts of futile hope. This eternity kept going on even as I saw the murderer lying at my feet, still indistinct, a formless heap, and that eternity lasted to the furthest limits that it could reach bearing a child in its arms, then it fused—whistling inaudibly—with time again, and then it seemed to me as if the

murderer was breathing something and I thought I heard the words "Young Sir," and when I heard them, I heard him whispering and I took in his words passively like a record takes up the sound being engraved into it. "Young Sir," I heard the man on his knees whispering, and now my eyes looked down and saw only his eyes and saw those eyes, that a moment ago had stared so fixedly and murderously, quavering fearfully now, and now too my ears heard his voice coming through louder and heard him begging desperately: "Please don't run off, please don't chase me away, young Sir, I beseech you—listen to me!"

Thus speaks the rescuing voice in a dream and from that moment onward I felt—still leaning half unconsciously against the kitchen door—completely weightless and two dimensional like a shadow, and it seemed to me as if the corridor and the kneeling man and I were rocking and drifting through the clouds, through peculiarly green clouds. For a while we glided on up into the sky but then I felt (this time without shuddering) the kitchen-door key in my back again, and then the flight stopped, the clouds froze into green walls and it seemed as if I was dreaming that I had woken up and that a man was kneeling in front of me, and the man was on his knees in front of me and he lowered his head as I looked at him, like his predecessors had lowered their heads, and he stared at the tips of my gleaming light-yellow custom-made shoes, and then, in a series of hesitant little jerks, he raised his head again, but now he looked past my lips. "Young Sir," I heard him go on, and he spoke faster and faster. "Young Sir," he blurted. "You're the benefactor of the whole community; you feed the poor and protect the needy. You're the active hand of our Saviour: dear, gentle, young Sir, I beg you, have mercy on me and listen to me!"

"You can have something to eat," I heard a voice that must have been mine, speaking like a faint, distant echo of my thoughts, and I didn't know if I was dreaming or waking even though I still felt completely weightless and two-dimensional and still saw the man in front of me and the green corridor in only two dimensions. "I can give you some pork and cabbage and dumplings," I heard my voice speak and in the meantime my hands opened the kitchen door mechanically, filling the corridor with the aroma of roast meat.

The kneeling man, sniffing the air, seemed to bend over a little but he didn't glance over to the stove where the roast with all the

fixings was keeping warm and showing forth in all its splendor. "I beg you to intercede for me with your father, young Sir," he answered. "Forgive my rashly barging in this way, young Sir, but you're my only hope!" It was really a dream after all.

"Can I show you something, dear young Sir?" the man asked.

My head nodded. The man was still kneeling and I still didn't feel my body.

"Would you be so awfully kind and turn on the light, good young Sir, it's so dark in here," the man asked. The light-switch was next to the staircase. My back peeled off the kitchen door and again it seemed to me as if I was flying: I felt neither the floor under my feet—gliding over the floor like a dream—nor the man's body that I brushed against in passing; but now that I was past him and the door to the room with the window facing the street and also the rescuing apartment door were in front of me, now that I touched the switch and perceived the vague, soft outlines of the open house-gate through the milky glass of the apartment door—now I woke from my dazed state and felt the sweat on my forehead and the weight of my limbs and the blood throbbing in my arteries and the trembling in the hollow of my knees and the heavy pain in the pit of my stomach that was gradually diminishing, and I heard the beams in the corridor creaking and felt the porcelain switch cold between my fingers and heard my breath whistle and felt my body relieved and realized that I was saved and guessed that I had had a terrific adventure; and now I was happy after all that I'd broken my father's rule, and suddenly I was tremendously proud.

I turned on the light and as the corridor lit up in the bright light the kneeling man jumped up in a single movement onto his feet and then he—whom I had thought my murderer—became a magician; and this time I knew exactly that I wasn't dreaming. He was a magician: all at once he held a little white ball between his fingers that he'd pulled out of nowhere, and he flicked it into the air and immediately pulled another little ball out of some invisible pocket at his right shoulder and flicked that into the air too, and while he threw the two balls alternately one after the other from one hand to the next in such a way that they always seemed about to collide at the apex of the parabola, he suddenly popped a third ball out of his mouth and let it leap into the ring of circling balls and quickly added a fourth ball to the company that he'd pulled out of another invisible pocket—this time up

around his left shoulder—so that now four little balls were dancing apparently weightlessly through the air, four blissfully silent little birds fluttering gracefully past each other, magical chicks, wingless, flying, hovering, voicelessly jubilant things; and the dance got more and more rapid and mad, and now there weren't four, there were six balls that were whirling about because the two hands too whirled about in the mad circle; now they were turning flat around the head of the magician—a halo, because it was a miracle; I'd never seen anything like it before. I know you can see magicians and fire-eaters and sword-swallowers at the fairs too and these were members of a magical guild that surely was not entirely of this world; but what I had seen of their accomplishments up to that moment was nothing compared to the unleashing of this magic that stopped as marvellously as it had begun: just as the words at the end of a story fall softly into silence, so with a gentle plunking sound one ball after the other fell into the hollow of his right hand; once more the hand was raised and revealed a little ball pinned between each pair of fingers, then his left moved in a lazy swing through the air and, without touching his right hand, dissolved the little balls into thin air: vanished, they had vanished; his right hand was as open and empty as his left; they showed their tops and their palms and then they smiled, the hands smiled at this marvel, and the man made a deep bow. I clapped like mad. "I want to thank you very much too, young Sir, for lending me these little birds," the man said and moved quickly towards me. "Would you care to reach into your jacket pockets." My hands plunged into my pockets. The miracle was complete: in each one of my pockets there were two tiny little balls. For a moment I was seized by a feeling of horror, but only for a moment: the miraculous dance had been so blessedly beautiful that this man simply couldn't be a bad magician. If he had asked me to let him tie me up and blindfold me, I would have given myself up to him without the least suspicion. But he didn't ask that of me; now that he could have demanded anything of me, he started to beg again and I gradually began to understand what it was he wanted of me. My father, he asked, should give him the chance this evening to show his skill to the audience before the movie started, and I was supposed to put in a good word for him with my father. "Oh, gentle young Sir," he blurted, "if I could then pass the hat around, young Sir, and get a little bit of capital, even

if the money were ever so little it would still be a start; I really need a couple of bicycle tires, a shirt and a tie. You haven't got any idea, young Sir, what a difference it makes, to dress yourself up a bit. Even if everyone only gave me a few pennies, it would still amount to something. The opening of a movie theater, that doesn't happen every day, that would be my great chance, young Sir, my great, great chance—I implore you!"

I took him into the kitchen, though I had strict orders never to do so, and gave him my slice of the pork roast, heaped dumplings and cabbage over the meat, and then gave the man two more helpings which he gulped down ravenously. When my father came home in a good mood from a patient who was recovering with unexpected rapidity, it didn't take long for me to persuade him. In good moments he could be well disposed towards artists and even vagrants; he considered himself a poet-painter (on Sundays he painted landscapes with mountains and meadows and he had composed an opera libretto, "The Swan Maiden"), and my enthusiastic description moved him so much that he—though he otherwise handed out punishment with authoritarian strictness and without mercy—forgave my gross failings (I didn't tell him that I'd taken the man into the kitchen) and even allowed me to attend the performance of the magician and the first act of the film. "To be sure, you did something that is completely against the rules, that could have cost you your life and that I really should have punished you for with two weeks' house arrest," he said. "But since everything came out well in the end, we won't do anything to cloud this day's happiness." Then he said that everybody, including this particular juggler, had a right to a fair chance in life, and I asked him what I hadn't wanted to ask the magician, namely what kind of a thing such a chance really was since till then I had only heard the word used to describe ski-jumps.* "It's a little like that with one's chance in life," my father explained. "It's the possibility of letting somebody prove how far he can get. And we're going to give him that chance." I was unspeakably proud of my father. "We'll give him a chance," he had said. We—that meant him and me. We sat in the smoking room in the heavy leather easy chairs next to the hammered bronze smoking table, and Father was puffing his

---

*In German, the word "Chance" (= chance in English) and "Schanze" (= ski-jump) are pronounced identically.

Havana cigar and I sniffed the smell and was grown-up and was giving him, the magician, a chance, and here inside it was now The Isle of Dreams, and lying deep in the easy chair and barely hearing my father's scolding words that I shouldn't sprawl there like a farmer, I dozed off in exhaustion.

In the evening, then, the hall of the movie theater, formerly a storeroom, was filled with buzzing, perfume and rustling; on the pale blue painted walls there were the oval frames with smiling ladies and beaming men and the front wall was completely covered with a curtain that shimmered in all the colors of the rainbow. The performance was sold out; everybody who belonged to good society in our town was there and I was the only child that was allowed to come along, the only child out of hundreds of children; not even the mayor's son, who was just as old as I, was there. At that time I would have let myself be nailed to the cross for my father. I looked around for my protegé, the magician, whom we were going to give a chance, but I didn't see him. The pianist played a march, then my father stepped forward, leaned slightly against the piano and, with his left hand in his pocket, gave a short speech: It bore witness to the infinite interest in the arts in our dear little town, so he said, that even during this grave economic crisis it was devoting itself to the muses and to their youngest companion, Cinematographia; that it had built a handsome temple for the joy, entertainment and instruction of all its citizens; and then the pianist hammered out a fanfare, and my father explained that he thought he could speak for everyone present that they would approve his giving a talented artist who was just passing through an opportunity to show his skill in exchange for whatever little something anyone cared to give; and then the magnificent curtain moved back and my protegé stepped forward and bowed, but not so deep as he'd done for me at noon. I sat next to my father in the first row which in those days was still considered to be the best seat in a movie theater; my protegé stood in front of me, scarcely a meter away, and I nodded to him encouragingly. The audience clapped generously; my protegé made another bow, then, so it seemed to me, he jolted himself; his face seemed to me somehow strangely changed; it grew tense and now his arms swung out too but he didn't reach, as I had expected him too, into the nothing of the invisible pocket near his shoulder, he reached into his left jacket pocket and pulled out a little ball and another one out of his right

pocket; and while he was throwing the two little balls from hand to hand, I was surprised to see that he didn't pop the third one out of his mouth but pulled it out of the open neck of his shirt; and even though he seemed to be satisfied with only three balls, now he missed one ball and he let it—and then the others too along with it—fall as if their wings had been paralysed and roll through the hall. The juggler turned pale as chalk and I felt a sudden pain shooting through my heart. "Well, well, well, just take it easy, that can happen to anybody," my father said to calm me, and he said it out loud and my love for him that was hardly five hours old turned into passion. One of the little balls had rolled up to my feet; the man bent down for it; he almost knelt in front of me and now I saw that big beads of perspiration covered his forehead and that his hands trembled and—this almost revolted me—that he only managed with difficulty to suppress a violent burp. Despite his slip-up, the audience remained benevolently quiet except for a few giggles and still remained generous when a second attempt failed in the same way as the first; and I remained calm too, I had complete confidence in my magician; yes, I was convinced that he was just pretending to be so clumsy in order to surprise the audience suddenly with some unheard-of marvel. I had faith in the man who was bending down in front of me again in order to pick up a ball that rolled off once more; I had faith in him and I looked straight into his eyes: I wanted him to see me and to feel how unshakable my faith in him and his skill was; and now he looked at me too with the little ball in his hand and I smiled at him and he tried to smile back at me and then I saw with horror that his smile was a wretched, helpless grimace, a mask to cover a terrible fear, and although I didn't understand anything and didn't know what to do, I was utterly convinced that this magician was in reality not a proper magician at all and that something dreadful—at that time I still had no conception of embarrassment—was going to happen; and then I was flooded by piercing shame like a boiling stream. For after all he was my protegé; after all I had been the one who had recommended him to my father so that he would then, relying on my testimony, pass on that recommendation to the audience; and so this man's disgrace became in reality my disgrace and I was almost deathly ashamed of it and I was ashamed to have put my wonderful father into such a bad position, and I thought that it probably was my duty now to

119

stand up and justify my father, to explain the whole thing, and now that the man's fluttering hands missed the balls for a third time, I felt like jumping up and grabbing him by the collar and dragging him out of the movie theater, screaming and swearing and spitting and protesting that I had been victimized by a mean character, a lousy swindler and fraud, but when the man put the little balls wearily into his pocket, fighting down as he did so a burp that was almost an attack of vomiting, and put an old hat upside down on his head, got out a tennis ball from behind the curtain, put it onto the split tip of his shoe in order to pitch it into the open hat amid a silence that had now grown icy cold, and when even this really simple little trick failed miserably, my mortification gave way abruptly to another, far more suffocating kind of shame: that of pity. If I had realized only a moment ago—with the rage of one deceived—that this was no magician but just an ordinary human being too, nothing more than I was myself, then I felt now that this human being was being publicly tortured, that something was being killed in his soul, and that tore my heart open and my sympathy with the man who was like me grew so intense that I was suddenly the man who stood in front of the silent, now scornfully hostile audience and offered himself up to them; it was I who was exposing myself to a crowd inexorable in its glacial silence: trembling, no longer a human being, a ridiculous, miserable ruin; and it was I who now placed the ball a second time onto the split tip of my shoe and I knew that I would miss the hat once again; and I sat in my seat in the first row and the disgrace and torture of the man who had failed were so very much my own shame that I was he and I wanted to run away, dive outside and crawl under the weeds growing by the brook out there or race over to the Giant's Rock and jump down from there to my death; I wished that the earth would swallow me up and yet I sat there in my seat overcome as never before by any other hostile force, by shame, and the juggler once again pitched the ball past his hat; then he bent his head wearily and let his hat fall to the ground and let it lie there and went, with eyes almost closed, slowly up the corridor-like passageway to the door, and now, as if according to plan, the audience applauded madly and voices cried out: "Bravo!" and "Encore!" and "Good-bye" and "Come again!" and the clapping hands and the words were now followed by coins, a rain of pennies—the collection, the tip, the capital—that now hailed down on the

man's back and chest and head, and I thought that now at least he had got something out of it after all and that he would bend down now to pick up the aftermath of being stoned with pennies, and this thought made me feel a little calmer; but the man went up the passage-way, a walking rock, slowly and without looking around, dragging the soles of his feet, and at that moment I understood him. He *was* the magician after all and he had put them all to the test and they had not come up to his standard; he had only shown me what he could do and now he was leaving, never to come back to this place that wasn't worthy of him. Oh, now he was leaving and I really should go with him! All the suffering of the ten years of my boyhood, and that didn't mean hunger and want and starvation—on the contrary, it meant the terrible, hundred-fold satiety that excluded all the magic of a fearfully and intensely awaited fullfilment: a satiety which I paid for by remaining within the walls of my class-conscious father's rules and taboos, walls that locked me into a bourgeois world that, despite its mean riches, was empty and cold and blocked my way into any region of my longing—all that suffering rose up in me and pressed me to follow the man and to fall on my knees in front of him and to beg his forgiveness for the outrage that had been committed upon him, and to ask for forgiveness for my father too who now called out in his bass voice (and I could have strangled him for it): "Don't forget your splendid top hat, you great artist, you!" and on top of that made a gesture in front of this orgiastic audience that served as much to excuse himself as to humiliate even more profoundly the man who had failed. Run after him, hurry after him, fall on my knees in front of him and beseech him to take me with him and go away with him, away, away, to a place where I would be allowed to be a child like all the other children, where you could get dirty and play with the sons of factory workers and peasants and could embrace your friends and hit your enemies in the face, even if you didn't get roast meat every day and fruit and chocolate and if there wasn't a smoking room there with leather easy chairs and a hammered bronze smoking table. Away from this paternal house which with all its superfluity of culinary pleasures and clothes and gifts was just one big cruel prison fortress which I hated, hated, hated with an intense hatred, just as I now hated the daily roast and the daily chocolate and the leather chairs and smoking tables; I wanted to get away, away, just get away, out into the

world, wherever there might be adventures, magic, ghosts, where people went hungry and froze and suffered and where a piece of bread might be something magnificent, away to the nearby isle of my dreams where the mysterious other world lay. Oh, I envied and admired them all now, all those men who had squatted and greedily gulped down left-overs on the uppermost step that was covered with brownish yellow material with a lily pattern and that was already a little worn; I envied and admired them as much as I loathed that clean, arrogant young snot who told them to sit down on the steps and fed them garbage, and as much as I loathed the domineering father who had forced the disgusting job on the lazy student in order to improve him; I wanted to get away and I knew that it was my only and last chance. He hadn't been given a chance; he didn't need one. It was my chance and I realized now already that I had lost it and wouldn't possess the strength anymore to jump up and follow him. The lights went out; the laughter died down; the pianist played a romantic waltz; the curtain glided back and a broad, white screen became visible in the cosy darkness; it purred and hummed and a bundle of light flickered and while—marvel upon marvel—a living man in a cutaway and a living lady in a magnificently glittering dress danced towards each other, one last strip of trembling light shot into the hall: the magician had closed the door after him again; and I knew that I had irretrivably missed my chance and that I would never see him again, and while for that reason I felt an aching but already almost sweet pain, I started to perceive with growing joy how after the couple had found each other in the dance and separated again, the screen was suddenly covered with waving palms and ocean and hibiscus and ships' masts, and I was there, I was there— the only child in the whole town—and I owed that entirely to my father, and I sought out his hand in order to press it gratefully while on the screen a ship weighed anchor and sailed with me across the south seas which I'd never seen before towards a shore covered with wreaths of flowers and corals . . .

122

IN A DARK WORLD

STEFAN HERMLIN

I got to know Hermann R. in the summer of 1933. The man who arranged the meeting had left us right away. It was still completely light outside and a breeze blew in through the open window. We had sat down, each with a glass of beer, at a table under the radio that was blaring out march music. There weren't any other customers in the little Friedenau bar at this early hour of the evening. The bartender was lazily rinsing out glasses behind the counter. Between him and our conversation there rose up a wall of martial noise from the radio. From somewhere or other people I didn't know had sent Hermann R. to me and to the illegal group of which I was the leader. He was our new "instructor."

From then on we met often, every week actually. Sometimes Hermann disappeared for a while. I guessed that he was off on difficult and daring missions. I waited impatiently for the postcard with the agreed-on message from which I would be able to decipher when and where he wanted to meet me—at the Zoo Station, in the Potsdamerstrasse or on the Alexanderplatz. Once or twice he would casually mention Amsterdam and Paris— cities that I hadn't been to then and whose names sounded fantastic to my ear. I followed our rule and never asked him any questions about his personal life or business or trips. If some event or situation wasn't clear to me, he would think about it for a moment. While he bent his handsome, dark-haired head to one side, his eyes seemed to lose focus, but only because he was concentrating on something wonderful, something remote, something that only he was able to see. He made his explanations in a quiet, hurried, and then momentarily halting voice, explanations that seemed infallible and definitive because they tied together a mass of surprising and (to me) unfamiliar facts into a convincing proof. I loved and admired Hermann R. who

was so much more mature, cooler and more knowledgeable though he was only a few years older than I was.

Usually we only met for a few minutes. Conspiracy has its rules, and Hermann rarely had time to spare. "Well, take care . . . ," he said, squinting good-humoredly at me with his dark eyes, and was up and off on his bike. Sometimes our meetings lasted only for a moment: those were the times when Hermann brought me things for my group, a few leaflets or newspapers printed on very thin paper or other printed matter that was disguised as Reclam paperbacks. Sometimes he included a new book by Heinrich Mann that had been published abroad. On these occasions we would meet at the precise minute we had agreed on in some part of Schöneberg or at a bench in the Tiergarten. We both came with bikes and briefcases. My briefcase was empty. We exchanged the briefcases unobtrusively and went our own ways.

Sometimes Hermann had more time. Then we would take interminable walks through Berlin at night, pushing our bikes along next to us, from Steglitz to the Kurfürstendamm and then back down the Charlottenburger Chaussee to the Lustgarten and even further up into the northern districts of Berlin. We talked and talked. It didn't bother me that I didn't know anything about Hermann, about his past, about where he lived, or that I didn't even know if the name with which I addressed him was his real name. Most of the time of course we talked politics, about the preparations for war that the Nazis were making, about the street battles in Paris and Vienna during February, about the arrests, about the coming, inevitable revolution. We discussed books, concerts, exhibitions, boxing matches.

Sometimes we talked about girls too. Hermann knew my girlfriend because she was a member of my group. I didn't know if he had anybody; he talked about girls without any kind of reserve, but without any of that boasting suggestiveness either that young people sometimes like and that always repelled me. Two or three times he mentioned a younger sister in a tone of naive admiration. "What a girl!" he said and raised his eyebrows. Once, looking at me jokingly out of the side of his eyes, he added: "Actually, you'd really suit each other . . ." I was embarrassed because his voice had made it seem as if he was in earnest. "I don't know, but I think so . . . ," he answered. But then we were already off on some other subject.

124

We were young and we viewed our times more seriously than most people our age; we wanted to change those times, and we loved, and we didn't know what the future held in store for us: turmoil, intense pain, disillusion and death. We fought as well as we could but we didn't have the faintest idea of the real nature of our opponent.

I heard about Hermann's being arrested in the late fall of 1935, half a year before I left the country. Nobody knew anything about the circumstances of his arrest. Apparently somebody had squealed. It wasn't known just where Hermann was imprisoned —probably in Prinz-Albrechtstrasse. There were no other arrests among our adherents. Hermann hadn't named any names, that much was certain. We hadn't expected it to be any different.

In the years afterwards I would sometimes hear his alternately rushing and hesitating voice in my dreams, would see him sometimes standing before me in some foreign country or city being bombed or in the barracks of some concentration camp. His face grew increasingly indistinct but I always knew that it was his. It was mischievous, thoughtful, or simply tormented and dead.

Shortly after the end of the war and my return to a smashed Berlin I went to an exhibition of documents and pictures from the German resistance. On one of the walls I suddenly saw Hermann R.'s face. It emerged simultaneously out of the fog of the blown up photograph and the fog of my memory. A brief comment under the picture noted that Hermann R. had been shot in 1940 at the Buchenwald stone quarry. I was already sure at that moment that I was going to write something about him, that I would protect that smile on the blurred photograph from vanishing altogether. How many of those who had known him were still alive ... How many of those who were alive still remembered him ... I had known him, even if only for a little while; it was my duty to give an account of that. How I was going to do it, I really didn't know. It wasn't pressing but remained clearly visible in the background and made itself felt from time to time. While I was investigating the histories of other friends, I had also asked about Hermann—though without much luck. The information I got from survivors of the concentration camp—there were two or three who remembered him—was shadowy.

The case grew more pressing when a few years later I was

trying to write a little book about people in my generation who had fought against Hitler and died. I was delving into Plutarch and reading Livy and Suetonius again for the first time since my schooldays. I had a vision of something that would emulate the prose of those historians; they had abstained from false pathos and unseemly prolixity for the sake of the grandeur of their subject. I set up a list of names and Hermann's was among them.

I wanted to find out if any of his relatives could still be reached. My investigations yielded the information that his mother had died in Berlin during the war; that his sister, the sister about whom he had on occasion spoken to me so approvingly and invitingly, had left the country; that she had moved to London only two years ago as the wife of a British officer. She was now a Mrs. Young and I had her address.

I wrote to her explaining my plans in a fairly comprehensive letter. The portrait, I wrote, that I was proposing to make of Hermann ought to be put into relief; I needed details about Hermann's childhood and youth, about that whole part of his life prior to our first meeting. I asked her to let me look at whatever letters and documents that might have survived. And I expressed my hope that my name wouldn't be unfamiliar to her because of the friendship that her brother had shown me. "That friendship," I concluded, "surely justifies my expectation that you will support my plan."

I didn't have to wait long for an answer. She said that she had run across my name here and there and that she still remembered well how warmly her brother had spoken of me, but even so she was reluctant to part with the mementos that were left and it was difficult to have copies made; in short, she thought it would be best to discuss the matter sometime in London, expecially since there was no chance of her coming to Berlin in the foreseeable future. There was an unmistakeable note of reserve about her letter. It won't be an easy job, I thought.

It so happened that three months later I had to go to London for a variety of reasons. I notified Mrs. Young of my visit well in advance. I hadn't been in London since the last years before the war; it was a city to which I felt attached in a number of ways, a city which I knew well from several visits but with which I did not feel familiar—a distant relative whom as a child one loves shyly and uneasily.

I took a cab from the railway station to a little hotel in

Kensington. I had soon taken care of the business that was the actual reason for my trip. Next morning I called up Mrs. Young.

"This is she," said a voice. "What can I do for you?" I was so taken aback that I couldn't say anything, and the voice went on: "Excuse me, of course, I know who you are and what you want. I've often thought about your letter."

"Maybe we could . . .", I said but the voice interrupted me.

"Hermann often talked to me about you," she said slowly. "Or actually not so often because I hardly saw him any more; my mother and I only saw him rarely and didn't really know what it was he was doing. Actually he never mentioned your name, but spoke of a special friend, and when you wrote I realized that you were that friend."

"Yes," I said. "I was that friend."

Her voice hurried forward at times and at times hesitated. After a while I noticed that I was holding my breath every time she spoke so as to listen to that voice, so as to find another voice in hers, a voice that of course had been deeper and surer and that once had said: "Actually, you'd really suit each other . . ."

"I would really like," I said, "to talk to you about Hermann."

"My God," she said, "how long ago that is. Hermann, oh my God. My big brother who didn't exactly wear himself out for us. He'd rather change the world. And then came that disaster that anybody could see would happen."

"He thought," I said, "about you too. Especially about you. He . . ."

"I know what you mean," the voice said. "Since then we've learned a lot of things we didn't know then."

"Perhaps we could meet, Mrs. Young," I said then. "I would be happy if I could pay you a visit."

There was a rustling sound in the receiver. "That's not possible at the present moment unfortunately," the voice said after a while. "I'm busy all day long."

"Maybe it would be more convenient tomorrow," I said. "Or the day after tomorrow."

"You don't give up easy, do you?" the voice said in a tone of mocking admiration. I felt myself tremble because it was Hermann's voice that I had just heard, but at the same time the voice of a woman, of his sister who perhaps looked like him, whose praises he had sung to me and had seen in his imagination standing next to me. "Why all this rush? Why bother anyway to

drag all these things back into the light of day? Let the dead rest in peace. We suffered all of us enough then."

"I'll come to see you whenever you like," I said bitterly. "Tomorrow or the day after tomorrow or some other day. My visa's good for another two weeks."

"I see that it won't be easy to get rid of you." The voice tried to sound joking but I only heard the irritation in it. "Listen to me. It's just not possible here at home. Let's meet instead somewhere in town. Tonight at eight." She gave me the name of a restaurant in Soho that I knew.

"I'll be there at eight," I said. "You'll find me there. I'll have the 'Financial Times' lying on the table in front of me. I don't suppose there'll be too many people coming into that place with the 'Financial Times.' "

She gave a quick laugh and hung up.

I killed time as well as I could, let myself be invited by my friend D. to the Saville Club, walked slowly through Albany in order to see once again who had lived there and when, read a pile of newspapers in Hyde Park, got to the restaurant at ten minutes to eight and found it pretty full. I told the waiter that I was expecting a lady to join me. I drank a campari and kept an eye on the door. It was almost eight-thirty when the waiter came up to my table and said that unless he was mistaken, I must be the gentleman whom a lady wished to speak to on the telephone; this way, please, over there is the booth.

"I'm really sorry," the voice said. "But I'm afraid I won't be able to come."

"I don't mind waiting a while," I answered.

"I've thought it over," she said. "I don't feel like coming. I can't stand getting excited. Anyway, it's so long ago, what's the point of the whole thing. . . ."

"I owe it to him," I said. "Don't you understand that?"

"I understand you perfectly," the voice said. "But I doubt if you understand me. My life has changed; everything is completely different now and I'm glad that it is. If you write about Hermann and your book is published over there, that might even make things difficult for me." The voice now didn't resemble any other voice in the slightest. It came from an icy distance. It suddenly stopped.

"I think," I said, "there's no reason for you to be worried. Who

is going to connect you with a certain Hermann R. if you don't choose to have them make the connection?"

"There are lots of people," the voice said, "who like nothing better than putting their noses into other people's business. Aren't you aware of that? Quite a lot of people here know that I'm German, that I come from Berlin and what my maiden name was."

A dumb, dead feeling rose up in me. "You can't be serious," I said. "I've come to London because of Hermann—not just because of Hermann, to be sure, but mainly because of him."

"I'm really sorry," the voice said. "I'm sincerely sorry. I feel for you, even though you're one of those people who is always stirring up things in the past and not leaving the world in peace."

"What 'world' do you mean?" I asked. "Maybe things would have been quieter and more reasonable in the world if people like Hermann had had something to say about it. But they killed him."

"I don't want to argue with you," the voice said. "And I don't want to talk you out of anything. But don't count on my help."

"Wait," I said. "Wait. Think it over for a moment . . ."

"It's my final word," the voice said. "Except, one more thing . . . Actually I really don't feel like telling you this. But maybe it's better if you know: when he was arrested, Hermann didn't believe in it anymore."

"Didn't believe in what anymore?" I asked and felt a coldness in myself.

"He didn't believe in it anymore," the voice said. "In his ideas, in your ideas. He didn't believe in the whole thing anymore. He didn't believe anymore that it was worth it. I saw him once more in prison before they took him away to Buchenwald. He told me himself."

"You're lying," I said. "Now you've killed him for the second time. But you won't succeed."

"Don't get all mushy," the voice said. "Good night."

The line went dead, a buzzing welled up, a thousand indistinct voices whispered.

When I opened the door of the telephone booth I stumbled. I made it to my table and sat down. A thousand confused thoughts whirled in my head or none at all. I ordered another Campari.

129

When the waiter brought it, he said: "I think the lady wants to talk to you again." I rushed back to the telephone booth.

"I really wouldn't like us to part abruptly like this," the voice said. "You're an idealist and can't understand that normal people try to arrange their lives according to the demands of the times. Don't be angry with me . . ."

"I told you before," I replied, "you've killed him for the second time. I probably exaggerated a little. But you reported him to the police."

Again the voices whispered. A dull, hollow silence spread out between us. Then Mrs. Young said: "Yes." There was a pause.

"What do you know about it," she said, "you don't know anything, you with your idiotic idealism. I was six years younger than Hermann but old enough to know what he was doing and where he was going. I didn't want to get him killed—it's not at all the way you think—he was my brother after all. He was only supposed to get a warning and find out that you have to take your family into consideration. They were talking about protective custody in those days—you remember—and prisoners were supposed to think things over, so they said, and become members of the new community. I didn't want to be deprived of the possibility of going to the University because of him; I didn't want to have my life ruined. My mother didn't know anything about it to her dying day. And he didn't suspect anything either . . ."

I slowly took the receiver from my ear, let it hang from the cord and went quietly out of the booth. Then I paid my bill and left the restaurant.

I walked through the streets as if in a trance. Sometimes a thought awakened in me: maybe Hermann suspected me. I woke up now here, now there. In my semiconscious state, I recognized a street, a square.

The sound of jazz was coming out of a Lyon's Corner House. Big cars stood darkly in front of the doors of Park Lane. A voice in the semi-darkness said: "Don't forget us, sir." I bent down and saw a man standing motionlessly and looking past me. He was wearing a sign on his chest. I went up closer and was able to read the inscription: PEOPLE LIVING IN A WORLD OF DARKNESS DESPERATELY NEED YOUR HELP. In smaller letters there was written underneath: The Royal School for the Blind, Leatherhead, Surrey. I searched my pockets for a couple of shillings.

A vault of dust, light and noise extended over the city. The reflection of distant streets burned in the nocturnal sky. I felt that now from somewhere very far away some silent, aching pain was traveling towards me. It had a long way to go and lots of time. But I was calm. It would reach me all-right.

A BIT OF THE SOUTH SEA

HERMANN KANT

On Sundays most people sleep longer than they do during the week—with us it was the other way around. During the week my mother would get up earlier than my father—on Sundays it was the other way around. When the alarm clock started rattling away at 5:00 in the morning my mother would emphatically turn over on her other side; but my father would crawl coughing out of the featherbed and feed the animals. In the process he would keep up a stream of talk and since he had a habit of making subtle distinctions in his speech you could hear clearly through the open window whether at that moment he was feeding the goats, the pig, the chickens or the rabbits.

During the week my father whistled in the intervals when he wasn't talking; but on Sundays he sang. And that was even worse. In the upper register all his efforts would turn to a kind of thin cawing, but in the lower his singing always ended in a bitterly acute attack of coughing. "He smokes too much," my mother would then murmur into her pillow.

When he had finished taking care of the animals, my father would go into the kitchen and make himself a few sandwiches. Ever since he had read the grandiose words of a shipwrecked captain in some novel about the sea: "Women and children first!" he choraled out through the bedroom door every Sunday morning while cutting his bread, "Goats and chickens first!" ". . . and then the asses," my mother would reply, half asleep but promptly.

On Sunday mornings my mother was not especially well disposed towards my father and this is why: My father went every Sunday to the fish market in Altona. He didn't go in order to buy any fish, no, he only went "for the hell of it."

133

Since he had taken me along sometimes I knew quite well what drove him there: the fish market was the big world.

Up above on the terraces stood the stands with burnt almonds, coconuts, Edam cheese, licorice root, and licorice, further down the banana peddlers bawled themselves hoarse and ruined themselves—if one cared to believe them—by selling at suicidal cut-rate prices. Towards the right, in Eier-Cohr's bar, the first Sunday drinkers would meet the last Saturday drinkers and sing seafaring songs in a hundred languages, and towards the left one could buy Siamese cats and guinea pigs from New Guinea, and Rhesus monkeys and cockatoos, and goats from the Alpine provinces and even rabbits from Hamburg-Lurup. In the middle the farmers from Vierlanden and Geesthacht had set up their stands and haggled with the housewives from St. Georg and Fuhlsbüttel, and far below by the Elbe river, from where along with the morning mists the howling of the fog horns of the arriving and departing ships would drift upwards, the fishermen loaded their flounder and smelt and cod onto the rocking pontoons. Here below in the furthest left-hand corner there stood the aquariums, and every one of my father's excursions to the fish market ended here.

That too I understood well, for as magnificent as the noisy confusion in the market might be, in front of the glass walls of the aquariums it was soon forgotten. Even the names of all the spotted, checkered, dotted, speckled, striped, jagged or completely and utterly indescribable fishes seemed to have been invented by Jack London and Joseph Conrad.

My father knew them all and he knew exactly in what watery corner of the world these colorful swimmers were at home.

It was lucky that the market closed at ten because otherwise he would never have come back to land on time.

My mother was grouchy enough anyway when she heard him rattling about the kitchen on Sunday mornings; but she only got really mad when she noticed that another "business Sunday" was coming round again.

The thing about these "business Sundays" was this: the goats, the chickens, the rabbits and the pig, they were useful animals, said my father, and my mother really had nothing against this sort of useful animal which helped to make the

soup thicker, but my father said that the whole caboodle
didn't give him any pleasure if he couldn't have "a little bit o'
somethin' extra."

What he called "a little bit o' somethin' extra" my mother
called short and sweet "luxury." She, too, was for chickens
but not for the kind that laid wrens' eggs and looked like day
old chicks in a pan and only got into the barnyard because
they had breeding.

She'd also have been the last to say anything against rabbits
but she really couldn't grasp what the point was of those
spindly things that seemed to consist only of eyes. And then
the pigeons, oh my goodness, they couldn't do anything but
bespatter the roof and fly around like crazy in a circle, but
they were genuine . . . ! "What do you think we are, Rockefeller?" she asked, and my father said no, because then of course
he wouldn't just have ten pigeons . . .

To be sure even my father wasn't able to stand it for too
awfully long with his genuine pure-breds; after three or four
months he had his fill of looking at them and then he needed
something new.

It always started with his beginning to agree with my
mother when she was finding fault with these luxurious creatures, and then one day he would say that he was thinking of
taking them the next chance that he had to the fish market.
And that's when a "business Sunday" came round, a real day
of crisis.

For—and this had established itself slowly—actually my
father didn't go to the fish market at all in order to sell the
Tottenham pure-bred dwarf hens or the medium sized broad-
eared Silver-Damascene rabbits; I mean, he did sell them,
but only in order to have a bit of money in his pocket so
as to be able to look around again for "a little bit o' somethin'
extra." When he was out on one of these excursions my
mother would dread the moment he came back and dig into
his rucksack and triumphantly present her with a new but now
wholly and utterly genuine pure-bred animal. But he really
did have a knack for digging up the most impractical kinds of
creatures and you really could understand why my mother
groaned and wrung her hands when she set her eyes on some
unspeakably wretched blue-blooded creature.

If it had just been those crazy pigeons or rabbits that might

have been tolerable but it got to be more and more bizarre. Once my father let a gigantic Persian cat out of his rucksack—at least the seller had said that it was a Persian cat—which quite obviously was afraid of mice; then another time he pulled a Guatamalan parakeet out of a paper bag which compensated for its inability to speak with an uncanny gift for popping millet husks through the bars of its cage into the room; and finally he dragged a Greek turtle with a pedigree into the house which he tied to a long string and allowed to take walks in the garden where it always hid itself under a leaf of lettuce—just long enough for my mother to come along and pick it.

My mother said that on the day when my father would trundle a baboon out of his rucksack, on that day she'd set fire to the house and move away with the kids to her mother's house in Finkenwerder. My father didn't bring a baboon home but the idea he had on his next to last business Sunday wasn't bad either. My mother was watching with arms crossed as he lifted his rucksack onto the kitchen table with careful movements. He had a big glass box in it and his pockets full of jam glasses. He put the glasses on the table and with each glass he uttered a sonorous word in a tone as if they were lumps of gold. "Scalares," he said, and "Malabarbarblings" and "Neonfishes" and finally even "Guppies."

There they were, all the miniature fishes from the aquarium on the Sunday market, and my mother asked what on earth we had to say to that. She kept on shaking her head all the time and finally she said that she was ashamed ever to have done any harm to an honest flounder when she looked at all of those downright indecently formed and colored fishes.

But she couldn't get at my father that way; he really had "something extra" now and he began to fix up the aquarium. Water had to be warmed—"The poor buggers are gonna catch cold," he said—fine sand had to be brought and washed—my mother groaned: "Sand washed!?" Instead, he really ought to see to it that the brats scrubbed their necks properly...

But my father didn't rest until the magical fishes had plopped into the aquarium.

And when we were finally sitting down to dinner I saw quite well that my mother too was looking in a really interested way at the colorful little flitting fishes. When the big sailfin moved

along the glass window once again, she poured the pudding sauce onto my father's hand. My father saw his chance.

"Yes," he said, "it's only natural for that to muddle you up; it's really something nice, all those fine animals, what?"

And then he wiped the raspberry juice into his Sunday handkerchief and declared that an aquarium like this was, so to speak, a bit of the south sea in our raw northern parts and no one needed to be ashamed if that made them confused. And then he handed his pudding plate to my mother once again and she very carefully poured some sauce into it.

Naturally on that day we didn't budge from the aquarium anymore and by evening all the fishes had received suitable names. The iridescent sailfin for instance was now baptized Alphons after the snobbish druggist's apprentice, who when he had a new tie on always sauntered past our hedge so slowly that my sister would notice him, and the mouthbreeder was called Hulda, like the fat woman who owned the grocery store.

When we were then finally lying in bed, my father remarked that he was already feeling happy anticipating the big eyes of the neighbors, ha, when they got wind of this. . . For that was part and parcel of his search for "a little somethin' extra": that the neighbors should make their pilgrimage to our house and marvel at his rarities. Then he would sit for hours with them on old boxes, roll his own cigarettes and do what my mother called "looking up the chickens' rears," and one could hear him say triumphantly: "Yessir, by golly, you won't find a pure-bred cock like this one every day."

In fact the news about the aquarium really did spread quickly and for a time it looked as if a real shortage of salt had broken out because the neighboring women kept on coming all the time for a spoonful and they only went away after they had marveled thoroughly at our new possession.

Their enthusiasm only waned when they found out why of late they had been receiving their mail only after considerable delay: the mailman was only persuaded by my mother to move from our south sea back onto his job after several mornings.

When my father found out about the effects of the water-wonder on the mailman he said, full of satisfaction, that that's how it was and that whoever had "somethin' extra" became in the eyes of others a bit of "somethin' extra" himself and people would come to see that person then as well.

How right he was.

It started with Jonathan Kraulig. It was Thursday evening, we were just about to start with supper when he came.

None of us would ever have called anyone else but him Jonathan; that protracted name would very soon have been shortened to "Jonny," but Jonathan couldn't possibly be called anything but Jonathan. He was poor, and pious in an extraordinary way. In earlier days, so my father said, he had been neither poor nor religious, by no means, then he had owned a large coal business and had drunk a great deal. In those days he'd also been called Jonny. But the consumption of coal in our settlement had not kept pace with Jonny's consumption of alcohol and one day he had declared bankruptcy and started a new sect.

Jonathan came to us. He wore as always a massive black cape, now wet with the rain, and cracked sandals from which he would not part even in deepest winter.

He explained without beating around the bush that he had come because of the fish but then he noticed that my father was lying on the sofa and wasn't smoking.

Jonathan knew that the one was as unusual as the other and so he asked worriedly: "My dear Paul, have you caught some kind of disease?" "Yes," said my father ceremoniously, "my dear Jonathan, I'm lying prostrate with the flu."

My mother who knew my father and Jonathan very well fiddled nervously with the coffee cups but Jonathan had now turned too much missionary to perceive it.

"Well now," he said softly, "that really ought to give you a bit of leisure time to take a look into the Good Book. . ."

Yes, my father answered with gentle malice, it was a real joy that the flu should force one to bed at the right moment so that one might finally find time to concern oneself with such matters. With that he opened his eyes wide like a little baby, so that my older sister ran into the bedroom giggling.

Jonathan overlooked that too. "If it's all-right with you," he continued, "then we'll take a look together into the Good Book and drive out the wretched flu. . ."

At the same time he fumbled about under his wet cape for the Good Book which he always carried about with him. But my father said, no, they'd better leave that alone for now, since in this place they didn't have the proper devotion to it.

That drove my other sister into the bedroom, and my mother who had busied herself up to now with filling the oven full of

coal briquettes now began to pull them out again and stack them neatly back into the box. When I noticed that she was determined to repeat this trick again, I considered how I might get unobtrusively into the bedroom. Then there was a knock at the main entrance and a little later the Health Commissioner Dr. Pfauch stood in the little kitchen.

My father looked at my mother but no, she hadn't ordered the doctor; to get a doctor because of the flu just wasn't done at our house and certainly not this doctor, the fancy Health Commissioner, whom we only knew because he always drove his car to the nudist colony in the little forest nearby—that wouldn't have occurred to her even if we'd had scarlet fever. The doctor did not leave us in suspense for long. He was obviously a straightforward fellow; he said energetically, "Evening!", shoved his damp hunting cap into my mother's hand, sat himself astride a chair and trumpeted:

"Well, my boy, where are we hiding that chamber pot full of sea creatures?"

The "my boy" was my father and by "chamber pot" he seemed to refer to the aquarium, because when he had spotted it behind Jonathan's cape he hunched up next to the glass case and pressed his big nose against the pane.

"Did you put him through a clothes press to make him so nice and flat?" he bellowed when he saw Alphons, the sailfin. "A really first-rate specimen!"

That it was a first-rate specimen my father certainly accepted but as to the chamber pot . . . I saw that he was rolling himself a cigarette after all and that in the process he was flaring his nostrils.

"Well," he finally said with an unmistakable look at the massive stomach of the medicine man, "it's a pity that it isn't possible to put us through a clothes press too, then we'd take up a lot less room."

It grew pretty quiet in the kitchen and my little sister had a lucky minute when she put her head through the bedroom door and asked if we weren't going to have supper soon, and besides, there was somebody else outside.

That "somebody else," or more precisely "she" was already in the kitchen; it was Alice. We actually didn't get along at all with Alice because she was always throwing stones from her garden into ours, but at this moment she was welcome.

In her younger years Alice had sung in a hippodrome in the

Kleine Freiheit and from that period on had retained the look of a hustler as well as a pretty hoarse voice.

She didn't bother for long about Jonathan, she knew him already from the time when he was still called Jonny. She only pulled his ear and croaked: "Be ye greeted, pious man!"

But she examined the Health Commissioner carefully and said in a rough but still friendly tone: "Oh, you're the Uncle Doctor with that snazzy carwhatchamacallit! My God, it's a long time since I knew the anatomical gents . . or did we perhaps have the pleasure sometime?"

No, the doctor growled, and said that he wasn't quite as old yet as he looked. Even Jonathan smiled softly and sourly. But Alice quickly remembered that she had actually come because of the "darling little fishes" and she squatted in front of the aquarium and repeated over and over again: "Oh God, oh God, no, how fabulous!"

Since the fishes were getting their due again my father's face relaxed. But even so some doubts about the usefulness of his latest acquisition seemed in the meantime to have penetrated to him and the next visitor was not at all the proper one to remove them.

The mouthbreeder's namesake, Hulda the grocer, limped into the overcrowded kitchen.

For me Hulda was a witch. It was a long time since she herself had stood behind the store counter; her legs couldn't take it anymore because she was so fat that she had to get herself an electric wheelchair in order to be able to collect the money from customers who were behind in their payments. And in this consisted her only interest in the business; to watch over the prompt payment of the credit customers.

In her store one didn't simply settle one's accounts the next time one bought something; instead, one had to climb up a flight of stairs and enter a room in which it was always inordinately hot and in which it smelled as if all the various odors of this huckster joint had settled there forever. Here Hulda squatted in the semi-darkness and took in the money. And since it was her manner not to accept a penny without first giving a lecture about the vanity of Mammon to whoever was paying, my mother used to send me up there whenever something had to be paid.

No doubt about it, she was a witch. Even now, as she was standing in the harsh light of the kitchen lamp, that impression

didn't diminish a whit. At first she let her rather mean little eyes wander over the kitchen cabinet on which supper was set out and only when she was convinced that we hadn't bought anything from the competition did she look around for the aquarium. "Well, well," she said after Jonathan and Alice had assiduously made room for her, for they were just as much in the red with the witch as we were, "well, well, that's really quite remarkable and it must have cost money too, eh?" Not that she wasn't in the habit of thinking of other things besides filthy lucre, for after all, she couldn't take it with her into the grave either; yes, yes, she was thinking a great deal of late about death and she really did want to leave everything in good order behind her, and somebody had told her that we had acquired something quite wonderful and by pure chance she discovered in her little book that a certain sum was still owing and money was really a curse and just how much had those fish cost?

The appearance of Pastor Meier relieved my father for the moment of the need for making a reply. The Pastor surveyed this unwonted meeting with mildly questioning eyes, wished everybody cheerfully a very good evening—to be sure not without a sideways glance, quick as lightning, towards Jonathan, a glance with which he wanted to make clear that he wished it to be understood that that fellow, that charlatan of souls was not to be included in "everybody"—and then he said that he had gathered that my father had collected God's scaly creation in beauteous variety in a vitreous container and that these profoundly heartwarming tidings had led him down the dark, rainy path. That Pastor Meier "gathered something" surprised nobody; there was absolutely nothing in our surroundings that he didn't gather; my father had brought into circulation the name of "our dear Lord's Pinkerton" for him because there was no meat fried in a thousand pots of which this shepherd of souls did not have knowledge.

And the business with the rainy path must have been true as well because the laced boots of the Pastor looked as if he'd been wandering about for two hours through a sodden clay pit. My mother couldn't take her eyes off those smudgy preacher's boots anymore and she winced each time that a lump of clay dropped from them and presently landed under the wide soles of the spiritual visitor.

Pastor Meier seemed to be training himself a bit for the next

parish meeting because he declaimed at us an extraordinary mixture of otherwordly promises of salvation and down-to-earth idioms, and he couldn't stop making up new analogies out of the actions and appearance of our pure-bred tropical fish.

Jonathan had wrapped himself up in his cape as if it were a toga and attempted now and again to force a mocking smile into his sectarian face, ravaged during the "Jonny years"; Alice commented at every second analogy of the preacher in a hoarse and emotional voice that that was just too fabulous; the Health Commissioner bellowed now and then merrily that his colleague had really put that famously, and what he didn't find famous he found capital or fantastic; Hulda, the witch, was in the meantime furtively gauging the value of our kitchen furnishings and she could at any time have given us a pretty accurate estimate for it, though she always nodded heartily with her triple chin when Pastor Meier began to talk about the vanity of earthly goods.

But my father and my mother only exchanged looks, nothing more, and it must have been at just this moment that I understood what the writers of fiction mean when they speak of eloquent glances.

The light of the lamp struggled through the kitchen air as if through a November fog in Hamburg; it smelled of sweaty Pastor and hospital carbolic acid and Jonathan's vegetarian garlic and Alice's nasty "Parfong," and Brinkmann's cheapest tobacco and the thousand goods in Hulda's witch's den. And was it hot!

Sometime late at night my little sister squeezed into the kitchen again and asked right in the middle of the Pastor's analogy of the faithful mouth breeder and the gluttonous swordfish in a sleepy and whimpering voice when all these visitors would finally be going because she was ready to drop from hunger.

The Pastor got up immediately and signalled to the others with a warning expression as if exhorting his church choir, mildly but emphatically, to sing a hymn, and he said, while rubbing a last lump of clay into the kitchen floor, that none should get in the way of little children coming to the table. He drove our visitors ahead of him out of the door whether, like Hulda for example, they had anything left to say or not, and on the threshold he turned around and asked, while the fumes circled about and the lamp illuminated his head, whether he

might perhaps bring along his own little children next time—he had seven, and six of them could walk—so that they too might look upon this watery parable, or just how had my father called that container in such a cute folksy way, "A bit o' somethin' extra," that was the expression he had used, wasn't it? Yes, said my father, now even hoarser than Alice, that was it.

Next Sunday my father went to the fish market once again and in the evening a dog lay behind our garden door, shaggy, alert and with a sire in every village.

IMAGINARY MONOLOGUE

GÜNTER KUNERT

I'm not denying anything. It all comes under the statute of limitations anyway. I admit that I've snatched a few forest rangers since 1830. They smelled terrible and usually tasted like tobacco, hartshorn and unwashed loden, and that should be accounted enough punishment for my appetite. But I haven't touched another forest ranger for more than a hundred years now. Looking back at it, I get sick thinking of those full-bearded green shapes, crazy about trees, their ears overgrown with thick, bushy hair, listening raptly to nerve-wracking bird noises. I've got much too delicate a sensibility to be able to stand this unceasing screeching cuckooing trilling whistling warbling. But those forest rangers, ever since they've existed—or, rather, ever since I've known them—stand spell-bound as if hearing the grandest music of Liszt Toselli while enveloped by the morning mists, with a first ray of sunshine penetrating the moldering branches. Meanwhile my hand stretches out softly from the center of the lake where I'm at home and I grab them by their green necks and put them out of their romantic misery. I don't deny it. But even so it's not prosecutable under the statute of limitations. And there were never any witnesses in the vicinity. Potential circumstantial evidence like remains of clothing shoulder-bones indigestible shoe leather has long since dissolved in the quagmire. And there's no net fine enough to trap an infusorium which, by reacting to birdsong, might reveal what transformations of matter it has undergone.

Forest rangers are boring. If you crack their skulls, you find nothing but hunting junk. Virtually nothing new about the great, vast world on dryland. It's a long time since I've talked to a human being.

A few days ago something was swimming around down here, a queer creature like I'd never seen before: instead of feet it swam with flippers, there were two round bulges protruding from its back, its face consisted practically of only one big flat eye, two curved tubes hung down from its mouth, and little air-bubbles were always coming out of it! At first I thought it was a kind of strayed seacow without an udder until I addressed it and it stopped dead in terror and then in a mad dash climbed to the surface. Then I recognized it: it was a human being. I reached out after him with my gigantic iron hand, happened to hit up against a rapidly rotating screw jutting out of the stern of a boat and would have had my fingers torn off if I weren't made of iron. As it was, it only scratched off a little of the rust that I'm covered all over with. There was a time when I used to clean off the rust myself once in a while in order to take pleasure in my smooth iron rump but I soon outgrew that youthful vanity. The rust returned after a little while anyway, and so I let it grow until it formed a thick rough bark around my body—the color of dying embers. I still remember what heat is: fire, I saw it for the first and simultaneously last time shortly after I was born. There's no mystery whatever about my origins.

My mother was a simple miller's daughter but my father was of the very highest ancestry. He wished to preserve his incognito at the time and actually so should I now too if I weren't compelled by my respect for science and my liking for Dr. Mullberger to disclose unreservedly everything that concerns me.

When in the summer of 1719 this miller's daughter went out to pick blueberries and was filling her little basket, a noble gentleman rode down that lonely path, a gentleman for whom basket miller's daughter and jumping off his horse was a single act. Before the (to date chaste) maiden was even able to stand up—drowsy as she was from the sticky heat of the forest and stunned by the intense sunlight—it was already too late. With impunity the horseman had ravished her from behind. And as she meanwhile piteously beseeched her ravisher for his name so that her child would at least know that much about its father, a voice behind her bellowed rudely: "Theirs is not to reason why, theirs is but to do and die!"

At that moment she realized whom she had to thank for her

subsequent fate: King Frederick William I who had been riding from village to village on this sweaty day in July in the year of Our Lord 1719 checking up on his subjects—unrecognized, so he thought. Not much later it became obvious that her excursion into the forest had borne fruit—whose consistency, however, was something of a mystery. For the weight of the life growing in her made it impossible for the miller's daughter after only three months to stay on her feet. She spent six months in bed before giving birth to twins: there were two of us, you see. Me, Ironjack, and him, Nickelpeter. About him, more later. When the midwife pulled me out into the world and lifted me up, she was so surprised at my weight that she dropped me out of fright. I heard her scream that the brat had fallen on her foot: Ow, she was bleeding, the instep of her foot must be broken . . . Miller's daughter, Miller's daughter, what is it that you've given birth to?! And my dear embarrassed mother replied that the noble sire had looked quite normal insofar as he'd been visible during conception: a big, fat man in a blue jerkin. His broad shoes with real silver buckles were what was most vivid in her memory. Meanwhile the midwife was moaning: Lord, help us, the kids are made of metal! You're a witch, Miller's daughter, you've been carrying on with the devil . . . And off she rushed straight to the Tax Office to register a formal accusation. Shortly thereafter legal proceedings were instituted which concluded with the death sentence: the said Miller's daughter, together with her two homunculi, conceived by her of Beelzebub as she herself had admitted on the rack, were to be sewn up in a tight bag and dropped into the biggest pond far removed from the city limits. And whereas she had sought to inculpate the King in this satanic intercourse, she was in addition to be deprived of her civil rights by reason of lèse majesté.

And so we were immersed: the three of us. Our mother drowned. We, her metallic sons, of course didn't. Any sort of pulmonary breathing turned out to be superfluous. We only felt a voracious appetite every now and then. Then we would devour fish and since that time these waters are uninhabited. We grew. With our powerful claws we grabbed the wild animals that came to the water's edge to drink. Nickelpeter was the first to grab a forest ranger but we gobbled him up together. We divided everything up between us. In the evenings, as it got murkier and

murkier under the water, we would ponder and speculate about our own materiality, without being able to arrive at any explanation. Only later was it analysed for me scientifically, after my brother had already emigrated to England. This is how it happened.

One whole burning summer long the water level of our pond dropped lower and lower—it must have been 1760—and we could hardly stand up without risk of being seen. So we spent most of the time resting and daydreaming in the mud. A farmer, seized by the absurd hope of catching a barbel or a stickleback, rocked back and forth above us in the square shadow of his dinghy. We pulled him down to us and found out from the trembling fellow that a war had been going on for seven years already. The fields weren't being worked and people were going hungry. Pressed for more, he stammered: The war's against Austria. Frederick William I's son is personally leading our troops.

Our half-brother! What's he made of: iron or copper or what? We wanted to know and got for an answer: Ah cain't understan' yor question, sirs. But all metal stuff is bein' collected and melted down for cannon and shot.

While chewing pensively on the meagre bones of the farmer, we considered how odd it was that our half-brother, a certain Fritz, was made of real flesh and blood. Nickelpeter, a rather timorous character, was afraid of being melted down as soon as the water dropped further and we would be discovered. He wanted to forestall the violent breakdown of his personality into militant spherical masses and made up his mind to escape that very night through one of the brooks running out of our pond. He seemed to have disappeared without a trace, seemed to have vanished unnoticed God knows where, until I found out from an Englishman—who though tough on the outside, was quite tender on the inside—that my brother was now in Loch Ness. He's often seen there but he isn't caught because the British S.P.C.A. has officially declared him a "Royal Monster" and hence in need of preservation. Our mutual physio-chemical origins which I hadn't understood because of my poor scientific training were only clarified in the 20th century however.

My rustbark kept on growing, my iron face was covered with lichen and algae which I removed once a year by means of a scraper. I carried out this process hidden among the rushes and

bent over the water, which I used as a mirror, scraping off the annoying green muck from my cheeks. I had hardly shoved my head out into the air this time, blinking in the bright sunlight, snorting and dripping water out of my ears and mouth, with my knuckles pressed into the sandy beach, when I suddenly heard somebody yelling:

Hold it, you over there! You're getting my fishing lines all fouled up, you damned lout!

I shouted over to him that the pond belonged to me, that I was the terrible Ironjack and that I didn't allow anybody to mock me. But the guy in the boat answered: We Germans fear God alone, and nothing else in the world. I'm Professor Emeritus Andreas Schulmann and fish wherever the law allows!

I: The only reason there's no law against it here is because there aren't any fish anymore. What time do we have now? I mean: what year is it?

He: It's 1912. It seems to me you must be a foreigner. From somewhere along the eastern shore of the Baltic, with some Mongoloid blood as the shape of your skull seems to suggest.

I explained to him that I was born in the area, but he shook his tangled white mane: Nonsense. I'm a geneticist. I know you much more thoroughly than you know yourself.

What's a geneticist? I asked, and he explained it to me, twirling his pince-nez on its black band. He struck me as really the only possible person to explain my incomprehensible genesis. He listened breathlessly to my confession, soon tears rose into his eyes and he muttered excitedly: A Hohenzollern, a real Hohenzollern! The striking forehead, the shield of world-embracing designs, mindful of the grandeur of the Empire, the stern nose, the chin—yes, Your Royal Highness has convinced me! Your Royal Highness, I am entirely at your service!

I: Why is it that I'm made of iron?

He: A remarkable but by no means mystical process. As far as is known to posterity, His Majesty Frederick William I possessed an iron character which probably served as a genetic catalyst. At that time the King was undergoing mercury treatment for his gout—in other words, being medicated with quicksilver—prescribed for him by a medical science still in its infancy. His character, acting as a catalyst, must have structurally transformed the quicksilver circulating in his body, and in his testicles as well, into iron or, respectively, nickel. An astonish-

ing and most royal result. The spermatozoa, now of the same chemical composition as metal, but alive, couldn't produce anything other than metallic beings, an iron man: You, my Prince!

I was so dumbfounded that I neglected to internalize this remarkable scholar, something that would have aided the development of my personality enormously. Instead, I simply gaped while he seized his oars, bade me a respectful farewell and in a flash was swallowed up by the reeds—rustling mockingly—instead of by me. He was the first to get away undigested. Thus this second of confusion and lack of decisiveness proved to be the cardinal error of my life—as it later turned out.

I must have dozed off for a while after settling back comfortably once again in the mud, pondering the mystery (now unveiled) of my earthly existence, an existence which I could only enjoy in a submerged state because on land my weight impedes all of my movements. I slept for at most a few little years. I woke up suddenly and with a jolt. Thought I'd heard distant thunder. Rolled over grudgingly on my other side. Then another shock wave jolted me wide awake. Inky slime whirled up into my eyes, the all too perceptible crashing noises of explosions broke out close by—not above but below the surface—and forced me to rise up. It was raining up there. On the shore stood men in black uniforms. One of them yelled: there he is, Oberscharführer! And the man so designated put a funnel to his lips and addressed me:

Hey, you listen to me, Comrade Ironjack! I'm Oberscharführer Schulmann! My father told me about your pristine steely German might. Now that Final Victory is nearly at hand we've got to make use of all our reserves of strength. Your steely strength too. The country needs fellows like you. If you refuse to do your duty we've got even better things than hand grenades. We've got underwater detonation bombs. Not a dry eye after you use those! We've managed to take care of the defeatists so far, get it? So, OK, tomorrow morning a crane will come and pick you up. A toothbrush and a change of underwear will be enough. Sieg Heil!

The dark shapes slipped away under the trees. Billions of little drops of water made them invisible. As the forest stood silent in the rain before me like a murky three-dimensional tapestry, I

almost doubted that anybody had been there. But my environment was still utterly convulsed and obscured by the explosions. Underwater detonating bombs, eh? I thought about whether Schulmann jr. wasn't actually right to ask for my help. Oughtn't I to be grateful to my country for the forest rangers? And after all the country couldn't be held responsible for their unappetizing nasty and felt-like taste. Didn't I have my countrymen to thank for those robust girls who went out looking for mushrooms and who practically melted in your mouth? Being German means: Being easy to digest! In spite of my iron constitution: Underwater detonating bombs, eh? I decided to be a loyal subject of my fatherland, which I knew only in a fluid state. They would undoubtedly send me into action along the coast in order to sink ships or something like that. One blow from my fist against the hull and the cruiser would go to the bottom. I was sure of getting a medal. I already saw myself with the Order of the Black Eagle or with the Golden Fleece, soldered onto my freshly de-rusted chest, towering out of the waves of the German Atlantic, a living monument to victory, girded by the raging surf, a Germanic Poseidon, the source and fount of a new myth of the sea-conquering tribe of Teutons.

As if charged with an ambivalent tension almost like electricity, I sleeplessly waited for dawn. It came. But no Schulmann jr., no vehicle to transport me away. This was the greatest disappointment of the last few decades and the reason why I withdrew resentfully into the relaxing mud, there to reflect upon the geopolitical role which inexplicable circumstances had prevented me from playing. Shouldn't I just utterly renounce all earthly pursuits? Nevermore to emerge to the surface? Simply rust away sadly, to be discovered in future millennia, an unsightly lump of scrap iron on which once the fate of Prussia hinged? Serves them right: if they don't want me, they can and should lick my...even if they get blood-poisoning in their tongue in the process.

I stuck to my decision for a long time, until something came diving down to me, a queer shape that might credibly have been an udderless seacow till I spoke to it and it took off in horror for the surface. Then I noticed: it was a human being. I made a grab for him. Went up after him. A boat sped away leaving a wake of loud screams behind. An uneasy presentiment filtered through to me. The loudmouths in the speedboat would doubtlessly

broadcast their encounter with me through the whole world. My peace had departed. Handgrenades, eh? Underwater detonating bombs, what? Who knows what kind of monstrosities they'd invented.

I waited in the deepest spot in the lake for what I had imagined would come. I didn't have to wait long until the hull of a ship floated past above me, large and oval shaped, a rubber ellipse. As I was peering up there, they lowered a can on a string. The cap was off and an amber-colored fluid oozed in delicate clouds out of the container. Then my memory stopped functioning. Suddenly it was night.

When it grew light again, I was lying at the bottom of a tiled pool in lukewarm water, with the taste of perfumed soap in my mouth, free of the algae and mussels that had inhabited my back and derrière, and enveloped by a net of steel wire. Over the edge of the pool a bald head, with glasses, beard, and looking like a seadog, peered down at me: You, Dr. Mullberger, and you said: Good morning, Ironjack. How do you feel? And I answered: Where am I? How did I get here?

Then you again: You are in a scientific research institute, my good fellow. I'd almost given up hope of finding you. For twenty years now we've had in our safe the report of an SS-Oberscharführer about an encounter with you. The report was never sent off because he died in action. A friend of the dead officer, a metallurgist, saved the report and after the end of the war delivered it to his company and they then passed it on to us for evaluation. Can you imagine, Ironjack, the number of ponds, puddles and bodies of water I've searched through? Because the dead officer had forgotten to make a note of the place. When I heard the news last evening of your surfacing in Devil's Pond, there was no time to be wasted. At four in the morning we reconnoitred the bottom with a mine-detector and—zammo! We got you. Anaesthetic in the water, wire cable round your neck, towed to shore, loaded on a truck and zowee: to the Institute. On the way back hordes of reporters and curious onlookers met us. We managed to steal a march on them. You can congratulate yourself. Now you can kiss rust goodbye.

Every morning Dr. Mullberger appeared at the pool. Out of various other little bottles he dropped various compounds into the water. Was it a solution of hydrochloric acid? A corrosion preventative? In any event I woke up one morning completely

clean and bright as a boy. Spread out along the bottom of the pool there lay a thin, coarse layer: my old rust. Proudly, I examined my limbs and they reflected so much light in the water that Dr. Mullberger had to approach me wearing sunglasses. Although I asked him every morning why he'd dragged me out of my home in the pond, he always shook his head and smiled: Just hold on, Ironjack. The future's already begun. We need you badly, old friend. How do you feel this morning?

Very fine, thanks, Doctor. Quite young. As if I hadn't been born in 1720, but only twenty years ago.

The next morning a girl's face leaned down over my shining iron nakedness.

As a child of the 18th century that made me feel an unsuspected embarrassment. I tried to hide myself, she tittered. She pushed herself out further over the edge of the pool in order to empty a little tube of milky viscous stuff and in the process showed a pair of naked shoulders. Still a little further. I lowered my eyes because her sweet little bulges weren't covered by anything either. I believe a reddish glint spread over my gleaming exterior. On the next day I had the courage to raise my eyes. And after a week I had gotten used to seeing her completely nude. Hence I wasn't dumbfounded when one morning she appeared in company with another girl, just as unpeeled as she was. The first was blonde, the other brunette. The third had freckles all over, the fourth was suntanned. With the eighth, I didn't even notice details anymore, and when there were about twenty of them camping around my pool, I could hardly manage to keep them apart. They didn't rouse my appetite in the least. Even when they took away the wire netting over my head and I could easily have reached up with my gigantic hand and pulled down a breakfast for myself. Incomprehensible: I'd lost all of my savagery. Maybe they'd mixed some hunger depressant in with the water. Or perhaps the lukewarm water just made me drowsy. I didn't even make a grab for them when they splashed around shamelessly on the surface. Not even when they dived. They got quite close, touched me with their little soft paws and in doing so set something in my breast moving like a steamhammer. They fluttered around me like mermaids nereids nixies sirens nymphs—or whatever other name you want to give to temptation—until I yielded to their incessant attack. Nine months later Dr. Mullberger comes up to my pool, nods smiles

says: Congratulations, Ironjack, you've become a father today. Precisely twenty times. Twelve daughters, eight sons.

I: Thanks, Doctor, I'm awfully embarrassed about it.

Nonsense, Ironjack. That's what you're here for. Oh my yes, I'd completely forgotten to inform you of the reason for your stay in our Institute. So now you know it.

I answered him that I'd confessed my life history to him in good faith, even the business with the forest rangers (though falling under the statute of limitations), while he . . . he kept quiet about his intentions of misusing me. Until now. Until he now delivered this lecture:

We're in need of people with constitutions like yours. Through people like you, Ironjack, we're getting in reach of that long sought-for ideal of an absolutely frictionless historical process. The present species of homo sapiens—that lacrimose, eternally hungry, eternally unsatisfied creature torn by conflicting emotions—will be gradually replaced by a species sprung from your seed. Only an iron humanity is ordained to rule the universe, and I, Dr. Horst Mullberger, will be its prophet!

He makes a gesture with his right hand, hides his left hand behind his back: a clumsy movement on his part and I perceive that he's hiding a little bottle from me: full of the same amber-colored substance which I remember only too well. Asked about it, he replies curtly:

You've done your duty. You can go back now to your pond.

Suddenly it's as if a yellow fog is seething down through the water and no matter how far I retreat into the opposite corner—still it reaches me. As I gradually lose consciousness I see how kind Dr. Mullberger keeps on dumping bottle after bottle into the water and, dropping off, I wonder what's the point of the overdose. . .

Epilog: Advertisement in the Classified Section of the "Daily Mail": Circa two tons of highest quality iron (the faulty cast of a statue) for sale considerably below scrap iron price: Dr. H. Mullberger, Institute for Macrobiology.

THE STRANGE BETROTHAL
OF A TRUCKER

SIEGFRIED PITSCHMANN

That evening in September I suddenly got a rotten feeling that the ceiling in our temporary quarters might come crashing down on my head at any moment.

So I got dressed and went into the *Kastanienhof.*

Now you ought to know that by that time this tavern had long lost all its cachet of having been a gold-digger's hangout. Once upon a time, so they say, during the transition period after the war our journeymen were supposed to have had their drunken brawls and knifings here—those guys who went from job to job doing piece work and shamelessly and unfairly skimming the cream off the top of the quotas. But in the meantime that gang has practically died out and their remains are absorbed and kept in line by an army of decent and moderate folks. And, besides, I admit frankly that I suspect all this gold-digger nostalgia that people talk about in our industrial combine is a later glorification which a few journalistic exaggerations no doubt helped create.

But no more about that. As always it was pretty full and I went upstairs to the dance bar. I got a small table a little off to one side and I sat there and looked at the faces and listened to the metallic beat of the guitar.

I saw Thekla sitting over there on a bar-stool. I recognized her from the slight tenseness of her body and from her hair, hanging black and frayed down into her forehead with just a suggestion of gray at the parting. She was sitting self-confidently and carelessly on the high-legged stool and I admired her: her nocturnal metamorphosis was perfect.

To be sure, there were other women and girls here whom I knew but none of them, I'm convinced, can hold a candle to

Thekla. She was sitting alone, quite slim and at the same time muscular, in a light yellow wool dress, with black hair, and you couldn't tell her age (we guessed her to be in her early thirties), and I had always seen her alone when I met her in the evenings.

Well, come on, I thought, go on over and give your brigade leader a how-d'ye-do.

There were four of us, as I should explain to you, running the cement machines at Waschkaue and Thekla took care of the 500 liter mixer and was our brigade leader.

After forty-six she had been a salesgirl, a sales representative, a secretary and finally a clerk in our cadre executive, until suddenly a year and a half ago she impatiently put aside all her office files and got herself retrained as a machinist.

Thekla's fiancé was killed during the last days of the war soon after her father, an old locomotive engineer, had seen the last, terrible signal hoisted—he'd turned to fire and ashes in Dresden under that howling February sky cut through by aluminum wings. Her mother went to live later on with relatives in Stuttgart and Thekla was left alone.

She was pretty laconic and ran her machine with care and skill; if necessary she would help out on any other job too without making a big fuss about it and we three guys in her brigade who ran the fork-lifts and construction elevators would have gone through fire for her. And since we didn't find out much more about her, that's enough about that for the moment.

Thekla gave me a nod as I climbed up on the stool next to her.

"Bored, kiddo?" she said and her voice as always had that soft, velvety-rough quality that we interpreted and respected as the outward symbol of her independence.

I mumbled something. I never felt completely at ease when she was looking at me and, although she was hardly taller than I was, I was plagued by the feeling of shrivelling up each time I saw her. Under her extremely broad, arched eyebrows her eyes shone with the piercing color of blue-tempered steel polished to a fine grain. (I confess, with understandable reluctance, that at the beginning I fell hopelessly in love with Thekla; but naturally she casually pretended not to notice all my bashful and clumsy attempts and finally, after I had stumbled around like the knight of the mournfully unrequited countenance, I gave up.)

"Feel like dancing?" I said boldly.

For a moment she looked over her shoulder at the dance floor,

rocking with the rhythm of the guitar; she said: "Our little calves frolicking in the grass—look," and I looked over towards the dance floor too. I knew a lot of the boys and girls; like all of us they had worked hard and strenuously the whole week long as cement pourers and excavators, as carpenters or masons, and now they were moving about here in their good suits and dresses, drinking wine and filling the room with their after-work laughter.

Thekla suddenly grabbed her glass and emptied it with one swig, shaking her head half-contemptuously and, so it seemed to me, half-despairingly. She pushed the glass towards the woman who was tending bar.

"Dance. . ." she said. "Oh, kiddo, let's not."

She climbed down quickly from her stool; she said: "I've got to keep an eye on Lisa, you know. She's drinking too heavily."

She left and I followed her with my eyes as she steered diagonally through the throng of dancers, a little stiffly and without getting out of the way of the others.

And then, around ten, when I was sitting at my table again, Ignaz came in.

He stood near the door for a while, wrinkled his forehead and blinked strenuously, and in the process held his hand over his eyes as if he couldn't find his bearings in this merry turmoil of light and noise and movement. His tie was askew and he was trying angrily to set it straight.

When he saw the table with Lisa and Thekla, he finally got a somewhat sluggish, uncertain move on. He groped his way to the table but stood still three steps away from it, and it looked as if he was furiously ordering himself to turn around. Then he came over to me.

Ignaz was part of Thekla's cement mixer team that fed raw material to the gluttonous machine and he set a rugged pace for the work. Before the war he'd dug coal in a mine in Upper Silesia.

"Well, what's up, bonehead," he said, and that was his way of talking. He leaned heavily on the armrest of the chair and stared at my coffee cup. "Everything in a mess, eh?"

"Not at all," I said.

"Yeah," he said. "Everything's a mess. Lemme have a swig."

I pushed the cup over to him and watched as he emptied it with a grin. His face, dark brown and covered with thin,

scrawl-like wrinkles, gave one the impression of being very broad because his eyes were wide apart.

All at once he leaned forward and muttered: "They won't get me. Not them—you know." Nature had committed a kind of funny blunder in his case and one of his eyes was brownish green and the other tobacco brown; and when he got excited, the iris in one eye slid over a little and made him slightly cross-eyed.

Naturally Ignaz often got excited. Out there in Waschkaue you could hear him cursing and swearing if something went wrong with the deliveries or if the water ran out or the cement crew took too long over breakfast; then he rolled his "r's" in rage and, leaning against his cart, spat out long strings of curses. But he was our best man and I considered his obstinate griping an amiable aspect of his character.

"Well, what's the matter," he complained. "You think I'm dense or something?"

Not knowing what else to say, I answered: "No, of course not." And now I noticed that he must have been drinking quite a bit. (But we had rarely seen him drink anything.)

He raised his finger and said: "I've read a lot, you know, big thick books, get it? I can tell you what's what . . . I'm not going to get out on a limb and say anything about equal rights. Never, not me. Ignaz is going to keep his trap shut . . . But I'll tell you: it's all crap. Get it?"

I nodded vigorously. "Sure," I said and thought: just don't get him riled up, and I wondered what sort of trouble the alcohol had stirred up in him. I felt sorry for him.

"You stupid son of a bonehead, think I'm drunk, what?" he said spitefully and looked a little crosseyed. "I ain't drunk, buddy. Completely sober . . . Want me to walk a straight line?"

I said: "OK, you walk a straight line. You're sober."

"Nonsense," said Ignaz. He wanted to get up and did manage to but immediately let himself drop back into his chair. He ran his tongue over his broad lower lip that turned down at the corner.

"Listen, kid, " he said and his voice was suddenly completely cold and calm. He cut through the air wearily with his hand and said: "It's a mess, all of it—whether you believe it or not. First that shitty war. And then having to get out of Kattowitz. And then them bugs in my lungs . . . Souvenirs of the war, get it? Well, they smoked 'em out at least.

And then later I got married. But what does she do? Huh . . . ?

She beats it . . . not even a year, and I'm just starting to get going again, start working on a construction job—and she beats it. Took off . . . wanted to go to work again; and I told her to stay home. But she went anyway and got a job running the conveyor-belt on a coal excavating machine, get it? And then she started hitting the books and getting her qualifications. It wasn't good between us, kid; I was really patient but it always got worse, and then I lost my temper and let her have it and told her to get out and get married to her damned machine. And she left. Get that, kid? She left . . . Can't help wondering if she ever cared for me if she just went off like that . . ."

He stretched his elbows out on the table and said: "Well, what can you do—it doesn't matter . . " He squinted darkly over toward the dance floor where the boys were calmly letting their partners turn in circles around their outstretched fingers according to some unfathomable rule, while they recklessly banged the floor with the metallic edges of their heels. And then I noticed that he was always staring in one direction: there, where—a bright spot of color in the billowing tobacco smoke—Thekla's canary yellow dress was.

"You feel like another coffee?" I asked, but he didn't seem to hear me.

He said: "But it really bugged me . . . Damned broads. I really ate my heart out; I got burned: get it? Never again a woman, I said. I swore to myself . . . But I also thought that they're free and can go where they want and be whatever they like—and that's the way it should be. Sure. But they've let it go to their heads, kid."

He looked at me with his green and with his brown eye and he repeated: "They've let it go to their heads." And I tried to talk him out of it.

"Aah, what do you know about it," he shouted. "You don't know a damn thing about it! I swore . . . They won't get me . . . Do you think I haven't seen that she's got her eye on me? Huh?"

"Who's got her eye on you?" I said.

He said: "You think I'm stupid and an idiot, huh?—Like a maniac on the machine and bossing us around and giving me the eye. But not with Ignaz, you don't." He stared in her direction and then he muttered, without seeming to be aware that I would be able to hear him: "Those eyes . . . Have you put a spell on me with those eyes?"

Well, I'll be . . . , I thought with a ridiculous pang of

jealousy—that Thekla! Now I remembered too all those scenes between Ignaz and our foreman.

"We really needed her like a hole in the head," Ignaz complained on the very first day that Thekla took charge of the mixer. "Of all people this one's got to come here and tell us what to do, eh, you boneheads?"

He leaned on his shovel and squinted up to the mixing platform: he was waiting greedily for Thekla to make some kind of mistake. But Thekla didn't make any mistakes: she operated the machine calmly and confidently, and when she let the heavy hammer crash against the metal container in order to loosen the remains of the dry mix in it, he pulled a face and growled: "Sure, I might have known—another one of those broads who dumps her husband and prefers to get hitched up with a machine. Listen, kids, another one of those damned . . ."

He now began to wage a wild, unfair and grotesquely one-sided war against his machinist, swore and griped, but Thekla defended herself against all his wild talk and furious attacks with a remarkably dogged forbearance—something that I couldn't understand then.

Only once did she seem to lose her composure: when Ignaz smuggled big lumps into the gravel—a simple minded variety of personal sabotage—so that after every mixing cycle Thekla had to fish out the stuff laboriously with a scraper. The cement pourers on the intermediary platform cussed about the delays but Thekla didn't say anything although she was desperate because she couldn't prove anything against Ignaz and because she was afraid of endangering her reputation as a first-rate machinist; so she kept on working fast and strenuously and swallowed her tears.

That day Ignaz suddenly went silent and the grin of self-satisfaction that at first had suffused his face vanished behind a curtain of gloomy and thoughtful wrinkles.

All that went through my brain as he now pushed his chair back. He wavered a little and said: "Holy Vodka, do I feel thirsty . . . A couple of little shots'll do me good, eh?" And then he leaned down to me and whispered conspiratorially: "And after I've had my drinks, you know what I'll do—huh? Go over to her and tell her that I've read a lot and know what's what—in my noggin, get it? But that my heart's as cold as ice . . ."

160

There he stood, Ignaz, our eternally complaining trucker from the mixer at Waschkaue East, forty years old and already a little grey, and I didn't know what I should tell him. Of course the alcohol had been, as I thought, the cause of his confused and fragmentary confession, and I considered his mistrust and disgruntled misogyny exaggerated, but of course I felt sorry for him and I wondered how often we judge other people hard and unthinkingly or make fun of them without knowing what kind of memories and disappointments they're burdened down with. I would gladly have helped him or at least have said something nice to him, but I also realized that nothing could be done for him now anymore.

I finally said impatiently: "Come on, don't make a fool of yourself. Stay here."

But he just shook his head and see-sawed over to the bar with those absurd long strides of people who have had too much to drink, and I watched him without moving and thought: Let him run his thick head against the wall, what the hell!

Thekla was still sitting at the table. She had now put her arm carefully around Lisa and was patting her and trying to calm her down gently, and Lisa sat there all hunched up and in a daze, looking pathetic like a miserable plucked bird that will never chirp again. Her shoulders twitched; her eyes gazed dully in a drunken stupor that had long lost any semblance of elation, gazed at the empty wine bottles on the table and past them towards nowhere; and the guitar boomed in the amplifier and the young people danced unconcernedly past her table, and Lisa didn't hear anything and didn't see anything: it was enough to make your heart break. (Later on they told me that she worked with the underground construction crew and was Thekla's room-mate; and that evening her boyfriend had disappeared and left her without any reason or explanation whatever.)

When the music stopped, Ignaz came back from the bar. He careened past me, rudely squeezing his green eye shut, and I saw him steering towards Thekla's table.

He slouched up against the edge of the table, squinted a little cross-eyed and then said squeakily: "Well, what's up—you're really far gone in the dumps, eh, you little lush?"

"Cut it out," said Thekla. She still had her arm around Lisa's shoulders.

161

You goddamn bonehead, I thought, using his vocabulary in my anger. Is that what studying all those thick books has brought you to? And I got up.

But a few of the guys stood up too and shoved their way forward with their hands in their pockets, and all at once the air was charged with hostility.

Ignaz said: "I've got nothing to say to you, you black shrew," and he looked very cross-eyed.

"Cut it out," Thekla said once more.

We stood around looking grim; the music started up quickly and Ignaz looked mulishly at the guys and then at Lisa, who, not understanding what was going on, started to laugh madly, and then he repeated hoarsely and babbled drunkenly: "You little lush, eh?"

The guys whistled through their teeth. The waiter came and acted concerned and flicked his towel around, and the guys pushed a little closer up to Ignaz, and finally the towel-man retreated.

Thekla stayed in her seat; she said calmly: "Run along, buddy, you're drunk. We'll see each other tomorrow . . ." She looked attentively at Ignaz for a moment, and I saw her eyes.

Ignaz stammered something and then croaked: "You tryin' to threaten me, huh? With your brigade, huh?" And suddenly he swung out blindly with his arms and let fly absurd curses.

Our volunteer police force went to work precisely and almost noiselessly. They grabbed him without a fuss and while the guitar strummed away undisturbed the guys brought our rabid trucker down the stairs and he simply couldn't do anything against that polite but irresistibly masterful force.

In the garden in front of the house the colorful chairs and tables had been stacked together, two lanterns were burning sleepily and the blue neon sign glowed at the entrance. Under the sickly autumnal yellow of the chestnut trees some belated crickets were fiddling away intently and shrilly. It was a peaceful evening full of gently wafting aromas and quiet melancholy—at least that's how it was when I arrived.

Now, when I stepped out of the door (driven, I admit, by an indecent curiosity), the scene had changed into something warlike.

Ignaz was standing there with his arms hanging down, his head pushed forward and slightly bowed, and his eyes with their

madly sliding iris were streaked with red. He was standing near the door.

"Let me through, pal," Thekla said. She had Lisa by the arm and wanted to get out but Ignaz blocked her way.

"OK," the boys yelled, "let him have it, Blackie! Really give it to him!" They waited in a pretty large semi-circle and more and more joined them, all of them with a sure nose for a juicy scene; and the garden was dark with excitement and shouting.

"Let me through," said Thekla.

"Give it to him!" the guys yelled.

Thekla tried to push him gingerly aside, with her right elbow slightly bent. "Don't be a fool," she said. She was out in the light.

Near the house, you've got to imagine, a police car had stopped that had been called for prematurely either by the waiter or the manager who were feeling scared; and the engine was idling noisily while the headlights lit up the battleground with their low beams. We could see everything, just like in the night scenes in the movies.

The policemen stood next to their car and kept an eye on the scene from under their friendly and watchman-like shiny caps; and they grinned a little and they seemed to know that the boys wouldn't cause any trouble.

Ignaz had retreated a step and hissed: "You put 'em all up to it, you got 'em to throw me out and finish me off, huh!!! I'd like to get my hands on you—you with your equal rights, you!" And then he spat and hit Thekla's shoes.

At that moment something in her gave way. "Take that for your equal rights and for your crap," she screamed, "and for your nuttiness and all the rest!" And with a shock she saw (I think she was more shocked than Ignaz or me or anybody) how the trucker came crawling out from under a table and shook himself with surprise; her blow had come like a bolt out of the blue.

The boys stamped their feet and screamed for joy as Ignaz shook himself back into order.

He crawled forward all bent up and gasped: "Oh you she-devil, you damned black cement-eater . . . I'd like to cut you up into little pieces, if only I wanted to . . . Oh, if only I wanted to . . ." He swung his bony arms and suddenly he screamed: "Grab hold of me, you boneheads! I'll lose control of myself— and there won't be an unbroken bone . . ."

That seemed to act as a signal for our policemen, but Thekla waved them off and said weakly: "Leave me alone, comrades, just leave me . . ." and I saw, already prepared for an unheard-of turn of events, how she leaned against the gate-post and reached for her forehead. Lisa squatted next to her on the step and blinked stupidly at Ignaz.

He stood right up against Thekla and it looked bad for her but she didn't move an inch out of his way.

"What more do you want?" she said, and I noticed how her voice wavered, and at the same moment she started to hammer madly and clumsily with her fists against his chest.

Ignaz let his arms drop. He stood there looking pretty miserable and taken aback, without moving and stammering some strange gibberish made up of rage and helpless tenderness: "Oh you, you're something else . . . Blood! You hit me on my nose . . . Oh, you're something else . . ."

The guys and the police laughed. Of course they didn't know what the whole thing was really about, and I told myself that this was really the most unusual way for two people to get acquainted that one could ever see.

"Don't you understand?" Thekla shouted. "Haven't you understood anything?" And she shook him and kicked him.

Now that was something hard for our poor old Ignaz to understand, as I saw. He still stood there completely stunned and the cool light from the headlights flickered over his messed-up face and he squinted confusedly and helplessly cross-eyed while Thekla wiped his forehead and nose with a handkerchief and calmed him down with senseless, loving words.

Suddenly he turned around and yelled: "You boneheads, what are you standing around for like a bunch of fools and staring! Beat it—the show's over!"

And that is how the memorable, moving act of human insight and transformation was carried out, even if only by means of a barbaric short-circuit and under the sympathetically blinking eyes of our state; and we could leave the two to themselves, and so it came out right in the end.

SNOW WHITE

ERWIN STRITTMATTER

Uncle Phil worked in the county seat, but he didn't like working much and what he liked best was not working at all. On weekends he'd visit us and our grandparents in the country. His palms were damp, his fingernails chewed off, and when we greeted him we only let him have our hands reluctantly; and when we shrank away from his damp naked fingers, Phil would laugh like a zombie.

Uncle Phil possessed the gift of the gab and we eargerly soaked up all his fibs and hot air because we still believed that life in the city was elegant and exciting while our life in the country was ordinary and dull.

From his lips exquisite lies would drop glistening and gross half-truths would plunk down heavily, and the grownups would wink at each other as they listened to his crudely fabricated stories, but that didn't bother our uncle; it was enough for him to bask in the admiration of the children; and he was the hero of all his stories, conquering his opponents in verbal battle and firing off oaths and expostulations, because bad language often creates a semblance of truth and action.

There were weekends when Uncle Phil had already spent all his wages by Friday and then he would appear at our grandparents' with empty pockets and have to invent some story. In the story our poor uncle had invariably been held up, and he would often be held up and the hold-ups were always dramatic:

What, you wanna kill me? I ask.

Kill you, he says.

Stab me in the back, you snot?

In front it's dangerous, he says.

Throw your knife away, I says.

And he doesn't throw his knife away and I've got to jump him and I've got to roll my eyes like a lion and I've got to stomp up to

him and yell: Kiss off! Then he drops his knife and he's gone and my money too.

"The knife, Uncle Phil, show us the knife!"

Poor Uncle Phil had to plunge deeper into his forest of lies: he'd buried the knife so it couldn't be found, he had to lie, "because that would really be something if a cop comprehended me with a crook's knife!"

Father and the miners were drinking beer in our kitchen and they laughed at Uncle Phil for his imaginative accidents, but Grandmother defended her darling Phil and said pointedly: "He should know it, after all he was there," and Father and the miners laughed at Grandmother's naïveté and Grandmother spat on the floor in front of them. She took Uncle Phil up to the grandparents' own living room for a special welcoming meal, and Uncle Phil ate quickly and he ate, though he ate quickly, for a very long time.

The fabric of man is interwoven with passions and vices, just as the roots of trees are intermingled with a network of fungi, and no man has ever been asked how many passions and vices he would like to have before he slips into material life; and one man lugs lots of passions and vices behind him and another man only one passion and one vice, but the rest of humanity is dying to find out if you'll gain control over your passions and vices, or if they'll overcome you and trample you again into the dust.

Uncle Phil was free of all passion, but he was loaded down with three principal vices and various secondary ones, and his principal vices were reading, smoking and playing cards.

If after dinner there was no prospect of a game of cards with Father and Grandfather or with the two grandmothers, Uncle Phil would get up a head of steam, and the cigarette fumes would seem to billow out not only from his mouth but from his jacket pockets and buttonholes as well. Uncle Phil read like he ate, quickly and plentifully, and he built for himself a world out of smoke and words, and he disappeared into it; and just as when he ate he never put on weight, so, too, when he read he never put on any intellectual weight: he became aware without gaining in awareness.

First Uncle Phil would read the pile of back issues of the *Watchtower*. The *Watchtower* was a family newspaper and whoever subscribed to it was insured, and his dependents were supposed to be paid several hundred marks, "in the event of the insured's departing this life by death," so it said.

166

After the *Watchtower* Uncle Phil would reach for *Vobach's Fashion Journal for the German Home* and read it; and he would even fold out the pattern sheets and he would read the directions on the patterns for smartly cut pleated skirts, for he had to have read everything that could be read and he stored away the contents of the two piles of papers under his skull, and his skull was overgrown with unkempt hair that was always somewhat dirty.

Then Uncle Phil would resort to books he had already read several times, and specifically to the two volumes of *The Practical Home Doctor for Healthy and Sick Days.* I've seen sick people in my life but never a sick day; nevertheless, the two volumes rested on the clean linen in Mother's closet and were called Huelsen books because the name of the man who wrote them was Dr. von Huelsen. By means of colored fold-out pictures, Dr. von Huelsen instructed Uncle Phil in the muscular, skeletal and sexual life of man, and Uncle Phil studied especially the physiology of woman, and in contrast to Mother had no objection to our looking on over his shoulder.

Man consists primarily of vacant cavities, explained Dr. von Huelsen, and the chemical components of Homo sapiens have a value of only six marks and eighty pfennigs in gold.

This *VALUATION* of man as the result of scientific research became a by-word of my uncle's, and he would slip it in now and then into his conversations, and his conversations consisted of a hodge-podge of popularized scientific information: "Fashion is a constraint exercised upon people of unstable character, and those people of stable character who don't yield to fashion are made to appear ridiculous, and it's all a plot of business people. Yes, yes, and what is man? Vacant cavity after vacant cavity, with a chemical value of six marks eighty after being melted down."

We listened to this materialistic calculation and we shivered and we didn't suspect that a few years later some brutalized countrymen of ours would turn Von Huelsen's scientific view of man into reality by melting down people. Neither did we suspect that scientists—who fixed their gaze only on the narrow segment of their scientific specialty and who see in man only what Dr. von Huelsen saw—can become worse sinners against life than people who have no education at all.

After the two *HUELSEN BOOKS* Uncle Phil read the Almanac, and that was a book which accompanied us children throughout

our school years in the village, and now I'll say something about it here for interested readers because I toted it every day to school like the Bible; and the uninterested readers can skip to that point where I finish what I've got to say about it:

The Almanac contained a short outline of Prussian-Brandenburgian history as well as dates of births, reigns and deaths of all the unavoidable kings and generals, and judging by this historical outline one had to conclude that the Germanic tribes had made their appearance on earth only in order to prepare the way for the genuine Prussians.

Following the historical section there was a zoological section, in which the porcupine was treated as an important animal, probably because in our primer the first letter of the alphabet which we learned to read was the "p" in porcupine, and then there came various facts about domestic animals, especially about the cow as milk producer and about the significance of the horse as an animal for fieldwork and battle steed, and the zoological section closed with a description of the squirrel, the monkey of the Prussian-Brandenburgian forests, thereby providing a link with the zoology of the rest of the world.

The Flaeming, the Niederlausitz border-rampart and the Glogau-Baruth glacial valley combined to form a sort of geography in the Almanac, and in the section on cosmography we learned that the earth was a planet, the sun a fixed star and the moon a nocturnally luminous body which derived its light from the sun.

Along with the German oak, the section on botany dealt with the coconut palm which, despite the loss of the colonies, still grew in German Southwest Africa, and we were told that it was above all the *PALMIN* from the palm trees of which the "evil enemies" had deprived us by means of the Versailles Treaty. At the same time we were informed frivolously that the Ancient Germans had known practically no fruit at all, and that the monks had brought it to them after those old mead-imbibers had let themselves be Christianized, whereby we were supposed to recognize the important role of the Church in German fruit production.

My youngest brother, however, who attended school in the era of the Twelve-Year Reich, was taught that the Aryan Germans had need neither of Southern-European plums nor Roman wine, because they had long known the high vitamin content of wild

gooseberries and red currants, and they had cultivated wine in Grüneberg in Silesia and in Weissenfels and in Naumburg and in Meissen, too, "a little sour, to be sure, but all praise be to anything that makes you tough!"

And this is how the dear Germans, who are so fond of calling each other CULTURAL FERTILIZER or SALT OF THE EARTH, allowed themselves to be ruled on a pseudoscientific basis, and it is high time now that they should learn something, after all the hue and cry of their history, and begin to distinguish between pseudoscience and real science.

This was the nature of Uncle Phil's weekend emergency reading matter, but in the city he would read detective, wild west, love and sex stories as well as the works of the classic authors, because whatever books in the stream of days would wash up against Phil, he would fish them out and gnaw on them with his quick blue eyes.

And he read while he ate and while sitting on the toilet, and whenever he was bored going some place he read while he walked, and Goethe's WERTHER was for him a love story with a prolonged fatal exodus of the lover, and Manzoni's THE BE-TROTHED was for him another love story in which the author was always putting obstacles between the engagement and the wedding in order to make sure that he managed to get a full-length book.

Uncle Phil assiduously avoided the science called orthography though he dealt with it daily. He only wrote when he was in trouble, chiefly when he wanted to borrow money. Then he would prepare my mother for his attack with a letter already written during the working week: "My deer darling Lehni! Fate has arranged to leve me standin once agaihn without any mens in this world. I have lehnt everythin but my good disposishon to those who were want to call themself my friends and as punishmnt for my botomles genarosity I step naked thus befor you . ."

So, too, in his letters to my naive grandmother sent from the front in the First World War, Uncle Phil's requests and demands were always dressed up in piteous tales:

"Deer Mother!!!

Only you know how atached I was to my pocket wach, which Father gave me as a confermation present, however, now a horrible disastor has hapened to me and a stray fregment of a

shel has made mush of it in my vest poket and I can thanc the Dear Lord tht the fregment dameged only my wach but not my body. If it was to seme to you a matter of posibility, so send me by return of male a new timepiese, so that I know what hour struk when I have to jorney to the land from whose born no traveler reterns . . ."

Oh, if only Uncle Phil had had some sticktoitiveness and had taken a little more trouble over capricious Lady Orthography! He would have been able to create a kind of pulp literature made up of worn out images and turns of phrase and hackneyed dramatic scenes like those inflated word slingers and female journalists who "rest in the arms of Morpheus" when they sleep, and to whom Berlin, Dresden and Leningrad are too colorless and who therefore write about the "Athens on the Spree," "Florence on the Elbe" and the "Neva Metropolis." They don't marry but "forge matrimonial bonds," drink "juice of the grape" and "noble nectar" on such occasions, and don't sail off on the Berlin excursion boats but rather on the "holiday armada" to spend their "honeymoon." They turn fishermen into "St. Peter's disciples" and women riders into "Amazons" in order to simulate a classical education; they "create" victories and defeats, pillows for perambulators and wreaths for the dead, and they think they've "created a posture" for their own limitations when they call the Zeiss outlet on the Berlin Alexander Platz the "Mini Mecca for Camera Fans."

My Uncle Phil would easily have been able to handle the kind of bombast that's needed to babbitize language in this way.

Grandfather regarded Uncle Phil's pseudo-literary turns rather more skeptically:

"Shot the watch out of his vest pocket? Since when do soldiers wear vests?"

"He must mean the knitted cardigan that I sent him."

"What, my good cardigan?"

"It already had a hole in the sleeve."

"Sure, two holes in the sleeves. You of course won't be freezing for me in the winter."

There was an argument, but Uncle Phil got his replacement watch secretly from Grandmother anyway; and thereby the power of even the worst literature should be proved.

Our Step-Uncle was often in love but his income wasn't large enough to allow him to marry what Grandmother called a

"reasonable" woman, admitting thereby involuntarily that Uncle Phil was unreasonable. Phil changed his place of work more often than his handkerchief, and as soon as he lost his taste for a job he would find something to complain about.

Once Uncle Phil worked for a cloth-dyer, and then he would come for his weekend visit with a deathly yellow face and lemon-colored hands, and a week later he came dyed blue all over, and after another week he appeared loden-green in our kitchen.

With a little bit of stamina Uncle Phil would have been able to scrub off his various hues, but he wasn't fond of washing himself and, as I've said already, he loved it when we kids admired him. Grandmother however moaned and groaned about his unhealthy work, and this worry made it easier for Phil to leave his job at the dyer's when we stopped admiring him sufficiently because we'd grown used to his changing colors.

So Uncle Phil hired himself out as a night watchman at the dyers.

"You of all people are going to watch over something!" said Grandfather who knew what we all knew, namely how faint-hearted Phil was. But whatever his fears, Uncle Phil's main concern was to get a job at which he could read. He locked himself into his watchman's lodge so that the thieves stealing the cloth wouldn't be able to drag him off and in the morning he would in good conscience enter into his log: "Night passed as per regulation. No incidents to report." And there was nothing disingenuous about this report because if Uncle Phil was able to read and smoke then his night passed as per regulation, and whatever else happened on the factory grounds was, in Uncle Phil's view, none of his business. But the watchers of watchmen, the time-clocks strewn about the factory grounds—those embryos of our computers—which Uncle Phil ignored, took their revenge and betrayed him and deprived him of his cozy nights of reading.

During this period of nocturnal reading, Uncle Phil lived (or rather slept) with the family of a garbage collector, whose house, dating from the Middle Ages, stood at the end of the Friedrichstrasse in the county seat—an area where the bottom window ledges of the one-storied provincial houses weren't more than a foot above street level.

When I was a little boy going to the village school, I would

walk past these houses whenever I found myself in town because I liked looking into the rooms and watching what the people did and because I thought I was taking part in the city life which seemed so desirable to us children; and I would only too gladly have gone into one or the other of these rooms and sometimes I think that this particular desire of mine was so intense that later on I would go in and out of suchlike rooms more than was good for me. And I was not just looking for Uncle Phil to visit him in this kind of place but I myself had become déclassé and lived in the slums of German cities.

The neighbor of the garbage collector at whose place Uncle Phil lived ironed clothes for a living, and in her youth—that is, six or seven years before I got to know her and before she became my Aunt Elli—she had been a beauty, a kind of gypsy-like beauty.

A fine gentleman, as she always stressed, had made her pregnant "in the delirium of love," and then for transparent reasons he had become unavailable for the wedding; and since then my aunt-to-be had lived alone and waited for the availability of that gentleman, taking care of her daughter, my later cousin.

Aunt Elli's main room wasn't just the living room, bedroom and kitchen, but it also served as the place for doing the washing and ironing. A little sign posted at the entrance to the house, with its letters about to fall off in all directions, indicated that in the walk-out basement apartment gentlemen and ladies could have their clothing washed and ironed and that one could also have curtains stretched.

When Uncle Phil met this laundress, he stopped visiting us regularly. His empty wallet, which formerly he would have Mother or Grandmother fatten up furtively, now seemed to renew its contents elsewhere, and Grandfather said in order to annoy Grandmother that Uncle Phil was now living off "hot merchandise." But one Saturday Uncle Phil did put in an appearance again and kept on talking and talking and in the process he pulled a cigarette case with a conspicuous silver sheen out of his jacket pocket. With much ado Phil ceremoniously took a SWEET GIRL—in those days one of the cheapest brands of cigarettes—out of the case, and for the purpose of lighting the little tube of tobacco he pulled a shiny lighter out of the clutter of his jacket pocket and into the evening sunlight.

"What's that shiny thing you've got there, Uncle Phil?"

"It's something Elli gave me."

"Elli?"

"My bride."

Our imaginations caught fire at the thought of Uncle Phil's bride: she couldn't possibly be anything but a beautiful girl if she gave our Uncle such lovely silvery shiny things, a fairy-tale bride, a kind of Snow White.

Later on we discovered that the cigarette case and the lighter which had glittered so thrillingly and which had so inspired us had been intended originally for that "fine gentleman" who had been prevented from taking part in his wedding with Aunt Elli. Aunt Elli had waited and waited for the "gentleman," but one fine day she had gotten tired of waiting and she had presented the shiny things to Uncle Phil.

If one wanted to go straight to the county seat, one had to hoof it for thirteen kilometers, and one day our grandmother set out to go there carrying a basket full of provisions and a bunch of summer flowers. First, however, she walked five kilometers to the railway station in order to have herself joggled from there by way of a detour of 35 kilometers to Uncle Phil's wedding.

"That's the limit!" said Grandfather. "Who knows what kind of hen let this half-grown cock mount her?"

Weddings, weddings—what a role they play in the life of mankind! Aren't they treated like a re-enactment of birth, a birth after which man appears with two heads, four hands and four legs before his fellow men and life? And the parents of the bridegroom and bride invoke luck and they invoke fate, and they do so especially on the day of the wedding; luck or fate are supposed to arrange it in such a way that the two heads with which man will henceforth be supplied won't work against each other, that he won't use his four hands to beat himself up and that his four legs won't try to run away from each other; in short, that this bipartite man will work, hold together and that the young heads and legs which in time will grow out of him will find a good example in him.

A short time after the wedding, Uncle Phil appeared with Aunt Elli and his little step-daughter to introduce them to Grandfather and us, his dear relatives, and the Snow White of our children's imagination was damaged by reality: Aunt Elli was little and inclined to plumpness, her face was already lined

with crows' feet from worrying and it was faded from the steam of her washing and pressing. Aunt Elli's black hair led a life of its own and no matter how much she would stroke it back it would always escape out of the bun again. Or was it that Aunt Elli employed too few hairpins to get her exuberant gypsy-like hair under control? In any case Aunt Elli's cheeks were continually covered by black strands of hair as if by black chicken wings, and her way of walking too—with her feet turned inward—resembled that of a hen in a hurry.

Aunt Elli spoke an elegant Spremberg dialect and she liked to talk, and she was well versed in the customs and morals of the provincial town, and when they took an inspection tour through the village she admonished Uncle Phil, who was throwing stones into the village pond and in general taking part in our shenanigans: "Phil, take me arm and walk popper!"

"Popper" was pronounced in elegant Sprembergese fashion and meant "proper."

Aunt Elli didn't lack book-learning, as it's popularly called, but she found little time to read, and this is how she would tell the love story that had taken place between herself and our old friend Uncle Phil: "That's how it is: you're alone. You've made your MISTAKE, right?" (We kids looked at our likeable cousin, the MISTAKE.) "You look for a chance to redeem yourself and you pray to God, right? One fine day the Lord has mercy and he sends us our chance." (We looked at Uncle Phil, the messenger of the Lord.) "I felt so sorry for him, a man without parents in town. In the afternoons, after he'd slept long enough to recover from his night-time job" (the night-time job referred to Uncle Phil's hours of reading as a night watchman), "he'd look longingly into my window, right? It's summertime and it's warm, you know, and the window's open and you talk a little and you look each other in the eyes, right? One word leads to another but I'd never thought of marrying, until one night I gave him the bread anyway."

"What kind of bread, Aunt Elli?"

"The love bread, as they say, right?"

"There you've got it!" said Grandfather. "So he was standing there like a little beggar in front of the window because he'd frittered away all his money."

Aunt Elli defended Uncle Phil against Grandfather. Uncle Phil hadn't been a beggar. She hadn't handed him the bread with ground beef and onions through the window, because she knew

what was respectable, "right?" She had invited Uncle Phil into her room. "One thing leads to another, right? He came again and all at once we were in love."

Now we knew how love takes its course over bread with ground beef and onions and "throws a person in chains," as Aunt Elli was fond of saying.

That's how we unexpectedly inherited an aunt and a cousin in town, and thereafter it meant a black mark in Aunt Elli's book if we stayed in town with Mother's old friend—with whom she'd worked in the textile factory—instead of with our relatives, as it behooved a "popper" person, "right?"

We children distinguished between the uncles and aunts who had "always" belonged to us and those who had arrived after we were already busily swimming about in life, because their ARRIVAL seemed to have been determined by chance. For Uncle Phil could have married some girl from our village, one that Grandfather had found for him.

In fall we sowed the rye and in spring we planted the potatoes; we harvested the rye in summer and we harvested the potatoes in fall, and year after year there were straw piles in our fields and in fall there were bags full of potatoes standing by the potato fires in the fields—and that too—year after year.

And when the meadows had been hayed for the second time we let the cow and its new calf graze in them, and all that didn't bore us because it was life that was confronting us in its recurrent metamorphoses.

But we were bored by the village school and its curriculum that was repetitive all the five years long, because it didn't deal with life itself but with abstractions from life, and because it repels any man to be stuffed full with the same abstractions year after year. I wanted desperately to go to school in town, wanted, though I wasn't aware of it, to be confronted with new abstractions and stimulated to think my own thoughts, and I asked and begged for permission and finally my parents consented and I was sent to board with one of the friends of my Mother whom she had known when she worked in the factory. Mother's old friend and her husband were janitors in the municipal girl's school, and they lived in the basement of this institution, and my bed was set up in their bedroom.

Aunt Elli was offended: "Did you think their basement apartment was located higher up than ours? It would have been 'popperer' to have put up the boy with relatives, right?"

Right, right, but my parents didn't want to have me, too, living in Uncle Phil's and Aunt Elli's only room, and so to placate my aunt I would pay them visits now and then, especially because I found life in the washing and pressing establishment at the end of the Friedrichstrasse exciting and stimulating since part of my aunt's steady clientele was made up of girls of a certain profession. There were three of these professional houses in town and my aunt took special care with these ladies' laundry because it had to be cleaner than the underwear of the roomers and the "gentlemen lodgers."

These ladies of pleasure paid well and, as they say, they didn't turn every penny around twice; and the petty bourgeois turns his nose up at this and says: "Easy come, easy go"; and in those days I used to wish that their noses would stay turned up, and now that I think of it, I still do.

I, too, would get a little spending money from these ladies of pleasure when I happened to be visiting Aunt Elli and for that reason I visited her more and more often, so as to be there when the ladies picked up their laundry; and in this way I got to know all of the "approachable" ladies in town and they knew me. And when my uncle approached them for cigarettes or beer they would send me for wine to Bombel's Liquor Store because they didn't want to have anything to do with beer, and then later I'd be given a tip for getting the wine.

I got to know the new girls who came to town at the beginning of the month and I knew those who stayed longer and I knew this and that about their talents, for it hinged on these talents as to whether they would be engaged for longer than a month in their establishment; and I would greet those who stayed longer and I would greet those who had just arrived when I met them in the street, and I didn't pay any attention to the prejudices and horrified faces of my schoolmates. It even happened frequently that the girls would embrace me in the street and stroke my cheeks and kiss me and invite me to eat MERINGUES WITH WHIPPED CREAM in a café, and all that was so exciting, and the ladies of pleasure put my brain all in a whirl.

Aunt Elli had a didactic vein and I was an eager pupil; really, it looked as if she had entered the wrong profession and should have been a teacher. But life lets nothing escape that it has once set about doing and what life doesn't manage to accomplish in one generation it manages in the next. Perhaps our freedom—

our freedom as human beings—consists by and large in our being able to accelerate a little the pace of our intellectual development—the only thing that really matters in the end. In any event my aunt's daughter—my cousin, in other words—became in our age of many possibilities what her mother hadn't become, namely a certified teacher.

The unprotected end of the ironing board was singed all over and had burns that were light brown, dark brown and charcoal black—witnesses to the frequency and duration of the other jobs that Aunt Elli did in addition to ironing, because at this end of the ironing board rested the iron rack on which Aunt Elli would put the hot iron whenever she left the ironing board. Next to this rack there was a cup the size of a small chamberpot which contained coffee as black as ditch water and seasoned with a pinch of salt.

Grandmother reproached Aunt Elli for "throwing out piles of money" for this "black muck," as Grandmother called her coffee, and Aunt Elli justified herself: "You just don't understand that, Mother," and she pointed towards our work-shy Uncle Phil who was reading over by the window. "One man smokes and reads in order to raise himself a little out of the dirt, and another just drinks coffee, right?"

"What do you want to raise yourself out of the dirt for?" asked Grandmother. "That wouldn't agree with me. I'd really get dizzy doing that," and she spat in all directions as she always did when something didn't suit her.

Aunt Elli explained to me the individual parts of the under-clothing of those ladies who constituted her principal clientele: "So, this is a corset and it's only fashionable with women who find it necessary to push their stomachs in, right? And this here is a corselet and it's modern, and these are drawers, as you well know, and these over here are panties, the most modern of the modern." Then Aunt Elli spread out before me various kinds of bras and showed me their discreet padding and explained: "It's best when one doesn't need any of this, right?" She looked down along her flat pinafore and she drank down a gulp of coffee out of her big pot, and she sighed with pleasure after she had finished drinking and began to sing:

> "Oh, let me rest
> my head on your breast.

> Then she started to groan;
> but I ain't got one.
> What I had yesterday
> was made of hay.
> Then she started to roar:
> I won't do it no more."

Aunt Elli's singing too was like the clucking of a contented hen and she pattered back and forth along the ironing board, my poor aunt, and coffee spilled onto the starched dicky that she was just ironing. She ran in her flopping cloth slippers from the ironing board to the washtub which was always kept full of blue-gray suds and stood on the stove.

Aunt Elli tried to wash the coffee stain out of the dicky and she washed and rubbed for a while and she shuffled with the dicky over to the window and checked to see if the spot had disappeared, and while she did so she squinted with her eyes because she was short-sighted and finally she called me over to help and when I decided: "It's O.K.," she started ironing the "gentleman lodger's" dicky again, took another gulp of coffee and forgot about the dicky and rushed over to the stove and thrust a fork into the boiling potatoes in the oven. She tested how hot the other iron was that was heating in the opening of the space heater and then she stopped to reflect: "What was it I wanted to do?" and she remembered the dicky and she ran over to the ironing board and she saw the burn that the iron had made in the dicky, and she tore the iron away from the board, and she clapped her hands together over her head, stroked her hair—her black chicken wings—out of her face, took another gulp from her coffee cup, and threw the dicky into the fire.

There were always replacements for lost dickies like this, for there was enough laundry that had been left behind by GENTLEMEN LODGERS or roomers who had left town from one day to the next and hadn't found time to look after their earthly possessions.

Uncle Phil, who was just then staying home again from work pretending to be sick, sat unmoved by the window and took no part in the incineration of the dicky. He sat next to the commode, smoked and read and dwelt in far-away worlds. If it happened to be an exciting part of the trashy novel he was reading he would bend his index finger with the nail chewed down to the quick

and hold it under his left nostril and inhale the air excitedly and snort, and this snorting recurred at intervals of about half a minute and it lasted for as long as Uncle Phil's reading material retained its suspense. And when the plot of some dime novel didn't conclude to Uncle Phil's satisfaction, he would throw it against the wall, or the word-encased detective and his bankrobbers would clatter against a batch of flies that were just squatting down on the large framed photograph of Aunt Elli, which showed her in a condition prior to the MISTAKE. The little book dropped down, dropped onto the sewing machine table and from there onto a pile of freshly washed curtains and the squashed flies, too, dropped from the glazed photograph, dropped like black seeds of future vexation onto the white FINISHED laundry.

Uncle Phil immediately would start turning the pages of a new thriller, belch smoke and disappear in a blue cloud, like Pythia of yore, the fortuneteller of Delphi, who had disappeared from the Greek mountains in the smoke of her burning plaits.

At that time something happened in Cottbus, the neighboring county seat, that exceeded the theoretical horrors of Uncle Phil's thrillers: a girl, a student in the pre-school, had disappeared and she stayed disappeared, and the police investigated and investigated and only very gradually arrived at the conclusion that the caretaker of the school had "subjected her to immoral advances," as the two town papers considerately and turgidly informed the public; and he had felt a twinge of conscience after the "immoral advance" and had strangled the girl and cut the girl's corpse up into pieces and burned her in the school furnace.

The inhabitants of both towns and counties were horrified: a well-liked minor city employee had turned into a beast, had reverted to an animal state. Whom could one still trust? What class of people could one still count on as human beings without fear of being disappointed? What if suddenly all the minor city employees were to develop bestial characteristics and pounce on peaceful children?

In the patriotic newspaper that called itself *The Steel Helmet*, the fact that the caretaker was a member of the Social Democratic Party was seized upon as a ready occasion to warn readers of the "red peril" which paid homage to Darwin's teaching—the mistaken teaching that man was descended from the apes, in other words, from savage animals. *The Steel Helmet* also took

advantage of the opportunity to heap abuse on and discredit anyone whose views were politically to the left. In the Social-Democratic *Voice of the People,* on the other hand, the caretaker's bestiality was rationalized as the result of his fear of having to pay possible alimony, which a poorly salaried caretaker would not have been able to afford, and its discussion of the murder case culminated in the demand that the city administration kindly pay the lower grade municipal employees higher salaries, please.

My landlady, the wife of the janitor of the girls' school, wept and whined, and she called her husband, whose name was George but whom she—in the elegant speech of the county seat—called Georidge: "Georidge, if you was to cheat on me with some schoolgirl, I wouldn't know what I'd do . . ."

My landlord wiped the sweat off his bald head with a checkered handkerchief and said: "Ah, rot!"

In my aunt's laundry establishment, too, the sex murder was discussed thoroughly. Uncle Phil had just resigned from a job as storeroom clerk for a grocer because he wasn't allowed either to smoke or to read among the sacks of coffee and boxes of cheese; and now he was sitting at home and Aunt Elli had equipped him with a pail of water and set him in front of the curtain-stretching frames spiked with hundreds of sharp nails and made him sprinkle the curtains every now and then with water.

Aunt Elli ironed and took one gulp after another out of her big coffee cup, which every time was a signal for my uncle, the curtain watchman, to light up a new cigarette. Aunt Elli however talked with me—the docile nephew—about the sex murder.

"He made use of the girl; you know what that means, right?"

I nodded as if I knew all there was to know about raping girls.

"He made use of her and then he got scared and that made him go crazy and then he just did her in, right? . . . You know how that happens!"

My uncle, the specialist in all kinds of theoretical murder, interrupted; for in his opinion this was no case for provincial cops, no case for amateurs, it was a case for his serial-detective Harold Harst of "Scoootland Yard"—as he said—because it still hadn't been determined what the caretaker had used to strangle the poor girl with in the furnace room. To my Uncle Phil—who considered himself a member of Scotland Yard—it was obvious:

"He did her in with her own pigtails. Nothing simpler! What is man? Phlegm, callouses and water, vacant cavity upon vacant cavity—chemical value of 6.80 marks." Uncle Phil put his crooked index finger under his left nostril and snorted, for here suspense had arisen without the assistance of any reading matter, but Aunt Elli looked at him critically, took a big swallow out of her "ditch water" and said: "You just get busy sprinkling the curtains, Mister Scotland Yard, right?"

My thoughts wandered away from the murder case to a linguistic puzzle, for linguistic questions had fascinated me, because of my half-Sorbian ancestry, ever since I was a child. Here now I was interested in the double meaning of the sentence: "He made use of her." I knew that one made use of a person when one was in need, but here the helping verb "made" conferred a sense of instrumentality to the object of the preposition, in this instance of an instrument that had been employed and then thrown away. Beyond that it struck me that sexual making-use-of was something only men were charged with, never women. Mightn't there be women who made use of men? How was it, for instance, with my Aunt Elli? She was older (I don't know by how many years) than Uncle Phil and she was no longer the grandest of beauties, and she didn't have a hope that some man would come along who would raise her (with her MISTAKE that she was always mentioning) out of her living, cooking, ironing and washing quarters; and on the other hand, she wasn't old enough to be able to renounce love altogether. Hadn't she then, in her loneliness lured our down-at-heel Uncle Phil into her spider's web with steak tartare on bread in order to make use of him?

Perhaps that's how it was but Aunt Elli didn't make use of Uncle Phil like an instrument, and if she did, then she took care of the instrument, took care of it in view of those nights which she would otherwise have passed lovelessly, alone and full of longing; for although she didn't believe a word Uncle Phil said all day long, although during the day she viewed his actions with a critical eye, corrected him and tried to educate him, at night she believed for a whole hour long his sweet nothings, all his declarations of love, and the more pseudo-literary they were when they gushed out of Uncle Phil's virtually toothless mouth, the more credible they seemed to Aunt Elli.

Uncle Phil and Aunt Elli produced two children. The boy only

got to be half a year old but in Aunt Elli's stories he remained alive: "A little fellow like cream and honey, is all I can say, and what lovely little hands, right?" The girl lived and she turned into a fun-loving girl, and if you want to know how a canary sings, my cousin will show you, and if you feel like laughing at how this or that braggart or oaf in the village talks or walks, she'll show you that too. And if you want to know if she's still alive, I'll tell you: "Yes, she's still alive," and if you want to know where she lives, I won't tell you, because her husband is jealous. Aunt Elli allowed two children to be born although she couldn't count on Uncle Phil ever being able to feed even one; she allowed two kids to come into the world as witnesses to her happy hours during the night.

Every week a battalion of men would march up to the Employment Office of the provincial town, men in whose palms the callouses were coming loose, men who were unemployed, who stood in line and waited for the stamp that would officially confirm their blameless idleness.

It seemed like a miracle that my uncle should have got a job at this time delivering newspapers and magazines, but the reason for it was this: it would have been disgraceful for my aunt to know that my uncle was standing in an unemployment line, and so she, the owner of a laundry and ironing establishment, assumed the responsibility for making sure that whatever my uncle had contracted to deliver would be delivered as per regulation; she, as they say, stood bond for him.

Uncle Phil enjoyed delivering newspapers. He got into a lot of houses, and he saw this and that, and he found out in which houses on his route it wasn't quite "home sweet home" and he bragged of his knowledge, and in addition he got to know what women kept lovers and spent their time very pleasantly while the husband was in the factory and the children in school. All of this tickled my uncle's curiosity, and he gossiped a little here and a little there and took the chance to show off the wisdom he'd lifted from books and which he introduced by way of aphorisms, and some of the newspaper subscribers considered him an "educated man" who hadn't been intended "from the cradle on" to be a delivery boy, and my uncle had no objections about that, and did nothing to correct them when people considered him to be the victim of an unkind fate, and he pocketed the cigarettes which people gave him as consolation.

And in the taverns which Uncle Phil provided with newspapers he would now and then get a CHASER out of the glass that was used to trap the overflow from the beer spiggot, and when some generous steady souser was standing at the bar, my uncle would also get a shot of COTTBUS RYE out of a bottle into which the bartender had let the cork drop, and all this increased Uncle Phil's good humor and his gusto for life, and in all this Uncle Phil saw the proof that he was needed down on earth and that he was well liked.

But Uncle Phil wouldn't have been Uncle Phil if he hadn't tried to increase his pleasures in life, for however modest he was with respect to his clothing and cleanliness, he was immodest with respect to anything that he considered one of life's pleasures.

And Uncle Phil found an opportunity even as delivery boy to satisfy his lust for smoking and reading during the working hours: in the morning he would sit with his bag full of papers behind the hedges in Kaiser Wilhelm Square—for in spite of Ebert, the county seat still had a square by that name—sit down on a bench and read through for himself what he proposed to deliver to his clients, for it went against Uncle Phil's nature not to learn first-hand of the latest murders, and the name of this FIRST-HAND was the BERLIN MORNING POST, and after the MORNING POST the sun had risen and Uncle Phil really started to feel comfortable on his park bench and he would read other products of the Ullstein Publishing Company: THE CORAL, a monthly journal devoted to nature and technology. Uncle Phil read it down to the last advertisement: "Why don't you learn judo, the art of Japanese self-defence? The strongest opponent will fall victim to the edge of your hand! Toughen yourself up according to the instructions of our genuine Japanese instructor, Hukeiti Takayoto!"

After that Uncle Phil read the children's bi-monthly, MERRY FRIDOLIN. The pansies would smell sweetly in the flower beds and the blackbirds would chirp in the lilac trees and sometimes a nightingale would start out on one of her stanzas in the shade of a tree. Uncle Phil had it good. He was in fine spirits and he was smoking and he was reading. If by any chance one of his newspaper customers crossed the Wilhelm Square in the course of the morning, Uncle Phil would hand him his paper, but if it happened to be a barkeeper then Uncle Phil wouldn't hand him

his newspaper, for by means of this unceremonious manner of delivery Uncle Phil might have cheated himself out of a chaser of old overflow beer or out of a free shot of rye.

Sometimes it wasn't until early evening that Uncle Phil had provided all the subscribers with their copies of the morning paper and in this way he anticipated future conditions which have only been attained in 1970 in some of the villages in our Republic.

The shadows had already grown long and Uncle Phil took his delivery bag—which he really should have returned—along home. The agency had already closed for the day, so what do you want? And as it turned out, taking the delivery bag home also meant an increase in Uncle Phil's pleasures, a gift from God who seemed to love Phil greatly because Uncle Phil lived his life like the birds under the heavens and lilies in the fields. In the bag (who would have thought it?) there was enough reading matter for Uncle Phil's late evening hours: the YELLOW ULLSTEIN BOOKS, at one mark per book; Karl zu Eulenburg's MEN WITHOUT DESTINY, Vicki Baum's PEOPLE IN THE HOTEL, the first novel of a typist who was making a career for herself. Books with snappy titles like these helped to shorten my uncle's evenings agreeably, but when their contents, and especially their endings, didn't suit my uncle, then they too—without regard for their origins—flew against the wall of the room and received scratches and fly spots which naturally reduced their chances of being sold.

Of his salary as a newspaper delivery boy Uncle Phil rarely brought anything home, if you don't count the comic-grotesque masks which he bought for the whole family at Mardi Gras time; and if you disregard the foot-callous remover which some huckster at the fair talked him into buying; and if you also don't mention the walking-stick-umbrella combination which Uncle Phil bought for the autumn rains. But he didn't experience those rains any more as a member of the newspaper vending profession, for Uncle Phil, who, like every other person, represented a center of power, attracted these irregularities to himself, or both of these things happened, the former and the latter, as we must admit if we're to be honest dialecticians.

And it happened that Uncle Phil would return home more and more often merrier than MERRY FRIDOLIN, high as a lark on brandy or beer and belching smoke out of his nose and ears and

eager to jump into bed with Aunt Elli, at once if possible. Then it was awfully difficult for my hapless, tormented aunt to say no, because after all she understood that it wasn't merely she who liked my childlike uncle so much, but barkeepers were bewitched by him too and they had treated this bearded child to free beer again.

But the generosity of the barkeepers existed only in my uncle's stories. His heightened spirits and augmented libido were the result of the alcohol inherent in the beer and brandy which he had bought with the newspaper money he'd collected; for unfortunately among Uncle Phil's duties as newspaper delivery boy was the duty of collecting the monthly subscription fees.

The balance of debts not yet collected by Uncle Phil due to the intervention of a HIGHER POWER grew and grew, and it began to be noticed at the agency that a great many subscribers of my uncle's newspaper route were never at home. One day my aunt was requested by "registered letter" to appear at the agency and the wellspring of Uncle Phil's good humor and high spirits was stopped up, but my aunt, too, was deprived of her early evening pleasure, the only one which she still had except for her coffee. "No, I still believe that he really and truly loves me, right?" my aunt explained at the agency, and she also declared herself ready to take over the collection of the monthly subscription fees and she assumed responsibility for ensuring that Uncle Phil's debts would be liquidated.

My uncle's interest in delivering newspapers died away and all of my aunt's sermons and even those of my grandmother who had been called in to help weren't of any use, because Uncle Phil dedicated himself to being sick. That was always his escape when someone wanted to make him do something which he didn't enjoy doing any more. Now again it was Uncle Phil's hands that wouldn't function any more the way they should, and Uncle Phil showed them to everybody who wanted to see them: "Look at the knots of arthritis, like little billiard balls, what?"

Could Phil vouch for his actions with hands like that? Was it strange if these hands weren't able to distinguish something as thin as one newspaper from two or three exemplars of the same species?

With many of his customers my uncle had stuffed more newspapers into their mailboxes than they had ordered or wanted in order to finish up the bothersome delivery of the

newspapers as quickly as possible, because dragging his delivery bag around town spoiled his good mornings of reading. Let the subscribers divide the newspapers up among themselves and decide what belonged to whom.

My uncle's fingers actually did exhibit something like knots of arthritis, but nobody quite knew if these knots were new or already years old. As Uncle Phil told it, he got arthritis while working at the dyer's, and it seemed to be a kind of arthritis that varied according to my uncle's needs; in other words it grew worse when he wanted it to and it reduced poor old Phil to a pitiful cripple as soon as he found it necessary.

My aunt was seized with pity and from one day to the next she changed her life and in the mornings she hung the delivery bag over her shoulder in the agency and ran like a scared dwarf-hen through the streets and up and down the stairs of the houses. I met her once in a while when she was hurrying across the LONG BRIDGE or I met her near the post office which I had to pass on my way to school. The already grayish chicken wings—those disobedient strands of hair—hung down to her shoulders and her feet were turned inward and as she ran along they would get out of step with each other so that the poor hounded woman would stumble. "Oh God, my Phil" she called over to me with her breath whistling, "My Phil, you know, didn't deliver the newspapers popperly, right?"

I cursed Uncle Phil and used the expressions with which my grandfather belabored him: "lazy devil," "swine," but Aunt Elli immediately jumped to his defence: "No, now he's got arthritis; fair's fair, right?" and Aunt Elli was already rushing off, fearful that the kids, together with Uncle Phil, would be tearing their room apart during her absence.

So Uncle Phil stayed home as babysitter, and the kids would interrupt his reading least when he made them stay a long time in bed and when he gave them the iron, the rolling pin, starched men's shirt collars and a curtain so that they could play WEDDING in bed.

But finally the children were overcome by hunger and they threatened to leave their bed in the groom's collar and bride's veil. If a couple of marks were lying around the apartment which in her distraction Aunt Elli had forgotten to put into her purse, Uncle Phil would take them and carry them over to the pastry shop for meringues with whipped cream and Frankfurt coffee-cake, and he lived with the kids off the FAT OF THE LAND and

said to himself: "What do you get out of life otherwise, eh? What is man anyway? Phlegm, callouses and water . . ."

Meanwhile the water in the potato pot in the oven boiled away and the unpeeled potatoes quickly charred and gradually turned to ashes. Uncle Phil never peeled the potatoes. Peeling potatoes took away from his reading time and it deprived the children, as he explained, of the valuable potato vitamins located just under the skins.

Now Aunt Elli would do her washing and ironing in the evenings and at night, and while she worked she would drink black, salted coffee by the liter, and my uncle would lie in bed and read and snort and when he had finished a book he would coo at my aunt like an enamoured male guinea pig, and my aunt couldn't resist him, no, she couldn't resist him, and she lay down next to Uncle Phil . . . and when he was asleep, she got up again and washed and ironed for half the night and put the starched and ironed laundry in neat bundles on the ironing board and labeled the bundles: "For the lady from the WHITE HORSE"; or "For the gentleman who lives above Stoppras."

Uncle Phil was in charge of handing out the finished goods in his wife's business and when he ran out of SWEET GIRLS while reading and babysitting, he would take some open tobacco and use the labels from the laundry bundles as cigarette paper and make himself substitute cigarettes, and when the customers came to pick up their laundry Phil would get the laundry bundles mixed up and the customers would get annoyed and not come back.

Around this time it happened that while delivering the papers Aunt Elli got a splinter in her right hand while grabbing hold of a rotten staircase railing so as not to stumble over her own feet into the depths. At home she used the point of a pair of scissors to pull the splinter out of that part of the hand which is located right under the thumb and is called the ball, and she didn't pay any attention to the wound and that evening she put her hands into the grayish-blue lye water crawling with germs and containing the dirt of at least twenty-five customers, and she got an infection: blood poisoning.

The next morning she nevertheless ran with her papers up streets and down streets, up stairs and down stairs, and already she couldn't use her right arm any more and she distributed the newspapers with her left hand and then she ran home and washed and ironed with her left hand. Only late in the evening

did she go to bed and she lost consciousness and she died lying next to my uncle who, in his childlike belief in his own irresistibility assumed that my aunt had come to bed because of his amorous glances.

Aunt Elli's coffin stood in that part of the room where formerly stood the two chairs on whose backs the ironing board had rested. The wrinkles in my aunt's face had disappeared—probably because of the blood poisoning—and the undertaker's female assistant had tamed the eternally dangling strands of hair and her dwarf-hen's feet were concealed under the shroud. Aunt Elli's cheeks glowed faintly with pink and what caused this hue was known only by Death, who, disguised as a stubborn splinter, had lain in wait for my aunt in a stairwell. And suddenly we saw it, my sister and I: Snow White—our aunt as we had imagined her when we first heard about her from my uncle's lips.

That day my uncle didn't read. He behaved himself in a way that he must have read about many, many times: he grieved in the proper way—pseudo-literarily, and whenever anyone entered the room to extend his sympathy, he would pound his own chest with fistfulls of fingers chewed to the quick and he would pound himself on the forehead and he would wail like an abandoned dog, but this wailing, too, was just as phony as the one I heard many years later from the wailing women on the outskirts of Tbilissi. After his wails, which emerged five at a time from his throat, he would snort as he otherwise only did while consuming suspenseful reading matter, and after he snorted he kneeled down and kissed my aunt's poisoned hand, her forehead, raised himself up, pulled a pack of SWEET GIRLS out of his jacket pocket, opened it, lit a cigarette and thereby, in his own way, furnished the funeral incense, while I waited for his pat phrase: What is man. . . , but on this day my uncle seemed to have forgotten that phrase, a sign that his grief had caused some disturbance in his brain cells after all; and that was a consolation after everything that one had had to be an eye-witness to.

My aunt, however, looked past us with a tiny smile in the corners of her mouth and with her eyes closed, past all of us, past Grandmother, past me, past the smoking man whom she had made use of, and forward to, if nothing else, the death she had died.

AN EXAMPLE AND ME

ERNST BÖTTCHER

In order to get more skilled workers, the factory administration had come up with a new idea. They sent a circular letter out to all departments that skilled workers who took on a woman apprentice would receive a bonus. That bonus would be paid out when the woman came up to the specified work quota.

As is usually the case with new programs, not everybody volunteered at once; in fact, nobody volunteered. I wondered if I should take part. Sixty marks for the first month was nothing to spit at. There were women who wanted to qualify as skilled workers. I hesitated. And the other men were suspicious too.

"You'll never get rid of those broads again," said old man Morenz.

"There's sure to be a catch in it somewhere," warned another fellow worker.

I didn't go near the office. Because our old man would immediately grab me by the scruff of the neck and say: "Come on, as a party member you've got to give a good example."

Of course there were other party members too but I was the one he always picked on first; he knew that I couldn't say no. But we had to pick up our money in the office and nobody ever came late for that.

The old man must have been waiting for me. I went into the Union Office to pay my union dues. There he was sitting next to the shop steward who was collecting the money. If at least he hadn't pretended to be so pleased. "Man, Fatty, so there you are," he said. "Sure a long time since I've seen you in the office."

"But you recognized me anyway," I growled. The others grinned. I knew what they thought: Watch it, now the old man's got Fatty by the neck: now he's going to talk him into it.

The old man took me into his office and sent his secretary out. He didn't even try to make the thing palatable by talking first

about the 13th Plenary Session or the New Economic System. He even apologized to me as if I hadn't been able to sleep for days out of desire to take some woman on as an apprentice. "Don't be angry with me for not having talked with you earlier. But for a party member like you the whole thing's quite clear. What do you say, shouldn't you give them an example and get the show rolling? The factory manager, you know, has been calling me every day and wants to know what progress we've made with our women apprenticeship program. Today I told him that you were the first, and right up at the top of the heap again."

He had the gall to laugh right in my face while telling me this. So he had finessed me on that one all-right. And I couldn't even feel angry at this blond and rather excessively thin fellow.

I didn't say anything at first and let my head hang. Then I said: "Always me!"

The old man shrugged his shoulders and pulled a face. "Well, my boy, being party members puts an extra burden on us."

"Don't lecture me on top of it," I replied with a sigh.

"So you'll take on a female apprentice," he said expectantly.

"What kind are you planning to talk me into?" I asked.

"Tomorrow morning, Fatty. She's completely new. A young, really goodlooking girl," he said and winked.

After a restless night the new day broke and I went into the office with mixed feelings. The old man praised me to the skies. "Our Comrade Martach is a first-rate craftsman: conscientious, punctual and decent." He was speaking with extra emphasis because he knew I was standing right behind the slightly open door. I pushed the door open. "Ah, here he is already! Let me introduce you: This is Comrade Martach, and this. . .—what was your name again?—Of course: Miss Schulze, Rita Schulze."

A silly name, I thought, practically everybody was called Schulze. I sized her up from the side. I saw delicate hands, a black nest of hair that was twisted together on the top of her head. I cautiously shook her childlike hand and listened to see if no wind had come up outside that would blow away this little birdie like a rose leaf that's been plucked. The smell of perfume invaded my nose and I suddenly had to think of summer and green grass, and outside it was winter and damp and cold, and I of all people had to take her on.

"Mr. Martach, sir," she said like a child to the head teacher. I

went through the work area with her and thought: The best thing for you to do now is to go on six week's sick leave, then somebody else will get her. But then I thought that she would probably be better off with me after all. With old Morenz, for example, she wouldn't last long; he swore all day long and pretty unambiguously at that.

"You don't seem to be overjoyed, Mr. Martach, sir," she said.

I coughed. That "sir" stuff got on my nerves, but I didn't dare to ask her to be less formal. And the guys would laugh themselves silly if I were to say: "Miss Schulze, would you, if you don't mind, hand me the automatic cutter, please."

"Is it pretty formal around here?" she asked. And the way she smiled at me when she said that.

"No, we're all on a first-name basis," I said and thought: Why of all things do I have to have a name like Emil, a name out of the Middle Ages. The boys called me Minko or Fatty but this Rita girl wasn't going to call me Fatty.

"Emil?" she then said slowly. "Even though I've just met you I think you're really neat, Fatty. Please don't look so glum."

That "Fatty" really made me swallow hard but I made her a mental promise: We'll take that up again another time, Miss Schulze. After all I was in charge of the whole assembly.

At first I'd planned to let her sign her own "death warrant," that was the best way to get rid of her. But then later on I did drag the heavy chest of tools over from the check-out point to the boiler that we were supposed to tin-plate. I only gave her easy and simple work. I cursed myself for an ass because I caught myself looking around for her when she wasn't working right next to me. I felt really happy when I'd see her then somewhere on the boiler working away with her lower lip between her teeth and using the drill as if she'd never done anything else. Then she laughed and winked with an eye, and I turned around quickly again.

The job was a lot of fun, she said after three days. That it was fun for me to have her around as well, I wouldn't admit to myself. I didn't say anything at all to the boys about it. They thought I was really weighed down with a heavy burden and they were amazed at my patience. That's why I didn't praise Rita either: so that nobody else would have his appetite whetted. And she didn't want to believe that I was only twenty-six and still single.

Probably the right one just never crossed my path. One fine day she took my work jacket along and darned a hole and sewed a button on.

But soon the boys would always be hanging around near us. Some bugged her. The sixteen-year-old quality controller would be around our necks six or seven times a day. He acted like he was checking up on our boiler. But I noticed at once that he was checking Rita's sweater with his eyes. I only looked when nobody else was looking.

We ought to celebrate a little with the first bonus, she suggested.

I needed about an hour to get dressed; my tie just wouldn't fit right. I waited for her in front of the tavern. When she finally came, I felt like beating it. She hid her embarrassment and fixed my tie as if we'd been going out together for years.

"Well, Fatty," she said.

I coughed and took a look around. I didn't see any familiar faces. She peeled out of her coat at the coat check-room inside and I felt my knees go a little weak.

"I've never had so much fun on a job as with you, Fatty," she said.

I nodded and turned my wine glass in my hand.

"Are you satisfied with me?" she asked.

I nodded to myself. Now and then I'd look at her out of the corner of my eye in order to see her in her water-blue skin-tight knit dress with the pink scarf shimmering at the neck. I sat quite still and thought of my grandmother who had always gently scratched my neck when I was a boy.

After the fifth glass of Balkan Fire she said: "Every place I worked at before there were men who wouldn't leave you in peace. For some of them life is a kind of self-service store in which you can get girls just like cocoa or cigars."

I nodded to myself.

"But you're so different, almost funny," she said.

I saw the old man in my thoughts. "You've got to give them an example, Comrade."

And now I was sitting next to the example and I felt that I just wasn't up to it.

ON THE ROAD

WERNER BRÄUNIG

At any rate: we're off. There are the transport papers, there's the thermos bottle, here's the Autobahn. It's ten o'clock; this is the weather report. Reality and illusion, and so on.

In fact: it's raining. It's been raining since Zwickau, it let up a little before Leipzig, started up again at the Schkeuditz intersection and now it's beating down on the Elbe. The soporific sound of the windshield wipers, the monotony of the road. Just now Karl was thinking: if only I had somebody riding with me. My dear, my all too dear colleagues. And now—there was something standing at the edge of the Autobahn with a little suitcase next to it, standing there with a kerchief on and a little coat to keep out the rain that was whistling through the pines; and that was in the middle of the Flaeming. All around nothing but woods and heath. Nothing but pine trees and rain and sand and wind. Karl had his foot on the clutch already. Never before in his life had he seen a hitch-hiker in this part of the country.

She pushed her little suitcase up and climbed in. Karl said: "Hey, you'd better wring yourself out first." He started the truck moving. The trailer was pushing, there was a slight downslope on this stretch.

Sitting there in one of those sweaters, combing her hair; well, OK. How does a person get to this neck of the woods? You get out of a car or you're gotten out of it. There must be reasons for it, no doubt. The Flaeming is a slightly vaulted part of the southern land mass, formed during the ice age, relatively thinly settled, an area of pine forests. That's still floating in your memory. All sorts of things float around in your memory. And she'll start talking eventually. How about a cup of coffee, for instance, seeing as how the weather is what it is? She screwed the cup off the flask, drank in little swallows and said: "Not bad." For the moment she

193

didn't say any more. She only glanced at him sometimes from the side. That went on until they got close to Niemegk. Then Karl asked: "Where do you actually want to go?"

Just north, further north: that was, you might say, an answer of sorts. Rostock or Helsinki, who knows. Besides, she seemed to be bothered by something. Maybe some kind of trouble: who could tell? Cheer her up a little, if you only knew how. For example by singing, if you could sing. She could really put ideas into one's head, this one.

Or like this: once upon a time there was a guy whose fellow workers sent him off to study and in return during the summer vacation he went to work for three weeks in the outfit, to give his fellow workers a chance to have a vacation themselves. Now the outfit happened to be a transport firm, and it so happened that on his first trip this fellow was to bring two transformers from Zwickau to Magdeburg, this time without any return freight but with lots of speed. So he drives off and in Magdeburg he discovers to his great joy that the people there can use only one of his transformers. He calls up Zwickau: a little misunderstanding. The second transformer has got to go to Rostock. So our guy's off to the Baltic. When he gets there it's almost night and in that company nobody knows what's going on, but anyway after three hours they find an empty bed for him. Next day it turns out that they really are desperate for a transformer—but for a different model. Now Mr. Philipp Reis' invention is put into operation again.* For quite a while nobody knows what to do; they talk about driving back and then they change their mind, because for instance Eisenhüttenstadt is waiting for a transformer and it really wouldn't be that much of a detour from there. The rest is incredible but solidly vouched for. In Eisenhüttenstadt they did in fact need this particular model of transformer, except that they had already received one three weeks ago. Let's not go into the scene that our fellow made the next day back at his firm. Let's only say: from then on of course he had a nickname. Odysseus. Odysseus Meyer. Although his name was actually Karl. And isn't that really nice?

Anyway: she smiled. And said, if the story isn't true, at least it's imaginative. And wanted to know what Mr. Odysseus' major was. For her part she was studying architecture.

---

*In the GDR Reis is thought to be the inventor of the telephone.

Rain, hellish rain, filthy road. No: she hadn't asked about Penelope. The trailer looks pretty funny in the rear-view mirror. A Wartburg** passes by and some guy with a hat makes some signs that were no doubt meant to be very clear. Off the road and to the edge of the woods, out into the rain. What a mess!

She looked out of the cab and asked if she could help. "Not that I know of," said Karl. Put up the warning sign, got out the tools. But she came climbing out anyway. Had her kerchief on again, had put on Karl's old thick canvas jacket and rolled up the sleeves: an astonishing sight. And while Karl went to get the spare tire out of the truck, she had already set up the jack. Put it in at the right place. Karl loosened the nuts, she unscrewed them. Incidentally, she said, her name was Sabine. Work, so they say, brings people closer together: that's true. And now she had the obligatory grease stain on her face and helped to pull off the old tire and put the new one on. She did it just like that. Naturally Karl asked if she had done something like that before, maybe on a car. She smiled and said: "Not that I know of."

That was in the vicinity of Beelitz, and they were both wet to the skin. Somewhere they got themselves back into a semblance of order and warmed up a little. Then they passed by Potsdam on the right, and Nauen as well, they ate lunch in Oranienburg. Although Sabine said that she didn't feel quite at ease in this part of the country. "I know—it's foolish. But always when I see people over forty in Weimar, for example, I always wonder: they had that concentration camp*** right in front of their noses and they can't say that they didn't know anything about it. But what was going through their minds back then and what, in heaven's name, is going through them now?"

Yes: there are things that one knows and still doesn't understand—perhaps doesn't want to understand. There are things which one can see and test and still can't comprehend. There is this girl, Sabine, and her case is as follows:

I was little and prayed near the water. It belonged to me and its name was the Rhine. . .

That was childhood. Then came the move into another city where everything was strange, into another country, and as it turned out later, into another world. When she was ten years old,

---

**A model of car manufactured in the GDR.
***The concentration camp Buchenwald was located very close to Weimar.

Sabine found out what that word "camp" really means. When she was thirteen, she went to visit Buchenwald with her school class. And now she knew what had happened to her father three months before she was born in that March of the year forty-five. Later on there was a time when she felt ashamed that she owed the advantages she received in this country to his death—she who hadn't done anything and hadn't prevented anything, because she hadn't even seen the light of day before he died. Probably from that time on the course of her life changed. She became more serious, stricter and sometimes, she now realizes, unjust. When her civics teacher talked about the "new, peaceful Germany," she embarrassed him by remarking: It doesn't mean there's peace just because people have stopped shooting. She worshiped Fidel Castro and Ernesto Che Guevara. She attacked those who were luke-warm, and that made her friends forever; but she attacked the careful ones even more fiercely, and that isolated her from most people. A few weeks before she was to graduate she distributed leaflets throughout her school that she had drawn up herself containing what were later called "sectarian and revisionist demands." During the subsequent investigation, she accused several teachers: "You're always talking about the struggle in order to hide all the more the fact that you're not doing anything yourself." She had applied for admission to the School of Architecture because her father had been an architect—she passed her general exam for graduation with a grade of "excellent" but she was informed that her application was turned down "for lack of study space." She grew distrustful and embittered.

Then a man turned up who had known her father in the camp. For a long time she had tried to find people who could give her information and supply the missing parts of the image in her mind, because she wanted to be like him: "Somebody who doesn't knuckle under; somebody whom you can rely on in the thick of battle without having to worry if he'll run away or desert or shoot you in the back." That was precisely the kind of image that Ernst Runge painted of her father—and yet it was different from what she had imagined until then: not so aggressive, not so heroic, grander. "He was a helpful and profoundly happy man up to the very end," said Runge—that was a touch that didn't seem to fit into her image of the anti-fascist struggle. About what he called her guerrilla attack in school, Runge said: "But, my

dear girl, we're not living in the Wild West here." Then her distrust welled up again. Even so she followed his advice and went to work for a year in a chemical industrial combine; Runge was head of the electrolysis section there. At first she was aloof and kept to herself. But after a few months she began to realize that this was a world into which she had never been really able to enter before. She suddenly understood what it means for somebody to work all his life long, frequently even in a profession that doesn't fully satisfy him. She found entry into a world in which day after day chlorine, carbide, or some sort of aluminium is produced, frequently under severe strain, and many a worker does more than he has to, worries about the production figures, about political work, union matters, job-skill improvement, even culture. For fifty years and more he gets up early in the morning, comes home in the evening, family, children, responsibilities, three weeks vacation per year and the weekends: that's the salt of the earth, that's what we live from. She talked about it with Runge. For the first time she had the feeling of really belonging somewhere and being useful. But here too she soon discovered contradictions: the transport foreman, a man who was capable of hard work and whose crew was always way ahead in the work competitions, told her bluntly that they had already managed to bring "quite a few wild-eyed revolutionaries to reason. As far as I'm concerned, the real thing is work, nothing but work, everything else is crap." They often got in each other's hair. When he was supposed to give an estimate of her performance in the brigade, he described her as intolerant and arrogant. Sabine had almost expected that—but she didn't understand why nobody in the brigade objected to that evaluation. She lapsed into a kind of paralysed indifference. She didn't even renew her application to the University. When he found out about it, Ernst Runge, otherwise always so sensible, got angry: "Who taught you to throw the towel in like that? Besides: the man has five kids and a sick wife; you're judging him just as superficially as he judged you. And the reason why the brigade didn't speak up in your behalf is because they know how hard he's got it and how you didn't stop to consider this." Sabine could only say: I didn't know that. Exactly, said Runge. And he showed her the written evaluation in which all that was left of that "intolerant and arrogant" was a mere "she sometimes judges too hastily." Runge also drove over with her to the

entrance examination. That's how she came to go to the University. . .

"Yes," said Karl, "I can understand that."

"Odysseus," she said, "I don't know; I don't understand it myself completely any more."

And then the road again, the main highway between north and south, and rain again. Who taught you to be modest? Yes, Karl understood a lot. When he returned to this job after his first year in the University, his pals at work wanted to know how he'd done. Three A's, five B's and one C—that's good enough for me. "So," Merten had said, the man who had introduced him to the mysteries of automotive repair, "so, a C's good enough for you. Who the hell taught you to be modest?" Yes, there were all sorts of parallels. Even if you had traveled a completely different road. That's how things are.

Anyway: architecture. And as was almost to be expected she had met somebody at the University who really seemed to be all of a piece. He didn't take anything back. He did what he said he'd do. He admitted it when he didn't know something—even though he was an instructor. He didn't start to stutter when he was asked touchy questions. He managed to get done what he believed was worth getting done. He had the right people behind him and there were a lot of those: and he had the right people against him and of those there weren't many.

His name was David Kroll and he got where he wanted to get. And of their love there was no end. David Kroll and Sabine Bach don't, to be sure, announce their engagement—engagements are petty bourgeois—they only say: look, friends, this is how it is with us. It was an unheard-of autumn, a fantastic winter, and only the spring wasn't quite up to par anymore. For he wrapped her up in silk and satin—there was nothing to be said against it. I love you. I need you. And only one thing, unfortunately, did he neglect to ask: namely, what *she* needs, what *she* expects from life, what *she* wants to make of herself in our world. Unnoticeably but irresistibly she saw that he didn't ask her—he took her. He ordered her life, he protected her; she stood at his side with her arms hanging. Nothing was good enough for her as far as he was concerned, and she changed her mind about some aspects of his steep, straight career after she noticed what unlimited resources his father had—the National Prize winner and city

builder. A cool summer. He heaped attentions on her, tenderness, he wanted her wholly for himself and yet he lost her.

They had planned for months to take advantage of the summer vacation in order to take a leisurely tour of the coast, to investigate and discover for themselves what had struck them as absolutely worth seeing in the books they had read during the winter: North German architecture, Backstein Gothic. They were already sitting in his Wartburg. They were already on the Autobahn. Baby, better watch it or things might go wrong. It simply isn't the right weather. It will probably be pretty difficult to find a room somewhere. (Didn't they have a tent in the trunk?) And look, he had the key to his father's—the National Prize winner's—amazing vacation house in his pocket. Finally we'd really have some time to ourselves, we'd finally be alone, we'd have peace and just about everything that we need. Then she asked him to stop. Then she got out. He stood out in the rain for a long time, tried to make her change her mind, didn't understand anything, didn't even lose his temper, not even that, and finally drove on. What else could he have done? What else could anybody do?

And this now is Neubrandenburg, the parting of the ways. The Stargard Gate and other gates. The old city wall. All sorts of new things too, all sorts of things worth seeing for a girl who had gone off just to get to see this area and its buildings and who knows what else.

"Well," she said. "Here we are."

"Yes," he said.

"Well, take it easy." She hesitated. "And thanks for the ride."

"Cut it out," he said. "My pleasure."

Saw her still standing in her short coat, one of those girls on the highway, waved once more, stepped on the gas. This is highway F96, it's three o'clock in the afternoon, the show's on the road. A dot on the side of the road, growing distant now in the rear-view mirror. Sabine Bach, Weimar, the Architectural Institute, he thought. Think it'll get there?

ONE VILLAGE AND MANY VILLAGES

WOLFGANG BUSCHMANN

I'd like to say a few things about life and this is how I'll begin: there are lots of organizations that are set up according to their purpose and special function: a society for classical antiquity, a stock company, a wedding party—and then human society in general as a separate category, and (this is something philosophers should pay attention to) as something living and breathing. Along with the requisite accommodations to live and breathe in, like ministries, banks, notary offices, registry offices, law courts, theaters, hospitals, car agencies, schools and smaller institutions. Included in the last category are—to give an example—public toilets. About which people naturally smile but have no reason to. Because doing it in the middle of the market place would be a public nuisance. Then the police would come.

So: order, organization and system down to the last detail, a labyrinth with road signs: that's society. In which you move and are moved. Something that's—from the point of view of space and time—Grand. You can't argue against that. We're only adding and padding a little bit here: that society is something small too. Something intimate. Not what you usually mean by intimate between a man and a woman, but rather peace of mind and security.

Alois Tuchscherer is sitting at the table and reading the paper. To be precise: the classifieds. To be more precise: the marriage ads. Since this sort of ad is divided by sex—like man and beast and the dioecious plants too—he's reading the female marriage ads. He's reading black on white: mature unmarried woman, one meter eighty, reliable, seeks acquaintance of suitable companion for marriage.

Alois looks down at himself and decides: he isn't suitable. He's one meter sixty tall, not specially attractive, rather skinny, with arms that are disproportionately long and legs that could be called straight only by somebody who is cross-eyed; by profession a railway signalman, hence the uniform with the red stripes. And single, otherwise he wouldn't be continuing to read: decent, warm-hearted woman, domestic and hard-working, wishes to get to know a loving gentleman. Yes, Alois says to himself, yes, and he opens the drawer, puts some paper on the table and thinks it over. And now, when he's finished thinking it over, the bureaucratic machinery is set in motion; modern and most discreet. You write to a number via the office that takes the ads, to a number that later on, if all goes well, you'll marry. For lack of opportunity.

On Wednesday the answer is in the mailbox. The woman's name is Olrun Wendrock and she lives in Mauersberg.

To get to Mauersberg you take the Annaberg bus through a number of villages. There are twenty-four houses there, including two inns. One of the inns is called "The Green Linden Tree," though there's a birch tree growing in front of it, and from it there's a path leading uphill, straight as an arrow to a house that stands by itself, a solitary house just like the woman who lives there. Just right for Alois; it gives him time to collect his thoughts.

What's he going to say? Then the door opens, quite suddenly, and a woman steps out into the doorway. And Alois says: How do you do? Then the door closes again. Alois has vanished behind the door. Pretty simple, wasn't it?

But for us it gets harder. Through the keyhole would be indecent if somebody caught us in the act. Likewise through the window and even worse through the wall. The walls have ears to hear your own shame. We don't much like to hear our own shame. Since from the political point of view this is an internal affair anyway, we'll rely, I think, on public opinion. Pietsch, the mailman, is public opinion. He delivers letters and newspapers, of the kind that are printed and of the kind that he issues directly out of his mouth.

Frieda Bischinski or anybody else in the village who is peeling potatoes of a morning in front of the house sees the yellow mail-bicycle coming towards them. It's an exercycle, as those bikes with the turned-up steering bars are called, and the

packages are dangling from it and Pietsch the mailman is sitting on top, pedalling away with regular movements and keeping a kind of orthopedic posture. When he arrives, he leans the bicycle against the wall of the house, opens his leather bag and pulls out letters and newspapers. While he's handing over the letters, he talks about the weather, and progresses—rather skillfuly—from this subject to the real point of interest.

That happens as follows: first he says: nice weather we're having today. Then he drops a word which, by bridging one thought with another, allows him to shift the scene, down to the lower half of the village about a kilometer away. Since you can't tell at that distance if it's raining there, he gives his report: it's nice weather down that way too—for after all he's been all over by this time today. The next intellectual gulf isn't that wide, so an associational bridge would be a waste. So Pietsch the mailman puts three good solid boards across it: the weather's good for the flowers, first board. At Alois' place the gladiolas are already blooming, second board. Then the third board, so that everybody can get across safely: by the way, Alois Tuchscherer is off a-wooing. Now Frieda Bischinski gets an earful and, if we pay attention, so do we.

That is, he's not exactly wooing. To be sure, Olrun, who's supposed to become his wife, has moved into the signalman's house and wanted to get married right away, but Alois stalled and said: For the time being, a symbiosis—an expression we owe to Schypulla, the teacher—a symbiosis is enough.

Symbiosis? a puzzled Frieda Bischinski asks. That's just what Pietsch the mailman was waiting for and he explains it graphically and—so everybody thinks—better than the teacher: Symbiosis is a love affair between a toad and a toadstool—they're living together but the registry office doesn't know about it officially yet.

You live together, you eat together, it's what is called a common-law marriage. That takes care of the biological end of things. Everything together from now on. Emphatically so, I insist. The main thing is to satisfy the material and cultural needs, things that the state, too, undertakes to support.

Since we accept the primacy of matter, we'll start by preference with the material needs. Just what they are is debatable. Whether they include a T.V., washing machine, revolving chair or the progressive short skirts that only reach down to who

knows where—I for one don't know of any greater need of this kind than an automobile. You can never tell what else will still be needed, but today it is an automobile. That's what they call this need, until they satisfy it anyway; afterwards it's a car.

So Alois wants to buy an automobile and, all excited by it, has to tell Olrun about it when he appears again in his signalman's house. If the journalists had anything to say about it, he'd now have to say: Olrun, we want to satisfy our material needs. But nobody says that. That would mean ignoring the realities of life. So Alois says just as he comes into the room: Olrun, great to have an automobile, eh?

I don't know, Olrun replies and wants to start telling him about all sorts of fatal accidents when Alois interrupts her gently and diplomatically, sure that she'll agree: A real bargain, a once in a lifetime deal, belongs to Waldane.

Next day Waldane drives up in it. An old heap, Pietsch the mailman says, looking over the fence. But that's just his envy talking—him with his bicycle. And Waldane, the businessman, doesn't have much time. Fills out the bill of sale, two or three words of advice, hop in, it's easy as pie, have a good trip, he's off.

So there now is the automobile standing in the middle of the yard and without any set of directions. The body's red, four wheels with spikes, one spare screwed on in back, Dixi model, built in 1923. And the driving test is twenty-five years back, always hoofing it up to now. Let's see what the encyclopedia has to say, Alois says and leafs through the reference work under A, Australia, Austro-Hungarian Monarchy, Automobile: Greek, from auto meaning "self," see Autobiography and Autodidact. That's all just academic. An automobile doesn't just drive itself. You'll notice it's got a dashboard in front with lots of knobs and switches—almost as many as a telegraph office.

And today, Saturday, the test drive.

With the tank filled up, Olrun and Alois sit in the shag covered seats. O.K., Alois, you can start.

Alois shifts into first gear, lets the clutch out, a little jolt forward. Driving is terrific. Up the village street all by itself, past the firehouse, then along the long boulevard with the cherry trees on each side, noisy with birds. The landscape pushes past as if it was flying, trees, houses. Until the road—what's the matter with the road?—ends in turns and twists. With teeth clenched and hanging on for dear life around the first curve. Step

on the brake, you feel like shouting to Alois. But he doesn't need to brake anymore. The car's stopped already, against a tree. A maple tree, I think. The doors open; Alois appears, black and blue around the eyes, and Olrun with a scratch, and Alois says in profound agreement with his life's companion: the car's got to go—it's a menace.

In our view, that's a wise decision they've made. Now they'll have more time for their cultural needs. But if anybody thinks that's much less risky, then he's dead wrong. If only because of the prejudice. Even Pietsch the mailman, by profession mailman and honorary cultural officer in the village, calls the theater a place to satisfy cultural needs—since we are talking so much about needs—when you need to go. But anyway Pietsch the mailman doesn't have the faintest idea about culture beyond theater tickets. He says: *Egmont* was written by Goethe when we all know it's by Schiller. He ought to be deposed, but who would deliver the tickets in that case?

So he stays in office and approaches Alois' house with a bundle of placards under his arm, bicycle-less and with long honorary steps, and speaking abruptly as is his wont on such occasions. Door open, two theater tickets, door closed.

What's being put on? Olrun inquired from the kitchen. *Hamlet,* by some unknown.

No matter, unknown or not, Olrun and Alois are going anyway. The theater's educational, so everybody says after all.

Next Sunday four and a half hours' education. To put it in a nutshell: To be or not to be, that is the question here.

And the fencing scenes are the high-point. Then there's real action on stage. Up and at 'em, my Prince. They're fencing. A hit, or so it appears. Until Laertes kills Hamlet. As he does the murderous deed, Olrun lets out a shrill scream and yells: Oh, my God! Everybody turns around. Alois gets red in the face and angry and says: You embarrass a man—never again to the theater with you.

But Alois, how can you say that? Especially to your wife.

No, "wife" is wrong. Wife means an entry at the registry office, a tax deduction and such-like formalities. Wife frequently still isn't understood properly; nor is husband. And I didn't want to talk about it in the usual, every-day sense anyway. What I did want to say, I've forgotten myself.

But I remember it right off when I see Alois coming out of the

laundry shack, with his railwayman's uniform covered by a flowery apron. In front of him he's carrying a mountain of laundry, that is, thirty centimeters in front of the apron (because he isn't used to the apron and he actually could rest the basket with the laundry up against his body without any problem, since after all the apron is there to protect his clothes)—anyway, the mountain of laundry in front of him: stockings, socks, pants to put over same and under same, handkerchiefs, bras, only for under, and slips for under dresses. You'd hardly believe it possible: real slips that he's washed and now is hanging up on the line. As he does so, he considers the lunch menu. And what is that menu, Alois? Hot cereal, says Alois and, with the shopping bag in his hand, he goes off to buy the cream of wheat, the cinnamon and the sugar, and all the other fixings.

What's happened to Olrun? Frieda Bischinski asks.

She's sitting in an easy chair with a book on her knees and can't find her way among all the Latin phrases. Placenta and all that other Latin stuff.

What's the meaning of all that? Frieda Bischinski asks the mailman further. Don't you know? Pietsch the mailman says. Something's on the way over there. Oh dear, oh dear, Frieda Bischinski shouts and shouts it out very loud because she's hard of hearing: His brother from Munich must be coming and Alois wants to fix everything up nice. No, no, the mailman says, it's the stork.

Oh, him, says Frieda Bischinski who isn't exactly fast on the uptake and still hasn't grasped what I want to say and what I'm concerned about. Oh, him, she says again and means Mr. Stork from the Life Insurance Company.

THE SECOND DESCRIPTION
OF MY FRIENDS

FRITZ RUDOLF FRIES

When I introduced chubby Margot (Margón, according to Villon) to them last evening, I didn't think twice about it. Margot dragged me through town and I dragged her hither and yon, to friends, into exhibitions, so why not into this apartment that I hadn't seen yet. They offered her a seat—leather and foam rubber, revolvable like a carrousel—and she immediately and unabashedly proceeded to examine the four walls of the place. She had difficulty sitting still anywhere; she only stopped a moment to look at Richard. Richard pulled his stiff leg off the hassock and the mechanical joint in the knee clicked, and there was a tiny pause in the conversation. That is, we couldn't manage to get a conversation going. Each one sent out a couple of sentences and hoped that somehow, somewhere, they would link up into a conversation. I was sitting next to Regine—it just happened that way—and we were able to talk facing sideways, in broken phrases. It was the first time that I'd been in their new apartment and they expected me to show rather more curiosity than I felt like showing, since they did have the new furniture and in the next room they had their new baby. Regine looked healthy and glowing with the happiness of being a mother again. And Sabine too would have changed in the meantime; she was going to school and she woke up nights when the baby screamed. The new baby had arrived according to plan, after they had moved; it was a boy and they had given him a name that I didn't seem to be able to remember. Exotic but somewhere out of the latitudes between Greenland and Labrador; who knows what book they read on their vacation gave them the idea.

Now, in the morning, I realize that the real reason why we couldn't get a conversation going was because they were put off

the moment they saw us. Margot had said that she was living in a dormitory and so they probably thought we had only come by in order to sleep with each other here. Because after ten o'clock in the evening the supervisor checked under the beds and in the closets, and I had no desire to play hide-and-seek with him. Now in the morning they're sitting without us in the kitchen: early Monday morning when you're still lazy and stupid from sleep and the autumn cold. They're now showing that they're hurt and that makes them simultaneously defenceless, lacking the weapons they had yesterday as hosts. The baby is getting its bottle; Sabine is chewing her bread with honey and studying Margot's appearance. Regine and Richard say, do you want some coffee, and we're standing at the door and say, no, we don't want any, we've got to go, and then we take two steps across the gleaming kitchen floor in order to say good-bye. I'm sure they must have a cleaning woman who makes things spic and span for them while the baby is in the day-care center; Sabine in school; Regine driving in her official car through the various city districts and inspecting kindergardens; Richard weighing the employees of the German Railways and drawing their attention to the start of an overweight problem. As if being fat, it occurs to me, could interfere with punching tickets in a train. That too was something we talked about yesterday, about improved methods of early diagnosis, a warning service that would put an end to a dozen diseases that would otherwise feed and multiply on the excess fat. Richard had listed the endogenous and exogenous factors and used the technical term—adiposity—and Margot laughed at that as if it was a joke and stopped and looked at Richard. And Richard found it hard not to look at her the way he looks at the girls from the Railways as he sits behind his desk in his white coat and the next patient in line is standing in front of him and exposes her heavy breasts, and Richard examines the roll of fat that's making her waistline disappear, examines it with his big heavy hand which he otherwise uses to lean on pieces of furniture and railings because he uses his walking-stick only in the street. I see that scene in my mind's eye though she isn't fat enough yet to be treated by Richard.

We had arrived after dark and so I hadn't been able to see much of the neighborhood, part of the western suburbs, part of our childhood for Regine and for me. I went to the window; it's one

of my idiosyncrasies always to look out of the window first in every apartment as if people only moved into an apartment because of the surroundings and not because they needed more room for a growing family or more comfort with growing prosperity. I could live for half a year sometimes, and even longer if I hadn't sold a picture, on what according to my calculations the two of them earned in a month. I still can't make up my mind to take on an amateur painting class, though Richard could arrange something like that for me. I'm sure the employees of the German Railways paint in their spare time; the onset of fat surely doesn't prevent them from doing that. On the contrary. Fat people are contemplative people. But I won't let my cousin's husband do me any favors. In a state that survives without nepotism, I don't want to make a beginning of it. Maybe it's just that I suspect the motives of railway employees who have seen too many faces, train after train, to be able to summon up enough patience for an individual portrait. And what does the archetypal traveler in our country look like? There are probably different species, I know, that vary according to the season and the landscape. Halle-Leipzig at the end of a work-day, or Berlin-Carlsbad. I've painted a picture of a family about to start off on a vacation, with their baggage stowed away in the train, a year's work in their faces and in the woman's the marks of over-work, family, preparations for the trip. That picture was recently shown at the big district exhibition; it was hanging somewhere off in a corner and none of the critics paid any attention to it. But maybe it's only because I've got something against traveling. Sometimes the view from the window is enough for me. It isn't easy for my fat Margot to drag me all over town when I come for a visit. Towards evening along the Elster Canal when the trees have silhouettes like in Beardsley's pictures. Or the little mermaid at City Hall, or the park downtown, the main post office, or more than anything else the covered passage-ways that filter the light so strangely and lure the passer-by into an indefinite past. That's how I've developed certain habits when I'm in town, habits on which Margot can rely.

I don't think that visiting this apartment is going to turn into a habit. Sitting on her chair Margot turns around so quickly that she has to push the hair out of her face. Once we hitch-hiked together for four days to Budapest. On the third day we got off

the main road into a village where a fair was being held. She would have slept with the hawker if he'd given her the carrousel. I shove my foot forward and try to stop Margot. It's true, she does behave pretty naively, as I notice especially tonight. I let Regine tell me about the neighborhood in front of the window. Here they don't have a courtyard in back anymore as they had in the old apartment; no coffin-maker's at the corner that in the summer would be veiled in impressionistic green by a tree. Out of the dampness of early autumn glistens the window of an indoor swimming pool which the city council erected on the site of the old water tower—the tower that in our childhood was for us an imaginary equivalent of the Eiffel Tower. Out of the second window in the living room, she said, you could see the two buildings that made up the school which we had attended for all eight grades; the gray dust of the courtyard, during recess the children, and in front near the fence the outhouse, painted green, and further to the left, half blocked from view, that pavillion-like building where they had collected old things for recycling for the Total War: bones and rags. Invisible, subterranean were the cellars, the last protection when there was an air raid. And in the first building the rooms on the ground floor where after '45 the People's Union had its meetings. There our mothers had gone to pick up their ration cards, the coupons for wood and coal and for ersatz materials, after the Block Leader was gone because the Americans had locked him up.

Our mothers were further up in the cemetery, squeezed in between a construction company and a factory so that there isn't much room left for the dead. The cemetery administration is economical and deposits them side by side; they prefer cremation to burial; and it smells of ashes there anyway because of the pollution of the factories. But all in all it's a quiet neighborhood; the tower of the suburban town hall makes it look like a post-card. The slow, reverberating, rich-sounding strokes of the Town Hall clock are interrupted by the brisk ringing of the church standing opposite: a reversal of the traditional time sense.

It's not a hopeless sort of town; I register my approval. Regine closes the windows, pulls the blinds down and draws the curtains shut—what a color, goes through my brain—and the impression of a windowless room sets in; and that makes me

restless. Margot has turned herself around now in such a way that she can pretend to be looking at my picture on the wall. I almost feel like going into the kitchen like I used to do, opening the refrigerator and getting out the Adelshof Vodka. But the drinks are now kept in the bar that's part of the book case. We have a choice. There's no vodka, just brands with something of a literary flavor. Margot comes to life again as the various brands are being counted up; as a future bookseller, she knows them all, and she's waiting for Campari. We drank Campari in Budapest at the expense of a crazy film director who wanted to discover Margot for the movies. He probably was only an advertising photographer. There isn't any Campari and so we choose between gin (without tonic) and whiskey and cognac, and Richard pours the drinks into glasses made of Bohemian glass. I still don't say anything about the new furniture—it's new and effortlessly comprehensible. The old furniture from Regine's parents' apartment is all gone, except for a pewter jug (an heirloom), except for a cupboard that looks like it came out of an antique shop in the Goethestrasse. I drink my gin and disappoint Regine's unspoken expectation that I'll praise the color combination of black leather (with which the seats are upholstered), book case with built-in bar (imported from Yugoslavia), and carpet (folk art, maybe from Mongolia). I don't say anything; I see how Margot is getting more and more impressed each time she makes a full turn on her revolving chair. Or perhaps the shine in her eyes is only from the whisky. Without warning, I start praising the furniture design of the twenties and thirties, the uncomplicated architectonic lines that were so obviously and unselfconsciously modern, without the grossly commercial touch of contemporary furniture that always seems to be pointing at itself and exclaiming shrilly: Modern! Top Grade Quality! If you're unlucky you have to glue the table legs back on again after they deliver it. I admit that the color scheme taken as a whole—except for the curtains—achieves what you'd call cosiness. Only the light is too stark; this isn't an operating room. Regine and Richard have both left the so-called furthermost front lines of medicine long ago. Later on Margot will turn off the main light and turn on the reading lamp on the sofa and lie down in her underwear as if we were setting up an advertising photo. But it won't work with me; I'm not sleeping with any

model in order to warm her up prior to a shot. The night turns cold and each of us counts for himself the strokes of the Town Hall clock.

Aha, Regine says in reaction to my remark about the furniture design of the thirties.

Richard seems to be considering thoughtfully the possibility of my being right. It might be that at some time in the past we agreed that every age puts its stamp on even the most trivial object it produces and now I come and praise the thirties when the only thing praiseworthy about the thirties is that they're behind us, that our fathers went to war and not we, that we've survived them and are able to sit here now, older than thirty and each one of us with his little problems in life and, I know, Regine and Richard cope with them in their own way.

I need another prescription: for headaches, I say; and Richard unscrews his fountain pen which he's still using because it's a wedding present from Regine. And because I'm always in quest of reality, I ask: What about the new patients? Richard doesn't react to the question; the fountain pen prescribes a new and better medicine. The echo of my question sounds like a challenge. Regine drinks in order to do something. I realize again that doctors have the sensitivity of generals. The strategy of attack is, whether victorious or not, always a work of art, virtually aesthetic, a question of skillfuly exploiting the moment. But the surgical attack on the body of the patient can be described in advance; before they cut us up, they give us information about the how's and the why's of the operation. Using simple words: the technical jargon would sound like complications to the layman. Everything is simple, clean and painless. However: the individual victory is a piece of luck; the general dying goes on. An irreversible law of Nature. So doctors use morphine as an easy way out and their injections for hospitalized flu patients are hedging bets against chance. If the case goes beyond the pre-calculated stage, the flu does what it wants and extinguishes the life of the patient behind the doctor's back. There remains the death certificate to be filled out—a prepared form with blanks—and everything else is a matter for the bureaucracy.

Regine in her TB sanatorium hadn't wanted to watch the dying any longer: the individual patient who dies. The dying despite every prognosis, despite the improved medicines, de-

spite the statistics that prove that tuberculosis is one of those diseases that can be conquered.

Medical diagnosis, Richard would say, must include the realization that disease is sometimes, with old people especially, stronger than the doctor.

But not a one of you, I would say, admits that once you've donned your white coats. Still the old magician who devotes himself to a new case in order to make up for his failure with the old case. And maybe chemistry has provided something that can be used against it, and what chemistry can't do you can't do either. Laying on of hands, prayers for recovery: that would be superstition of course. And so you believe what you've learned. A decent computer could reduce the number of public health organizations by half if it were programmed to provide free delivery of pills. That's what I'd say.

I take the prescription and thank him for it. Regine then goes ahead anyway and talks about her job, trips in the official car, traffic cops that turn out to be former patients; psychological tests for three year-olds. When her log is full, she goes to the capital and compares her findings with those of others. Surely not anti-authoritarian education in the kindergarden? I ask. The kindergarden teachers are against it, says Regine, and anyway: where do you think you're living? Early diagnosis of children, I'd say that keeps medical optimists young; with them you've got all the possibilities the future can bring. Struggling to prevent overweight problems is better than just waiting around in a clinic for the paralysed.

Did they pull back to their bases? I'd ask Margot one of these days. But she won't have an answer, not even a come-back, like: if you're looking for heroically struggling doctors, go to the movies.

When I ask about the official day of fasting, Margot laughs too loud for the second time this evening. Regine goes out into the kitchen and comes back with a plate of open-faced sandwiches, ham and cheese, dill pickles and pretzel sticks and we stuff countless calories into us, three to four hundred calories too many every day, Richard says; we drink gin and whiskey and the alcohol will cause the formation of dangerous fat cells in our bodies. I look benevolently at Margot; I can't imagine her being thin and even less can I imagine her being a professional nude model.

Into the silence that we've created while chewing and drinking, the baby screams from the next room. It's ten o'clock; it's got to have its bottle. Sabine has awakened and comes to the door. Her hair has gotten darker and is cut short. She stands in the door-frame, holding her body like a dancer in order to indicate to me that she's taking ballet lessons. Richard directs her back into the children's room with one of his looks. Margot isn't asked to take a look at the baby. Regine goes into the nursery alone. Margot smokes and empties her glass.

Richard bridges the interruption with music. He leaves the selection up to me, then puts the record on the new record-player himself, supporting himself with one hand on the back of the leather chair that Margot is sitting in . Armstrong with Ella. "Another season, another reason for making whoopee." Margot taps with the tip of her foot on the soft carpet, Richard goes back to his seat, one hand still on Margot's chair which makes half a turn as he lets go of it. "Now picture a little love nest."

When I ask about doctors who have left the country illegally, Richard doesn't know anything about it. Not his colleagues. Regine too doesn't know anything about it and what I know doesn't come from any legal source. Then Richard does come out with what he knows after all: 40,000 marks cash, that's the going market price. Isn't that, I would say, a deviant form of your profession—which tends towards skilled labor anyway—to hire seasonal workers for high pay and the promise of a vacation on the Riviera?

There are said to be specialists among them who have bequeathed the carrying out of special operations to their chief residents, and these latter have therefore had their first opportunity to fill out death certificates.

And I've gone too far again. When the guild's being attacked, they get their professional dander up, these doctors. And so I proceed to provoke my friends shamelessly. The very best medicine, I say, is the political medicine of Dr. Salvador Allende, a country doctor who goes into politics in order to be able to prescribe for all the children in his country half a liter of milk every day. Do you know him?

Regine looks at me as if I should have drunk milk myself instead of gin. Or take Doctor Che Guevara from Argentina, I say. All of them people who have understood something about

endogenous factors while you here are only concerned with exogenous ones.

I think you mean it the other way around, says Richard.

Regine leaves the room as if she was afraid that I wouldn't hold back now from mentioning our mothers' illnesses: and their utter inability to cure those illnesses. Two doctors in the family and—nothing! The massive application of medicines and the lethal result. Now they're lying over there, on the other side of the indoor swimming pool, ashes in metal containers and a gleaming gravestone.

Regine comes back with blankets and a freshly covered pillow. Richard opens curtains, blinds, windows. The evening's over. Margot doesn't know if she should help Regine in making up the bed on the sofa. Neither one of us asked Regine if we could spend the night here.

During the night I think, among other things, of the picture which I painted of Regine and Richard and which was so successful with the critics and public. There's a copy hanging on the wall. Richard in a white coat with a stethoscope in his hand as if it was some object that he wanted to display; Regine, whom I can't imagine in a white coat, in everyday dress; Sabine, four years old, in the middle, surprise in her eyes like in Otto Dix. The new realism of our painting, the new objectivity, as some of the critics wrote, derived essentially from this town, this picture. A picture that I couldn't paint again in the same style. Perhaps it's the distance between us, symbolized for me by the difference between their old and new apartments, that won't allow me to paint them like that again, impersonally, objectively. Is it Margot's fault or is it because I want to introduce myself into the picture, an observer who only sees when he participates? Or was I speculating on the innocence in Sabine's eyes? Art is political; I've realized that. That isn't any different today from what it was with Van Gogh or Manet. Only Manet's Olympia, placed in the show window like goods, is better than my picture because it's simultaneously foreground and background. Not a trace of an objectivity that claims to be honest, but isn't. And art can't be political if it doesn't tell it like it is. Thoughts of the night. In the dark I go over to the bar and pour myself a glass of lukewarm gin. They should have shown us the slides of their trip to the Black Sea last year, I say, when they made their new baby.

Don't be so angry, says Margot and presses her hip against mine. In the morning the alarm in the bedroom rings through all the walls of this modern apartment building from the thirties. Richard's electric razor trickles a little later through the wall. Then when we're in the kitchen, on the gleaming floor and are shaking hands, Margot has to suppress a desire to touch the baby. We take our jackets out of the front closet and are out in the street. Half past six in the morning, an undiscovered hour for me. The woods at the outer edge of the suburb, between the private homes, look as if I'd never seen them before. In front of the co-op store next to the post office are boxes with milkbottles in them. Margot pulls out a half-liter bottle and I put a coin in its place. Nobody was watching. We take the bottle to the edge of the woods; then Margot insists that each one of us takes only a little swallow each time, and so the bottle goes back and forth from mouth to mouth. Margot decides too late not to cut her classes in the trade school. As we're running across the canal bridge towards downtown later on, I wouldn't have minded if I'd made her pregnant this morning in the woods.

LETTERS

MANFRED JENDRYSCHIK

H., May 4

DEAR JONAS:

Don't be angry with me for not dropping by to see you again. I had so much to do—really. Are we going to make up again? Well, I got here all-right. Dead tired though. A ten hour trip, that's a real drag. Today it was really rough again, a rotten mean test which an instructor made us write. So naturally I got into a sweat. Tell me, when are we ever going to see each other again? Be a long time probably, what? Can't something be done to speed it up? Put a little strain on your brain and come up with something. Tell Gerd and Klaus that I'll be writing soon. I've only got two hands unfortunately.

AFFECTIONATELY,

H., May 11

DEAR JONAS:

You still haven't written to me. Didn't my letter reach you?

Well, on Whit-Sunday I'll be coming to R. and I won't be going back until Wednesday. I'll probably see you then.

In any case I'll drop by to see you. I can sleep in House II with Grit. You know, the one who was working with me in the student cafeteria. Pretty soon I'll get to thinking that you're really angry with me or something?

217

If you've got a heart you'll forgive me. As long as you won't write I'll send you very short letters.

See you then, okay? I'll bring you a big picture of me. If you aren't there I'll put it on the door.

LOVING GREETINGS,

H., May 26

DEAR JONAS:

Actually I ought to be furious by now that you've let me wait so long. Are you still mad at me? I can see already how you're swearing and having a fit. Don't know at all what I should think. You're really a brute and that could affect my studies if you don't write me soon and leave me in the dark even longer. Otherwise everything is fine. Our swimming pool has finally been opened and there's lots going on. Keep all your fingers crossed for me, the exams are coming up soon. Hey you, write this minute!

KISSES,

H., May 28

DEAR JONAS:

After taking a moment's rest to recover from your letter (the last sentence really made me go all red in the face), I'm replying to you at once.

You think I won't be able to get reduced-fare train tickets. It's got to work, you hear? Tell them that I don't have any parents and so I've only got you to visit. Tell them we're engaged or that I'm your bride or something, that'll make an impression. Then we'll save a lot of money. What's going on during Baltic Week? You know in summer I've got to work in a camp and then a couple of weeks somewhere else. Perhaps you can find some-

thing for me at your place. After all I've studied horticulture. And in September school starts again.

BEST GREETINGS,

H., June 5

MY DEAR JONAS:

I'm waiting for a letter again. Look, I've got to explain something to you. Don't know anymore if I've got my head screwed on right. Well, yesterday we had a meeting and to be precise I had a violent discussion about NATO radio stations etc. Because I've always been at it (listening to hit songs), the Teacher's Training College has decided that I should interrupt my studies for a year in order to gain maturity.

What do you say about that? The worst thing is that I don't know what I should do and where I should go.

In any case I'll go to R. Dear Jon, you've got to help me now, I love you. I've got good grades, but I don't have social maturity, so they say. Get everything started and then I'll come to you.

WITH KISSES,

P.S. I'm really down in the dumps and confused.

H., June 11

DEAR JON:

You've let me wait much too long. And you forgot my birthday too.

The fact that you're taking exams might excuse a lot but on top of that you're just a plain rotten correspondent.

In September I'll probably be starting in on a job but in August

we can take our vacation together. Does that make you happy? Back to this thing again: 1. I like listening to hit songs on the NATO radio stations and I've been criticized at meetings etc. 2. I overstayed once by three days the date I was supposed to leave for home. You ought to know that in this kind of College the number 1 rule is discipline and you know how I am, I'm not mature enough yet. 3. After my practice teaching in February when I was living in a teacher's dormitory, one of the apprentices offered me his reduced worker's return ticket. So at least the trip as far as Magdeburg was cheaper. Somehow that got out and now everybody is saying that I should've behaved myself like a teacher. I seduced a minor into committing fraud, horrible! Hopefully you've understood everything, Darling. What should I do, break out into tears maybe? The story is that I'm a dud and that sticks, and you can't help me either because our College is governed by the Ministry of Education.

Baby, it's enough to drive me nuts. Should I try correspondence school? Why haven't you sent me a picture of yourself? Haven't you got one? And how are Gerd and Klaus?

First of all you've got to get me a place to live. I'd like to be with you. Perhaps you don't believe that sometimes but it's the truth. That surprises you doesn't it?

Shouldn't really.

AU REVOIR, MON CHERI

H., June 15

DEAREST JON:

You're surprised that I'm writing to you again already, and on top of that by special delivery, aren't you? But I've got a big favor to ask of you, darling. I don't want to beat around the bush for a long time either. The thing is that I've got money problems, I haven't got a cent. I won't be getting my scholarship anymore next month, and I can't work yet, because I've got to pass the exams first. Please send me the money right away, okay? By

telegram if possible. You'll get it back for sure. Help me and I send you

MY LOVINGEST GREETINGS,

H., June 25

MY DEAR JON:

I could get a job in the county library but as long as I can't find a place to live where you are there isn't much hope. So you've got to put some effort into it. Hey, I've got blond hair now. I told you, didn't I? That I had blond hair once before; now I'm blond again. Looks much better, especially in summer. I'm gonna leave it that way permanently. The planning for the tent camp where I was supposed to go along has been botched, Leipzig U. has reserved the whole thing. That's typical. What should I do? Should I look for a job here? Now I'm at the end of my tether. With love, as always, and write at once, it's important.

H., July 3

MY DEAREST JON:

You think everything's simple. I've turned it over and over again in my mind whether or not I could write like that again, but you know that I haven't got a cent anymore. Please don't be angry and don't immediately suspect the worst. Actually I'm afraid about the future and about whether or not I can stay in R., or anywhere else.

Write to me quick what we're going to be doing in August. What do you think? And please help me, it's like sitting on coals though a hole's been burnt in my pocket. But I'm still going to take the exams. I've got a lot of books which I'll have sent after me later, about fifteen.

WITH LOVE,

221

R., September 10

DEAR JON:

Now the summer's gone and there isn't much news from you. And we didn't even say good-bye to each other properly.

You can take it easy in your parents' house. But I've got my damned shift to work. Pretty strenuous. By the way I'm writing this letter during the night shift, we've got a break now and I'm thinking of you. Whether I want to or not, at times like this I just get these ideas. Sometimes I feel you don't think very much of me because you hardly write. If so, tell me straight out. Or don't you know what you should think, huh? It's really very complicated.

I'm going to try to get a little more sleep at this table.

GREETINGS,

R., September 30

MY DEAREST JON:

You'll be coming soon, right? That really sends me. I'll stop by on Thursday to see if you're there already. Satisfied?

Yesterday I saw Peter, my ex-fiancé, on the street. Boy, did my heart shake. Hardly greeted me, the bastard.

KISSES IN ADVANCE,

R., December 22

DEAR JONAS:

You didn't expect that, did you? Well I'm simply writing to you because you just came into my mind.

222

Things aren't going too well with me. As you know, the problem of Peter and then the job. What I'd like best is to get out of here. You shouldn't consider this letter an attempt to make up. Only today I'm a little desperate, and I wanted to talk to somebody, nothing more.

GREETINGS,

B., April 9

DEAR JONAS:

As you can see, I'm now in the Capital and I'll certainly stay here. I'm staying with friends temporarily. And I'm earning my living as an administrative assistant.

How are you? Still the same preference for old women? That's bad, my dear! In any case you've just got to answer; after all it's not a matter of complete indifference to me. To be honest: I'm homesick for R. Tremendously even. Or for you. But I did give notice and I don't have a room anymore. You don't understand that? Me neither. Otherwise it's marvelous weather here. I'm staying close to the Schoenhauser Allee.

. . . . . .

B., April 14

DEAR JONAS:

Forgive me for just sending a postcard. I don't resent your giving me hell the way you did. You're absolutely right and I'll really send you the money order soon. I feel sort of abandoned, I really expected more from this place. I'd really like to have a talk with you again sometime. A silly wish?

MANY GREETINGS

P.S. Tell me, would you marry me?

B., May 25

DEAR JONAS:

I know (right away) you'll think I'm crazy, but even so I'm coming to you bawling and with a last request. I had an accident here. You know, I'm going to have a baby, for sure. Please help me now. There are some medical students in House III, can't you manage to get something for me? Or at least ask around what kind of things one can do against it? You're my only hope. I don't want the baby, the guy's married and I'm finished if the news spreads. Another thing: I left a few things in my old room; I'm enclosing a power of attorney. Will you send me the things? And will you help me?

GREETINGS,

P.S. Remember the power of attorney.

B., June 6

DEAR JONAS:

Many thanks for the package. Did my news shock you so much that you couldn't add a single line to it? Well, I went through a real moment of panic, forgive me. Now I'll try to bear it with dignity. Or stubborness. I'd like to go back to R., you can laugh if you like. A real rolling stone, what?

That's how things are with me. And you, what are you doing? Have you got together with somebody decent? I'm alone. Please answer me. Is that too much to ask?

MANY GREETINGS,

Manfred Jendryschik

B., August 19

DEAR JONAS:

I never thought that I'd ever read something from you again, so I'd like to thank you.

The doctor says that I'm in the fourth month, that sounds pretty important, doesn't it? I feel pretty important too, and hardly miserable anymore. Sometimes I really do look forward to having the baby. Only I'm a little homesick for you, but that shouldn't get us all excited, what the hell.

I wish you all the best now, dear Jon! I think I've put a lot of nonsense behind me; maybe we ought to start all over again, even if we never see each other again. I'll omit any remarks about the weather.

BEST GREETINGS,

PIMPUSH

JOACHIM NOWOTNY

Yeah, OK: Wally. She's a pretty strange girl, somewhere around fifty, well upholstered, sometimes crabby like a hen without chicks, sometimes all hepped up like she'd just got a love letter, but never at a loss for words, always getting after us young guys as soon as we stepped into the barracks after work. "Take off your boots! You still haven't showered! And who's supposed to hang up your coats for you?" She was like a record-player. Naturally we don't listen to her or if we do it's only to get a rise out of her. That usually makes for a first-class scene. Wally has a huge fit and we all laugh, and so everybody has a good time. For a long time we couldn't figure out why the poor girl worked herself to the bone like she did. Actually Wally's only supposed to keep the barracks clean—a job that requires a little elbow grease, I admit, but only keeps her busy until about the middle of the afternoon; but she stays on until evening. She cooks us another warm meal, quite of her own free will and especially because she thinks the cafeteria food isn't worth eating. We can't talk her out of it and we don't try to anymore because we flatter ourselves that she likes to be with us technicians despite the daily scene, and that she doesn't feel any longing to be in her old maid's room in the village.

With regard to the food, we have all kinds of surprises. Wally mixes up the principles of health food cooking with the recommendations of the TV chef and age-old Lausitz farm recipes. Usually some nameless steak is crackling in the pan or some soggy chop, spiced with herbs from the woods behind the camp as well as with imported nutmeg, or coddled eggs with wild thyme, or a vegetable stew without any recognizable vegetable is bubbling quietly on the stove: only Wally knows exactly what's in it. We don't ask a lot of questions but usually keep to a fixed ritual after we've sat down at the table. Silently we chew the first

bite, silently and deadly serious we look at each other a long time until somebody says in an emphatically calm tone of voice: "Oh well, you can eat anything if you're hungry enough." At that moment Wally usually smashes something on the stove, a spoon or a ladle, depending on what she's got in her hand. Then she exits in a huff. We grin at each other, dig into the food and are completely sure that her conniption isn't going to last for more than five minutes. Wally is incapable of eating her anger into herself; she's simply got to attack us with masses of furious words—she has to clear the air. With this kind of background noise the food tastes twice as good. The whole day long the rivetters and compressors are hammering away, the welding torches hiss, the cranes shriek—and all of that in the silence of the pine forest. Then you simply get lonesome for the sound of a human voice.

But once we really got ourselves in a fix. That was in March and there was still a lot of hard frost; we'd come off the shift and were as hungry as bears. A mountain of potatoes with the skins still on was steaming on the table, the vapor had condensed on the window panes and was running in big drops down the walls. We didn't much like this type of potato anyway but then to top it off we found on our plates a brown, gluey substance with a tough skin forming on the surface and smelling of some strange spice. That made even our foreman lose his composure. Completely breaking the rules of local etiquette, he asked: "What's that supposed to be?"

"Bon appetit," Wally answered smartly from the stove. "That's pimpush."

"Oh, sure!" we exclaimed. "Pimpush." And we looked at our foreman accusingly because he hadn't known that. Then we laughed and started peeling potatoes—a mountain for each one of us—and as we peeled our good humor gradually evaporated. We watched each other furtively; one of us after all had to be the first one, had to dip a potato into that brown stuff and eat it. Nobody got up the courage. Hunger was gnawing at our innards. One of us got so desperate that he finally ate his first potato without gravy. He chewed on it for a long time, opened his mouth, shifted the glob around in it and turned up his eyeballs. We watched this eloquent complaint in silence. As we expected, Wally then threw her spoon on the stove, but she

didn't whiz outside; instead she started to give us a long lecture that turned into a single sentence.

"You!" she said contemptuously and then again: "You! You're just spoiled, nothing else." Then her voice was lost in sobbing. She turned around quickly to the stove again, stirred something with her spoon in the pan, scraped the edges so that the noise made a shiver go down our spines. In the meantime the foreman tasted a little bit of this pimpush that he'd put on the tip of his knife. But he kept a poker face as he tasted it—that's how mean he was, not to give us any indication how the stuff tasted. But we didn't have any time to get excited about it because we could see clearly how in Wally's plump body something was struggling to escape: a fit of crying or maybe the beginnings of one. In any case she suddenly started to tremble so that her shoulders just heaved up and down. "Well, well," grumbled the foreman, "it's really not as bad as all that." And he quickly ate another knifetip's worth. We dug in now too; we could take anything, even this pimpush, anything but a howling woman. Luckily Wally recovered quickly; she wiped her eyes with the corners of her apron and then she sniffled: "Don't worry about it, boys. I can't get him out of my mind today, I just keep thinking about Siegmund: that's why I cooked the pimpush." As she gave us this curious explanation, she remained standing where she stood; and with her back turned to us, she told the rest of the story to the wall or, rather to the flickering shadows cast by the blazing fire in the stove. And it was only after she was well into the story that we realized that she was talking about the time right after the war, about the soldiers who had just been released from the camps and were wandering about, looking for their families and begging in the villages for food.

"What a sight they were!" said Wally. "My God, what a sight! In rags and emaciated, with wooden clogs and blisters on their heels, eyes like beaten dogs—what utter misery, boys; it was enough to make the angels weep. None of us could give them anything substantial; the war had passed through our village and hadn't left us anything. But they knocked again and again at the doors and gates and begged so that the tears just poured out of your eyes in pity. If one of them was standing outside you just had to stop up your ears or else you'd give away what you needed yourself to keep skin and bones together. For a while I

managed to hold out like that. At that time I lived in the darkest hole in the village hall, ever since they'd buried my mother; I rationed myself to one potato a day—I couldn't afford more if I was going to last until the next harvest. I stuffed sorrel and nettles down my gullet and tried to make do until one day Siegmund knocked at the door. He was such a spindly little guy, just skin and bones, with his ears hanging from his head like frozen laundry on the line, that I just couldn't stand it any more. It's possible that he might have managed to make it a little further; but at the other end of the village his legs would certainly have given out from hunger and weakness, he would have been a goner: I saw that at a glance. So I took him in, set up a make-shift bed for him on my old sofa (let people talk if they wanted to!) and cooked him up a whole kilo of potatoes at once. He had to eat them slowly, with coarse animal salt, just to be able to stay alive. Then I started bending his ear: Stay here, I said, I haven't got anybody either; we'll make it together, just trust me. And he looked at me, that kid, with his faithful dog's eyes, so gratefully and timidly that I could have hugged him to death for joy. Only that wouldn't have helped us. That very night I went off straight through the dark heath, always heading south towards the high land. There were supposed to be villages there where the farmers still had bacon in their pantries.

I went from farm to farm, begged and whined, but nobody gave me anything. They've got such terribly straight dung heaps there, as if they'd been fenced off and measured to the inch; they're real sticklers for orderliness. But they won't let you have a thing. Sure, when the city folks came, then they might have come out with some of their good stuff, in exchange for carpets and clocks, for gold jewelry and God knows what else. I only had myself and a few rags on my body; they didn't even turn around when I talked to them. When evening came my apron was as empty as a pond in winter. And I always had my Siegmund on my mind; what was to become of him if I couldn't do any better than that? I lay down in a barn in a field on some musty hay but I couldn't get to sleep from hunger and worry. Then I took off around the third hour, following the road back to the village; somewhere that day I'd seen an old woman planting onions. I scooped them out of the ground so that I'd at least have something. But before I could make it over the fence again, some vicious mutt attacked me—one of the kind that whips around

the corner like lightning without even a single bark and sinks his teeth right into you. The critter tore up my calf; just lucky I didn't have any stockings on. Well, I got away anyway and even felt grateful to the mutt that he'd gone after me so quietly because in those days they beat you mercilessly to a pulp if they caught you. I ripped a piece off my apron, wrapped it around my leg and hobbled off like that into the dawn, up over the mountain and into another village. Right at the first town it smelled of boiled potatoes and I felt the hunger bite into me with a thousand teeth, so I simply went in through the gate and up to the door of the feed kitchen. Then suddenly somebody opened the door from the inside, a kind of a wiry lout with fresh eyes and no more than sixteen years old; he didn't bat an eye when he saw me standing there like that, he just kept looking at my blouse that I'd stuffed full with the onions. Who knows what went through his head, that precocious little lout; in any case he dragged me by the arm into the dim feed kitchen, jumped all over me and wanted to throw me into the fresh feed even before I could grab a single potato. I screamed as loud as my lungs let me and defended myself with the feeble remains of my strength and screamed until the farmer came diving in; then I kept on screaming and screaming until he stuffed a few boiled potatoes into my mouth. But even then I still kept on screaming in between bites and the farmer finally chased the boy off to get me a quarter pound of low grade bacon. Only when I had it inside my blouse did I quiet down. On the way home I came past a water mill where I know the baker; I wanted to beg a small bag of coarse flour off him but he too wouldn't give me anything. The police was keeping close tabs on him. Luckily I suddenly remembered old Himpel— he was actually my father but we just called him Himpel because he'd left us already long before the war in order to drink up his money by himself. But the baker had been one of his drinking pals so I overcame my revulsion and softened him up with a few memories of the time before the war and pretended I was crying for my father and longing for the good old days when I had to go get Himpel from the bar but only got a hiding instead. The baker stopped kneading at once, blinked his eyes and swallowed a couple of times; then he gave me a small bag of coarse flour which I added to the onions and bacon. I took off right away, straight across the heath towards home. Sure, once in a while I howled on the way home because I'd stolen, lied and sold my

pride—something I'd never have done for myself. But down deep in my heart I felt really happy because now I could get my Siegmund back on his feet. I was going to make pimpush for him out of water, flour and bacon cracklings, out of onions and marjoram that grew wild behind the fire station."

Suddenly Wally stopped; she tugged nervously at her apron strings, pulled off her apron, made it into a ball with one hand and threw it into the corner of the barracks.

"He was gone," she screamed hoarsely. "Siegmund was gone—flown the coop like a bird—when I got back. He'd cooked himself the potatoes and taken them along, all of them; only the peels he'd left lying there. He'd deceived me, poor simple girl that I was with his dog's eyes. People had seen him march out of the village without a trace of a limp and quick as a tomcat in heat."

We all sat there stunned; we hadn't expected it to end that way. We stared at our half-empty plates and nobody knew what to do. But something had to happen; we couldn't just let the poor girl stand there with her heaving shoulders and hysterical weeping in her belly. Maybe one of us should have gotten up and just hugged her for once; at least that would have been something! But nobody did it; we just sat there as if glued to our chairs and felt embarrassed as one usually does at moments like that. Only the foreman was able to cope with the situation; he ladled pimpush off his plate and into his stomach as if he was eating raspberry pudding. Then he turned towards the stove and asked very casually: "You wouldn't happen to have any pimpush left in that pan, would you?"

And as Wally wiped the corners of her eyes and sniffled and nodded, we started to feel better again.

PODIRALLA JOINS THE CIRCUS

KRISTIAN PECH

Podiralla had packed his brother's tent on the back of his motorbike and had driven off to that little hole which, according to the travel guide, offered the pleasures of an unassuming landscape and peace, lots of peace. And peace was precisely what he needed or thought he needed. He wanted to camp near the lake that was as round as a bowl, and he wanted—as they have a way of saying—to take stock of himself: think things over, dream, dream, think things over. But Podiralla had lain for two days in front of his tent in the blazing sun and done nothing of all that. He had spread apricot jam on rolls that got harder every time. Had eaten, slept.

On the third day, Podiralla had gotten up at six, had strolled over to the village and come back with freshly baked rolls. As the tea water boiled, he suddenly pulled his head back. He listened; he heard the cows lowing, just as he must have heard them before, but now he thought about it, about being able to go and get warm milk fresh out of the udder. He dumped the tea water into the dewy grass and went, with his pot under his arm, in the direction of the enclosure.

The herd shied away and wallowed over towards the opposite fence. There was a milking stand over there. Podiralla trotted after them and said: "Don't get all excited!" and: "I'll get you." He really did get one. It seemed to be the laziest one; she only ran away slowly but even so she was quick enough to frustrate Podiralla's attempts every time. Though he was able to grab one of the teats of the bouncing udder a number of times, he was never able to get the pot between the cow's legs. As soon as he managed to refine his tactics, the black and white cow increased her speed.

Only then did it occur to Podiralla that somebody might be able to see him. But he would have known about it by now, he

thought and relaxed because his awful clumsiness would have occasioned peals of laughter. But since he needed a rest in order to catch his breath, he stopped and looked around in all directions. Over by the milking stand a girl was leaning or maybe a woman, he didn't know, dressed in blue work clothes. He couldn't tell if she was laughing. More likely she's furious, Podiralla told himself. She'll start screaming right away, and he'll jump over the electric fence, even higher and surer than before.

But she walked up to him slowly. He thought: nineteen and not bad. She thought: not bad and nineteen. She said: "Once again, the best laid plans of mice and men. Gimme your pot!" She squatted down under the black and white cow that had run away from Podiralla, milked the container full and gave it to him. She said: "I've by-passed the assembly of the collective farm. A vote would have been necessary for this kind of service. But it takes a while to drum the hundred members together. You shouldn't have to wait for your milk. I'm in a good mood." And she laughed.

Podiralla didn't know what to make of her; he was much too taken aback. He said "Thank You" and had the feeling that he should say more. After a few moments he stammered: "Don't think that I'm in the habit of stealing. That was just a lark today. But—can I come again?"

She brushed her black hair back. She made a grimace with her mouth. Her mouth went square and that looked funny. "We'll see."

There was a pause, a long pause. Podiralla was surprised when he heard her say: "You're already thinking about coming back and nobody has even mentioned going away yet."

He set the milk down in the grass. "What's the name of the cow I got the milk from?"

"Hyacinth."

Podiralla was asked to come along and she made that funny square mouth again. She ran over to the herd, pointed to a white cow and asked: "What's her name?"

Podiralla thought it over; he would have liked to mumble: silly game that you're playing with me. But he had started it after all. "How about—Ulla?"

She asked: "That must be the name of your girlfriend?"

"No, she hasn't got a name," he answered. The pause that

followed now was different from the first. Podiralla knew that he mustn't say anything now.

And then he heard her clear voice. "The cow's name is Vera, just like mine. And yours?"

"Bert."

"Don't tell me—Brecht. Then I'd want an autograph."

"No, Podiralla."

She said: "Nice. If I ever write a novel, I know what I'll call the hero."

And Vera started to laugh. She sat down in the grass, lay down, stood up again, and laughed and laughed.

"Mr. Podiralla, I'd like to be able, just once, to handle a cow with the terrific naïveté that you can. Boy, would that be fun." She sat down once more.

Podiralla said: "Now the milk's cold anyway and the rolls in my tent aren't warm anymore either." He sat down next to her. "Do you mind?" She said: hmm.

Through the trees noises drifted over to them from the campground. Vera asked: "Are you camping alone?"

"Yes," said Podiralla. "You know, I came to this lake because I wanted to be alone. I had a lot to settle with myself."

"Admit it: you're disillusioned with yourself and most of all with the world?" Vera asked. "You're like all men. Now it's time for you to tell me your tale of sorrows."

"No," said Podiralla. "I don't want to bore you." But he really hoped that she would insist. He simply had to tell her his story. She actually said: "Please." And he began: "Last week I graduated from high school, and I got a letter. In it, it said that my application for journalism school was—oh well—turned down. Not a chance. In September I'm joining the circus. I'm actually supposed to be working in some big combine in order to gain maturity and a sense of the collective, that's what they said. But if I've got to start working already, then I'd at least like to travel around with the circus."

Vera said: "That's a sadder story than any I've heard before. But don't feel bad if I start laughing. You? In the circus? That would really be something. Those poor animals.

"I'll be a driver or put up the tent or punch tickets."

"Why aren't they letting you study?" Vera asked.

Podiralla said: "I can, but only after working for a year. They told me I wasn't mature enough. But I hardly think that any of my

classmates were more mature. But they didn't rebel against the dishonesty of one of the teachers." Podiralla got up. The thing was still eating him.

Vera asked: "You going?"

"I want to have breakfast. Hey, what would you say if I came back tomorrow?"

"Good morning. Just like any other polite person."

They laughed.

Podiralla left. He must not stay any longer now. He had a feeling for things like that. You mustn't say everything at once. Then he thought: Let's see if I get a hankering for her. And how that sort of thing feels. And Vera thought: Guess I won't see him anymore.

Podiralla learned what hankering is. That must be what it was. He felt it two days later, on the third morning: if before he hadn't strained himself unduly, now he didn't feel like doing anything at all. He didn't go into the water at all anymore, didn't go to get any more rolls in the village, and if he managed to find one lying about that was stone-hard, he didn't cut it in half anymore and spread each white half with jam like he did before; he just ate the roll and the jam right out of the container with a spoon.

One thing he did do now: think things over and dream. But he wasn't the center of this process as he should have been—the desire to think about himself and to dream himself forward had driven him into this part of the world—but in the center stood black-haired Vera who could make a funny square mouth. Podiralla felt utterly miserable when he couldn't think of any other detail about her. If she were to walk through the camp ground, he wouldn't recognize her.

That afternoon he stood in front of her again or she in front of him. She asked: "Where's your pot?"

"I only brought myself along," he said.

She: "That's nice." She wiped her right hand clean on her working clothes and extended it to Podiralla. "I hope you don't mind but I've got to clean the animals first. It's absolutely necessary. You can tell me your story while I'm working if you like."

Podiralla lay down in the grass. From time to time the cows sniffed at him. One of them even licked his feet. He let them do it. He lay absolutely still and didn't say anything. Until late in the

afternoon. When he called Vera over, she was already finishing up for the day. "Hey, listen, I'd like to ask you something."

She said: "I'm listening."

"If somebody's always telling you: you've got to be absolutely honest, and then if he makes all sorts of promises because he has to, and makes promises that he can't keep and doesn't want to, and if you draw his attention to this fact, are you right about that?"

"Yes, of course," said Vera, "but does that have anything to do with me?"

"No."

"Then with what?" she asked.

He said: "Just something that interests me. Nothing else."

She seemed satisfied with that. Vera and Podiralla walked along the little river that led into the village. He had taken her by the hand so that she wouldn't be able to run away from him. So he said.

She thought: He's not in love; he still takes too much trouble to find a reason for everything he does. She had just finished thinking that out, when he asked: "You want to put your arm in mine so that you won't stumble?" She took his arm and laughed almost as loud and happily as that first day on the meadow. About what, he didn't know, and she wasn't going to tell him, ever; that is, unless he asked her to. But he just kept on walking by her side without a word.

"Why do you want to join the circus?" Vera looked down on the ground.

"I told you already why."

"What gave you the idea?"

"I thought, the world's a kind of high class circus anyway. That's how."

Vera looked at him. She felt like laughing again but she kept a straight face. "Tell me, are you high school kids all so mixed-up?" she asked.

Podiralla swallowed nervously; he let the arm that Vera was holding hang down lifelessly. The swampy ground under his feet gurgled.

"Of course not," he said heatedly, "but I'm like that; ever since twelfth grade I've been like that. How could I be any different?"

"Oh, Bert," she parried, "let's assume they treated you un-

fairly. They made a mistake. But you're making a thousand mistakes if that's how you philosophize about the world. That just doesn't work." She shoved him. "What you're doing with me—is that part of your circus?"

"No. How could you think that?"

The brook grew wider. Podiralla saw the first houses of the village. She said: "I could let you guess in which house I live, but you won't guess. Then you'll be even more unhappy." He didn't say a word; he stared into the village.

"You actually can't see it yet," she confessed. He said suddenly: "Then I just won't go. I'll get into a boat and row up and down the Elbe. Or . . ."

"That's not the point." Again his arm hung down lifelessly. The swampy ground gurgled under his feet.

"I'd like to tell you a little story," said Vera. "A few years ago a married couple moved into the house where I live. Bad things were said about both of them. In reality their story was simply magnificent—that's the only word for it. They got to know each other by talking over the fence in prison. It's true. The woman— she'd been sentenced for failing to show up at work—was practically reborn after she got to know him. The warden noticed it and quickly found out why. They didn't do anything. She got an early parole. Before they came to the village they got married. And now the woman is work brigadier."

Podiralla wanted to ask why she was telling him all this. But he didn't ask.

"I live here," she said. "On the second floor."

"I'm going," he said. "Goodbye!"

That very same evening he jumped into the lake that was as round as a bowl. He swam from one end to the other, again and again. And as fast as he could. Sometimes he climbed out in order to feel the sand under his feet for a few steps, and then he dove into water again like a happy frog in spring. When Podiralla was exhausted, he got dressed. He had turned ravenously hungry. He made himself a royal supper out of the food that he had managed to wheedle out of his neighbors in the camp, and he slept until late next day, Sunday.

Towards evening Vera came. She was wearing a white blouse and a light colored skirt; she had put up her hair and was swinging a tiny handbag.

"It's a real job to find you. Whom are you hiding your tent from?"

Podiralla went up to her quickly and held her hand for a very long time. "Greetings," he said.

She said: "I've never walked around the lake. Feel like it?"

"Yeah, let's." Podiralla put his arm around Vera's hips. He inhaled the smell of her hair.

She asked: "Well how's the circus?"

"You bug me; I'm going to get rid of you," said Podiralla. "I'm going to throw you in the water. To the hungry pikes." And he lifted her and cradled her in his arms. She let her head hang, her arms, her legs. She grew as light as a feather. He held her over the water and then put her down again at his side.

"I just don't enjoy it when you don't scream. You have to know first how unpleasantly a woman can scream before you talk about anything else. But anyway: how do you feel when you haven't got any solid ground under you and when you think that I've got it for both of us?"

"Pretty good," she said, "but it's got to get even better, Mr. Podiralla."

He kissed her. Two sails were dancing on the lake. The sails drew closer to each other and then drew apart again, but once one got behind the other.

Night fell and they vanished increasingly into it.

Podiralla said: "I'm not going to join the circus. I'll stay in this little hole."

"Don't sweet-talk me," Vera said. She leaned against a willow. "You don't have to sweet-talk me. I like you anyway."

Podiralla said: "Wait and see."

She kissed him. The sails had become invisible.

BIOGRAPHIES

List of abbreviations: A = autobiography; CB = children's book; D= documentary; E= essays; N= novel; P = poems; Pl = play; Pr = prose; S = short stories; Sa = satire.

BOBROWSKI, JOHANNES. Born in Tilsit in 1917, the son of working-class parents, he spent part of his youth in the German-Lithuanian border area near the Memel river. In 1928 he moved to Königsberg where he attended a famous humanistic high school and then went on to Berlin to begin studying art history, but in 1937 he was drafted into the Army. As a devout Christian, Bobrowski abhorred all that the Nazis stood for. After the war he was imprisoned in the USSR and was forced to work in a coal mine until 1949. Thereafter he returned to Berlin to take up an assistant editorship with a children's book publisher, and it was only in the last half-decade before his death in 1965 that Bobrowski began to publish seriously and to become known as one of the most sensitive poets and short story writers of the post-war period.
Major Publications: Sarmatische Zeit (1961) [P]; Schattenland Ströme (1962) [P]; Levins Mühle (1964) [N]; Boehlendorff und Mäusefest (1965) [S]; Litauische Claviere (1966) [N]; Wetterzeichen (1966) [P]; Der Mahner (1967) [S]; Windgesträuch (1970) [P].

BÖTTCHER, ERNST. Born in Nauendorf (Saale) in 1932, the son of working-class parents, Böttcher was originally trained as a plumber. He has also worked as a policeman and as a minor official in the City Government of Wismar, where he is now employed as a locksmith. He is married and the father of five children. Though only a part-time writer, Böttcher has produced short stories, articles, cabaret songs and poems.

Major Publication: Ein Beispiel und ich (1968) [L].

BRÄUNIG, WERNER. Born in Chemnitz in 1934, the son of working-class parents, Bräunig was apprenticed to a locksmith and subsequently worked at a variety of manual jobs, including coal and uranium mines, and a paper factory. The years 1951-52 he spent in West Germany, but decided to return to the GDR. From 1958 to 1961 he studied at the Johannes R. Becher Institute for Literary Study in Leipzig and he was

subsequently appointed lecturer in prose there. Bräunig's work has not always proved to the liking of the authorities: his famous chapter, "Rummelplatz" (1965) from his projected novel on uranium mining in the GDR was censured and the novel never appeared; so, too, with a film on the same subject for which he had written the scenario.

Major Publications: In diesem Sommer (1960) [S]; Gewöhnliche Leute (1969) [S]; Städte machen Leute (1969) [D]; Prosa schreiben (1968) [E]; Die einfachste Sache der Welt (1971) [S].

BREDEL, WILLI. Born in Hamburg in 1901, the son of working-class parents, Bredel became a metal worker at a very young age and soon revealed an active interest in politics, joining the Communist Party at the age of eighteen. In 1923 he was sentenced to two years imprisonment for his part in the October rising in Hamburg, and it was in prison that he began to write. After his release in 1925 he went to sea, traveling especially to Spain, Portugal, North Africa, and Italy. In 1928 he became editor of the *Hamburger Volkszeitung* and in 1930 he was again sentenced to two years imprisonment, this time for "literary high treason." After a visit to the USSR in 1932, he was arrested by the Nazis in 1933 and sent to the Hamburg-Fuhlsbüttel concentration camp. He survived thirteen months' incarceration there until he managed to escape first to Czechoslovakia and then to Moscow. There, together with Feuchtwanger and Brecht, he edited the anti-fascist literary journal, *Das Wort*. He also fought in the Spanish Civil War as a member of the International Brigade. Returning from his Russian exile in 1945, Bredel immediately assumed an important role in the establishment of socialist government and socialist culture in the Soviet Zone. His last years were laden with honors, including the Presidency of the German Academy of Arts in Berlin. He died in Berlin in 1964.

Major Publications: Maschinenfabrik N & K (1930) [N]; Begegnung am Ebro (1939) [N]; Verwandte und Bekannte (1941-53) [N]; Ein neues Kapitel (1959-65) [N].

BUSCHMANN, WOLFGANG. Born in Rittersberg (Silesia) in 1943, Buschmann attended a polytechnical high school before entering the Teachers Training Institute in Nossen. After teaching for seven years in Pobershau in the Erzgebirge, he attended the Johannes R. Becher Institute for Literary Study in Leipzig (1971-74), and subsequently returned to teaching in Zöblitz. He is best known as a writer of short stories, but he has also done translations from Polish, Czech and English.

Major Publications: Kater Lampe mit Zwischenspiel (1974) [S]; Die Geschichte vom Nussknacker Kunka (1975) [CB]; Die grosse Erfindung (1976) [CB].

CLAUDIUS, EDUARD. Born Eduard Schmidt in Gelsenkirchen in 1911,

the son of working-class parents, Claudius was apprenticed to a mason. Mistreated by his foreman, Claudius turned to writing as a means of seeking redress. He joined the Communist Party in 1932; and, after being jailed briefly by the Nazis, he emigrated to Switzerland in 1934. There he worked in close contact with the anti-fascist underground movement in Germany. Arrested for these activities in 1936 by the Swiss Police, he was nearly deported to Germany. Instead, he managed to escape and make his way to Spain. There he joined the International Brigade, was wounded, and eventually rose to the position of War Commissar. After the fall of Spain to Franco's forces, Claudius returned illegally to Switzerland in 1939, was captured and imprisoned. Only at the personal intercession of Hermann Hesse was Claudius spared the fate of being turned over to the Nazis, but he was nevertheless interned for the duration of the war. In 1945 Claudius returned to Germany and became press manager in the Bavarian Ministry of Denazification in Munich. In 1948 he moved to Potsdam where he still lives. He has been awarded various prizes, including the National Prize of the GDR in 1951, and has served in diplomatic positions abroad.

Major Publications: Das Opfer (1935) [S]; Grüne Oliven und nackte Berge (1945) [N]; Menschen an unserer Seite (1951) [N]; Von der Liebe soll man nicht nur sprechen (1957) [N]; Das Mädchen "Sanfte Wolke" (1962) [S]; Ruhelose Jahre (1968) [A].

FRIES, FRITZ RUDOLF. Born in Bilbao (Spain) in 1935, the son of a German father and a Spanish mother, Fries grew up in Leipzig and attended the University there, specializing in Germanic and Romance languages. After finishing his studies in 1958, he worked as an interpreter and translator, often at international socialist congresses. From 1960 to 1966 he was an assistant at the German Academy of Sciences in Berlin, and since then he has earned a living as a writer and translator. Considered the most promising of the youngest generation of GDR writers in the West, Fries was for some time completely ignored in his own country.

Major Publications: Der Weg nach Oobliadooh (1966) [N]; Der Fernseh-krieg (1969) [S]; Leipzig am Morgen (1969) [S]; Seestücke (1973) [D]; Das Papierschiff (1974) [N].

FÜHMANN, FRANZ. Born in Rokytnice (Czechoslovakia) in 1922, the son of middle-class parents, Fühmann as a boy was a passionate pan-Germanist and admirer of the Nazis. Immediately after graduating from high school, he joined the German Army and fought in the Greek and Russian campaigns; but he also found time to write a volume of ardently pro-Nazi poetry, published in Hamburg in 1942. Imprisoned by the Russians after the war, he was re-educated in an anti-fascist school from which he emerged as a convinced Communist as he had earlier been a

Nazi. Since his return to East Germany in 1949, he has been one of the most unswervingly loyal, as well as gifted, literary servants of the regime; and he has been rewarded with numerous prizes and offices. His work is frequently autobiographical in nature, full of the guilt of someone who had been tempted into the worship of false gods; and his evocations and memories of childhood in Nazi surroundings are some of the most poignant of the post-War period.

Major Publications: Gefühle der Klage, Trauer, Ratlosigkeit (1942) [P]; Die Nelke Nikos (1953) [P]; Stürzende Schatten (1958) [S]; Kabeljau und Blauer Peter (1961) [D]; Spuk (1961) [S]; Die heute Vierzig sind (1961) [S]; Das Judenauto (1962) [S]; Böhmen am Meer (1962) [S]; König Oedipus (1966) [S]; Der Jongleur im Kino (1970) [S]; 22 Tage oder Die Hälfte eines Lebens (1973) [A]; Prometheus (1973) [N].

HERMLIN, STEFAN. Born Rudolf Leder in Chemnitz in 1915, the son of middle-class parents, Hermlin was already active in Communist youth organizations as a boy, and after the Nazis came to power he stayed on in the Communist underground until 1936. After taking part in the Spanish Civil War, Hermlin enlisted in the French Army to fight the Nazis. With the fall of France he managed to escape to Switzerland where he was interned for the duration of the hostilities. In 1945 he first returned to Frankfurt, where he worked in radio broadcasting, but two years later he decided to move to the Soviet Zone. Hermlin is best known as a poet and translator but he has also written numerous short stories, including the notorious "Die Kommandeuse," the only contemporaneous story in the GDR to deal with the June 17, 1953 workers' uprising. He has been a frequent critic of Government cultural policy but has just as frequently exercised self-criticism after being reprimanded by the Party.

Major Publications: Zwölf Balladen von den grossen Städten (1945) [P]; Der Leutnant Yorck von Wartenburg (1946) [S]; Zweiundzwanzig Balladen (1947) [P]; Die Zeit der Gemeinsamkeit (1950) [S]; Das Mansfelder Oratorium (1950) [oratorio]; Die Kommandeuse (1953) [S]; Begegnungen (1960) [E]; Tradition und Modern (1965) [E]; In einer dunklen Welt (1966) [S]; Erzählungen (1966, 1970) [S].

HEYM, STEFAN. Born Hellmuth Fliegel in Chemnitz in 1913, the son of middle-class parents, Heym very early developed an interest in leftist causes. The Nazi takeover occurred while Heym was a student in Berlin, forcing him into exile in Prague, where he lived until 1935. In that year Heym was awarded a fellowship to the University of Chicago and subsequently took his M.A. degree there. After a brief career in journalism, editing the anti-Nazi German language weekly, "Deutsches Volksecho," in New York, Heym joined the US Army, saw action in

France and at the end of the war was stationed in Munich, where he helped to found the "Neue Zeitung." Profoundly disillusioned with the U.S. and its policies in Germany, he returned his citizenship and commission to President Eisenhower and departed for the GDR in 1952. But in the GDR, too, Heym has not always found the ideal state he sought, and in his later novels especially—none of which have been published in the GDR—he has bitterly, though indirectly, attacked the social and cultural policies of his country. He is perhaps the most remarkable "dissident" writer of his generation; and remarkable, too, in that, during the years of exile and immediately following, he wrote English and German with equal fluency.

Major Publications: Die Hinrichtung (1935) [Pl]; Hostages (1942) [N]; The Crusaders (1948) [N]; The Eyes of Reason (1951) [N]; Goldsborough (1953) [N]; The Lenz Papers (1965) [N]; Lasalle (1969) [N]; Die Schmähschrift (1970) [N]; Der König David Bericht (1972) [N].

JENDRYSCHIK, MANFRED. Born in Dessau in 1943, the son of middle-class parents, Jendryschik became a member of the Dessauer Circle of Writing Workers at seventeen. After graduating from high school, he first worked as a transport worker, then in the book business. From 1962 to 1967 he studied German literature and art history in Rostock, where he also led a group of writing workers and students. Thereafter he became an assistant editor in Halle, and since 1970 he has been the head of the Dessauer Circle of Writing Workers.

Major Publications: Glas und Ahorn (1967) [S]; Johanna oder Die Wege des Dr. Kanuga (1973) [N]; Die Fackel und der Bart (1971) [S]; Lokaltermine (1974) [E].

KANT, HERMANN. Born in Hamburg in 1926, Kant is the son of working-class parents and was trained to become an electrician. After serving in the war, he was imprisoned in Poland until 1949; there, however, he was re-educated in an anti-fascist school and also met Anna Seghers, who advised him to study at a university. Following her advice, Kant first attended the "Workers & Farmers Faculty" at the University of Greifswald (the subject of his later novel, *Die Aula*), and later enrolled in the Humboldt University in Berlin, where he studied German literature from 1952 to 1956. During the first years after leaving the University, Kant worked as an editor, but he now earns his living as an independent writer, having received more literary prizes and awards than any other writer of his generation.

Major Publications: Ein bisschen Südsee (1962) [S]; Die Aula (1964) [N]; Frau Atlas und Herr Atlas (1969) [S]; Das Impressum (1969, 1972) [N]; Die Gefährten (1971) [A]; Eine Übertretung (1973) [Sa].

KUNERT, GÜNTER. Born in Berlin in 1929, Kunert was excluded from

military service during the Second World War on "racial" grounds. After 1945 he studied at the Academy of Applied Arts in Berlin-Weissensee, but soon began to write and publish satirical poems and stories which attracted the attention of Johannes R. Becher. Kunert has traveled widely, both in East and West (including the US), and is frequently critical of aspects of GDR cultural policy. He is best known as a poet and short story writer but has also written for radio and the film. *Major Publications:* Wegschilder und Mauerinschriften (1950) [P]; Der ewige Detektiv (1954) [Sa]; Tagwerke (1960) [P]; Das kreuzbrave Liederbuch (1961) [P]; Der ungebetene Gast (1965) [P]; Im Namen der Hüte (1967) [N]; Kramen in Fächern (1968) [S]; Die Beerdigung findet in aller Stille statt (1968) [S]; Offener Ausgang (1972) [P]; Die geheime Bibliothek (1973) [S]; Gast aus England (1973) [N].

NOWOTNY, JOACHIM. Born in Rietschen (Silesia) in 1933, the son of lower middle-class parents, Nowotny was first apprenticed to a carpenter. Retrained at a "Workers & Farmers Faculty," he then studied German Literature at the University of Leipzig from 1954 to 1958. After working briefly as an editor and trying to make a go of it as an independent writer, he accepted a teaching position at the Johannes R. Becher Institute for Literary Study in Leipzig.
Major Publications: Hochwasser im Dorf (1963) [CB]; Labyrinth ohne Schrecken (1967) [S]; Der Riese im Paradies (1969) [CB]; Sonntag unter Leuten (1972) [S].

PECH, KRISTIAN. Born in Frankenthal (Oberlausitz, Silesia) in 1946, Pech attended the Goethe-Oberschule in Bischofswerda (1961-65), where he was also apprenticed as an agricultural technician. In 1965-66, before doing his military service, he worked as a volunteer reporter for the "Sächsische Zeitung" in Dresden. This led to the study of journalism at the University of Leipzig (1967-70), where he also worked for a short time in a brewery. Best known as a poet and writer of short stories, he has made his living since 1971 as a writer, first in Leipzig and now in Cottbus. He has travelled extensively in the USSR, Poland, and Austria.
Major Publications: Gedichte (1971) [P]; Das Brot-und-Knochen-Haus (1972) [P]; Der Landsitz (1975) [S]; Abschweifungen über Bäume (1976) [P].

PITSCHMANN, SIEGFRIED. Born in Grünberg (Silesia) in 1930, the son of working-class parents, Pitschmann attended but did not graduate from high school. After the post-war expulsions from Silesia, he moved to Mühlhausen where he first worked as an unskilled laborer and later as an apprentice watchmaker. During this period he also joined a writers' group in Thuringia and attended a writers' seminar. In 1957-58 he

246

worked briefly as a cement worker and machine operator in the soft-coal mine "Schwarze Pumpe." Aside from writing short stories, Pitschmann has also gained a considerable reputation as a radio playwright.
Major Publications: Ein Mann steht vor der Tür (1960, with Brigitte Reimann) [Pl]; Wunderbare Verlobung eines Karrenmannes (1961) [S]; Kontrapunkte (1968) [Pr]; Männer und Frauen (1974) [S].

SEGHERS, ANNA. Born Netty Reiling in Mainz in 1900, the daughter of a wealthy art and antique dealer, Seghers studied philology, history, art history, and sinology in Cologne and Heidelberg. She received her doctorate in 1924 from Heidelberg, writing a dissertation on Rembrandt and the Jews. A year later she married the Hungarian author, Lazlo Radvanyi, and in 1928 she joined the Communist Party. In the same year she published *Aufstand der Fischer von St. Barbara* (using the pseudonym Seghers, the name of a Dutch seventeenth century painter), for which she was awarded the Kleist Prize in 1929. Though arrested in 1933 by the Nazis, she managed to escape with her children first to France and later to Mexico. During her years of exile Seghers took an active role in fighting the fascist regime in Germany, both through her own writing and as a participant in various Writers' Congresses and exile groups. After her return to Germany in 1947, she soon became involved in shaping cultural policy in the Soviet Zone. Though her best work (notably the novel *Das siebte Kreuz*) was written during the period of exile, she has continued to publish fiction and expository prose, and over the years has been showered with a variety of honors and prizes, including the Lenin Peace Prize, the Büchner Prize, the National Prize of the GDR (three times), and an honorary doctorate from the University of Jena.
Major Publications: Aufstand der Fischer von St. Barbara (1928) [S], filmed by Piscator in 1934; Auf dem Wege zur amerikanischen Botschaft (1930) [S]; Die Rettung (1937) [N]; Das siebte Kreuz (1942) [N]; Die Toten bleiben jung (1949) [N]; Transit (1944) [N]; Die Entscheidung (1959) [N]; Das Vertrauen (1968) [N]; Sonderbare Begegnungen (1973) [S].

STRITTMATTER, ERWIN. Born in Spremberg in 1912, the son of agricultural working-class parents, Strittmatter spent his formative years in a small Silesian village. There he attended high school until he was sixteen, after which he was apprenticed to a baker. While working at various odd jobs, the young Strittmatter sought to educate himself further and enlisted in the Socialist Youth Movement. In 1934 he was arrested briefly for actions hostile to the Nazi regime. Drafted into the army at the outbreak of the war, Strittmatter served at various fronts until he deserted shortly before the German surrender. As a result of the post-war land redistribution program, Strittmatter was able to start

farming on his own; in 1947 he joined the SED, served as councilman for his region, and began writing for a local paper. One of his early plays, "Katzgraben," attracted Brecht's attention, something which undoubtedly helped Strittmatter in his rapid rise to fame in the 1950's. Since that time he has served on numerous literary committees, often as president or chairman, and has received several prestigious prizes and awards, including the National Prize (three times). He is probably the closest thing that East Germany has to a genuinely popular establishment writer.

Major Publications: Ochsenkutscher (1950) [N]; Katzgraben (1953) [Pl]; Tinko (1954) [N]; Der Wundertäter (Part 1: 1957; Part 2: 1973) [N]; Die Holländerbraut (1960) [Pl]; Ole Bienkopp (1963) [N]; Ein Dienstag im September (1970) [Pr]; Schulzenhofer Kramkalender (1967) [Pr]; ¾ hundert Kleingeschichten (1971) [S]; Die blaue Nachtigall (1972) [S].

UHSE, BODO. Born in Rastatt in 1904, the son of an officer in the Prussian Army, Uhse was an intensely patriotic youth and joined the National Socialist Party in the early 1920's. By 1927 he had risen to the editorship of a Nazi paper in Ingolstadt and by 1928 to the chief editorship of the Nazi daily in Itzehoe. Two years later, however, he broke with the Nazis and subsequently joined the Communist Party. The years of exile and war Uhse spent in Paris, Spain (with the International Brigade), the United States, and Mexico. From Mexico, where he edited the literary section of "Freies Deutschland," Uhse returned to Berlin in 1948. He became chief editor of the journal "Aufbau" until 1958 and then a few months before his death in 1963, of the prestigious literary journal *Sinn und Form.*

Major Publications: Söldner und Soldat (1935) [N]: Leutnant Bertram (1944) [N]; Die heilige Kunigunde im Schnee (1949) [S]; Die Patrioten (1954) [N]; Mexikanische Erzählungen (1956) [S]; Gestalten und Probleme (1959) [E]; Sonntagsträumerei in der Alameda (1961) [S].

WEISKOPF, FRANZ CARL (also pseudonyms: Petr Buk and F.W.L. Kovacs). Born in Prague in 1900, the son of middle-class parents, Weiskopf graduated from a German language high school and at the age of eighteen was drafted into the Imperial Austrian Army. After the war he studied German and History at the University of Prague, joined the Socialist student movement and co-edited the leftist student journal "Avantgarda." He became a professional journalist after receiving his doctorate in 1923, first in Prague where he was repeatedly charged with "literary treason," and after 1928 in Berlin. He returned to Czechoslovakia in 1933 to assume the editorship of the "Arbeiter-Illustrierte Zeitung", but was forced to leave again in 1939, first to Paris and then on to the United States. There he worked with the Committee for Exiled Writers and assisted numerous German writers in escaping from the

Nazis. After the war he stayed on in the U.S. as a member of the Czech diplomatic staff, and subsequently served as Czech ambassador to Stockholm and Peking. In 1953, however, Weiskopf left Czechoslovakia for East Berlin and a full time career as a writer; he died there in 1955. *Major Publications:* Die Versuchung (1937) [N]; Abschied vom Frieden (1946-55) [N]; Das Anekdotenbuch (1954) [anecdotes]; Verteidigung der deutschen Sprache (1955) [E]; Literarische Streifzüge (1956) [E].

SELECTED BIBLIOGRAPHY

BRETTSCHNEIDER, WERNER. Zwischen literarischer Autonomie und Staatsdienst: Die Literatur in der DDR. Second Edition. Berlin: Erich Schmidt Verlag, 1974.

BLUMENSATH, HEINZ und CHRISTEL ÜBACH. Einführung in die Literaturgeschichte der DDR. Stuttgart: J.B. Metzler Verlag, 1975.

FRANKE, KONRAD. Die Literatur der Deutschen Demokratischen Republik. München: Kindler Verlag, 1971.

GEERDTS, HANS JÜRGEN. Literatur der DDR in Einzeldarstellungen. Stuttgart: Alfred Kröner Verlag, 1972.

GRANSOW, VOLKER. Kulturpolitik in der DDR. Berlin: Verlag Volker Spiess, 1975.

HAGER, KURT. Die entwickelte sozialistische Gesellschaft: Aufgaben der Gesellschaftswissenschaften nach dem VIII. Parteitag der SED. Berlin: Dietz Verlag, 1972.

HELLER, ILSE und HANS-THOMAS KRAUSE. Kulturelle Zusammenarbeit DDR-UdSSR. Berlin: Staatsverlag der DDR, 1967.

HASSE, HORST, H. J. GEERDTS, E. KÜHNE et al. Geschichte der Literatur der Deutschen Demokratischen Republik. Berlin: VEB Volk und Wissen Verlag, 1976.

HUEBENER, THEODORE. The Literature of East Germany. New York: Frederick Ungar Publishing Co., 1970.

KORALL, HARALD. Literatur 71: Almanach. Halle: Mitteldeutscher Verlag, 1971.

MAYER, HANS. Ansichten: Zur Literatur der Zeit. Reinbek bei Hamburg: Rowohlt Verlag, 1962.

Meyers Taschenlexikon: Schriftsteller der DDR. Leipzig: VEB Bibliographisches Institut, 1974.

RADDATZ, FRITZ J. Traditionen und Tendenzen: Materialien zur Literatur der DDR. Frankfurt am Main: Suhrkamp Verlag, 1972.

REICH-RANICKI, MARCEL. Deutsche Literatur in West und Ost: Prosa seit 1945. München: R. Piper & Co. Verlag, 1966.

SCHMITT, HANS-JÜRGEN. ed. Einführung in Theorie, Geschichte und Funktion der DDR-Literatur. Stuttgart: J.B. Metzler Verlag, 1975.